"Why are you doing this?" Jeanne whispered fiercely.

Black Eagle shrugged nonchalantly, his face an impassive mask. But there was nothing dispassionate or nonchalant in the fires burning in his midnight eyes. "It is the custom."

Jeanne stared blindly at the knife. Her mind refused to accept what he was saying. "Will it take long?" An involuntary whimper escaped from her throat.

"No. Only a few seconds." His voice was deep and husky, tinged with regret.

She felt a curious pull at her innards. He could not mean to torture and kill her, or could he?

He smiled, as if he were amused, and began to walk toward her, very slowly, twirling the knife in his fingers. "Are you ready?"

The scent of him filled her nostrils when she dared to inhale. He gently slipped his hand slowly up the side of her neck....

Dear Reader,

It's March Madness time again! Each year we pick the best and brightest new stars in historical romance and bring them to you in one action-packed month!

When the hunt for a spy throws the cynical Duke of Avon and Emily Fairfax together in *The Heart's Desire* by Gayle Wilson, one night of passion is all they are allowed. Yet their dangerous attraction is too hard to resist.

Anton Neubauer's first glimpse of *Rain Shadow* was in a wild West show. Although Anton knew she could never be the wife he needed, why was the Indian-raised white woman the only one he desired? A wonderful tale by Cheryl St.John.

My Lord Beaumont by Madris Dupree brings us a wonderful love story for readers with a penchant for adventure. Rakish Lord Adrian Beaumont rescues stowaway Danny Cooper from certain death, but finds that beneath her rough exterior is an extraordinary young woman willing to go to any lengths for her true love.

And rounding out March is Emily French's *Capture*, the story of Jeanne de la Rocque, who is captured by Algonquin Indians, and Black Eagle, the warrior whose dreams foretell Jeanne's part in an ancient prophecy.

We hope you enjoy all of our 1994 March Madness titles and look for next month's wherever Harlequin Historical books are sold!

Sincerely,

Tracy Farrell
Senior Editor

Please address questions and book requests to:
Reader Service
U.S.: P.O. Box 1325, Buffalo, NY 14269
Canadian: P.O. Box 1050, Niagara Falls, Ont. L2E 7G7

EMILY FRENCH

CAPTURE

Harlequin Books

TORONTO • NEW YORK • LONDON
AMSTERDAM • PARIS • SYDNEY • HAMBURG
STOCKHOLM • ATHENS • TOKYO • MILAN
MADRID • WARSAW • BUDAPEST • AUCKLAND

ISBN 0-373-28814-X

CAPTURE

EMILY FRENCH

A woman of infinite interests, Emily French has a living passion for the past. She feels it is a vital element of the present and a compelling route to the future. An inveterate traveler, Emily has explored underground caverns in Europe, mustered cattle by helicopter in Australia, climbed a pyramid in Egypt, shared a tent with the bedouin in Africa and gone bicycle riding in China. Emily confesses there are many strange things in the world, but nothing more wonderful or complex than the love between a man and a woman.

To the Menominee people of Wisconsin,
whose history, legend and courageous struggle for
survival in a changing world epitomize the spirit
and endurance of the human race

Prologue

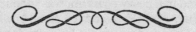

"I ascend in a column of smoke that billows upward from the fireside. I rise in the air on a stream of light, floating, floating...." The young boy sat cross-legged, dark eyes opaque, recounting his vision, his charcoal-smeared face in the shadows. Wise Speaker sprinkled more tobacco on the fire.

"Looking down, I see that one side of the stream has become dark, while the other has the glow of a new day. The parts mingle as the stream of light bears me along. I become one with the stream. This sacred place has a guardian, an enormous black creature whose wings whip the air. He has one foot in the stream and one upon dry land."

Wise Speaker drew deeply on his pipe, pleased that the boy's fasting dream was a strong one. The boy was treading on the threshold of the spirit world, a place that encompassed powerful forces.

"Ride into the inner world, journey in the mind's eye to places unknown," Wise Speaker murmured softly.

"I breathe deeply, and the energies of the eagle seem to rise within me. I can feel its vibrancy. I am the eagle with soaring wings who flies to the top of the universe, confined only by the curve of the sky. Far below I see the earth. I am the hunter ... waiting ... watching ...." The boy's voice faded as he withdrew into his secret dream.

Sometime later, he slowly became aware of his heavy limbs, and of the wise man on the other side of the fire. "What does it mean, Wise Speaker?" The boy wriggled in anticipation, unable to suppress a shiver.

The medicine man was silent, thoughtful. His hulking figure, cloaked in a heavy bearskin, was silhouetted against the blazing fire. He held the carved stone bowl of his pipe firmly in one hand and tapped the long wooden stem against his swarthy chin. "The eye does not see. The ear does not hear. Only the spirit knows...."

Disappointed, the boy drooped. He had fasted for four days to clear his mind, and the dream had seemed so real he had found it difficult to return to the fireside. His spirit had wanted to stay with the vision. He would fast some more. He clamped his jaw shut with determination. Staring down at the ground, deep in his own thoughts, he almost missed Wise Speaker's announcement.

"Black Eagle has favored you. He has given a sign that he will guide and protect you the rest of your life. This guardian spirit is a strong totem, giving you the power to cure or to harm, granting you the ability to prophesy. In return, there will be many obligations. Are you willing to accept Black Eagle on your personal drum? To be worthy of this honor? To praise him by your daily actions?"

The boy stared at Wise Speaker. The old one's expression was enigmatic. "I will," he promised, awed by the power that would be his. The ways of the manito, the spirits, were strange.

"I am grateful you chose me, Black Eagle," the boy said proudly. "I hope I will always be worthy of you."

Wise Speaker nodded his head, pleased. "From this day forward, you will be known as Black Eagle."

Chapter One

"Papa?" Jeanne leaned forward, ignoring the precarious tilt of the canoe and the disapproving grunt of the Algonquin guide. "Are you all right, Papa?" she queried, her soft, musical voice sharp with anxiety. There was no response from her father.

"*Mon Dieu!* Do you want to capsize us! Keep still, *ma'mselle!*" The man's voice was harsh, thick with a French village dialect.

Jeanne clenched her jaws together, her slim shoulders hunching in protest, willing herself to remain motionless. The wind was coming up, churning the ice-cold water into little waves. Still locked within winter's cold, the forest seemed to recede from the forest's edge into an endless green void.

In the distance, an isolated group of mountains rose against the darkening sky. Jeanne heard a bird cry out in alarm as the canoe passed. The sound seemed to come from far away. The thought made her frown. A sharp burst of wind sent loose tendrils of hair whipping around her face. Wrapping her arms around herself to ward off the chill, she lifted her face to the sky. This American sun was so different from the paler French one. Even the clouds seemed flat and ominous, stretched in a wind-smoothed front across the icy arch of the sky, as if a thunderstorm might be brewing.

Touched by some nameless dread, she felt a prickly fear race through her. Her father gave a restless movement, as though in pain, and the French trapper, Émile, muttered something unintelligible beneath his breath. The Algonquin guide stared straight ahead, dark and aloof, his shoulders moving rhythmically as he paddled steadily.

Jeanne straightened cautiously. The feeling of foreboding would not go away, and she concentrated on the movement and timing and balance of the paddle.

Her papa was dying. She knew it. He was dying in the midst of this hostile wilderness, with only herself, the French trapper and an Indian guide! Someday, Papa was fond of saying, the skeptics would recognize that there had arisen among them a prophet, a dreamer of dreams. Someday, the heathens in this wilderness would hear the voice of God through Étienne de la Rocque, fourth son of a duke.

Dreams, Jeanne decided, huddling against the bundle of damp, stinking furs stacked against her aching back. *Nothing but dreams.* The reality was this dreadful canoe, in which for weeks its four occupants ate, slept and carried their equipment. Reality was the food hastily prepared, the river water surging and sucking at the paddles, the misery of sudden spring squalls, the stench of rotting hides. Reality was the weariness, the utter isolation from civilization. Reality was the dying man opposite, his face shiny with perspiration, occasionally emitting mewing, kittenlike cries as he lay in the grip of fever.

As the canoe rounded a bend, Jeanne fastened her eyes on a shaft of April sunlight, transparent as ale, that lit a small clearing.

"Pull over there," she commanded, trying to infuse some authority into her voice.

The French trapper stiffened and glared at her. He was a thick-chested, grubby-looking man of indeterminate years, wearing a hide jacket trimmed with beaver, and water-

stained breeches thrust into fur-lined boots. He spat in the
water to indicate his contempt. Jeanne felt her heart sink.
For an instant she crumpled. He is only a guide, she reminded herself sternly. As her shoulders squared, her voice
took back authority, too. She let her eyes challenge him.

"My father is dying," she heard herself say calmly. "It is
going to storm. We will shelter here, in the forest. The trees
will give greater protection."

For an instant, a dark, angry expression flicked across the
trapper's face. Then it was gone. He shrugged and dipped
his head. "Yes, *ma'mselle*."

A rapid exchange in Algonquin occurred between the two
men before the canoe turned toward the riverbank.

While the de la Rocques had wintered at the small settlement at Mont Real, Jeanne had whiled away many hours
talking with some of the native women. During that time,
she had acquired the rudiments of the Algonquin language,
sufficient at any rate for her to understand the gist of the
conversation between Émile and the guide.

It seemed Falling Feathers was reluctant to make camp
along this particular stretch of the river. Something to do
with the young braves of many tribes known to travel this
territory with each spring melt in swift, small parties to win
coups. Jeanne shrugged. War parties or no war parties,
Papa needed to rest.

When a makeshift camp had been set up and Étienne de
la Rocque lay, fevered and delirious, Jeanne considered the
situation. Inspired by his newly discovered missionary zeal,
Papa had taken passage to Quebec in the spring of 1637. It
was now the spring of 1640. The intervening years had not
been kind to the de la Rocques. First, baby Jacques had
succumbed to the grippe, then little Jean-Paul. They had
been followed in quick succession by Thérèse, Pierre and
Gabrielle. The settlement on the Saint Lawrence had proved
to be too much for Mama's frail strength. Last autumn,

weakened by the constant cupping the surgeon had pre-
scribed to lessen her melancholy, she had died within hours
of giving birth to a stillborn son.

Papa had wanted to go somewhere where he would be free
to follow the way of the Lord. It seemed that this freedom
had been purchased at very great cost. All he had left was
one daughter, herself, Jeanne Marie, his firstborn. Strange,
scrawny and thin as she was, she could not remember a day's
sickness in all of her seventeen years.

A shiver ran through Jeanne, a little drift of thoughts ed-
dying in her head. Pictures in her mind. Polished oak par-
quet floors. The smell of old leather bookbindings. Happy,
laughing faces...

She rose abruptly. "We will remain here until Papa is
well." The moment of recall, of sadness and loss, was gone,
lost in the exigencies of the present.

During the night, the storm burst over them with mind-
less ferocity, flapping at their rough brush-and-sailcloth
shelter. But by morning it had passed, leaving the air behind it still and clear. The first red-gold tint of dawn had
barely seeped through the clearing when Jeanne rose quietly. The silence was broken by the snoring of the trapper,
the sound of Papa's wheezing, and the soft cluck-cluck of a
bird.

Jeanne dressed quickly, needing only to slip on her gown
over the linen chemise in which she had slept. The gown was
trimmed with dark brown silk braid, and had a high-waisted
velvet bodice, full sleeves and wide cuffs. The underskirt
was water-stained and soiled with mud, and the double lace
collar was limp and grimy. She walked down to the river's
edge, her skirts sending shivers of motion over puddles that
lay on the still-frozen ground.

The daylight grew and swiftly overspread all things. The
cluck-cluck of the bird sounded closer. It was answered almost immediately by the call of the bird's mate, even closer.

Jeanne remained motionless while the sound wove itself into the background of her thoughts. She was, in fact, hardly aware of it, until that feeling of unease washed over her once more. She turned, listening intently. She allowed her gaze to wander idly about the clearing. Inwardly her heart was pounding.

She had learned in France, as a child, to trust her instincts. The awareness, the catching, somehow, of what was still to happen... She felt the hairs on her arms and neck raise in a rippling shiver. She could sense something. Something as strong and touchable as the trees, which still dripped moisture from last night's storm. The sudden yip of a fox, and the soft bird sound ceased quite suddenly. She spun around.

Falling Feathers, the Algonquin guide, was standing there, his face inscrutable, his eyes dark, unblinking.

"The old moon calls." His head tilted toward Étienne de la Rocque.

Jeanne's skin grew cold and clammy. Suddenly she knew what was behind this vague feeling of apprehension she was experiencing, and it could be summed up in a word. *Fear.* Fear of the future. The future that she somehow knew was in this raw new land. A future very different from the one she had envisaged.

Kneeling at her father's side, she gently touched his burning forehead.

"Papa?"

"Daughter..." he muttered, as though unable to get his thoughts into words. Death was upon him visibly.

"Papa!" Her harsh intake of breath was as clear as a scream.

His lips and skin were bluish. His hands, also bluish, moved restlessly.

"I am not going to die," he whispered. "Not yet. Not before I..." He raised a limp hand to touch the high cheekbones in the face bent anxiously over his.

It was an arresting face, broad, with a square chin, a wide mouth, and slanting hazel eyes. Not a pretty face. The cheekbones were too high, and boldly sculpted, and the smooth, pale skin, which accompanied the chestnut hair, had become sadly freckled during their extended travels.

"Hush. Do not talk. You are wasting your strength."

"No. I must. I have not very long now, and I must..." Étienne de la Rocque coughed agonizingly, wheezing and choking.

Jeanne gently sponged his forehead with a damp cloth.

"This world has not anything to offer me now, and it has not in a long time." He had stopped coughing now, and was looking weak and drained.

"Papa! What about the mission? Your plans?" In spite of her best efforts, her voice was rising, thready with tears.

"Daughter, I—"

Étienne de la Rocque gave a breathy gasp, and Jeanne looked wildly around for help. Neither Émile nor Falling Feathers was in sight. She pulled the sick, fragile man forward, propping his head against her shoulder. Her body was slender, and her hips were slim, but her strength was wiry.

"I have nothing to leave you, Jeanne. Nothing but dreams. Worthless dreams. Go back to France. To your grandfather. Promise?"

Jeanne's eyes were glittering with moisture, and her mouth was trembling. *"Oui, Papa,"* she said obediently.

Étienne de la Rocque closed his eyes, shivered convulsively, and was still.

Jeanne gathered him close, softly praying. *Be not afraid for the arrow that flieth by day...*

A terrible feeling of emptiness washed over her as she realized her father would not speak again. Étienne de la

Rocque was dead. Weak, ambitious, thwarted Étienne. But a true visionary, warm and caring. Oh, Papa, Jeanne thought dazedly. How strange you could be, how terrible and wonderful.

For a long moment she was silent, her eyes stinging with tears. She had a sudden sad knowledge that all her life she would remember this scene, the dim wilderness, and herself sitting so still, the dead man in her arms.

With an enormous effort, she blinked, swallowed hard, racked by the loss. But more tears filled her eyes, and helplessly she let them run down her cheeks, for she did not have the strength to wipe them away.

She glanced upward, toward the sky, which seemed to push down on her until she wanted to gasp for air. Leaden clouds were piled up in the sky, holding rain in their depths. A gray mist rose from the river. Water sparkled and glittered everywhere, testimony to the night's storm.

How odd, she thought as she sat quietly rocking her father in the cradle of her arms, there was a lone eagle circling directly above. Watching... waiting...

She felt the hairs raise on her arms and neck in a rippling shiver of anticipation. She knew the danger today lay not in the sky, but in the forest.

Two hours later, Étienne de la Rocque's body lay beneath the soil of the land that had offered so much promise in faraway France. His meager possessions, wrapped in two small bundles, were stowed in their usual place in the canoe. The haste seemed indecent to Jeanne, but both Émile and Falling Feathers were keen to return to the safety of the river.

Her eyes dry now, she had just accepted the trapper's hand to scramble into the canoe when he grunted and fell forward. An arrow protruded from his back, its feathered shaft quivering. The odor of blood, sharp, hot, vividly salty, filled the air as Jeanne bent to assist the trapper. The sound of foxes yipping sent fear churning in her belly. Holding the canoe steady with one hand, she pulled at Émile's arm with the other.

"Get into the canoe! Falling Feathers, help me!"

She dared a glance over one shoulder. Her heart stopped beating. Three painted Indians stood at the edge of the clearing, heads red, hands painted indigo. Black streaks of paint covered their naked chests.

"The musket. Get the musket." Émile grunted in pain.

Jeanne was so frightened she found it hard to breathe, and her hands trembled as she pulled the heavy rifle from the bow, where the trapper had placed it in order to assist her into the canoe. Half in, half out of the canoe, Émile sagged against her, breathing heavily.

Falling Feathers was leaning over the far side, striking with his paddle at another member of the war party, who had come splashing through the shallow water. Jeanne could hear their hoarse cries as the two men locked in mortal combat. She raised the rifle to her shoulder, pointed it in the direction of the three fearsome men moving toward her, and carefully squeezed the trigger.

The rifle cracked, a puff of smoke rising from the barrel. Jeanne jerked backward, her shoulder hitting the canoe. She heard the thud as the ball hit one of the men. She gagged. One of the Indians was holding his shoulder, where red splotches appeared, adding bright color to his decorations. He shook his head at his companions, evidently to make light of the wound.

Jeanne heard the sound of water splashing behind her. She glanced back. Two more Indians, lean as starving hounds and bright with war paint, were wading toward her, hatchets raised. She clutched the empty weapon, groping in the canoe for the powder horn and shot pouch. Her hands shook as she tried to spill the fine French powder into the priming pan of the weapon.

"Leave me! *Fuyez! Vite!*" gasped the trapper. As Jeanne hesitated, a bloodcurdling war cry burst from one of the Indians. *"Allez-vous en, s'il vous plaît..."*

Jeanne turned and ran.

The water dragged at her skirts, impeding her progress. Her legs felt as if they were leaden poles as she tried to quicken her pace. She was afraid to look around. The men yipped to each other. A single hoarse yell pealed out, somehow trenchant and triumphant. Other yells, not so wild and strange, muffled the first one. The splashing stopped. Silence clapped down.

No more sounds caught her ears, but Jeanne was certain that the Indians would follow her, knowing it would be easy to take her whenever they wished. She clambered up the bank, grasping at tree roots, sliding and slipping in the mud. She was trembling so much, she could scarcely stand. She looked back furtively. She could no longer see either the Algonquin or the trapper, only the war party carelessly tipping the cargo from the canoe. Gathering up her wet skirts in one hand, Jeanne ran into the forest.

She ran until she was doubled over, gasping for breath. She ran until she fell. Rose again, and ran once more. Agonizing pain bit into her chest with every labored breath. Briars tore at her hair and clothes. Aspen branches whipped and stung her face, cutting her lip. Tree roots snagged her boots, tripping her. When her heart felt ready to burst, and she had fallen countless times, Jeanne crawled into the underbrush to curl into a trembling ball.

She lay there, breathing in great gulps, trying to get enough oxygen to keep the world from receding down an endless black tunnel. When she succeeded, she buried her face in the pine needles, digging her fingers into them, wanting nothing so much as that they might hide her. The sharp pine needles, piercing her wrists and cheeks, and her hot, heaving breast, seemed to give her security.

This was only a nightmare, from which she would awake in safety, she told herself. She wanted to be in bed, back in France, back at the château. There she could pull the covers over her head and call for Mama. She strained to hear any sound. Only the sound of jays scolding one another disturbed the stillness.

Alone. Never, never before in her lifetime, had she ever been quite so alone. She felt her body convulse in a shudder. The suspense grew unbearable. The snap of a twig sounded nearby. Jeanne's body stiffened. Then she quivered a little. Cautiously and noiselessly she raised herself upon her elbows and peeped through the brush.

A pair of moccasins, plain and unadorned, was firmly planted in the opening. Jeanne's eyes followed leggings of tanned deerskin up past a bulging breechclout, over a brown muscular wall streaked with blood and paint, to meet depthless eyes that gleamed like obsidian. His hair was raven black, his scalp lock bound with the dried band-patterned skin of a snake whose rattles hung down against the Indian's red-dyed skull. His high-bridged nose gave prominence to his cheekbones, giving his face a straight, sharp-cut profile. The curve of his jaw was unyielding. His firm lips were set in a straight line. Jeanne saw the blood throb in his powerful neck, the ripple of muscles as he breathed deeply.

Seconds passed. Seconds that became long, intolerable minutes in which their eyes locked. Fear sat like a stone in her stomach, slowly moving upward until she thought she would choke with it. She felt her face blanch and all her blood rush back to her heart with sickening force. Jeanne scrambled to her feet, mute, staring at him, her trembling hands stealing up toward her bosom, as if to ward off a mortal blow. Openmouthed, she drew a tremulous breath and tasted the hot, salty blood from her cut lip.

Jeanne gasped when he lunged for her, too swift for her to move a hand. One arm crushed around her like a coiled band; the other, hard across her breast and neck, forced her head back. She tried to wrestle away, but she was utterly powerless. His dark face bent down closer and closer, so close that all that lay between their mouths was the mingled heat of their breath. Jeanne felt pinned by those night-dark eyes, unable to move.

She ceased trying to struggle, like a stricken creature paralyzed by the piercing, hypnotic eyes of a snake. Yet, in spite of her terror, if he meant death to her, she did not welcome it. She had not realized just how much she had grown to love life until she faced certain death.

"No! No!" she screamed desperately. She balled her hands into fists, striking wildly. With a strength she had not realized she possessed, she wrestled for freedom.

Her fist smashed down on the painted face, and she saw the savage stare of the man's dark eyes. Twisting and turning, she lashed out with her boots, feeling one strike a shinbone. She threw her knee into the Indian's body and twisted. The Indian loosened his grip, grunting in apparent surprise at her almost feral resistance.

Jeanne fought frantically, feeling her skirts ripping as her assailant tried to keep a grip on her writhing body. A blow struck her mouth, splitting the skin so that blood ran down her chin in a long, thin red line.

Her fingers closed on the hatchet slung over one of his muscular shoulders. As she tugged at the weapon, the gunshot wound began to bleed more heavily. She could feel its wet warmth, smell its odor. With a desperate surge of strength, Jeanne jabbed the injury with her chin.

Suddenly she was free, the hatchet in her hand. They faced one another, breathing heavily. She pressed her lips together to stop their trembling, and with all her strength, she forced herself not to scream. She clenched the hatchet tightly with both hands. Her nerve had revived, despite the terror that clawed at her stomach. She could not outrun the Indians. She could never escape.

So, with the courage of fatalism, she stood defiant, her eyes fixed on her captor. She stood her ground, giving him stare for stare. She saw the white edging of teeth as the man met the challenge, the subtle shifting of his body. He was a tremendous specimen, all flowing, silent power. Jeanne needed every ounce of courage she possessed to continue looking at him.

His image condensed between the sky and the forest, restricting her breathing. For a moment Jeanne and the warrior stood there, transfixed, stunned by the pulsing spiritual bond that surged between them.

Suddenly the spell was broken. Three other members of the war party cat-footed through the brush to join them. Jeanne was surrounded by Indians. A few paces apart, they slowly circled around her, whooping, dancing, clearly enjoying themselves.

Her captor did not join in the game. He stood immobile, oblivious of the blood streaming down his arm, watching her, his face expressionless, his eyes impenetrable. Their intensity mesmerized her, and that was more frightening than any physical attack.

Jeanne's nerve broke there. She could no longer meet those terrible black eyes that seemed to be probing her every thought. With a scream, she launched herself at her captor. As light on his feet as a dancing master, he nimbly sidestepped the attack.

Plainly enjoying this new game, the rest of the war party began to hoot and shout, dancing around her, mocking her, darting in and out like irritating insects, tormenting her with their coup sticks. Her death did not seem to be their purpose. Rather, it was as if they were counting their bravery by the number of times they could touch her with their weapons. The noise swirled about her ears, making her giddy.

Jeanne spun wildly, striking out with the hatchet. Nausea almost overwhelmed her when she felt it connect, sliding through flesh, and heard the sickening sound of bone crunching.

She did not see the death blow coming her way. Was only vaguely aware of running feet, her captor slamming into another man, knocking a tomahawk aside from its deadly course. In a haze, she heard an angry flow of words she partly understood.

She could hear their voices, and she was still standing erect. But she could not move her arms. No matter how much she willed them to move, they would not budge.

"I say we should kill her now," one brave said softly.

Jeanne felt strong fingers bite into her shoulder. "No. She has shown spirit and courage such as I have never seen in a woman before. She should have the honor to..."

Although the men spoke Algonquin, some words were different from the language she had learned in Mont Real. Jeanne strained her ears, translating the Indians' dialect as they spoke. It seemed the man she had shot was arguing with someone called Thunderclap on her behalf.

"On the Other Side cries out for revenge, Black Eagle. Kill her now!" the first warrior said again. The rest of the braves grunted in agreement.

Jeanne closed her eyes and pressed a hand to her heaving breast, sucking air into her lungs. Her breath came in with an audible rush when she opened her eyes once more.

An older man had joined the group. He seemed to have drifted in, his movements like smoke on a windless day. On his shaved head he wore a dyed deer roach, spread so that each hair stood up and quivered like the tail of a red fox. He was tall and spare, and a white-edged scar ran along his swarthy cheek, puckering his mouth into a permanent grin. Across his forehead there lay another scar the length of the blade of a skinning knife. He checked the argument with a gesture. When he spoke, his voice commanded attention.

"Consider well, Black Eagle," the older man said, "this woman has killed On the Other Side. Our companion has died not in battle, nor in winning a coup. He has been struck down by this pale daughter of the moon."

Black Eagle stood his ground, balanced lightly on the balls of his feet, his voice husky and low with anguish. "True. Yellow Feather does well to remind me. I would not want On the Other Side's spirit to go home in shame. Bested by a woman." The other Indians stared at him, then began nodding.

Black Eagle stood motionless, staring hard at Jeanne. In the light, dappled by the overhead leaves, hints of gold caressed him like a lover, emphasizing the shift and coil of powerful muscles beneath smooth skin. She thought of a sleek forest animal, patiently awaiting its prey, forcing itself to restrain those powerful muscles and strength.

His dark eyes, flanking a high-bridged nose, seemed to penetrate into her soul. An odd feeling that was unlike anything she had ever experienced lanced through Jeanne. Her lips trembled in dismay. She could not help it.

"On the Other Side was not only the brother of my heart, but also the son of my mother's brother," he continued, each word carefully delivered, absorbing their entire attention. "I drank at his mother's breast when my parents drowned in the great flood. For more moons than I can count, I have shared his mother's fireside. There is nothing—nothing, I tell you—that I would not do for Singing Bird, after all she has done for me. I know she will grieve at the manner of his death."

"He is right," Thunderclap said.

"Black Eagle's words are wise," said the other.

He meant her to die! The very deliberateness of his speech served to give a decisive finality to his remarks. In that moment, Jeanne hated him fiercely. Hated him with every ounce of feeling she possessed. She gave a sharp movement of protest, a ragged sound dragged from her throat. Then, as though the movement had reminded him of her presence, Black Eagle spoke again.

"When you underestimate an enemy, he is all around you. This woman has succeeded in wounding me, also. My spirit felt the brush of death from the long stick of this woman. See, the blood drips from the wound. It falls from me to paint her pale face. Her blood mingles with my own. Whether you wish it or not, this has already happened."

Jeanne shrank away as a long, sinewy finger flicked her jaw. There was a muttering and a fearsome scowling and shaking of heads. Jeanne looked at the menacing figures. Then there crept over her a colder apprehension than when she had taken it for granted that she was soon to die. All the stories of settlers tortured and burned by savages came crowding into her head.

In a daze, she heard Black Eagle's eloquent argument. He was claiming her! Something about a dream! A dream known only to his spirit. The secret desire of his spirit manifested by a dream.

There was an excited gabble as the young men turned to look at Jeanne. Yellow Feather gave her a sudden appraising scrutiny. He shrugged.

"The daughter of the moon has strength and courage and would breed fine sons," Black Eagle was saying. "But if we take this woman captive, her life belongs first to Singing Bird. That is the custom."

Taut and strained, Jeanne never took her eyes from Black Eagle's face. He stood there, swaying slightly. His expression was cold, composed, yet oddly alert. His eyes met hers. That strangely direct gaze, which had disturbed her before, seemed to pierce the secret recesses of her mind. She shud-

dered. Her hands moved compulsively, tightening around
each other. She felt the world whirl giddily around her, and
closed her eyes against the tide of red that seemed to flow in
front of her vision.

Chapter Two

When she regained her senses, the warriors had wrapped their dead companion in birchbark in preparation for burial. All their ebullience was gone. Now they were silent, preoccupied with their tasks. The two younger men were twisting lengths of fiber, making a cord to tie around the enshrouded cadaver, pausing at intervals to softly sing a death chant for On the Other Side.

Yellow Feather squatted beside a log, mashing some soft pine bark into a pulp. Black Eagle sat on the log, pressing one blue-painted hand against his shoulder, staring at her. From the brightness of the blood flowing freely through his fingers, Jeanne surmised that the ball had just been removed from the wound.

As her mind cleared, Jeanne realized her wrists were tied behind her back, and that a piece of cord encircled her neck. She gave an experimental wriggle. At her slight movement, four pairs of dark eyes turned on her. Feeling an overwhelming urge to stay alive, she lay perfectly still, watching the men. They resumed their tasks. The oldest warrior carefully mixed some pine resin with the coniferous pulp before applying the concoction to Black Eagle's wound. He then bound the antiseptic poultice firmly to the young man's shoulder with strips of inner bark.

Jeanne lifted her eyes to Black Eagle's face, meeting his gaze. His narrowed eyes gleamed like gems in his painted face. The searching intensity of his glance made Jeanne shiver. Something in his eyes was making her blood shimmer wildly through her body, leaving chaos in its wake.

His male grace and power tugged at her senses. She felt as though she were on the edge of a cliff and had only to spread her wings and fly... or fall endlessly, spinning away into infinity like a snowflake on the wind. She turned away abruptly.

The sun was high when the party was joined by two other warriors and Émile, trotting behind like a dog at the end of a neck thong. The face of the trapper was swollen and bruised, with minor cuts. Where his right eye should have been, a puffed, dark purple bulge showed. His other eye, however, gleamed with hard and sullen light. His shirt had been torn away and hung in bloody tatters around his waist.

A hard shove sent Émile staggering. He groaned and fell onto his hands and knees, kneeling, head inclined, like a sheep about to be slaughtered. He slid sideways, breathing heavily. Jeanne could see the ragged laceration made by the arrow, the slow seeping of blood.

"Émile?" she whispered.

Desperately the trapper's eyes rolled backward until Jeanne could read in them their awful admission of abject fear.

"*Taisez-vous.* Draw no attention to us," he whispered in return.

Little by little, inching forward on elbows and knees, Jeanne pulled herself toward Émile. Her progress was crablike but steady—until she felt a foot rip into her ribs. She rolled with the blow, surrendering to the pain with a whimper. Thunderclap leaned down, his deer-tail headpiece trembling on his painted skull. He grasped the line that held her neck.

"Come," he commanded brusquely, impatiently.

The young warrior jerked hard on the rope, causing the rough fibers to bite into the flesh of Jeanne's neck, bringing her to her knees in the mud. She rose awkwardly to her feet, wavering unsteadily. Every fiber of her being cried out for her to move, yet she stood as if rooted to the ground.

Hands lashed together behind her back, Jeanne, head held as high as the cruel tug of the rope would permit, fought back tears. The tears that scalded her eyes were caused mostly by anger. Anger because her legs refused to comply with the commands of her mind. If she wanted to live, she must do as they asked.

"Move!" she ordered her dormant muscles furiously. "Move!"

In an explosive burst of pure will, her limbs obeyed, and she stumbled in Thunderclap's wake. Cautiously Jeanne turned her eyes toward Émile. Two of the braves had hoisted him to his feet. Now draped in fur mantles and laden with their war bags and weapons, they were arranging themselves in a single file.

The brave called Black Eagle halted in front of her, taking the thong from Thunderclap. "It is the duty of the son of Singing Bird's heart and breast to deliver the daughter of the moon for judgment, to keep her from harm." He spoke softly, his eyes never leaving Jeanne's face.

Raising her eyes to the warrior's grim visage, Jeanne met the half-lidded stare. "If I am to be spared, then why not free me?" she whispered in the same tongue.

Black Eagle blinked rapidly. He seemed to be caught off stride by Jeanne's use of Algonquin. "Even if I could free you, I would not."

"Then kill me now, I beg of you." Her voice was a mere thread of sound.

Tilting his head imperceptibly, he continued in an equally hushed voice. "Come. For now, you are to be spared. When it is time, death will find you."

Jeanne stared at him. "What will you do with me now?" She asked the question not out of fear of death, but out of fear of the unknown.

"There is no escape. Show that you are not lacking in courage. Follow in my footsteps. Go where I go."

Black Eagle did not speak again, only bending to hoist his arrow quiver and war bag over his undamaged shoulder, to clamp his deer roach low on his forehead. Tomahawk thrust into his waistband, bow in one hand and Jeanne's leading rein in the other, he joined the others. Yellow Feather took his place at the head of the line, the other warriors and the captives following behind like shadows.

That long afternoon was part of the same never-changing picture. The rain pelted down on them, slanting in against Jeanne's back. Her skirts grew heavy with the weight of it, and her boots squelched water with each step. Trudging wearily along behind Black Eagle into the dank darkness of the forest, Jeanne felt her strength ebbing fast. Tears stung her eyes. She had not eaten that morning. Her mouth was parched, and her lips were sore. A wave of despair swept through her, so intense it bordered on pain. How she hated the gray sky and the rain and the mud and the green, dripping trees. But most of all she hated the man in front of her. She hated his dark face, the set of his features, his bottomless eyes.

Just when Jeanne, gripped by a deadly fatigue, felt she could go no farther, the Indians stopped by a wall of weathered limestone. The liquid sounds of a waterfall reminded Jeanne how thirsty she was. She stumbled, jerking the neck line, and coughed as it bit into her neck. She lurched forward to ease the constriction on her throat and abruptly felt herself bump into the living column of strength that was Black Eagle.

Again she was aware of the enormous animal strength of the man as he gripped her upper arms to steady her. When he brought his face close to hers, she felt a brief wave of heat flood through her. His flat black eyes captured hers in an instant recognition of the current that flowed between them.

"Oh!" she croaked through the hot ashes and sand at the back of her throat. Confused by the shock of his touch, she felt her cheeks flush. Aware of the need for total silence, she simply stared up at him, unable to tear her eyes from his gaze. Her every sense trembled, absorbing some of his vitality.

Insects do this, she realized suddenly. They fly toward brightness, only to find it deadly. Instinctively she backed away, her eyes widening.

Silently Black Eagle removed the rope from around Jeanne's neck, then untied the lashings around her wrists.

"Follow me close and make no sound. Step only where I step." In a slight crouch, he began to move forward, glancing back once to see that she was following.

Jeanne obeyed his command. Rubbing her wrists to restore circulation, she carefully planted her feet in the exact spot his moccasins trod. Gliding around a twisting passage in the rock, they came to a wide, roomlike space under an overhanging ledge. Meltwater shot in a waterfall over the cavern, splashing into a pool below, effectively hiding the shelter.

Limp and exhausted, Jeanne huddled against the wall, letting her weary body slide to the floor. That was all she had strength for. Émile fell beside her, barely conscious. Jeanne heard the scrape of flint. There was an orange flash that limned Yellow Feather's scarred face. His bleak expression turned Jeanne's blood to ice.

The party must have camped there previously, for Thunderclap was kneeling, breaking some dry twigs from a bundle at the rear of the cave. He put them on smoldering shavings and blew gently until there was a steady flame. Carefully he fed the fire, first with small sticks, soon with larger, broken branches of maple. It was a low fire, warm and comforting. Jeanne noticed that the dried hardwood gave off almost no smoke.

Black Eagle waited until the fire lit the cavern with a pale glow. Then, in slow, deliberate movements, he removed his deer roach, leaned his bow against the wall, dropped his war bag and quiver on the cave's sandy floor and advanced upon Jeanne. Halting two feet away, he unemotionally surveyed his captive. "If you give me your oath not to try to escape, you may remain unbound."

Jeanne remained silent, unable to offer reassurance. Her mind retreated from the thought of her remaining a captive. She would rather die. But what could she do without a weapon, and with her wrists bound? Where could she run to if she did escape? Her frustration kept her mouth closed in a tight line.

Black Eagle neither replied, nor moved, nor changed expression. His ebony eyes glittered in the firelight. There was a disturbing quality in his glance, a subtle suggestion of force about him that Jeanne felt without being able to define it in understandable terms. But there was no ignoring him. She felt the radiating force of his presence, a thing to be reckoned with. She remained stubbornly silent.

"You are a foolish woman," he said in a deceptively soft voice.

Jeanne swallowed. The movement was painful. For what seemed an eternity, Black Eagle gazed at the pale face streaked with dirt and blood, the defiant eyes of living color, the pulse beating in the slender throat.

"Do you court death so eagerly? Perhaps the manito will be kind, and Singing Bird will grant your wish." He squatted beside her, pulled her arms behind her back, and fastened the cord about her wrists so that her fingers could not touch the knots. Strong fingers grasped her boots. Jeanne gave a token, futile kick. She felt the cord bite into her ankles. "You will neither drink nor eat until you give your word," he told her stiffly. His face an expressionless mask, Black Eagle joined his companions.

Jeanne tried to move into a more comfortable position, but the motion only caused the ropes around her wrists and feet to tighten. Black Eagle had, in some way, connected them, and she realized this was a punishment for her silent rebellion. The bitter defiance drained out of Jeanne as she watched the Indians eating dried deer meat and handfuls of crushed grain.

Thick black misery rose to fill her heart. Her thirst had become almost unbearable. She swallowed to ease the constriction of her throat and turned away to stare up at the changing colors on the slender cones hanging from the ceiling. The cathedral roof of the cave was filled with molten color. Jeanne had been in caves before, but never one as strangely colored as this.

In her fanciful mind, the colors merged, and, in the depths of the cave, strange, ever-changing shapes melted and reformed and melted again. There were voices, soft and hushed. Jeanne looked again at the six Indians squatting around the fire. Yellow Feather was checking the binding on Black Eagle's shoulder. Black Eagle faced in her direction. The flickering light threw shadows of his hawklike nose across his deeply sculptured cheekbones. Jeanne could see the glitter of his eyes as he watched her.

"Émile?" Cautiously she whispered to the trapper. He made no reply. She did not know whether he was asleep or dead.

The misery of Jeanne's thoughts mixed with the dark weight of exhaustion. She slept with her head on her knees. Huddled there, she woke with a start, shivering. Her neck was stiff, and her shoulders ached. The cursed ropes added to her discomfort and fatigue. She should think and plan how she might escape, but she did not have the energy. All she wanted to do was crawl into a soft bed and sleep.

Tomorrow. There was always tomorrow, and then she would decide what to do. She wanted to escape, and she would, somehow. But for tonight, all she wanted was to sleep—and mercifully find forgetfulness.

It could have been minutes, hours, or it could have been seconds later. Someone was tugging at her shoulders, shaking her. Jeanne wrenched open her eyelids. One of the young warriors stood over her. Her head ached. Her entire body ached. She felt as if she had been picked up and smashed against a wall. Her arms were stiff, and there was no feeling in her hands. Sometime, somehow, her feet had been released from their bonds. Struggling painfully to her feet, knees sagging, Jeanne felt hope drain out of her. She belonged to her captors now.

The young brave circled around her, viewing her from different angles. Watchful, apprehensive, Jeanne looked about her, searching for Black Eagle. He was nowhere in sight. The brave reached out and tentatively touched her hair, as though it were a living thing. Jeanne snapped her head away. He sniffed, expelling a quick breath through his nostrils. His lips curled upward, and he turned to the trapper.

Émile moaned as the Indian roused him, opened his one good eye, and then closed it again. A sudden kick in the spine made him struggle to his feet. The young brave stuffed some dried deer meat into the trapper's mouth and turned to do the same to Jeanne. His action was stayed by Black Eagle's hand on his arm.

"No, Stands Fast. The woman does not require food until the shell is broken, the fire is liquid in her bones, and she runs with the wind," he announced quite casually.

Stands Fast ruminated on this for a moment. "To be sure, she has the look of a runaway, and will no doubt try to escape at the first chance. But you who can track a squirrel along a log or the trail of a feather falling in the forest would soon recapture her. Without food, she will not survive the journey to our lodge. Nor suffer just punishment for the death of On the Other Side."

His protest went unheeded. Black Eagle shrugged. "On the Other Side will not weep and moan on the night winds, demanding revenge. She is a fighter, too, this one. She needs to be closely watched. If I am to deliver her alive to Singing Bird, I would have her accepting her lot. Unless you have changed your mind?" he said, turning to Jeanne. His head was tipped back, and his ebony eyes were looking down his beak of a nose in challenge, waiting.

The moment stretched itself wire-fine, to the point of breaking. Jeanne opened her mouth to speak, and found she could produce only a croak.

Without another word, Black Eagle took the lead rope. Jeanne followed quickly to keep the cord from tightening around her neck.

The new day was a repetition of the one before. Rain and drizzle soaked Jeanne's clothes, making walking difficult. She had no awareness of time. Living consisted of putting one weary foot in front of another, with a grim determination not to fall to the ground.

She wanted to live, but it took all her concentrated efforts to remain upright. Her pinioned arms ached from the unaccustomed strain, and she found herself growing lightheaded as the day wore on. Cursing her weak body, Jeanne paused and straightened, trying to ease the sharp cramp in her lower back. A jerk on the neck line kept her moving.

"Is there no end to this?" she asked. There was no reply.

By late afternoon, the world swayed gently. Jeanne's body felt light and weightless, all the weight having somehow transferred itself to her feet, which were as heavy as lead blocks.

The rain had eased when they came to a large lake, as glassy as some great irregular window in the crust of the earth. The placid, shimmering surface seemed gray and lifeless, the water oily-smooth. There was a vaporous wisp hanging just above the surface. Ringed by snow-capped mountains, it had an air of quiet majesty in its sheer wild, rugged beauty. An unending sweep of colossal trees sloped in an unbroken wall right down to the lake shore.

An owl hooted. The line stopped, the braves tense, listening. The woods seemed breathless. It was like being entombed.

Jeanne could see Black Eagle's mouth clamped like a mussel shell as his dark eyes searched the forest. For several minutes he stood still, listening, absorbing the sounds around him, watching the trees on the far side of the lake. Somewhere in the trees, two flicker woodpeckers were talking.

The sounds ended suddenly on excited *wick-wick* cries, followed by the *rat-tat* of their efforts to dig insects from tree bark. Farther away than the sound of the flickers, Jeanne heard a squirrel chatter in alarm, as if it had scurried around the trunk of a tree after something startled it. One of the Indians looked up at the sky and grunted.

The line continued.

It was almost dark when the party stopped to make camp in a grove of beech trees where the ground was relatively free of underbrush. Jeanne stood dully as Black Eagle released her bonds. The pain of renewed circulation returned her to awareness, and his face suddenly came back into focus. Except for traces of red ocher dye, the rain had washed away most of his war paint. He did not look nearly so fearsome.

"I welcome your spirit, little vixen, but your continued well-being depends upon your acceptance of my name vision, my secret dream. I need your word." His voice was soft, almost gentle.

Jeanne stood uncertainly, reasoning very slowly, woodenly. One part of her urged acquiescence to his wish, which was almost a command. The other half of her reminded her that French aristocrats did not parley with savages. The very thought was sacrilege. *This is,* Jeanne suddenly imagined her father whispering in her ear, *a time for compromise.* Black Eagle seemed of uncanny perception, for he answered her unspoken thought before it was clearly formed.

"Now I have your word, I will get you food. Sit."

His matter-of-fact acknowledgment of her unspoken surrender nettled Jeanne. She stood uncertainly. Her tongue held ready a blunt refusal, but she did not utter it. She had a glimpse of the futility of refusing to comply. Although her mind ran indignantly against compulsion, her muscles involuntarily moved to obey.

It irritated her further that she should feel in the least constrained to obey the calmly expressed wish of this quiet-spoken savage. Hating him with every fiber of her being, she swallowed. There was no point in prevaricating further. Accepting his offer of a gourd of water, a handful of pounded wild rice and several strips of dried meat, Jeanne sat against the bole of a tree. Watching a thin sliver of moon appear, she made herself chew the provisions slowly. It was the best food she had ever eaten.

She was stiff and cold and exhausted, her hands were swollen and painful, and her feet ached intolerably. But she was alive and free of her bonds! Free to run! But where?

The meager meal had restored her youthful buoyancy and natural vigor.

With sudden decisiveness, Jeanne twitched at a grimy cuff that was almost separated from its sleeve. She tore it off and threw it on the ground. The sodden, once-exquisite fili-greed collar of fine Brussels lace joined it. If she was to sur-vive, she had to conserve her strength. That meant making walking as easy as possible.

Tired, chilled to the marrow, shivering inside her damp dress, Jeanne distastefully eyed the bedraggled garment, rent in numerous places by brambles and twigs. A surrep-titious glance in the direction of the campfire made her daring. The Indians were huddled around the fire, talking softly to each other in their singsong voices. Their long shadows danced like demons in the flickering firelight. Émile was lying on the far side of them, eyes closed, un-moving.

Jeanne stood up and stripped off her heavy, wet velvet underskirt and wide ruffled petticoat. It felt as though an immense weight had been lifted from her. She sat and re-moved her fine kid-leather boots, wincing as the blistered flesh on her heels peeled away with the remnants of her tat-tered stockings. Her body made a pale flash of movement under the dark trees as she rubbed herself with the piece of lace. It was damp, too, but the rubbing warmed her a little. Clad only in the tight-fitting bodice of her gown and a sin-gle shift, she shivered in the cold night air.

Small clouds drifted across the face of the moon like a flock of sheep. Full of fear and hatred of the captors car-rying her southward to some ghastly, unknown fate, Jeanne searched the heavens for familiar comfort and reassurance. She recognized the constellation of the Bear and let her eye travel far off the end of its pouring lip to the North Star. Papa had told her that it was the only constant guiding star in the sky.

If she could escape, perhaps she could follow it. An insane notion—but one she clung to. She lay down and curled tightly into a ball for warmth. The pattern of the stars swayed above her eyes. Soon she felt as if she were drifting through the night sky.

The moonlight, the flickering fire, the moving shadows, disappeared into a dream. The wind stopped rustling in the trees. Later, warmth crept into her body, and she had an illusion of being wrapped in comfort. She awoke in the first daylight to find Black Eagle lying beside her. Their bodies were cocooned in his fur mantle. Dawn had tinted the sky a translucent pink. The sun was rising, the birds were calling, she was still alive, and the day was somehow miraculous.

Jeanne lay perfectly still, conscious that his eyes were on her. His eyes were so black that their pupils seemed almost invisible. His dark face gave no clue to his thoughts. Jeanne thought errantly that he had what Papa had called *a gambler's immobility of countenance.* He looked at her a long time, earnestly, searchingly, pinning her with his gaze. He turned toward her, slowly, imperceptibly. She felt his hand gently touch her split and swollen lip.

All power to move appeared to have gone from her limbs. She lay still and quiet, too frightened to shift, to breathe. His fingers slid lightly over her cheek, across her nose to the other cheek, then down to rest on her neck.

Jeanne's eyes widened as she felt a quiver in the fingers that lightly touched her shoulder. That repressed sign of the man's pent-up feeling gave her an odd thrill, affected her strangely, stirred the very roots of her being.

"No," she managed to whisper, pressing a hand against the rockhard chest that seemed to crush her.

His face looming above her in the half darkness, Black Eagle was systematically unbraiding her hair, untangling, threading, his fingers learning the texture, his eyes absorbing the vibrancy of her fiery mane. She could feel the steady beating of his heart against her hand. He looked down into her dazed hazel eyes.

When he spoke, his voice was low, almost inaudible, and his breath was warm against her skin.

"There is a strangeness about you, daughter of the moon. The sunset is trapped in your hair, the colors of the world hide in your eyes, falling leaves dwell in your pale skin, and the voice of the turtle sings in your words. It excites me to know the Eternal Person, in disguise."

Jeanne could smell his excitement, the faintly musky male odor mingled with the aroma of bear grease. She could feel his excitement in the long length of the body pressed against hers, solid and muscular and hard, the fullness of him, the maleness of him.

She had never before felt a man's body. Not like this, so close that she could hear the rumble of his breathing, smell the man-smell of him, feel the throbbing rigidity of his body. Jeanne was not sure what was happening. All she knew was that it sent a wild swirling into the pit of her belly.

Driven by an impulse to protest, she rolled away and attempted to rise. Before she could pull herself upright, Black Eagle was on his feet, superb in his muscled strength. Then his lips parted slightly in what was, in that stonelike face, almost the equivalent of a smile.

"It is not wise to know a woman before it is decreed. The singing in my blood must be denied for now. I will wait for what is rightfully mine." With these arrogant words, he strode into the bushes.

When the sun rose, it was a beautiful day. Black Eagle returned to Jeanne's side, carrying several bulbous brown roots. Perching himself comfortably on a log, he took out his knife and split the roots. With the point of his knife, he offered one to her. When they had finished the roots, Black Eagle rose, gripped Jeanne tightly by the wrist and led her forward.

"Come," he said, leading her to a small fresh-flowing spring. They knelt and drank. Jeanne splashed her face and hands. But when she started to rise and go back to the camp, Black Eagle caught her arm and held her back. In his hand he held a piece of cord.

Jeanne's eyes opened, stretching wide at the sight. Her face whitened, ludicrous with shock. Like the face of a child. Like the face of a hurt child, slapped while offering a kiss. The tremor of her mouth was an uncontrollable thing. She stood there, willow-slender, as motionless as stone. Staring at him, eyes gone crystalline with dismay, she slowly raised her wrists.

To her amazement, Black Eagle wordlessly shook his head, smiled, put up his hand and stroked her bright hair.

There was a sudden explosion of warmth in her veins, and a little brushfire leapt and blazed across her cheeks. She could feel her nerve ends come alive, twanging like harp-strings in a slow, dissonant, off-tempo response. Her wide, sensual mouth split into a gamine grin of relief. She snatched the cord, looping it, bunching her hair into a fox-tail over her back. Golden lights sparkled in her eyes as she tipped her face back to the sky, giving in to the miracle of being alive.

Eagerly, without any protest, Jeanne followed Black Eagle when Yellow Feather cupped his hands around his mouth and gave the low, trembling cry of a hoot owl, the signal to leave. Until now, the rain had killed their trail. Today, however, a tall warrior with a bear-claw necklace dropped behind. Gently swaying a long, thin willow wand from side to side, he carefully obliterated all signs of their passing.

The party traveled in this way for days, stopping only for brief periods to rest and eat. Jeanne lost all sense of time as day merged into night, night into day. She traveled steadily, youth and determination delivering energy in a smooth-flowing stream as her body adjusted to the constant strain. But each night she lay exhausted, afraid to sleep until she felt the hard length of Black Eagle pressed against her body as he settled himself beside her.

He must have sensed her fear, for once he murmured, "Hush...go to sleep. I am here."

Lying cradled against warm flesh, encircled in the safety and comfort of his arms, she gave a ragged sigh and relaxed against him. Thirty seconds later she was asleep.

Émile did not fare so well. Each day when she sought out the trapper he seemed weaker. He was skeletal, his face gray. His cheeks were dark hollows, and his eyes were lost in their cavernous sockets. Jeanne feared that the arrow must have pierced some vital organ, because he had developed a constant wheeze as his tortured lungs dragged in air, and sometimes there were bloodstains on his beard.

Black Eagle guarded his captive well. It seemed he knew that she had not given up making plans to escape, that they were fools to trust her! She was no longer bound, but she had no doubt that she was still a prisoner.

He treated her as if she were a piece of property, keeping her in sight at all times. When Stands Fast offered her some wrinkled walnuts, Black Eagle watched with sharp, bright eyes. When Thunderclap complained her feet were leaving a spatter of blood on the trail, Black Eagle gave her a spare pair of moccasins from his war bag to wear. Later, he sprinkled some poplar buds he had crushed between his fingers on her blistered heels, stuffing sedge grass into the moccasins as padding. But not once did he attempt to touch her more intimately.

Yellow Feather continued to check Black Eagle's shoulder, although it no longer seemed to trouble the young brave. Late one afternoon they came upon a small buck deer standing and drinking in a pool of water. It turned and stared at them, its ears moving as gently as the wings of some huge white moth. The deer wheeled away. Black Eagle took two long bounds after it and threw his war lance.

The lance made a flat thud, and the buck collapsed in the middle of a jump that would have carried it to safety. Stands Fast and the brave with the bear-claw necklace, Little Bear, helped Black Eagle clean the buck. They hooted softly in derision when they observed that Jeanne turned away from the nauseous sight with her hand over her mouth.

Late one afternoon, when the setting sun appeared to be sinking into the farther end of the long westward reach of the river they had been following, they came upon a small group of lodges huddled on the shore.

"Barricade Falls," said Black Eagle. "Dwelling place of the Rice People. We have arrived." Black Eagle dropped the noose around her neck once more.

Chapter Three

A multitude of people gathered to greet the returning war party. Men, women, children and dogs ran to meet them. Shouts of welcome turned to wails of despair when Yellow Feather struck the side of his own head.

"Ours has been a trail of death," he cried as he held up both hands in a dramatic gesture. "On the Other Side has been lost to us. Singing Bird, we bring only this weak creature and one miserable she-prisoner in return." Yellow Feather indicated Jeanne. "This one sent your son to the spirit world."

The crowd cleared, allowing the passage of an old, withered crone. Her face was a mass of wrinkles. To Jeanne, she seemed immensely old. Yet she did not shuffle or hunch her back, but strode upright like a woman half her age. She stepped forward, beating her head with her fists, chanting shrilly, her ululating moans taken up by the other women.

Behind her was an ancient warrior with a face like an apple that had hung through a dozen frosts upon its limb. He hobbled to stand in front of Jeanne, as though every step cost him painful effort. For all his hobbling, he moved with a confidence that seemed to come from great wisdom and a sureness of his place within the tribe. He peered at her, his eyes dark and troubled. Other members of the People came to stand near Singing Bird, hissing at the two captives.

A feathery wave of terror washed over Jeanne. This was the moment she had been both dreading and anticipating. This marked the culmination of all those agonized hours of travel—the threshold of death, or maybe some torture too horrible to contemplate. Would she be confronted with a situation beyond her power to cope with, or to bear?

She had eaten and slept with death for weeks. She could not keep it up. She knew that. She shrank back against Black Eagle, seeking protection.

Her throat quivered. "I am afraid," she said, her voice breaking over the words, splintering into planes and angles. It was as though time were oddly out of joint, a horrid dream, and she did not know how to set it right.

Black Eagle was so close, his breath stirred her foxtail. "Be strong. Show no fear. It is Singing Bird, mother of On the Other Side, she who will decide your fate. Go to her."

The words struck fear in Jeanne's heart. So her time had come, she thought dazedly as, encouraged by a gentle pressure against her spine, she took a step forward. Two steps. Her mouth was dry as sand. Her tongue stuck to the roof of it.

Mortal fear twisted inside her. It beat about her head like hidden wings. For all the harshness she had endured since her capture, Black Eagle had protected her from the warriors, seen to her comfort in many small ways. She had begun to accept the small attentions, to enjoy this vast land. Things had happened so swiftly, so ruthlessly, that she still verged upon the incredulous.

Between her past mode of life and the new lay a vast gulf of distance, of custom. Her whole world had changed, but she was nothing if not adaptable. She had begun to feel comfortable in the company of Black Eagle, to look to him for protection. *Show no fear.* She took another step forward, tilting her head back, straightening her spine.

The old woman looked at Jeanne. She did not say anything. She did not need to. Her eyes said enough. They were the eyes of an ancient she-eagle, icy with contempt.

Singing Bird made a half turn away from Jeanne. Then she whirled, lunged forward all at once, hurling herself against Jeanne. Her face was twisted with rage, and her moving hands were invisible with speed.

Jeanne felt the piercing of her flesh, streaks of fire moving down her face, and Singing Bird's hands came away with bloody nails. Singing Bird caught the front of Jeanne's bodice in one hand and slapped her face, right and left and right again, so that her head jerked upon her neck.

The other women screamed encouragement to Singing Bird, darting at Jeanne from all sides, shoving and pushing so that her slender figure was borne to earth. She felt a hard foot find her ribs, and all the breath left her body. She managed to get to her feet, screaming as someone grabbed her long foxtail and jerked her backward. Black Eagle's voice cut across the cacophony of sound.

"Is this one going to snap and bite like a vixen cornered, or is she going to wail like a small child?"

Jeanne turned toward that voice she recognized all too easily. Black Eagle's arms were folded, his legs were spread, and there was a quality about his expressionless face that warned her to expect no assistance from him.

Their eyes met, his hard and glittering, hers flashing, ignited by the fires of hatred. She would have raked out his eyes had she been able to reach them. Then, a blow struck her. Another. She stumbled. Quickly, Jeanne scrambled out of the way of the next blow.

"When a papoose cries, sweet maple is the only answer."

Now, she knew, he was taunting her mercilessly. Rage mounted up and beat about her ears as she rushed blindly toward the group of women. To stand still was to be murdered. But she was seventeen years old, and she did not want

to die. Not now, with vengeance against Black Eagle un-
earned, with revenge still before her. And especially not in
this stupid, ignominious way, put to death by this *canaille*
for the crime of self-protection! She was so enraged, she
raised her leg and gave a kick that sent one of the women
sprawling.

"Eyah!"

The victory shout burst from Jeanne's throat, primitive
as any war whoop. Her will to live forced her to stand her
ground, to give blow for blow. She heard a sharp cracking
sound, like the snapping of a pipe stem—or a bone breaking. Then a stone whistled past her head. Another hit her
shoulder.

The missiles continued to rain down on Jeanne, forcing
her to give ground, to cover her face with hands and fore-
arms, with no chance to offer a return blow. The women
screamed abuse. *To every thing there is a season, and a time
to every purpose... A time to be born, and a time to die...*
Jeanne dared not think of that. She dared not think at all
now. When you cling to life by a thread, you have no
strength to look beyond. She needed all her will to keep her
feet in motion.

Jeanne shouted again. "Eyah!" It was a high note, shrill
with animal terror. What she needed to do was to vanish into
thin air or have the ground open up and swallow her. Since
both were clearly impossible, she took the available alter-
native. She fell into a crouch, like a cat. She had watched
some boys fight once, in France. The smaller boy had beaten
the larger one. What had he done? Yes! He had not stood
still. And he had put his arms up, like so.

"Eyah!"

Protecting her face in her huddled arms, Jeanne tucked
her chin down behind her left shoulder and leapt into the
fray. She bobbed, weaved, ducked and sidestepped through
the throng of women, using all her wiry strength to run to-

ward the man who continued to mock her. A roar went up as she reached Black Eagle. She glared at the others. They moved back, back...

Black Eagle's words were lost beneath the women's caterwauling, but to Jeanne they sounded like "Well done." Which was impossible, of course. Triumph beat through her veins in waves. She had done it! She really had!

Then it ended. All at once, with no interval of transition, the triumph drained out of her, leaving her trembling, cold and sick, unaware of the rapid currents swirling around her.

The ancient warrior pushed his way through the women to stand beside Black Eagle. He raised one hand, and the din subsided. With his other hand, he motioned to Singing Bird.

"Come," he commanded.

Singing Bird obeyed, rocking back and forth, tearing at her clothes.

"There is fire in this she-prisoner. You all saw it." He gestured suddenly. "I, Wise Speaker, have walked in the place of the spirits. I recognize their power. Surely she has been sent by the manito, the spirits, for reasons we do not yet understand. For that reason, for the moment, she should live."

Every head turned to Jeanne. She stared back at them like a trapped animal. She watched them with a curious detachment as, one after the other, they nodded. Her mind was far too blank to read the admiration in their eyes.

Jeanne looked at Black Eagle. He slowly turned his head away from her, turned to look over her head at the women behind her. It seemed he had turned his gaze away, as if shifting position, not as though he were trying to avoid looking at her. But she saw the barest glimmer of recognition in his eyes, a hint of a nod.

It was enough. Her anger was pushed into a corner of her mind, to be brought out later, when her survival was not at stake. She marched straight to Singing Bird and stood arrow-straight before her. A wave of sickening rebellion against everything she had endured swept over her. She felt irrevocably alone, humiliatingly helpless in the struggle to survive.

"It is for you to decide, Singing Bird." Jeanne gestured defiantly. "You can seek revenge for the death of your son. You can have me killed, but you cannot crush my spirit! I will still be free! Free as the wind!"

Singing Bird's eyes were dark and sullen, but the former blaze of hatred had died out of them. She bowed her head.

"As Wise Speaker says, the ways of the manito are strange." Her voice was gruff, guttural. "Enough have died. The People can decide your future."

Jeanne had been in the wigwam a long time. Until the sun had set, she had heard the rumble of voices debating her fate, but she had not been able make out what they said. And now it was night. It had been dark for over an hour. The fire on the hearthstone had been stirred and stoked against the chill that pierced the bone and its acrid smoke stung her nostrils and throat.

She leaned back against a pole and closed her eyes. She was not hungry anymore. Just before dark, a young girl had brought her food. Hesitantly she had approached Jeanne, a birchbark container of food in one hand. With her other, she had fingered a small amulet hanging from her neck by a leather thong, as though to invoke protection, or to ward off unknown spirits. She had stopped several feet away, reluctant to come closer, pushing the container toward Jeanne. Its contents had been surprisingly good, a broth of moose flesh and wild rice, hot and savoury. Jeanne had eaten every scrap. It had put the strength back into her.

The yellow glow of the fire spread softly through the lodge. Jeanne lay there, listening. Then, after a while, the rhythm of a drum came over to her. She could hear the beats of it, as if they were stamping themselves out in the air before her eyes. The sound had no melodic line. It was crashing, savage. Slow chanting began. She shivered, wrapping her arms tightly about her.

The rattling sound of the door flap being lifted brought Jeanne's head up sharply, and she held her breath. Had the People decided? Had they changed their minds? Was she to be tortured to death?

The face of Black Eagle came into view, painted as it had been the first time she saw him. Fearsome. Dangerous. She stared at him. In the shadows of the lodge, he seemed taut, strained, ready to pounce, like some jungle animal that has already flexed its muscles yet remains unmoving, waiting for its prey.

"Come," he said, gesturing toward the open doorway.

There was no mistaking the command, and Jeanne tried to still the trembling of her hands as she slowly stood, standing just out of his reach. She could see his knife, interlaced ribbons, feathers and decorations of war decorating its haft, dangling from one hand. She wanted to scream in denial, but she could not.

Black Eagle moved to see her better in the dim light. He towered above her, so close that her nostrils were assailed by the tobacco he had been smoking. Jeanne suddenly felt as helpless as a bird sighted by an eagle.

As she met his half-lidded stare, she could sense undercurrents of such intensity, that she took a step backward. She stood perfectly still, hands clasped tightly together to still their trembling, afraid to move a muscle, her eyes wide open.

"Why are you doing this?" she whispered fiercely. "Why?"

The fire flamed merrily, throwing dancing shadows across his face, his long, lean figure making an even blacker shadow on the floor. Black Eagle shrugged nonchalantly, his face an impassive mask. But there was nothing simple or dispassionate or nonchalant in the fires burning in his midnight eyes. His gaze was as hot as the fire's coals.

"It is the custom," he said gravely.

Jeanne stared blindly at the knife. Her mind refused to accept what he was saying. "Will it take long?" An involuntary whimper escaped from her throat.

"No, only a few seconds." His voice was deep and husky, tinged with regret.

Their gazes clashed, and for one tense, silent moment they stared deeply into each other's eyes. Jeanne saw the reflected red flames of the fire burning there and watched his pupils dilate with some emotion, that was both a fear—and a hope. The hope was greater than the fear. She gazed at him, and felt a curious pull at her innards. He could not mean to torture and kill her, or could he? Yes, she thought. He did.

"Why not do it now?" she asked. Her eyes flickered to the knife.

Black Eagle shrugged. "It makes no difference to me. I thought that perhaps you would prefer to share in the ceremony." He stepped forward.

Jeanne found herself in the grip of an overwhelming need to turn and run. Instead, she stood like stone, her heart crying out in torment, her face giving no indication of the turmoil within. He smiled, as if he were amused, and began to walk toward her, very slowly, twirling the knife in his fingers.

She stood rooted to the spot, transfixed, her gaze riveted upon the blade. He was standing in front of her now.

"Are you ready?" he asked calmly.

He was so close she could feel the heat from his body. The scent of him filled her nostrils when she dared to inhale. He gently slid his hand slowly up the side of her neck.

Jeanne froze. She felt unable to breathe, unable to move. His nearness, his touch seemed to immobilize every part of her body. Helplessly she raised her eyes to his. His eyes gleamed with mockery. He took a strand of the fox-fire hair that tumbled from her face between his fingers, slowly rubbing it, as if enjoying the sensation. He twisted his hand into her hair and held her head still as he cut off a lock of hair.

"That was not too painful, was it?" He held the curl up like a trophy.

Jeanne abruptly jerked away from him, as if she had been scalded. Color flooded her cheeks. A wave of rage swept through her, so fierce that she began to tremble from the force of it.

"Oh." It was more of a gasp. "You *imbécile*. Do you know how frightened I was? What I thought you were going to do?" she demanded hotly. The sudden release of tension made her want to knock the knowing smirk from his face. For an instant she stood still, knowing it was useless to try to match his superior strength. Then her volatile temper exploded, robbing her of caution.

Giving in to the ferocious anger pulsing through her, she clenched her hands and began to hit him. She pummelled his chest and kicked wildly at his shins. He grinned at her fury, making no attempt to parry the blows until a flying fist struck his partly healed shoulder.

He shoved his knife into his waistband, and his free hand snaked out to seize her wrist. Slowly, deliberately, he started to pull her toward him.

Belatedly sense returned to Jeanne. She frantically tried to take a step back, to put some distance between them, but it was too late. He had already wrapped his hard, muscular arms around her, firmly anchoring her against him. She felt the powerful strength of his thighs hard against her, was excruciatingly aware of her breasts crushed against his chest.

She tried to twist out of his grasp, but he jerked her upward so that her toes barely reached the floor. His superior size and strength easily kept her his captive. He would not even let her hurt herself fighting him; he simply held her tightly until she exhausted herself and lay limply against him, gasping for breath.

"So small and pale, yet with so much spirit," he murmured hoarsely, his lean body arching against hers.

Breath coming in sobs, Jeanne hung from his hands, aware of eyes that burned like coals in the darkness, conscious of the long, brown body, the smooth, powerful muscles that coiled and uncoiled in the flat, hard belly moving against hers. She squirmed involuntarily against him, digging her nails into his back in an effort to destroy his compelling rhythm.

"This is wrong," he said thickly, pushing her away roughly. "The manito are testing my strength, my manhood. They have stolen my secret dream and changed it to a living thing, to test, to torment, to see whether I am worthy."

Jeanne took a shaking step backward, her heart squeezing painfully inside her. With his weight gone, she felt a strange sense of loss. For a moment she struggled with words, unable to mouth them. Then, as her voice returned, she asked, her voice surprisingly steady, "Why should the spirits need to test you?"

"It is the way of the spirits. They have set the price of my acceptance as a medicine man. I have to pay for giving you my protection, for behaving in an unacceptable manner," he said heavily. "On the Other Side was as a brother to me. His body lies far away. For four days, custom decrees we will address his spirit so that he can travel the way of the manito. This piece of hair from the one who struck him down will be placed with articles he valued during his lifetime. There is no doubt your protection is strong, or you would not be alive. It will be a sign of grief, a promise of reparation, to help him on his journey.''

There was pain buried deep in his words, Jeanne sensed. Black Eagle was not, she realized with a start, as invulnerable as he pretended to be, and she found a part of herself wanting to reach out and soothe whatever ache haunted him.

"Come," he said again, grasping her arm, dragging her along with him.

Jeanne was fully aware of the unyielding strength of his fingers, of the futility of struggling to gain release. She went.

There were sullen mutters from a few women as Black Eagle led her toward the center of the lodges, where a large fire blazed. Everyone was looking at her. Jeanne could feel their curious eyes, and lifted her chin defiantly.

That she was still alive was incredible. That she was so bold as to be defiant was a source of curiosity, and not a little fear. Everyone knew that her life had been spared because of Black Eagle's secret dream. Her own audacity in challenging the women had supported that decision.

What course of action would Wise Speaker take? Had she not killed one of their favorite sons? And Black Eagle! Had not her magic stick pierced his shoulder, leaving a hole as large as a man's hand? Had he not apologized to Singing Bird for his improper behavior in preventing the killer of On the Other Side suffering instant punishment?

Jeanne understood most of the chatter. What she could not understand, she could guess. Cheeks flaming, hazel eyes flashing points of fire, she returned their stares. She would let no one see her fear of them.

"Black Eagle! At last! We thought you were lost!"

"Or hiding!"

"What took you so long, Black Eagle? Did the fiery-headed squaw prick your tongue? Was she gentle with you?''

"We were just coming to look for you. Yellow Feather was fearful lest the pale daughter of the moon had spilled your blood!"

A chorus of good-natured badinage greeted them as the other members of the war party joined Black Eagle, forming a circle around the pair. Black Eagle shook his head, refusing to be drawn in, and he kept a firm grip on Jeanne's wrist. They continued to chaff Black Eagle as he strode forward.

Jeanne quickened her step so that she walked at Black Eagle's side. After all, she was Jeanne de la Rocque, granddaughter of a duke, of aristocratic race and blood. She might have been taken captive, forced to march for endless days, reduced to wearing rags... she might have had to kill to survive, to engage in bestial fisticuffs, to be manhandled, and, worst of all to be kept on a lead by her tormentor... but she would remember Papa's motto: *"I will contrive!"*

Her stride was checked, and she stumbled, when she noticed the Frenchman kneeling, huddled against a pole.

The trapper was a pitiful sight. Straggly black hair and a dark beard matted with blood and grime hid most of his features. His wrists were chafed raw where they had been bound. His garments were ragged, mottled with filth, his breeches torn nearly to the waist on one side.

He had lost weight since their capture, and his thinly fleshed ribs showed through the tattered shreds of his shirt. Where the arrow had entered his shoulder, Jeanne could see an ugly, festering inflammation.

"Émile!" Jeanne turned to Black Eagle, her eyes pleading. "Black Eagle, let me go to him, *s'il vous plaît*. He's sick. He will die if unattended...."

"Take care, woman. I am but a man. For the good of all, I respect and obey the laws of the tribe."

The uncompromising finality in his tone stung. Jeanne flinched as he roughly shoved her forward to stand in front of the fire pit.

"Do not shame me. Or is that what you want?"

Jeanne's eyes burned with tears, and she did not see Black Eagle shift to stand protectively behind her as the old medicine man drew near. The other warriors fell back to allow him through. Wise Speaker stepped closer.

He moved in a slow manner, as if contemplating each step. He shuffled over to Jeanne, looked at her thoughtfully for a while, then made flowing one-handed motions over her. His wise old face, seamed and lined, wavered in front of Jeanne. It was a brave and intelligent face. She stared at him, fascinated, her tears gone.

Wise Speaker had never taken a mate. He had maintained a reserve that added to his stature. Everyone regarded him with awe. He had seen more than seventy snows. They stared at each other, the young girl and the ancient wise man, studying each other with equal intensity. Jeanne returned his look with a frank curiosity. This seemed to surprise him, and the puckered skin of his face contracted around his wide mouth.

Jeanne was unaware that the children of the tribe were always a little afraid of him. They learned quickly that even their elders held him in awe, and his aloof manner did not encourage familiarity. The gulf widened when mothers threatened to call the Wise Speaker if they misbehaved. It was not until they gained the maturity of adulthood that members of the tribe came to temper their fear with respect.

His face came so close to Jeanne's that she could feel the warmth of the man's breath on her cheeks. She looked steadily into the hard black eyes in his sallow face.

Why, he was just like *Grand-père!* Wise Speaker's hair was gray, hanging straight and loose down about his shoulders, where it should have been curled, dressed into pigtails and tied with velvet ribbons. A wide lace collar should have replaced quill and bone.

The fur mantle draped over one shoulder should have been trimmed with gold braid and buttons. And instead of leggings, he should have worn a fitted doublet with matching Spanish breeches; and boots worn with butterfly boot leathers, spurs and clogs should be worn instead of moccasins; but he still reminded her of *Grand-père!*

His eyes crinkled in the same way, disappearing into manifold creases of skin when he wanted to hide the secrets of his eyes. For this reason, Jeanne felt secure in the presence of Wise Speaker. She felt a new courage.

There was an expectant hush, disturbed only by the crackle of the fire as the gathered people waited for Wise Speaker's reaction. He did not move, other than to narrow his eyes to mere slits. The People watched Wise Speaker in fear and fascination.

A sudden breeze tugged at Jeanne's chemise, lifting the folds and wrapping it around her legs with a rustle as faint as the wind sighing through the trees. As though this were the sign for which he had been waiting, Wise Speaker lifted one hand.

"The wind blows. It has been blowing over the Land of the Turtle for a long time, and it is growing. It will be a whirlwind soon. A strange wind that talks darkly inside a man's heart." He paused, playing on the emotions of his audience. "There are voices in it," Wise Speaker went on. "Voices of people. The words take fire, and the wind of discontent snatches them up and sends them like sparks throughout the land. The wind grows, it becomes a gale."

A shudder ran through Jeanne as Wise Speaker's voice became more impassioned.

"There is muttering in that wind now," he went on, "anger in that gale. The manito know this and have sent this girl to catch the rising wind, to share the destiny of our people. I see more people than grasses of the valley. The rising wind of the People's anger covers the Land of the Turtle like snow. It is then, through this girl's spirit, that the story of On the Other Side will be told.''

Dropping his hand, Wise Speaker drew a pouch from beneath his robe. He fixed Black Eagle with an unwavering stare, then handed him the packet.

With a gravity befitting the importance of the task, Black Eagle withdrew a portion of tobacco from the leather and dropped it into the glowing embers. The watchers leaned forward anxiously, and expelled their breaths in one communal sigh as brightly colored flames leaped upward in a dazzling display. Wise Speaker nodded, satisfied.

Jeanne felt the vibrations of the dull thud of spear butts pounding the ground just as the drums began to beat a sharp tattoo in rhythmic counterpoint. She gasped as, appearing from nowhere, a frightful figure leapt so close that the fire's roaring flames seemed to envelop him in their midst.

The man's features were hard, strong, sharp, their impact increased dramatically by bright red paint streaked over prominent cheekbones and the contour of a strong chin. Surmounted by an eerie white skull that appeared to hang within the fire itself, the leaping figure seemed to absorb all the lambent energy of the fire.

The young man's final lunge brought him directly in front of the powerful man of magic as the dull, thudding rhythm and the excited counterpoint ended with a flourish. The old medicine man and the young warrior stood facing each other.

"I, Cornstalk, say that the spirit of On the Other Side cries for revenge. It will not just bring bad luck to defy custom and let this girl live, it will drive the protective manito away.''

Black Eagle stepped forward. "No, Cornstalk. Protective spirits are not angered by kindness," he protested.

Wise Speaker lifted his arm and stared up at the crescent moon. "On the Other Side now treads the threshold of the spirit world. Only the manito know what road he follows." His rebuke was as gentle as a breeze whispering through grass.

Cornstalk bowed his head and returned to his place. Black Eagle, too, acknowledged the reprimand, stepping back beside Jeanne, jaw clenched, rigid with tension.

Spellbound, Jeanne watched as Wise Speaker began an impassioned appeal to the ethereal world of the spirits. His smooth, flowing motions were eloquent. Every subtle movement of posture, every nuance of gesture, made her tremble. By the time he was through, his people knew they were surrounded by the essences of their protective totems and a host of other unknown spirits.

Jeanne shivered and closed her eyes. A jumble of confusing visions tumbled through her mind. She was dreaming. She was running across a darkened expanse of grass. She saw the shrouded shapes, smelled the sickening stench of burnt flesh. She thought she could hear a man's voice, warm, rich, full of urgency. She struggled to reach the owner of the voice, but slowly other sounds impinged on her consciousness.

She sobbed and uttered a hoarse cry as she wrenched open her eyes.

Émile hung there in front of her, on his hands and knees. Like a dog. Like a whipped dog. He opened his mouth. There was a rustling in the Frenchman's throat. A sound like dry leaves blowing down a cobbled street on an autumn day. A rattle. Louder now, again.

Then, abruptly, no sound at all.

Jeanne's mind recoiled in horror, in outrage, but she seemed unable to move, as though transfixed by a force beyond her capacity to resist. Sickness choked up in her, and she swayed, fighting a sudden rush of dizziness.

"As surely as night follows day, that, too, was destined by the spirits," Black Eagle said. His voice was harsh, but the hand on her arm was gentle.

Chapter Four

Jeanne shot a quick glance at the group of women working nearby. Singing Bird, her face black with the resinous charcoal of mourning, sat on a log, watching the children play. Beside her sat Graceful One, who was to have been married upon the return of On the Other Side. With her dreams as shattered as the arm broken in the skirmish with Jeanne, Graceful One had withdrawn into herself, neither speaking nor eating, her eyes twin dark stars, eclipsed by grief. Her mother, Mountain Wolf Woman, was helping the other women.

Mountain Wolf Woman blamed Jeanne not only for the loss of her daughter's betrothed, but also for her daughter's fragile hold on reality. She wasted no opportunity to show her dislike. Jeanne's ears still buzzed from the blow received only that morning, when she had torn a piece of hide she had been given to scrape.

Giving the women another surreptitious look, Jeanne moved a few steps farther away. She swept sky, river and sloping forest with a quick eye. The land stretched out before her to the rim of the world. She followed the rapid movement of an eagle as it dropped to earth. Above, the clouds piled up, fleecy-white and great-domed with feathery silver edges, scudding before the south wind, and all between was blue.

Down on the river, swollen high from the spring floods, the women were gathering cattail roots, prizing them loose from the marshy edge with their sharp digging sticks. The tender shoots at the top would be used as vegetables. Later in the season, the flowering heads of brilliant yellow pollen would be used to make doughy unleavened bread.

When the tops dried, fuzz would be collected for medicinal purposes, and baskets, mats and ropes made from the tough leaves and stalks. It was said that if the pollen drifted in the wind, the people on whose heads it rested would live to see their children's children.

As Jeanne snapped off the foot-high shoots where they joined the root, a thought struck her. Père Xavier had told Papa in Mont Real that anger had made Mama ill. He said that anger at losing all but one of her children had given her a troubled heart.

Papa had stoutly maintained that the heart has its reasons, which are quite unknown to the head. But Père Xavier insisted the outward manifestation of melancholy meant that this wicked emotion was suppressed, locked inside Mama's mind, transferring hostility to her unborn babe, endangering its soul. The only cure was cupping to relieve this intense emotional state.

Privately Jeanne thought the blood letting had only made Mama worse. If Mama had been well, *le petit enfant* might have been strong and healthy. The need to care for a new infant would have ensured that Mama's depression lifted.

Jeanne reminded herself that she, too, had lost parents, brothers and sisters, but her suffering had not robbed her of spirit. No, another voice said inside her head. You are not numb with sorrow, Jeanne de la Rocque. You are overwhelmed by an all-consuming hatred, so great that it sweeps everything else before it. It eats into your heart like a canker. It blazes like the flame at the core of life itself, which is wicked, evil.

As Jeanne absently moved along the mounds of roots, she peeled and discarded the outermost layer of the cattails, stacking the remaining white portion into a plaited cedar basket. Her thoughts troubled, she gradually distanced herself from the women. She was feeling guilty. Mountain Wolf Woman was right, Jeanne admitted to herself. It was true. She had caused sadness and distress.

With a flash of insight so overwhelming she felt her blood drain and a chill crawl down her spine, Jeanne realized the vicious treatment she received from the women might be their way of dealing with the hurt. What else had the good Jesuit told Papa? *Whatsoever a man soweth, that shall he also reap.* Her knees were weak, and she was shaking so hard she dropped her basket.

Face ashen, Jeanne looked at Singing Bird and frowned. The woman was thin and drawn. The flesh of her once-smooth face hung from her bones, and her black hair, hanging loose as a sign of mourning, was heavily streaked with gray. Jeanne's thoughts ran through the evening of her arrival at the lodge from beginning to end, then over them again, stalling at the moment when Émile had died.

Wise Speaker had added more tobacco to the firepit, studying the colors that arced forth.

"This woman must not die," he had pronounced, his voice low, yet audible to the hushed gathering. "She walks fearlessly and with pride. In the secret dream of your vision quest, she came to you, Black Eagle. She will have need of powerful protection. Will you, Black Eagle, be responsible for her?"

Jeanne frowned, her russet eyebrows knitting as she recalled the moment that Black Eagle had faced Wise Speaker.

His voice deep, strong and even, his eyes black and fierce, he had announced gravely, "I will. The desires of the man-ito baffle us all. They must be appeased. I, Black Eagle, have sworn to Singing Bird that I will provide for her. In all but birth, she is my mother. She will share my fireside and enjoy my protection. As the first gift of a son to his mother, I give to Singing Bird this pale, spotted daughter of the moon. The prisoner is hers to do with as she will."

There had been surprised gasps and murmured conversations. This was unexpected—or was it? Wise Speaker had nodded, reached out and grasped Black Eagle's forearm. "She is your destiny, Black Eagle. She is the future of the People. Guard that future well."

As Jeanne listened to the old man, she felt a sudden chill. She did not think she liked the idea that her destiny was ordained. Why did she need protection? She heard the whispered comments of the people and wondered at the subject of discussion.

It seemed there were divisions within the tribe. Singing Bird was of the Turtle Society. Black Eagle was of the Great Ancestral Bear. By giving her to Singing Bird, Black Eagle had shown great foresight. With her limited knowledge of the language, Jeanne found it all too confusing.

She felt Black Eagle's fingers dig into her wrist and heard him say, "Tomorrow, I will purify myself and seek the advice of my protective spirits. Go, now, with Singing Bird. Obey her in all things...."

Restoring the spilled contents to the basket, Jeanne discovered she had been holding her breath, and released it. What would the old woman have done if Black Eagle had not promised to care for her? Too old and barren to attract another mate, Singing Bird would have died without the protection of Black Eagle. Jeanne struggled with her conscience.

Graceful One was also overburdened with grief. The blank look in her lovely almond-shaped eyes made Jeanne feel uncomfortable—and guilty. Perhaps her emotional disturbance was a combination of shock and pain, a numb ache that deadened her mind. *Whatsoever a man soweth that shall he also reap.* Jeanne de la Rocque's harvest would be as barren as a bundle of sheaves, fit only for dry tinder!

Then an idea struck Jeanne. It hit her so suddenly, a flush of excitement rushed over her. It was not a great service, but it was something tangible that she could do for Graceful One, and the personal risk to her gave it meaning.

Her guilt gone, Jeanne ran with sinewy grace along the narrow trail and up the path toward the point, which the women always took when they went to check the maple syrup pans. The act of running away imposed its immediate penalty. She was beset by fears she had not imagined. Thoughts of war parties and further kidnappings haunted her.

Shadowed terrors filled the thickets on every hand, waiting to spring out upon her. The harsh laughing call of a great spotted woodpecker filled the air. She strained her ears to listen for the sounds of pursuit. Breathing hard, she clenched her teeth against the hammering impulse to stop.

As she rounded the point and started up the long trail to the high shelf above, a partridge broke cover, fluttering in front of her. In panic, Jeanne strayed from the path. Suddenly her foot was seized. She fell headlong.

The grip on her ankle told her what it was that had so savagely gripped her even before she had recovered enough to run her hands down her leg. She had carelessly stepped into one of the hunter's traps. The carved tread-bar jaws had not cut deeply into her flesh, but were inexorably fastened upon her foot, just below the ankle.

The springs of the trap were too strong for her to loosen and the log to which the deadfall was stapled too heavy for her to drag. She was caught like any wild animal, condemned to lie here at the mercy of the dangers of the day until the falling of night exposed her to yet more fearful dangers.

From where she lay, Jeanne could see where the river gathered momentum to rush over the lip of a high bank in a broad sheet of white water. She could hear the thundering roar of the cataract as it cascaded into a foaming pool worn out of the rock at the base, creating a constant spray of mist and whirlpools where it met its twin, which poured over a similar cliff. She knew that beyond the waterfall the swift currents of the combined watercourse bubbled over rocks as it flowed into a great lake.

Jeanne watched a pair of red kites take wing from their nest high in a tree across the river and fly rapidly into the sky. They spread long reddish wings and deeply forked tails and soared down to the rocky falls.

The sun was settling into a hazy horizon and making golden streamers of the clouds, the colors shifting through the spectrum of golds and bronzes, then reds to a deep mauve, when a shadow appeared against the afternoon sky. Jeanne tried to scream, but could only whimper.

"Going somewhere?"

The high cheekbones, the long face, the hawklike nose, all receded into the background, overpowered by the heavily lashed, angry eyes that moved slowly over Jeanne.

With a sudden great throb of incredulous and shamed delight, Jeanne realized that it was Black Eagle. She had not seen him since that terrible night over a week ago when he had handed her over to the care of Singing Bird.

During the four-day period of mourning for On the Other Side, he had slept in the purification lodge, and he had departed on a hunting trip with Stands Fast and Thunderclap immediately after the birchbark spirit bundle had been ceremoniously laid to rest.

Black Eagle fell to one knee beside her, waiting silently for an answer. Jeanne backed away as his hands found the trap, sensing that another battle was at hand. She doubted he would believe she was not trying to run away.

"Can you stand up?" The glance he shot her was quick, yet his eyes seemed to take in everything about her, from her bushy, untamed hair to her small bare feet.

"Yes. I am not hurt. Just caught."

He took her by the shoulders and lifted her to her feet. "Now hang on to me." He held her upright against him to get a better purchase on the snare as he felt with his moccasins for the hinges of the trap and, pressing against her, thrust his full weight on them. The lever fell open, releasing Jeanne's foot. She was free.

The tumult within Jeanne made her frantically anxious to appear calm. She stood on one leg and tried the toe of her cramped foot against the ground. "I am sure nothing is broken."

Black Eagle grasped her in his arms and swung back to the path. Jeanne pressed her face in the hollow of his shoulder, against his neck, to escape the scrape of branches. His physical presence, like his gust of rage, was real. The masculine smell and roughness of him were real. The straining, convulsive embrace in which they were clasped was real.

The excitement and terror and pain of the past weeks had made her seem able to think with a sudden, extraordinary clarity. He must sense the half terrified, half shamed, yet wholly unknown excitement that suffused her. Her arms tightened about him. Her moan was a welcome.

Black Eagle recoiled. His start of dismay filled her with a greater dismay. She could not see his expression clearly in the dim light, but she could sense the eagerness with which he released her.

Jeanne removed her hand from his arm and stood unassisted. The breeze ruffled the spiked ends of Black Eagle's roach, and when he turned to look at Jeanne, a burning resentment flared for a moment in both their eyes.

She was suddenly struck by a fear that he knew her feelings, but then, made all the more nervous by the discovery of her own excitement, she stammered wildly, "I saw some comfrey growing up here on the way to the maple trees yesterday. Singing Bird mentioned this morning that she wanted some fresh leaves for Graceful One's arm." Jeanne's voice trailed off weakly at the improvised half-lie, but Black Eagle did not seem to notice.

"You still have marks of many colors on your face from the blows of the women." Black Eagle looked at her bruised and swollen face, her split lips, noting the high color on her cheeks. "There would seem to be fresh marks since I last saw you. Has Singing Bird been beating you?"

"No. I fell," she managed in a strangled voice.

"In that case, I will walk back with you."

He motioned for her to precede him, and she did so haughtily. Looking neither left nor right, her head high on her long, slim neck, she carried her pride like a jester at a fair, wrapped in nothing but rags and dignity.

Jeanne did not know why she lied. It was not fear of retribution from Singing Bird, nor was it a desire to keep secret the treatment she had received from Black Eagle. It was more that she did not want to face the bitter humiliation she had suffered at the women's hands. She shrank from the thought.

Her guilt and shame at lying lay heavy on her conscience. If she admitted it to herself, she knew intuitively, her hate would dissipate. Her life was different now, she was different. She was to live among strangers with foreign ways. She dared not give in to the despair she felt. She needed the hate within. Without the hate, she would be empty.

"You are in luck," Brave Eagle said. "There is some comfrey. Best not to go back empty-handed, hmm?"

Jeanne let a small, grateful smile cross her lips, knelt and deftly twisted off some of the large green leaves. When she had harvested a sizable bundle, she folded the edge of her chemise, knotting it to form a carrying basket.

That meant her pale, slender legs were exposed to the man's curious gaze, but she shrugged away her conventional scruples and accepted the inevitable. Haggard and disheveled as she was, she was certainly unalluring and unattractive enough to be safe!

Unaware that a ray of afternoon sunlight stole through the overhanging fern fronds and fell on her hair so that it blazed as bright as fire, Jeanne placed some tender new shoots of peppergrass on top of one of the comfrey leaves, using them as a wrapper.

Black Eagle stood watching her, his arms crossed. They walked slowly back to the women, each lost in thought. Jeanne sensed Black Eagle's withdrawal, but she was glad he was with her when they were met by a group of women coming toward them, sticks in hand.

Black Eagle strode forward to greet Singing Bird, laying both hands upon her shoulders, bending to rest his forehead against hers in greeting.

"Mother of my heart, the son of your breast has returned safe from the hunt."

"Black Eagle." Singing Bird acknowledged his homage with a light touch to the side of his face.

"All goes well with you?"

Black Eagle straightened, looking closely at the woman who had replaced in his heart the mother he no longer remembered.

"Aye," she replied. The word was gruff, guttural, but he understood.

"It was thoughtful of you, Singing Bird, to come to meet the hunter on his return, and to bring with you such a welcome."

He indicated the women's sharp-pointed digging sticks. A flash of white teeth gleamed briefly as he turned toward Jeanne, standing uncertainly behind him.

"But this Little Turtle beat you to it. She waited for me, her errand delayed. You will forgive her tardiness when you see she has picked the first spring shoots of the peppergrass to flavor the elk I have brought you."

Jeanne blanched as the women giggled at the name he had called her. Little Turtle. Did it have some significance? She knew that Black Eagle belonged to the Great Ancestral Bear Society while Singing Bird, his aunt by marriage, belonged to the Turtle Society. She was not sure of the meaning of the separate tribal divisions, but the women clearly thought her new nickname funny. They giggled again, softly, hiding their mouths behind their hands, while Singing Bird and Mountain Wolf Woman exchanged meaningful glances.

"You need not mock me, Black Eagle. Without your interference, I would now be safe in France. Miserable life is no more welcome than miserable death." Jeanne lifted her face and glared at him with loathing and contempt.

Black Eagle met her look, his face set.

"I must always long to be free, to escape at the first opportunity, so yet I stand and refuse to grovel."

"You want to live, do you not?" His voice was strained, dangerous. His black eyes gleamed at her, as if fires had been banked in their depths.

She lifted her chin obstinately, her face bloodless, like the effigy on a tomb. "I want to live, yes. But not without freedom. Not starved and beaten and threatened with death at every turn. Not surrounded by those who hate me. I will fight to escape with my last breath!"

Her surge of temper gave way to the devastating loneliness Jeanne had kept at bay during the past days. She started walking toward Mountain Wolf Woman, then stopped and said, speaking the words slowly, impressively, and with great dignity, "I have brought some comfrey, a plant used for healing where I used to live. It will help reduce the swelling of Graceful One's arm. Perhaps, when the pain in her body lessens, so, too, will the pain in her mind and the spirit of your daughter will return from where it wanders."

Mountain Wolf Woman's black lashes flickered. Her lips twisted. Her eyes were two hard, disembodied, glittering stones. Jeanne felt the woman's resentment and despair.

Turning toward Singing Bird, Jeanne continued quietly, her tone flat. "I am sorry your son walks in the spirit world. When you see Graceful One free and whole again, it may be that your pain, too, will fade, and you will not need to strike at others when your pain is more than you can bear."

Singing Bird looked at Jeanne with those old she-eagle's eyes. A flicker of admiration supplanted the hatred in her eyes. This crazy old woman grudgingly approved of her. Jeanne could see that.

The thought was strangely comforting. Summoning her fading courage, Jeanne faced Black Eagle once more.

"My family is beyond all earthly care. I am alone. Alone in a strange land, among strange people. Your ways are new. I am small, weak, and ignorant. But do you think, because I am small, weak, and ignorant of your customs, that I need to be punished? To be laughed at?"

"They are not laughing at you now, are they?"

Jeanne stood very still and stared at the women. No, the women were not laughing now. They were watching her. Graceful One's eyes were glazed and unfocused, but Mountain Wolf Woman's gaze was steady, and Singing Bird seemed to be regarding her with something of the peculiar satisfaction with which a mother views the work of her own child. Jeanne stood very still, savoring the feeling. It was a good one, very deep and strong and quiet, and the name of it was *respect*.

Black Eagle put out his hand and touched Jeanne's smooth cheek, letting his hand rest there as lightly as a breath. "Life never brings a man what he wants, and seldom what he expects, but in the flux of time all things run together finally, and one learns acceptance."

She brought her own hand up slowly and closed it over his fingers. She drew them down and away from her face, turning them over until she held his hand, palm up. "A choice cannot be made if there is none to make. It is a long way home to France," she said, her shoulders stiff, her chin held at a proud angle. "I would like to learn the ways of your people, but I leave when I will it."

"You forget that you are no longer free to come and go as you please. You belong to me now."

"No, I belong to Singing Bird." Jeanne smiled gently, dropped his hand and went to stand beside Graceful One, feeling a glow of warmth and satisfaction she had not felt for a long time.

"Take the water bag and bring in more water, Turtle. We are nearly out." Singing Bird stirred up the fire and put some stones in it.

Jeanne laid the collecting basket she had been weaving on the pole bed lashed to the inside framework of the lodge and picked up an otter-skin water bag.

Beyond the bark partition that divided the wigwam into private sleeping quarters, she could see Black Eagle sitting, legs outstretched before the fire, delicately threading some fresh feathers into the haft of his war club. She had to step over his legs to reach the door.

Black Eagle ignored her. Since the day he had rescued her from the trap, it was as though she no longer existed. Today was no different. The impassivity of his gaze kindled in her a flare of resentment.

Jeanne hurried the short distance down to the river and quickly filled the water bag. She splashed handfuls of water on her face. The day was unseasonably warm for late spring, and the river sparkled an invitation.

Impulsively Jeanne unbuttoned her tight bodice and splashed into the water. It was cool and refreshing, and washing off the dust and grime of months was a welcome pleasure. She swam upstream and felt the current growing stronger and the water colder as she reached the center of the river. She rolled over on her back and, cradled by the buoyant water, let the flow carry her downstream.

When the swift current started to drag, Jeanne remembered the falls beyond the bend, dived and swam to the far side. She waded back to the shore, to a narrow strip of sand between the river and a steep cliff, and sat down to let the sun dry her. The sparkling water reflected the bright sun up at her, while the almost white sandstone bounced light and heat down, adding to the intense glare.

Jeanne closed her eyes. For the first time in many months, she was completely relaxed and content, so content she did not hear the footfall creep closer, silently and slowly, inch by inch.

The touch of a hand on her thigh brought Jeanne bolt upright. Stands Fast was squatting beside her. Fascinated by the intensity of concentration reflected on his face, she allowed her eyes to move slowly over the taut, sharply angled planes. She saw the muscle flex in his jaw, the pulse beat at his temple. She felt a warmth emanating from him that disconcerted her.

She waited, tense, watching him intently. When he did not move, she scrambled to her knees. "You crept up on me!" she cried accusingly, modestly pulling her bodice together.

Jeanne was flushed with embarrassment at the realization of where his eyes had fallen, and her skin had a rosy glow even to the swell of her breasts where she clutched the fabric.

"I did not expect to find you alone and unguarded. I wished to give you this." Stands Fast held out a strand of shell beads threaded to form a delicate pattern.

"Would it not be better to offer your gifts to Singing Bird?" Black Eagle's words cut like a knife.

Jeanne was startled to see Black Eagle standing at the water's edge. He stood there, motionless, poised, waiting, as though expecting some imminent, sudden occurrence, such as an arrow or a buck plunging from a thicket. His dark brows were drawn together in an intense frown, his eyes were pinpoints of light, and the powerful muscles in his arms and chest were corded with strain. Stands Fast winced.

Aware of the tension between the two men as their glances met and held, Jeanne kept her gaze intently on the face of Black Eagle as she exclaimed indignantly, "And why should Stands Fast not offer me a gift? I think it is an especially delightful gesture of welcome."

The pinpoints flickered. Black Eagle was now standing so close she could see the large black pupils, the converging faint streaks of light within the dark brown of his eyes.

His features stiffening warningly, he responded, "It is not. It is an insult. And you are no better, flaunting yourself in this manner before an unmarried man."

Realizing from the darkness of his glance that he was very angry, Jeanne felt a sudden tightening in her throat. Her own ready anger flared.

"Thank you, Stands Fast. I accept your gift." She slipped it over her head so that the ornament rested on her small breasts. "It is very pretty." She glanced down, then flushed, noting how her wet chemise accentuated her breasts, the curve of her waist, the thrust of her pelvic mound.

Holding Black Eagle's glare, Stands Fast said with a menacing tone of his own, "I think Little Turtle and I will wait here a little while longer."

Black Eagle stood his ground stiffly. His face was blankly unrevealing, the twitching of a small muscle in his cheek the only change in his demeanor. "I do not think that would be a good idea."

Realizing incredulously that the conversation between the two men had abruptly reached a volatile stage, Jeanne turned to Stands Fast.

"I—I do think I should go back to the lodge now, Stands Fast. I am supposed to be doing an errand for Singing Bird. It has taken far longer than I realized. Perhaps you would like to call at the lodge, later?"

Stands Fast looked down into her face, a small smile curling the corners of his mouth, as he replied, "I will call and pay my respects to Singing Bird this very evening!"

His expression stiff and relentless, Black Eagle stood immobile as Jeanne waded out in the water, until she stood waist-deep, feeling the drag of the current. She filled her lungs with air, plunged in and swam upstream in long, clean strokes, racing through the water like a pale arrow of gold. Jeanne swam, scarcely making a splash, her feet flutter-kicking, driving her on, trailing an iridescent wake of bubbles behind her. She turned to the far bank, allowing her feet to trail downward until they touched bottom. Slowly she angled her way across the current, stepped out upon the bank, and stood there, shivering a little.

A woman came out of the woods carrying a log on her back. It was a burden that would have taxed a strong man, but she bore it with apparent ease. She was tall, slender, graceful. Her leather dress was smudged with earth and smoke and pine bark, but her hair and skin were clean. Jeanne recognized her as Rattle, wife of Leaning Wood.

Rattle came to a stop and, without laying down the log, spoke to Jeanne. "I passed Black Eagle earlier on. He was looking for you. Did he find you?"

"Yes, he did." Jeanne's voice was sharp.

Outrage flooded her senses. How dare that man make it so public that he was guarding her! How dare he intimate that she was flaunting herself to the young men of the tribe! Ignoring the trembling that still beset her limbs, Jeanne pulled herself to her full, meager height. Anger flooding her pale face with color, she added, "So did Stands Fast!"

"Stands Fast?" Rattle asked.

"Yes. He gave me this!" Satisfaction in her tone, Jeanne indicated the necklet, glistening with moisture, shining like diamonds in the sunlight.

Rattle looked at the purple-and-white necklace, almost as though she did not believe what she saw.

"Stands Fast gave you that? And you accepted?"

Doubts flooded Jeanne. "Should I not have?"

"Yes, of course. It is just that when Black Eagle gave you to Singing Bird and named you Little Turtle, we all thought...that is...Black Eagle must be—" Rattle giggled. "Leaning Wood will be amazed. I must go tell him!"

Jeanne watched Rattle hurry off, her brow creasing. A small voice inside her head whispered that she had done Black Eagle an injustice. Perhaps he had only been following Wise Speaker's advice. Cursing her stubborn temper, she retraced her steps along the shore, looking for the water bag.

When Jeanne delivered the filled otterskin to Singing Bird, the old woman studied the trinket Jeanne wore closely.

"Stands Fast gave it to me," Jeanne told her defiantly.

The older woman's only response was a grunt, but later, Jeanne saw Singing Bird smiling. It was partly the withdrawn, ageless expression of a woman wise beyond specific knowledge, and partly the excited expression of a child who shares a secret and fears that appreciation will not be properly given.

Chapter Five

That evening, Stands Fast came calling. As he bent to enter the doorway, an errant gust of wind swept into the lodge, setting the woven mats astir, rustling Black Eagle's war roach, which hung on a peg. A distant rumble of thunder echoed the mood within.

Jeanne's eyes turned slowly to Black Eagle, who was politely standing to greet the visitor. He had avoided her all afternoon, speaking only to Singing Bird during the evening meal. Her throat ached slightly with the effort to suppress tears, and she had a sudden, intense desire to cry.

She did not know why he was treating her like this when she had tried to make amends for unknowingly breaking some custom. She had tidied the lodge, shaking out the bark-cloth weavings and folding the furs neatly on the sleeping platforms. She had chopped artichokes and shredded dandelion and clover leaves for Singing Bird to add to the meat bubbling in the large cooking hide suspended on a frame over the fire. She had helped Singing Bird thicken the stew with ground rice stored from the previous harvest. The offending necklet was tucked in the furs on her sleeping platform. And she had braided her newly washed hair, Indian-fashion.

When he had seen her hair, Black Eagle had seemed upset, clenching his fists at his sides. Nervously Jeanne crossed to stand beside Singing Bird, staring at Black Eagle and Stands Fast, who were facing each other like gladiators. Then, as a cord pulled so taut it breaks from the strain, she felt her breath leave her body in a rush when Black Eagle waved his hand toward the fireplace.

"Greetings to you, Stand Fast. Welcome to our lodge," he said courteously, his smile guarded.

Stands Fast walked toward the two women, smiling. A shirt of soft deerskin embroidered with dyed quills hung to his hips, and ribbon appliqué and seed beads decorated his leggings and moccasins.

By comparison, Black Eagle was plainly dressed. His garments, soft from many wearings, faded from numerous washings, were unadorned. His only embellishment was a single eagle feather, the quill end swiveling in a bone socket attached to his scalp lock, allowing the feather to swing freely as he moved.

"Please accept this token, Singing Bird," Stands Fast said without preamble as he handed Singing Bird a finely crafted wooden bowl.

It was round and strong, but of uniformly fine thinness, polished to enhance the subtle pattern of the wood's grain.

"Why, thank you, Stands Fast. That was thoughtful of you." Singing Bird appraised him shrewdly, a broad smile warming her face. She ran her fingertips over the smooth finish, noting the perfect shape and symmetry.

"Sit down and join us." She pointed to the fur rugs scattered in front of the fireplace.

Stands Fast sat down beside Jeanne, far enough away that their knees did not touch, but close enough for her to be acutely aware of him, to smell the warm, musky scent of his skin. The dark eyes that looked into hers held her, compelled her to recognize his animal magnetism, drew from her a feeling as ancient as life itself.

Jeanne forced her eyes away, fixing them on Black Eagle. A tight knot of fear formed in her stomach. He was staring at her, eyes like two black stones.

"Turtle, offer our guest a drink." Singing Bird's gruff command reminded Jeanne of her surroundings.

Carefully adding some ground acorns to the water heating in a pot over the fire, Jeanne gently stirred the plant material with a long piece of antler until it sank, then dropped a piece of crystallized maple sugar into small bowls before adding the infusion.

As she gave Stands Fast a cup of the amber liquid, he touched her hand. She pulled it back a little, her eyes wide with surprise, then left it. But her heart beat with a warning. This was not right. He gave her hand a gentle squeeze, then took the cup and drank.

Jeanne looked at Black Eagle again. A long moment passed. She grasped the bone ladle, scooped out more liquid nervously, spilling some, embarrassed. Her hand shook as she held a cup to Black Eagle. She gave him a tentative smile.

There was no softening in his heavy-lidded gaze as he stared at her, but relief washed over her when he turned to Singing Bird.

"You have taught your new charge well, mother of my heart. The flavor of acorn and sweet maple is just right."

Singing Bird's murmur of approval was lost in the rattle of the deer-hide door cover. It was Thunderclap and Little Bear.

"We have come, bearing gifts for Singing Bird," they chorused in unison.

Black Eagle's expression did not lighten. If anything, his scowl deepened. However, he remained the perfect host, offering the ebullient pair a seat and a refreshment. They took places on either side of Jeanne, forcing Stands Fast, who had politely stood to greet the newcomers, to surrender his position.

"Greetings, Little Turtle. We have come to visit you!"

"We heard from Leaning Wood that Singing Bird was receiving callers—"

"And accepting gifts! You move fast, Little Turtle!"

Bewildered by the attention she was receiving, Jeanne closed her eyes, hearing the words of greeting echo in her mind, seeing again the fleeting shadow of anger cross Black Eagle's face.

Singing Bird beamed in satisfaction, her smile of hospitality broadened by her delight with her gifts. Thunderclap had presented her with a small container, exquisitely decorated. Carved out of wood into the shape of a small bird, the effigy had designs of feathers carved on it. The overall composition gave the impression of movement, of plumage rippling. Little Bear's gift was a heavy pile of dark fur. Singing Bird grinned widely when she shook out the mantle, made from an entire bear hide, and flung it over her shoulders.

"Your gifts are welcome and very beautiful," Singing Bird said. "Visitors always bring a little excitement, and we have not had visitors for a while. Not since On the Other Side was lost to us. You were all his childhood companions and grieved at the manner of his death. It is not good that a warrior should join the spirits when the longing and the lust and the dreaming are in him still. I was saddened that this was so. I was angry that so small and pale a female had the strength to steal the breath from my son."

Jeanne bent her head. A wave of guilt and remorse swept over her.

"But the spirit of the east wind has entered my dreams and reminded me that it was a lock of hair from Little Turtle that was the first item placed in my son's spirit bundle. That this was a sign that her heart was free from malice."

Jeanne winced. She lifted her hand to her forehead and sneaked a peek at Black Eagle under her lashes. Narrow black eyes slanted back at her.

"Now you are all here, I will tell you a dream-story told to me by your spirit-brother, On the Other Side." Singing Bird looked into the five young faces, and lowered her voice to a whisper.

"In a northern village of the Rice People dwelt a young girl so exquisitely beautiful that she attracted hosts of admirers. The fame of her beauty spread far and wide, and warriors and hunters thronged to her father's lodge in order to behold her."

Jeanne fixed her eyes on Singing Bird in surprise when the old woman's voice altered subtly as she continued her narrative.

"By universal consent, she received the name of Red Bird. One of the braves who was most assiduous in paying her his addresses was called Flash in the Sky because of the richness of his costume and the nobility of his features. He stood straight as a pine tree, head high with pride.

"Desiring to know his fate, the young man confided the secret of his love for Red Bird to another of her suitors, and proposed that they both should approach her and ask her hand in marriage. But the coquettish maiden dismissed the young braves disdainfully and, to add to the indignity of her refusal, repeated it in public outside her father's lodge."

Singing Bird paused to let her eyes travel over the four braves, who sat with downcast eyes, on to Jeanne, who waited expectantly, hands folded in her lap, eyes wide.

"Flash in the Sky, who was extremely sensitive, was so humiliated and mortified that he fell into ill health. A deep melancholy settled on his mind. He refused all nourishment, and for hours he would sit with his eyes fixed on the ground in moody contemplation. A profound sense of disgrace seized him, and notwithstanding the arguments of his relations and comrades, he sank deeper into lethargy.''

Singing Bird had settled now into a chanting rhythm, and Jeanne, seated between Thunderclap and Little Bear, wriggled self-consciously. She glanced at Black Eagle, staring with undisguised curiosity, caught his steady gaze and lowered her own, allowing herself to be absorbed by the tale once more.

''Flash in the Sky appealed to his guardian spirit to revenge him on the maiden who had thus cast him into despondency. He kneaded snow over a framework of animal bones, molding it into the shape of a man, which he dressed and covered with beads and feathers. By magic art he animated this figure, placed a bow and arrows in its hands, and bestowed on it the name of Hairy Serpent.

''The brilliant appearance of Hairy Serpent caused him to be received by all with the most marked distinction. But none was so struck by the bearing of the noble-looking stranger as Red Bird. Her mother requested him to accept the hospitality of her lodge, which he duly graced with his presence. But, being unable to approach too closely to the hearth, on which a great fire was burning, he placed a boy between him and the blaze, in order that he should run no risk of melting.''

Singing Bird paused, peering around the smoke-filled lodge, and sensed rather than saw that she had her listeners' undivided attention. Jeanne made a strangled sound as she fell under the spell of the storyteller.

''Soon the news that Hairy Serpent was to wed Red Bird ran through the encampment. On the following day, Hairy Serpent announced his intention of undertaking a long journey. The two set out. A rough and rugged road had to be traversed by the newly wedded pair. On every hand they encountered obstacles, and the unfortunate Red Bird, whose feet were cut and bleeding, found the greatest difficulty in keeping up with her more active husband. Finally, the sun came out and shone in all his strength.

"Red Bird was glad and sang, forgetting her discomforts. But a strange transformation overcame her husband. At first he attempted to keep in the shade, to avoid the golden beams that he knew meant death to him, but all to no avail. The air became gradually warmer, and slowly he dissolved and fell to pieces, so that his frenzied wife now only beheld his garments, the bones that had composed his framework, and the gaudy plumes and beads with which he had been bedecked. Long she sought his real self, thinking that some trick had been played upon her, but at length, exhausted with fatigue and sorrow, she cast herself on the ground and, with his name on her lips, breathed her last. So was Flash in the Sky avenged."

Thunderclap chuckled. Little Bear nodded in agreement, chuckling also, a mischievous grin on his round face. Stands Fast grinned, too. Black Eagle leveled a sharp look at Jeanne, then turned back to Singing Bird, a polite smile on his face.

Jeanne looked down at the ground, trying to make up her mind about the meaning of Singing Bird's dream-story. She knew it had something to do with Black Eagle and herself. She knew he was angry with her but she did not know why.

Black Eagle smiled gently across at Singing Bird. "That was a wonderful story. It is good to know that On the Other Side still walks in your dreams." He even clapped Stands Fast on the shoulder as they walked to the door together, but Jeanne noticed that the tension across his shoulders had not eased.

The next evening, in addition to Stands Fast, Thunderclap and Little Bear, the lodge of Black Eagle was visited by Cornstalk and Watchful Fox, both laden with gifts for

Singing Bird. Watchful Fox was the son of Yellow Feather and Good Woman.

Jeanne knew his mother. Good Woman had shown Jeanne how to fashion the birchbark vessel used for gathering roots and plants. Jeanne had felt clumsy, all thumbs. Her feeble attempts, all unsuccessful, had ensured a blow on the ears from Mountain Wolf Woman. But Good Woman, her fingers long, deft and powerful, had patiently demonstrated how to shape the truncated pyramid so that it did not unravel. Jeanne felt such a warm rush of feeling for the caring, sensitive woman that she smiled sunnily at Watchful Fox.

Discussion centered on the imminent departure of the People for the annual sugar camp. For several days, the entire tribe would be busy rendering the liquid drained from the maple trees down to a crystallized form of lump sugar.

"When the first sugar of the year is cooked, the People always offer a small amount to the manito. The Offering of the First Fruits is a very special ceremony. Especially for those of us who are unwed." Thunderclap's mouth widened in his lean face, and there were crinkles at the corners of his eyes. "Are you going to join in the dancing this year, Black Eagle?"

The eagle feather swirled rapidly as Black Eagle shook his head. "I think not. I think I will be like Wise Speaker and reserve my strength for the work of the manito." He regarded Jeanne thoughtfully. "No gifts will be given, nor songs sung by me. This I have sworn."

Watchful Fox frowned as if puzzled, and stared at Black Eagle. "What do you do when you want something so much you are sure you must have it? Do you wait? Do you pray? Do you hope for someone to give it to you? Do you just sit and shiver? Or do you reach for it?" His voice was a hoarse whisper.

Black Eagle eyed Watchful Fox narrowly. He looked for a long time, and his face was grave. Then, very slowly and quietly, he said, "Such thoughts would cause me pain, but my guardian spirit is strong. He would not have me dishonor him by choosing a wife unwisely."

"Be careful it is not pride, or bigotry or cowardice, that tempers your conduct!" Singing Bird shouted, her voice caustic. "You had better marry a frog or mouse or some other animal than take pride to bed. What is pride good for?"

Singing Bird began handing out bowls of mint-flavoured tea. Jeanne tasted hers and made a face. Singing Bird had added at least two sugar lumps. Something must have upset her terribly. Jeanne watched Black Eagle as he downed the formidable concoction almost at a gulp, hot as it was. Then he laughed. He tipped back his head and laughed. A rich, warm, masculine sound.

Jeanne's heart tripped a beat. She realized it was the first time she had heard Black Eagle laugh.

"Singing Bird, you are the best joking relative a man could have! I agree! The joke is on me! I will have another cup of your wonderful brew!"

After the tea-drinking ceremony, Thunderclap suggested a hand game, which consisted of hiding two small objects in the hands of the players. Singing Bird produced a piece of bone wound with string and a small red pebble.

The game was entered into with great gusto, the men making bets on who would be the winner. Singing Bird offered to keep score.

Jeanne had a quick eye and guessed the correct hands in which the objects were hidden. She clapped her hands with excitement, gurgling with laughter the second time she guessed correctly. Her enthusiasm was contagious.

Even Black Eagle lost his scowl and laughed uproariously at Jeanne's antics when Cornstalk sprang up, holding his hands clenched high above Jeanne's head. With catlike grace, her slender form outlined by her thin linen chemise, she leapt in her efforts to reach the prize, to find it had been tossed to Thunderclap.

When all the young men joined the new game, Jeanne spun like a doll. Giddy with laughter and the attention, she could not remember ever having had so much fun.

And every time she turned around, she saw Black Eagle's gleaming teeth and flashing dark eyes concentrated on her. Unexpected shocks of excitement coursed through her when she fell against him and felt that hard, hot body press against her.

For an instant, Black Eagle held her, then thrust her away as though he had touched a hot coal. This brought broad grins and knowing glances, and was obvious enough to make Jeanne blush.

With a fiendish, wild hoot, Black Eagle responded, spinning her around. His hearty slap on her rump brought a shriek from Jeanne and loud guffaws from the men.

After they had gone, Jeanne lay under her warm pile of furs, trying to solve the puzzle. She was not sure of the significance of the gifts given to Singing Bird. She did know that it had upset Black Eagle. She also knew that Watchful Fox had listened to the anecdotes related by the returning war party, and that he admired her. He had whispered that her hair was the color of a red fox. Stands Fast had told her that her skin was as soft as down. Little Bear maintained that her eyes reminded him of spring flowers, and Thunderclap said that her laugh was just like sunshine.

Only Black Eagle had not complimented her. His eyes had followed her, though, Jeanne thought bitterly. Watching her figure, which was as straight as a stick. Looking down his nose at the freckles she knew were splattered all over her face. But he had suddenly changed—from a slightly pom-

pous young man to one with his fellows. Had Singing Bird
pressed a sore spot?

The question bothered her all next day as she silently
helped the women cut and strip the saplings to be used to
transport the People's belongings to the sugar camp. Jeanne
hacked angrily at the base of a young aspen, then attacked
a second sapling.

Surely she had been spared for a special reason. Yet she
felt besieged and harassed by any number of conflicting
emotions, one of which was a vague sense of anxiety about
Black Eagle. There had been something about his actions
the night before that had unnerved her. And still did, when
she thought about it. Her uneasiness was strange, since he
was no different from the other warriors.

Besides her confusion where Black Eagle was concerned,
she was having to contend with an unreasonable sense of
guilt about her own reactions the night before. To her anger and astonishment, she found herself in the frame of
mind that might afflict a wife who had betrayed her husband with another man. This notion was patently ridicu-
lous, she thought to herself.

In the first place, Black Eagle was not her husband. In
fact, he had categorically stated that he intended to remain
unwed. And in the second place, she had not entirely given
up the idea of escape. So why was she behaving like such an
idiot now? The internal debate continued as she dragged the
poles to where some of the women were stripping the bark
and smoothing the shafts.

It was a very subdued Jeanne who sat beside Graceful
One when the women stopped working to enjoy a midday
rest. Spring had waved her transforming wand over the re-
gion. The hills were bright green with new-leaved birch and
alder and maple. The air was full of those aromatic exuda-
tions the forest throws off when it is in the full tide of the
growing time. The river sparkled in warm sunshine under an

unflecked arch of blue. All that was left of winter were the white caps on the faraway mountains, snow-filled chasms on distant rocky peaks.

"Little Bear has visited the lodge of Black Eagle for two nights!"

As though it could be contained no longer, the accusation burst from Sweet Breeze. Her face was flushed from a combination of strenuous activity and emotion, and the flawless copper of her complexion was heightened along her elegant cheekbones.

"Why, yes, Sweet Breeze, he has." Jeanne spoke very slowly and clearly, employing deliberately the somewhat ornate usages of emphasis that the French used habitually. "But so, too, did several other friends of Black Eagle. They brought Singing Bird gifts." Jeanne permitted herself an expression that was almost a smile. "We had such fun."

Sweet Breeze fairly flounced away at Jeanne's response. Jeanne's sable-fringed hazel eyes met the dark, enigmatic ones of Singing Bird briefly before they traveled to Graceful One's face. There is not any justice in this world, she thought bitterly. Why could not Graceful One have squealed in outrage like Sweet Breeze, instead of curling in upon herself, weaving silence like a protective cocoon securely around her? Her arm was healing well within the hardened-birchbark binding. But her spirit showed no sign of returning to dwell within the shell of her body.

Jeanne sat there, looking at Graceful One. Then, suddenly, impulsively, she put out her hand.

"Try some of this, Graceful One."

She proffered a piece of her dried, sugar-encrusted cherry cake, wrapping the girl's fingers around the sweet treat.

"If only she would speak, and tell me what she dreams of, I might be able to send away the demon that torments her." Good Woman sighed and looked at Graceful One.

The young woman was sitting quietly in the circle formed by the women, obediently eating the treat put in her hands. But she remained indifferent to the conversation, her eyes vacant.

"It has happened before that a maiden has lost the man she was to wed, and shall again," Mountain Wolf Woman said. "Yet I know of none who have done what my daughter is doing!" In addition to pain, there was mild reproof in her voice.

"You cannot think that Graceful One is doing this deliberately!" The words burst from Jeanne before she could halt their flow. A tide of blood mounted in her cheeks at her own impertinence. Her gaze dropped. One bare foot peeped from beneath the ragged hem of her linen chemise as she twisted her toe in the dirt.

"Poking your nose in things that do not concern you can be very unhealthy, pale spotted one." Sweet Breeze tossed her head, her mouth set in an unbecoming line.

Jeanne frowned. Then she shrugged. The shrug was a work of art, a small, very Gallic masterpiece. It all but stated, *"I have talked too much, but what is done is done."*

"You are like the she-wolf whose cub has been threatened, Mountain Wolf Woman," Singing Bird said soothingly. Compassion softened the jet of her she-eagle eyes as she glanced toward Graceful One. "You must allow for the part of her that grieves to say farewell to my son on his journey to the spirit world. Her spirit is only delayed. It will return."

Jeanne could scarcely dare believe Singing Bird was coming to her defense when she continued, her expression solemn. "Little Turtle has come into our lodge. She has not sprung from an acorn to be everywhere shaped like the oak." Singing Bird poked Good Woman's firm-muscled arm, eyed it ruefully, waited until the laughter of the others applauding her joke died away before offering her own smile. "This one has talent, a deft touch. She has made the son of my heart, Black Eagle, laugh aloud for the first time in many moons. If she has caused heartache, she has also the healing gift of laughter. She is learning well. A few more years of experience in the ways of the People, and she will be very competent."

There was a short silence. It was true that Jeanne, with her slender arms and legs, could not be described as sturdy. She was not as strong as the women of the People. Her slight frame could not support a powerful musculature, but she was surprisingly dexterous and limber. She had learned useful household skills, and was becoming proficient with the language. Her complexion was turning from pale and colorless to a rich, golden brown, healthy and glowing, her freckles blending until hers was truly a face of fallen leaves.

It was a very happy Jeanne who returned to her allotted tasks when the women resumed their labors. The poles were measured into lengths and marked. The marked sections were put in a small fire, turned to char the shaft all around. With a notched scraper, the blackened section was shaved away.

Jeanne and Rattle continued to char and scrape until the upper piece broke off. More charring and scraping brought it to a sharp, fire-hardened point. Then they started on the next one.

By midafternoon, Jeanne's euphoria had worn off, and she was pleased when Singing Bird asked her to return to the lodge for a supply of soaproot. She was skipping along, humming under her breath, when a flicker of movement caught her eye.

For several minutes she stood still, listening, absorbing the sounds around her. All was peaceful. She was about to resume her trip when she saw the flash of movement a hundred yards from where she had left the forest.

A red fox was moving in and out of the bushes at the edge of the trees, hunting mice. Jeanne watched the gleam of the sun on its coat as the plumed tail whisked in and out of the bushes. Then the fox was gone. A flock of pigeons swooped low across the open space and scattered into the trees.

Jeanne turned away and jogged along the path. A flood of liquid notes brought her attention to a pair of redwings scolding her with their *chick-chick* when she passed too close to their shrub. Once beyond it, they changed to a loud, clear, flowing song that was sung first by one and then by the other in an alternating response.

Jeanne stopped, sucked in her breath, and surprised herself with the whistling sound she produced. She tried again. Pursing her lips, she sucked in her breath, but managed to produce only a faint windy whistle.

The next time she got more volume, but filled her lungs so full of air that she had to expel it, making a loud whistle. It was much closer to the sound of the birds. Jeanne was surprised when a mimicking bush warbler repeated the sound she had made.

Curious, she deviated from the path. Her bare feet padded softly over the moist earth. Eyes alert for the warbler, she again made the sound. An answer came from nearby.

She stepped over a fallen tree from which the bark had been prized. This lay on the ground with the outer bark facing up. A canoe form was placed on the bark, which was weighted down with rocks, while the two sides of the bark were held upright by means of posts driven into the ground. Lengths of cedar were stacked beside it. Someone was building a canoe! Black Eagle!

He was standing there gently blowing air through his lips, the sound a whole chorus in one burst of melody. "You called?"

"Oh!" Jeanne said.

Black Eagle's song became a turkey's gobble, the hoot of an owl, the yip of a fox. "You called. I answered." His amused confidence irritated Jeanne.

"I am leaving. I never should have stopped. I have not reached the end of my journey." She turned to go.

Black Eagle put a restraining hand on her arm. Jeanne shrugged it off violently. She was still angry with him.

"Do not touch me," she warned, in a voice that was not as commanding as she would have liked.

He did not release her. "You are very bashful," he observed, arching his dark black eyebrows. "Like a maiden who is not accustomed to being touched by a man. Yet you encourage the young men to visit with gifts. And you have not needed to visit the women's lodge."

His tone startled Jeanne. He sounded like a man who had been mortally wounded. She looked at him. Really looked at him. His face was drawn into harsh lines, making him seem so menacing that her heart plummeted to her toes.

Jeanne knew it was the custom of the women to isolate themselves during the period of their monthly flow. The women's curse meant females suffered partial ostracism. Men feared the mysterious life force that enabled a woman to bring forth life. When a woman bled, it meant she had cast out the life-giving forces. The women avoided men during their menses by retiring to a special lodge. Jeanne's body had responded to stress by ceasing its monthly cycle.

Not since she had stood beside Papa in the muddy graveyard and watched the bundle that had been Mama and her poor dead baby slide into the black pit had her body proved her womanhood. And that had been over six months ago!

Jeanne lifted her tawny head in an unconscious gesture of dignity. "Because there has been no need for me to visit the women's lodge, that does not make me less a woman!"

Black Eagle's right hand settled lightly on her shoulder. His left slid down her bodice, fingers tiptoeing across her chest, over the softly rounded curves.

"You are indeed a woman," he murmured, and let the palm of his hand press hard against the nipple.

Chapter Six

Jeanne gasped as Black Eagle pulled her to him, held her locked against him. His hands slid possessively over her. With one hand at the small of her back and the other between her shoulder blades, he molded her against him with effortless expertise. He was so big, so strong. The masculine sound and smell and shape of him surrounded her. Jeanne shuddered at the contact with his hard, muscled body and instinctively began to struggle.

"Stop that!" she said fiercely, twisting and arching her back. She struggled with him in fear, in disgust.

Then the fear became terror, and the disgust shame, because of what was happening inside her. The sudden explosion of warmth along her veins. The slackening, the incurving ache, the breath-strangle, the heart-hammer, the loosening of loins, the irresistible thrust forward so that their bodies arched and curved and fitted into one another. There were dark woodwinds in her blood, trumpets, drums. Jeanne felt helpless and dizzy, fighting the almost overpowering urge to close her eyes and relax against him.

Instead, she held herself taut and glared at him with furious, disparaging hazel eyes. "I will speak of this to Singing Bird, and to Wise Speaker," she cried.

Black Eagle laughed. It was a low, scornful sound.

"And I will tell them that you invited my attentions. That you whistled and called until I was compelled to answer. That you sought me out in the forest. They laugh now because I make no move to ensure you are mine. By right of conquest you are mine. A right I foolishly ceded."

His gaze skimmed over her critically, noting the flecked eyes and softly trembling mouth.

Jeanne cringed at the bitterness of his look. She managed to lever her hands against his chest and push at him with her palms.

Black Eagle's hold was inexorable. He did not let her go. He held her closer and buried his lips against the slender, graceful curve of her neck. She felt him nibbling the sensitive skin with his teeth, then soothing it with his lips. She whimpered. She was not used to being touched or caressed, and the surge of intense sensation rioting through her was both terrifying and darkly thrilling.

Jeanne gave an involuntary gasp as Black Eagle pushed her roughly away, his sinewy hands clenching into tight fists at his sides as if he were willing himself not to touch her.

"You are disgustingly eager, Little Turtle!"

Trembling with the effort, a muscle leaping in his taut jaw, he moved to the partly built canoe and gripped the frame with both hands.

When he spoke again, his low voice was strained. "Did Cornstalk touch you like that? Did Thunderclap stroke you as I did? Do you find Stands Fast more to your liking, Little Turtle? Do you?" The words seemed torn from him in fierce anguish.

The *imbécile!* Consternation warred with mounting fury, leaving Jeanne in a turmoil as she glared up at him. "I am not a tramp, but you are a fool," she managed in a strangled voice, temper choking her.

She darted to the pile of cedar stacked by the canoe frame, snatched up a length, and struck at him with all her might.

He caught the descending blow with one hand and, with skin stretched across his teeth in derision, twisted the stick from her grasp.

Jeanne grabbed a maul lying beside a wedge and swung it at him. He inclined his head no single fraction of an inch more than was necessary to evade its swing. The maul flew from her fingers, hit the canoe behind him, and rebounded to his feet. He stuck his toe against it before it came to rest, and accelerated its roll back toward her.

As Jeanne looked about wildly for another weapon, Black Eagle's mocking glance went to his hatchet, leaning beside a tree. She came at him with it. He held her against him, her arms pinioned to her sides, until she dropped the toma-hawk. He was grinning. His physical superiority fired her into an infantile frenzy. She writhed in his grasp and bent, striving to sink her teeth into one of his restraining hands. He chuckled, more amused than ever. He shoved her away and stood watching her, his arms folded. She whirled and fled, driven headlong by the whiplash of temper out of the clearing.

Jeanne paused at the edge of the woods, panting, listen-ing for his pursuit. But the empty pathway behind her re-mained clear. The fool! The stupid fool! If she could just punish him for his crass stupidity!

She considered that idea for approximately thirty sec-onds, which was, after all, a respectable enough length of time for a girl in her present circumstances to consider a problem that directly concerned her. Because it was going to shape—or, more likely, distort—what was going to hap-pen to her next.

Then the idea came to her. The absolutely perfect, or perfectly appalling, stratagem. She could not decide which it was. Regardless, Black Eagle would find that she, Jeanne de la Rocque, was not the usual captive! She would think like the enemy! She would outwit, if only for a short time, that stupid man!

Gambling upon a shrewd belief that his pursuit would not start at once, Jeanne worked her way through the trees, taking infinite care to make no sound. Once down to the bank of the stream she began to run, doe-swift, agile, to where the birchbark canoes were kept. Sliding one into the water, she grasped a paddle and carefully maneuvered the canoe into the current.

She had escaped! It was uncommonly soothing to be once again in charge of her own destiny, even if it was only for a short while. Feeling light and cheerful, she paddled downstream.

A faint breath of an offshore breeze fanned her. Jeanne guided the canoe to a small islet set in midstream. A look of impish mischief crossed her face. Even if the canoe was missed, the People would scour the bank for signs. They would not search for her right under their noses!

Jeanne lay back and gave herself up to dreamy contemplation of the sky. By all the rules of the game, Black Eagle would wait for a while, and then he would start to track her down. How long before he found her? One hour? Two? She had a momentary qualm when she thought of Singing Bird. The woman had indicated an acceptance and a trust that had warmed Jeanne's lonely heart. Maybe she would understand.

In the meantime, she was tired, content to lie there and plot revenge on Black Eagle. As she lay so, before she was aware of it, her eyes closed.

She wakened with a start at a cold touch of moisture on her face. Rain—great, pattering drops. Overhead, an ominously black cloud hid the face of the sun. Between the small island and the settlement was a darkening of the river's surface. Jeanne reached for her paddle.

The black cloud let fall long gray streamers of rain. There was scarcely a stirring of the air, but that did not deceive her. There was a growing chill, and there was that broken line sweeping down the river. Behind that wind loomed a spring squall, the black gale dreaded by the People.

Jeanne drove hard on the paddle. She was not afraid, but there rose in her a peculiar tense feeling. Ahead lay a ticklish bit of business.

The birchbark canoe seemed to shrink to pitiful dimensions in the face of that snarling line of wind-harried water. Jeanne could hear the distant murmur of it presently, and gusty puffs of wind began to strike her.

Then it swept up to her, a ripple, a chop, and very close behind the short, steep combers whipped by the wind, tops white, bubbling froth. Immediately she began to lose ground, but that did not alarm her. If she could keep the canoe bow-on, there was an even chance that the squall would blow itself out before she hit the rapids.

But keeping the canoe bow-on proved a task for stout arms. The wind would catch all that forward part, which thrust clear as she topped a wave, and twist it aside, tending always to throw her broadside into a trough. White froth began to splash aboard. The river churned. The current was so strong, and the waves were so short and steep, that the canoe would rise over the crest of a tall one and dip its bow deep in the next, or leap clear to strike with a slap that made Jeanne's heart jump. She was being beaten farther down the river, and her arms were growing tired. And there was no slackening of the wind.

The combined rain and slaps of spray soaked her thoroughly. A puddle gathered about her knees, sloshing as the craft pitched, killing the natural buoyancy of the canoe so that it dived harder. Tossing and spinning, in a continuous roll, the canoe hit the rapids. Crouching on her knees, Jeanne dropped the paddle to grip the sides. Sit tight and hang on! Wood is buoyant. No river that ever ran can sink a canoe!

What about the falls?

Jeanne felt a rock scrape the side of the canoe. The light craft went into an unremitting spin. Her head swam with the movement. She felt airborne, shooting off the top of the world in a white burst of spray. A foamy cloud engulfed her....

Suddenly she saw a young man standing before her. His face was long and thin, with prominent cheekbones and hollowed cheeks. He held out his hand. His fingers closed over hers, his grasp cold but firm.

"I am On the Other Side," he said. "I saw you gazing upward at me, and have come to ask you to go with me along the river of light. I will take you to the lodge of silent memory. You will be happy there."

Jeanne trembled violently, but she did not say anything. She did not know what to say. She felt the pull, the drag of the water, but could not draw back. She turned to tell On the Other Side she was not yet ready. But no! He was gone!

In his place was a beaver, all long teeth and narrow eyes, who peered at her from within his lodge on the river's edge, beating his flattened, rudderlike tail in agitation. *Go elsewhere!*

Jeanne shook her head in confusion, looked away, looked back—into the face of a bear. Yes, undeniably a bear, round and plump, its dark fur heaving like the storm-waves on the river. She could hear it growl.

This image, too, yielded its place, between one whitecap and the next, to that of a wolf. Sharp-jawed, with ears flattened, it was a turbulent likeness of a wrathful Mountain Wolf Woman.

The shape dissolved to form a bird of some sort. Partridge? Crane? Jeanne was not sure. She could not see its plumage or its size clearly. But its warbling, melodic trill was a magic medley of sound.

Soon a host of birds of various sizes and colors whirred down to the water bird, wings fluttering. Their songs—warbles, trills, and squawks—filled the air as they squabbled for position with a display of puffed-up feathers. Hands outstretched, Jeanne took a step closer.

A huge bird swooped down and landed at her feet, blocking her way. She eyed it warily. It was an eagle. Large and black, huge wings flapping, feathered talons curled, preventing her from joining the stream of light.

Jeanne stepped back, closer to the bank, away from the fearful creature. It dissolved, shimmering for a moment on the fitful water, to reemerge, chimeralike as a snarling bobcat...a chattering squirrel...a swiftly moving otter...a wide-eyed owl...a hissing serpent....

Terrified, Jeanne clutched the edge of the bank, clawing herself away from the creatures that stopped her entering the stream of light. Above the roil and roar of the water the snarl, howl, hoot, whistle, shriek and hiss of these watery beasts merged into a single refrain, repeating over and over again in unison: *"No, too soon. No, too soon!"*

Out of the cacophony of sound, Jeanne identified the voice of the snapping turtle. It was lying beneath her feet. Its strong, hook-shaped, downturned beak grasped her rib cage, lifted her away from the hungry river, to the safety of the embankment. Jeanne tried to thank the creature. It was gone! Only ripples spreading in ever-widening circles told her it was not a figment of her imagination, a dream.

"She is still alive!" The man's voice sounded exultant.

"Turtle, I did not mean it!"

Jeanne frowned. It was Black Eagle's voice. Though what he did not mean, she was not sure. The words echoed in her head like waves on the seashore. She lay facedown, a hand outflung by her cheek.

"Little Turtle," he said again, and the pain in his voice was unmistakable.

Someone turned her over with infinite care. Jeanne opened her eyes. There were vague pictures moving in the light-flooded depths of space. Faces blurred above her. She tried to identify them, until some of the yellow-white began to spill out of the sky, and the blue crept back in and deepened. She closed her eyes again.

"Turtle, can you hear me?"

Black Eagle sounded greatly concerned about something. *Of course I can hear you!* Her lips framed the words, but he did not seem able to hear her.

Jeanne grimaced, eyelids fluttering, concentrating on the words he was saying.

"It is all my fault. I betrayed my guardian spirit." Black Eagle's voice was a ragged whisper.

"Non. Taquinerie. Vous comprends?"

Jeanne heard her words, but they were in French. Black Eagle would not know what she said. Why could she not think of the Algonquin words? Perhaps she had not heard the People's word for teasing? She knew they did tease. They joked a lot.

A wave of pain hit her, and she forgot what she had been thinking about.

"Turtle, can you move?" The sound of Yellow Feather's voice seemed oddly out of place.

She tried to sit up but gasped, almost fainting with the pain that lanced through her side. She hurt, all over. Suddenly she remembered the white water...the roar of the falls...the cold breath of the spirit world. She did not want to remember. She wanted to close her eyes and forget, sink into the oblivion that would end all her pain.

Black Eagle spoke again, his voice harsh, raw. "Why did you do it?"

She moved her head in negation. *Do what?* She found she could open both her eyes. Her forehead knotted in puzzlement, then smoothed as the edges of the pictures came into focus. They were like those funny puppets that the crazy artist who had traveled through the village with the tinkers had made from colored silk. Only these figures moved jerkily, and above them was the pale glimmer of the morning sun.

Fingers glided over her, lingering on a bruise forming under her right breast. Gentle pressure to it caused Jeanne to gasp. Her breath was short and sharp and tortured. Her hand came up to push the pain away.

"Easy. Just a moment longer." It was Yellow Feather's voice again.

A hand pressed lightly over her side, sensitive fingers telling Yellow Feather what he wanted to know. A faint moan escaped her lips.

"How bad is it?"

"She has some cracked ribs."

"We will have to get her back to the lodge," Black Eagle muttered. He sounded distressed. Why was he upset?

"Shall we make a carry-bed?" Surely that was Little Bear's voice!

Moth-wing lashes flickered. Jeanne's eyes opened. Black Eagle was bending over her, face as dark and grim as the bird of prey after which he was named. She tried to smile up at him. She put both hands to her forehead, pressing on the temples, fighting a wave of dizziness.

Carefully, his cheekbones jutting under taut flesh, Black Eagle gathered Jeanne in his arms and got to his feet. Her head lolled back against his shoulder.

Then her eyes closed again and the fog took her.

* * *

Jeanne stretched herself in the narrow pole bed and, without opening her eyes, thought of that other bed of hers, in Rouen. That was a wide bed, with an embroidered coverlet on it, with fine linen sheets and wool blankets.

There was a carved wooden screen she could pull round from behind the bedhead, if the wind turned to the north and the chimney smoked, or the draft came around the shutters on the windows. By her bedside there was a stand, on which the maid would set water and towels morning and night, and beyond that again the big carved chest against the arras, in which lay, carefully folded with sprigs of lavender, a number of linen chemises, her best gown of blue-green brocade, and the workaday ones of fine wool and velvet.

A cupboard on the wall held a mirror, her ribbons, silk stockings and a cake of scented soap from Versailles. A larger chest beside the door held her winter cloak, together with the muff Papa had brought home from Paris…and her leather shoes with the ribbon rosettes…and the sewing box with the sign of the de la Rocque's blazoned on it, azure-blue on black....

Sharing the bed would be Gabrielle and Thérèse, curled up in sleep, while she lay waiting for Pierre and sometimes little Jean-Paul to come rushing in from the nursery to join them. Where were they now? Were they in heaven with Papa and Mama, and baby Jacques, and that other poor, nameless babe? Or were they with On the Other Side in the lodge of silent memory? Or were those places one and the same?

Jeanne sighed and turned herself onto her side, staring at her present surroundings. It was a special wigwam at the site of the sugar camp. The pole bed on which she lay was lashed to the inside framework of the lodge. The mattress was a series of yielding wrist-thick saplings covered with a thick tangle of skins and furs. Beyond a bark partition, Jeanne knew, there were other sleeping compartments.

The wooden ribs of the lodge were bound together with moose-hide lashings and covered with thick elm bark. A hole in the middle of the roof served to carry off the smoke from the fire burning in the center of the floor. Long woven cattail mats were thickly scattered about on the floor.

Bundles of dried deer meat and herbs and bark baskets filled with dried berries hung from the wooden ribs that supported the house. Skins, two jackrabbits and several partridges dangled on this bent network of bound branches.

The air was pungent with odors of tanning elk hide, wild crab apples and the dried sweet grass Singing Bird used for baskets. Jeanne sniffed the familiar spicy sweetness of boiling cranberries and hickory nuts. Oh, but that delicious smell made her feel hungry!

Jeanne gingerly felt her rib cage, winced, and pushed herself into a sitting position, the fur covering dropping away. She swung her feet off the bed and sat upright, her hands pressed down on the bed on either side of her.

The cooler air raised goose bumps on her naked flesh, and she reached for her new elkskin tunic, then paused, running her hands over her slight breasts, past her small waist and flat belly to her slim hips.

I am the same as I was three years gone, though I am now in my eighteenth year. Yet she felt as if there were an empty, hollow void at the center of her, deeper than loneliness and worse than grief. She shook her head in self-rebuke.

A new land. A new people. They could be hers. She knew it. Why pine for what was past?

Jeanne nursed her chin on her hand and pondered this. It was time to be quit of all the uncertainties, all the useless regrets. To think for herself, learn new skills, adapt, change, marry, bear children. *A boy, with eyes like night.* Jeanne felt a queer sensation pass over her body at the errant thought. She shivered in anticipation.

Pulling the tunic over her head, Jeanne marveled at the softness of the garment. Beautifully decorated with red-and-yellow quillwork that Good Woman had designed and embroidered, the bottom of the tunic fell to her knees. She admired the bone-and-beadwork-trimmed edges on the leggings given to her by Sky Woman. Wife to Crayfish, Sky Woman was as famous for the fine detail of her needlework as her husband was for his fishing skills.

Jeanne slipped her narrow feet into the matching moccasins presented by Rattle. Tucked away in the fringed deerskin shoulder bag that Mountain Wolf Woman had added to her collection of gifts were the wampum necklet, a precious pot of vermilion paint donated by Singing Bird, and a special contribution from Yellow Feather, the carapace of a small turtle.

The turtle had been found in the skeletal remains of the ill-fated canoe. To the People, it was an omen, a sign. When she had told Singing Bird about her experience, that one had immediately told Black Eagle, who had called Wise Speaker. The response had been amazing. As soon as she had been well enough, visitors had called each day, bearing gifts, wanting to hear her story. She who had come as a captive, a pale daughter of the moon, had not only survived Barricade Falls, but had also attracted the spirits who sent dreams, and been granted a vision!

What did Jeanne know of visions? Nothing at all! They were probably no more than a dream sent by the spirits when you were awake rather than asleep! She did know she was prone to strange premonitions. She did know that there were pernicious spirits, as well as charitable ones. She also knew that both had been present in her vision! Still, the little turtle shell was a good beginning. It boded well for her future.

Outside the lodge, the whole world was washed in sunlight. Looking out from under the shadow that the maple branches made was like staring into a haze of gold. Over the field of low, waving grass, insects danced, suspended like motes in the light, and the air droned with their humming. On the branches above her, a blue jay scolded noisily, and a cardinal flashed from leaf shade to tree shadow tracing a trajectory-like flame across the sunny places.

Jeanne started toward where she knew the People were making sugar. She walked slowly, prolonging the moment before she would see Black Eagle again, half out of fear and half out of the unconscious desire to preserve it.

It was odd that she was so nervous now about meeting Black Eagle, when she was fully dressed. After all, he had been her constant companion for weeks, seen her in all states of undress, tended to her bodily comforts, fed and cared for her, awake and asleep. If she could find the cause, she reasoned sensibly, perhaps she could stop this uncomfortable inward quaking.

Jeanne had been looking forward to this day, and now that it was here she was almost terrified. It was as if an overpowering sense of excitement, danger and fascination had possessed her. Silly goose. She had been here before with the women.

She remembered well the rich, welcome smell of the sweet sap. Traverse cuts had been made in the maple trees, three or four feet above the ground, when the first crows returned from their winter dwelling place. Jeanne had helped the women drive cedar spikes into the cuts at an angle that would direct the flow of sap into the birchbark vessels placed on the ground. That had been before her misadventure!

Thunderclap had told her that, for the first time in his life, Black Eagle had forgotten caution. His lips had drawn back in a terrible snarl when he saw Prickly Man looking in wonder at her sodden, seminaked body.

Little Bear agreed. He had heard Black Eagle roar, "Dog!" And, according to Stands Fast, Black Eagle had caught Prickly Man in his unyielding grip, forcing him backward over his bent knee, down and down, hands tightening, crushing out life, until Yellow Feather intervened.

Jeanne could not remember Black Eagle pulling off his shirt and wrapping her in its folds so that they covered her, shielding her both from the cold wind and from curious eyes. She could remember the pain. The bitter taste of willow bark. The heat burning her skin . . . the blessed relief of cool water. . . .

Pictures flashed into her mind. Black Eagle holding a cup to her lips. Now he was frowning, biting his lip, bathing her face, stroking her damp hair with his long, sinewy fingers.

"You shall not die!"

Then he was gone. Wise Speaker. The ancient man hovering, mumbling. Black Eagle again. Herself putting up her arms, drawing his face down to hers, wrapping her arms around his neck, aching with a growing need and emptiness she had never before experienced. Wakening to find Black Eagle sitting there, watching, waiting . . .

As Jeanne drew closer to the sugar-bush activities, she gave up trying to piece it all together in her mind. She did not know what to think. It was too soon to tell. She did know that the next two or three weeks would be spent tapping the trees and boiling the sap down into maple syrup until finally only the sweet sugar was left. When it began to granulate, it would be poured into wooden troughs and stirred until it solidified.

There he was! Striding to meet her, moving easily, as always, straight and tall, all grace and balance and endurance, his moccasined feet making no sound. The stubborn, ruthless set of his chin, the hard, straight, handsome mouth, set Jeanne's heart beating faster. She stood stiffly, waiting for him to reach her. He was before her then, waiting, and with a great effort, Jeanne raised her face and met his eyes.

Black Eagle took his time, looking her over, his face revealing little of his thoughts. His eyes narrowed. "You are well enough?" he asked abruptly.

She grinned at him then, her face the picture of mischief, half gamine and half sprite. "Sure. I could eat a horse!"

"A horse?"

Jeanne suppressed a chuckle. "It is like saying I am so hungry I could eat, oh, a whole moose."

Black Eagle hooted with disbelief. "Then you would not only be greedy, you would be ill!"

Mon Dieu! And she had thought the man had a sense of humor! With a flash of irritation, she turned away and found herself face-to-face with a young girl. The child's dark hair was pulled back from her forehead and braided very tightly. Her eyes were wide and soft and clear, and her mouth was so sensitive it seemed on the verge of trembling. Jeanne held out her hand to her.

"Hello!" Jeanne said. "You are the little girl who brought me such a delicious meal the night I first arrived!"

The child edged closer, her hands behind her. Black Eagle frowned at her, and then suddenly his expression changed. "Why, She Is Playful, what is this secret thing you hide behind your back? Is it something Little Turtle can eat? Something smaller than a moose? A bear, perhaps? Something Little Turtle can get her teeth into?"

There was a softness in Black Eagle's voice as he uttered his little joke, and the sound of it made a warm glow run through Jeanne's body.

She Is Playful's seven-year-old face clouded. Awkwardly she pulled a brown-and-white-speckled frog from behind her back and clasped it in her hands, appealing silently and eloquently to Jeanne.

Jeanne laughed and flashed a bright smile at Black Eagle. "A frog! What an unusual pet!" She crouched, knees bent, hands splayed, and jumped up and down mockingly.

"How high can you jump, little frog? Can you jump as high as Little Turtle?"

She Is Playful smiled, and her small face was transformed. Her eyes lit and she giggled and cast a mischievous, triumphant glance at Black Eagle. The grave child was gone, a delightful hoyden in her place. She edged a little closer to Jeanne, and waved to a little boy standing some way away.

"Owl has the sister of this one," She Is Playful contributed eagerly.

Owl's comical, round little face, with snub nose and eyes that squinted as though in harsh sunlight, split into a grin. Because some of his teeth were missing, the new front ones looked unnaturally large. He was a sturdy eight-year-old, and when the baby roundness left him he would grow as big and bony and strong as his father, Leaning Wood.

"Do not bother Turtle and Black Eagle, children." Rattle rushed over and began to push Owl and his sister away. "Those frogs are a pest."

"Let them stay." Jeanne's eyes were dancing as she knelt and stroked the small creatures. "They are very fine," she said softly, her face level with the children's. "Do they have names?"

"Of course they have names. This one is Big Chief. And this one, Little Chief."

Owl made his momentous announcement slowly, his eyes solemn. It was easy to see his resemblance to his namesake! Jeanne nodded with the earnestness the occasion demanded. "Very good names."

"Take them away, children. Show them to your grandmother." Rattle chased the children, her high voice floating in the wind.

Jeanne turned to Black Eagle, her face alight with laughter. The children's eagerness for friendship, and their awkward little attempts to make friends by bringing to her at once their most treasured possessions, were infinitely touching. Rattle, too, had been wholehearted, generous. Jeanne had warmly accepted her gift and friendship.

Black Eagle opened his mouth as though to say something, but closed it again as they were hailed by Yellow Feather, and the moment was lost. The leader of the war party was not given to any form of demonstration, but the look on his scarred face as he strode toward them was one of welcome. His nod was no more than an inclination of his head, but the eyes he turned to Jeanne were direct and kindly. His brief "It is good to see you well enough to join the sugar bush camp" was accompanied by a twisted caricature of a smile that Jeanne thought was rarely used.

"Well enough to eat a whole moose!" Somehow, in a way she did not understand, Black Eagle's little joke gave her a feeling of triumph.

Chapter Seven

"Will you be there to watch the men play in the ball game tomorrow, Turtle?" Garrulous Rattle! That one never drew breath! She talked while lightly packing granulated sugar into carved wooden molds.

"Yes, if we finish cleaning up the sugar bush camp today," Jeanne answered.

Jeanne was trying to remove some of the sticky sap that still hung in strings from the stirring paddle with wood ashes and a stone. Her side ached. She had a smudge of black soot right down the front of her new tunic. And Black Eagle had offered to carry a laden basket for Sweet Breeze when that one had flashed a bright smile at him, lowering her hungry eyes in a maidenly fashion.

Simpleton that he was! Surely he was aware that Sweet Breeze wanted him to dance at the celebration of the Offering of the First Fruits? Could he not see that Sweet Breeze lusted after a man—any man?

"To whom will you throw your basket at the end of the Beggar's Dance?" Rattle's voice intruded into Jeanne's dark, bitter thoughts.

"I do not think I will take part in the dancing." Surely her voice sounded too strained and taut? She swallowed to dislodge the lump in her throat. "My side is still tender," she said to excuse herself.

Rattle looked up, startled. "You have worked as hard as any of us this past week, Turtle. The purple marks on your face and arms have turned to a sickly yellow and are almost faded away. That is a poor defense!"

Jeanne did not deign to answer. Instead, she concentrated on a stubborn piece of congealed sugar.

"What do you think, Red Leaf?" Rattle asked.

Red Leaf wrinkled her small nose, rubbed her swollen belly with a sticky finger and considered the question carefully.

"I think Turtle does not want to dance, because she is afraid."

Jeanne struck her hands together, her color high. "I am afraid of nothing! Nobody!"

"I think you are afraid that when it comes time to throw your basket, while you will have many suitors to choose from, the one you want will not be there!"

Jeanne leapt to her feet. "That is absurd!"

Rattle giggled. It was a high-pitched little-girl giggle. Red Leaf ignored her. "Or, if he is there, that Sweet Breeze or one of the other maidens will get him first!"

Again Jeanne struck her hands together. "Sweet Breeze is welcome to the lot of them!" She gave a sob that was strangled in her throat but expressive of her frustration. "Sweet Breeze has the right to throw her basket! You can laugh! But at least, each moon, she visits the women's lodge!"

Jeanne swung around and ran toward the path that led into the maple forest, then stopped and ran back to pick up her fringed deerskin bag.

Rattle and Red Leaf watched her, but neither was laughing.

Jeanne walked slowly down to a small lake nestled in a basin at the edge of the forest. *I am not going to cry. Noth-*

*ing and nobody can make me cry. Black Eagle is welcome
to Sweet Breeze. I do not care for him any more than I care
for Stands Fast.* She blinked furiously, kicking aside an in-
offensive thistle. Why was she so out of sorts?

At the lake's edge, she dropped onto a tuft of grass and
sat there, quite still. She did not weep, but shivered for a
while, convulsively clasping and unclasping her hands about
her upper arms. She shifted once, as stones cut into her legs.

Angrily she started slinging the stones. One hit a small
rock, shaped like a man's head, jutting out of the water. She
aimed the next one at the rock. It missed. She tried again.
This time the stone was short of the rock. She stood this
time. The stone flew wide of the mark, but closer to the
rock. Her next stone flew wide, but beyond the rock.

Suddenly a hand gripped her wrist, sinewy as a snake,
applying light pressure.

"You are doing it all wrong. You try too hard. The tree
that bends in the wind survives the gale. Let your wrist bend.
Keep your eye on the target and let the stone fly out of your
fingers to ride like a bird on the wind."

"Black Eagle! Why must you always sneak up on me!"
Jeanne let her indignant glance slide up him. A glance meant
to give him all the discomfort of being frozen and burned at
the same time.

His eyebrows went up. "I did not sneak! If you had been
listening, you would have heard me fifty paces away." His
eyes were mocking. "If I had not wanted you to hear me, I
would have crept as close as the breath in your nostrils before you knew I was there."

Jeanne turned away haughtily and pulled her wrist free.
"I would like to learn to move silently, with stealth, to be
able to track a creature of the forest, to hunt."

Black Eagle snorted. "Women do not hunt! Women prepare and preserve food, dress hides, make garments, weave
baskets! They do not hunt! That is men's work!"

"Why should women not hunt? Does it make you any less a man to help an old woman? To carry a small child? To care for the sick?"

"I am a member of the medicine lodge, of the first order. One day, if I please my guardian spirit, I hope to be promoted to the second order. If I keep peace and harmony within my spirit, it may be that eventually I shall rise to the fourth order and be as good a medicine man as Wise Speaker!"

Jeanne whirled and faced him. "And I suppose a woman cannot become a member of the medicine lodge, either?"

"Oh, yes, they can. There are no restrictions, if one has the calling to cure the sick!"

Jeanne felt a startled gasp escape her lips as the idea reached into her mind and twisted itself like an insidious snake through her thoughts. She shook her head.

"It is very difficult to understand. Where I grew up, women were allowed to join the hunt, but they were never encouraged to read and write, and so discover the arts of healing—not unless they practiced witchcraft!"

"What is this read and write?" Black Eagle gave her a blank, inquiring look.

"Writing is a strange skill only understood by priests and holy men, men of God. The Great Spirit. They make secret little wriggly lines. When they look at these strange wriggles, it is called reading. It helps them remember things."

"And witchcraft?"

Jeanne looked at him, and her mouth tightened. "That is a sort of black magic. Evil spirits. To curse and harm."

"The People do all of those things!" He spread out his hands.

"They do?" Jeanne scoffed, disbelieving.

"Yes." He seemed impatient at her skepticism. "Come, I will show you."

He held out his hand. Jeanne hesitated for only a moment before she reached out and placed her hand in his.

Black Eagle followed the small watercourse fed from the lake into the cool and peaceful woods. He pointed out the footprints of four deer that had come up from the stream in early morning, the scratch an opossum had left on a tree. They stopped by a steep rock wall over which the creek spilled in a cascading spray.

Jutting rocks whose jagged outlines were softened by a deep cushion of lush green moss separated the falling water bouncing from rock to rock into long, thin streams that splashed upward, creating veils of mist, and fell again. The water collected itself in a foaming pool that filled a shallow, rocky basin at the foot of the waterfall before it continued down to meet the larger waterway.

A gorge of rocky cliffs opened out of the dense thickets into a narrow, twisting canyon. Above, the sky seemed a winding stream of blue. The walls were red and bulged out in spruce-greened shelves, circling to meet the overhanging cliff, forming an oval depression. Jeanne was breathing hard when Black Eagle halted near some heavy underbrush.

"It is quite safe. Follow me." He slid into the hill.

On hands and knees, Jeanne followed him. In the dim light, she had the odd, lost feeling of one who has no way to measure distance or space. She stood up carefully, reaching with her arms overhead. Her hands touched nothing. Reaching to the sides, she felt nothing.

"Black Eagle?" Jeanne's voice, thin and thready, chased itself in mocking echoes that died slowly in the distance.

"I am here." Once more the echoes rolled away, bumping into each other. "Come." Needing no further invitation, Jeanne grasped his warm hand tightly.

One streak of light fell like a quivering arrow through a crack in the cave roof, illuminating the dark, shadowy reflections of an underground stream. The roof sloped down gently for about half the depth of the cavern, angling more sharply down to where the river disappeared toward the rear. Soft sand whispered underneath Jeanne's moccasins as she stepped closer to the water.

"Where does it go?" she whispered. The place felt holy.

"Far underground, where the ancient ones lie," Black Eagle said. Jeanne shivered. "This is a sacred site, known only to a few. It is here the People record their deeds so that those who come after will know. See, here is the sacred writing."

Now that her eyes were accustomed to the dim light, Jeanne could see that the rock walls and ceiling of the cave were covered with drawings. Figures of animals and figures strode the walls, while shooting stars and other celestial phenomena adorned the ceiling.

"Do you know what they mean?" Jeanne's voice was hushed.

Black Eagle's finger traced the outlines as he explained the pictures.

"Once, sun and his sister, moon, lived together in a wigwam in the east. Sun dressed himself to go hunting and took his bow and arrows and left. He was absent for such a long time that when his sister came out into the sky to look for her brother, she became alarmed. She traveled twenty days looking for the sun. Finally, he returned, bringing with him a bear he had shot.

"Sun's sister still comes up into the sky and travels for twenty days. Then she dies, and for four days nothing is seen of her. At the end of that time, however, she returns to life and travels twenty days more."

"What about these different moons?"

"The Spirit Keepers guard each of the moons of the year. See, this one is Big Winds Moon, this one Ripe Berries."

"And this one is Corn Planting Moon, and this one is Harvest!"

"Well done, Turtle. What is this one?" Black Eagle pointed to one of the lunar carvings.

Jeanne peered closely at the illustration, suddenly distracted by the close proximity of Black Eagle. His voice was so deep, so melodious, so pleasant. So near his breath warmed her face. If she took one step closer—? She felt her cheeks burn crimson at the thought, but she could not drive it from her mind. She was panting, terrified of herself, of she knew not what. . . .

"No," she said baldly.

"It is Long Snows Moon. The time when bears sleep, and women conceive."

Something moved in her throat, and she heard herself groan, as if she were in pain. She jerked herself upright. "How convenient. At least they will not freeze to death alone in the women's lodge!"

"Your tongue is sharp, Little Turtle. Come. We will return to the camp before you start snapping like your guardian spirit!"

They were back at the sugar camp when Black Eagle gently touched her shoulder. "If you really want to learn to throw accurately, go and see Fierce Man. He teaches the boys manly skills. And whenever I go to hunt, if you wish to come with me, you can take the opportunity to practice your tracking skills."

It was not much, but it was enough. Enough to make Jeanne's face light up like a beacon. To make her toes curl inside her moccasins!

The smile still lingered in her eyes while she leaf-wrapped some wild turnips and placed them next to the coals glowing in the fire pit. The wild turnips, small and pale yellow, were tender and had a sweet, tangy taste that would go well with the hare Singing Bird had skewered above the fire. Black Eagle enjoyed baked vegetables.

She could see him now, in her mind's eye. The strong white teeth biting into the pale flesh, which would melt into his mouth. The movement of his jaws, so strong, so sleek, so beautiful. The little knob at the base of his throat sliding, very gently and tantalizingly, up and down, as he swallowed the succulent morsel. In a dreamy haze, Jeanne closed her eyes to better absorb the picture she was creating.

Singing Bird, busy grating some snakeroot into a clay pot that already contained shredded tansy leaves, shook Jeanne out of her reverie.

"I could not find you today when I went to collect these." Singing Bird indicated the plants with her scraper.

"I went for a walk."

Jeanne did not elaborate, and Singing Bird did not ask. The easy camaraderie that was developing between them warmed Jeanne. For all her gruff manner, the older woman was kind in her own way, showing Jeanne where to find the different plants and herbs, their various uses, and how to prepare and preserve them.

Singing Bird spoke again. "Bright Path has not visited the women's lodge for many moons."

Jeanne was silent, but her eyebrows rose.

The older woman speculated further. "She is big with child."

Jeanne smiled faintly. "Yes, Bright Path has poor Dry Man searching for just the right piece of white cedar for a cradle board. She says if Dry Man does not soon start carving one, the child will have arrived!"

Singing Bird sighed. "That is not what I am trying to explain. Never mind, drink this," she said, handing Jeanne the evil-smelling concoction she had been stirring.

"What is it? You are not going to poison me after all this time?" Jeanne pulled a comical face.

"No, Little Turtle. But it will send you to the women's lodge in time for you to take part in the Offering of the First

Fruits festivities. To dance, and throw your basket at Black Eagle.''

"You know?'' Jeanne's eyes were wide. Was she so transparent?

Singing Bird shook her head. Tapped her fingers against her she-eagle eyes. "This old woman see things no one else does. Things only the spirit knows.'' She held up her hands. "When I walk with the spirits, I want you to be my hands. My eyes and my ears,'' she continued, "my voice, my mind.''

There was a long silence while Jeanne surveyed Singing Bird with a mixture of distress and dismay. "No,'' she said, her voice flat.

"You are always quick to snap, just like a little turtle.'' Singing Bird held out the drug once more. "We will speak of this again, when you are ready. When you know the trail your moccasins must tread.''

As she prepared for sleep that night, Jeanne reached for her deerhide bag. When she loosened the cord that drew the top together, something fell out. It was a small pebble, with hard, precise edges and smooth, flat planes. She turned it this way and that, watching its facets sparkle in the firelight. She held it at just the right angle for the prism to separate the firelight into the full spectrum of colors.

She caught her breath at the rainbow it cast on the ground. She looked into the fire. Tried again, this time with the stream of light arcing onto the turtle shell, transforming the carapace into a reflection of the stained glass windows of the chapel of her girlhood. Jeanne's hand shook. The rainbow disappeared.

The gleaming stone must have caught in her bag when she crawled through the hole to the sacred cave. She had not followed On the Other Side to the stream of light, but he had sent it to her, locked in this piece of crystal. It was a sign, just as the little turtle shell was a sign. A sign from her spirit? What kind of sign? She did not know. Only the spirit knew.

Excitement filled the air. It was almost tangible as the People began to prepare for the ball game. Thunderclap had found a tree that had been struck by lightning, leaving a black mark. His guardian spirits had instructed him to call the game, using clubs in the shape of this mark! The Thunderers had further told Thunderclap in a dream not to play himself, but to stand on the sidelines, offering prayers for Graceful One. While the game was being played, they would come.

Jeanne was particularly excited. Thunderclap had chosen her as his messenger, sending her with tobacco to invite the players. She had tripped around the compound with wings on her feet.

So infectious was her enthusiasm that even No Bone in His Back had accepted the invitation. Jeanne did not know what his name had been before Watchful Fox discovered his dreadful secret. She did know that No Bone in His Back was never included in the war parties. Nor was he involved in any of the activities enjoyed by the men. He had seemed surprised when she handed him Thunderclap's tobacco, and he had hesitated before taking it.

Mountain Wolf Woman despised No Bone in His Back. Her voice was sharp when she discussed the incident with Good Woman. It had been in his first year as a warrior that No Bone in His Back vowed to go down to their enemies, the Red Earth People, by himself, after a scalp.

Mountain Wolf Woman's head had tossed when she told how he had stayed away for a week and then come back with what he pretended was a scalp, but was in truth only squirrel fur. He had carried the "scalp" on a stick, singing. At first, the People had believed him, but Watchful Fox had seen the fake scalp and recognized the fraud.

That was how both young men had acquired their names.

The morning was clear and bright when Jeanne went down with the women to the lake to bathe. The sweet smells of wildflowers and heady pines filled the air, pierced by the shrieks of the children's laughter as they splashed in the shallows, or made turtles and frogs out of the mud.

Jeanne was rubbing soap made from wood ashes and fat into her bushy mane when she heard Rattle ask, "What are you thinking, Sweet Breeze?"

"Of men," the girl replied, and closed her eyes with a shiver. "I am thinking of how it would be to lie with a man...."

"Sweet Breeze!" Jeanne could not help the exclamation.

"Why so shocked?" Sweet Breeze turned her head to look at Jeanne and said mockingly, "Do not tell me you have never dreamed of a man taking you in his arms, and laying you down, with his strength leaping to meet and mingle with yours...and his leanness...his long back...his strong arms around you, and his strong thighs!"

"No!"

Jeanne's color rose. She repudiated the idea. "Of course I do not think of men like that!" She splashed her hair, rinsing off the soap.

Sweet Breeze snapped her fingers. "You lie. All women think of such things. Even Graceful One. Look at her! Hiding with the spirits!"

Jeanne squeezed her hair, looping it behind her ears. Graceful One stood so still.... Only her eyes showed she still lived. The slim, lovely body was a deserted château, the face was the face of absence, an empty reminder of a spirit blasted out of time by lightning. Her features were as lovely as ever, and her hair was glossy and shining.

Yet there was a suggestion about Graceful One now of a leaf touched by the fingers of tomorrow's decay. Jeanne felt a wave of affection for the young woman. Her blankness in grief was the only way she could keep at bay the thought of what was to have been...the thought that she could not face, the future that she could not contemplate. And yet she would have to bring herself to do so. Sometime she would have to pour out the grief, the pain.

Jeanne touched Graceful One's cheek, and smiled, more to herself than to anyone else. "You are right, Sweet Breeze. For some time, I have not known what ailed you. Now I know. It is the craving of she-wolves with the mating fever. I will even join you in the dance at the ceremonies next week and help you ease your hunger, if I can."

Sweet Breeze gave her a cold look. "I will get the man I want without any help from you, Little Turtle! It might be better if you attended to your own predicament."

Jeanne let a smile cross her lips at the gibe, but made no reply. Instead, she turned and spoke softly to the unseeing girl.

"Come, Graceful One. After I wash your hair, I will thread flowers through it, as I used to for Gabrielle. You will look very pretty at the ball game."

She was ascending the path to the sugar camp when Black Eagle met her, going down. His eyebrows lifted at the garland of flowers she had twined in her own hair. She stopped, hearing the sudden thunder of her heart, louder than the dogskin drums. Looked at him. A long, long look, with eyes bright as the newly risen sun.

"It is an Old World custom," she said defensively.

"And a charming one, too."

Eyes of living color in the broad yet delicate face met night-dark eyes, took in the harsh set of lips and the will betokened by the jut of nose and chin, noted the message concealed therein. Lost in an age-old mystery, neither seemed able to look away from the other.

"Come along, you two. You are blocking the path!"

Sky Woman broke the spell. She was a small, quick, wiry woman with snapping black eyes and weather-coarsened skin, her straight dark hair fastened in a tight knot on top of her head. Her laughter was quick and genuine, and her words were swift and to the point. Within a few minutes, she had dismissed Black Eagle, taken possession of Jeanne and reorganized the women and children, and was already planning how she could get Crayfish to persuade Black Eagle to join the Beggar's Dance.

By noon, the atmosphere of excitement had reached the point where Jeanne felt almost sick with tension. The playing field had been set, with mats for the spectators spread on the ground.

Jeanne's eyes watered when she saw the prizes hung on a horizontal bar between two upright poles. Among a variety of trinkets, she recognized some of her own brightly colored silk ribbons, some household items, one of her father's linen shirts, Émile's powder horn and pouch of gunpowder, and a gruesome object that she was sure was the trapper's scalp.

She shuddered and turned away. Her eyes full of tears, she walked straight into Black Eagle.

"Those are trophies from the war bags. By giving them away as prizes to the winners of the ball game, it is hoped that the spirits who hold on to the mind of Graceful One will return it to her."

Jeanne rubbed her palms along her hips in an unconscious gesture, inexplicably soothed by his explanation.

"Come, dry the storm clouds from your eyes."

Tremulously Jeanne raised her head and tried to smile at Black Eagle, but it was a pitiful attempt at best. "It is not for myself I cry."

"I know." He nodded, fiddling with the long racquet in his hand. Then, to Jeanne's amazement, he said, rather diffidently, "I came to inquire whether you were going to trill for the side of the Earth or those of the Sky?"

Jeanne's heart was pounding in her chest. It was almost like a throbbing pain. Could she rile him enough to trick him into taking part in the dance? He would be furious if he thought she was making a fool of him, but she had nothing to lose if her ruse did not work! And much to gain if it did!

A faint mocking smile played at the edges of her mouth. She shrugged. "It is not for me to say. I have not yet decided."

Black Eagle hit the bent end of the racquet, which formed a circular loop filled with a leather network, against his moccasin and grunted, not at all pleased with her answer. He did not like it one bit!

Jeanne's native sense of mischief got the better of her. She grinned impishly. "Whoever catches my basket at the dance will need the courage of a cougar, the strength of a bear, the cunning of a fox."

Black Eagle stood there, taut as a bowstring. His eyes narrowed as they raked her icily. "Clearly, you have chosen the Earth team!"

He turned and began to stalk away, back rigid.

Jeanne tilted her head, called after him. "He will also need the eye of an eagle, the swiftness of a hummingbird, and the wisdom of an owl!"

It said much for Black Eagle's displeasure that his stride did not break as he pivoted on the ball of one foot to face her, arms folded.

"Do not tempt me to beat you," he growled warningly through clenched teeth.

The whiteness of his knuckles as he gripped his racquet warned Jeanne she had gone too far. Black Eagle was not yet ready for such teasing! Jeanne watched him join his team, his injured pride evident in every long stride. Had she aggravated him enough to ensure his thoughts were of her and not the other maidens?

Jeanne listened carefully to Thunderclap's speech relating the difficulties Graceful One must endure if her spirit continued to wander. He called on Wise Speaker to appease the Thunderers with a gift of tobacco.

The ancient medicine man spoke to the Thunderers, saying, "You like tobacco, and we give it to you. Now we want you to give us what we want."

Jeanne watched Black Eagle as he stood talking to Thunderclap and Little Bear. They were smoking some of the tobacco in their long-stemmed pipes, the smoke curling around their roaches like little horns.

This was the signal for the feast for which the women had been preparing all morning. There was an abundance of wild rice, and a thick, fragrant stew, flavored with potatoes, onions, artichokes and lily bulbs. There was also a snapping turtle, as the Thunderers liked this delicacy and always came to a feast for which a snapping turtle had been cooked. Jeanne declined to taste this dish.

The two teams assembled. Thunderclap tossed the ball into the air and gave four loud whoops so that the Thunderers would know the game was beginning. The painted buckskin ball, half red and half blue, rose in the air, caught in one of the racquets and sped down the playing field toward the Earth team's goalpost. It was stolen during a pass by the Sky team, bringing the play toward the opposite end of the field. In the melee of flying racquets, Jeanne could scarcely distinguish one player from the other.

The play moved closer. She could identify Black Eagle as he twisted to avoid a blow from an opponent's racquet. He lunged for the ball, scooping it in his leather loop, running for the goalpost. Stands Fast was too slow! Black Eagle had scored! The crowd stamped and shouted until surely the Thunderers awoke!

Jeanne was on her feet. She moved her hand back and forth in front of her mouth and trilled loudly. By her side, Sweet Breeze jumped up and down. Beyond them, Acorn, laughing and clapping her hands, was cheering the Sky team.

As Black Eagle went to the sideline, where Thunderclap stood, waiting to present him with a prize, Sweet Breeze murmured to Jeanne, "Black Eagle will choose me to receive his trophy. He knows what this woman's gift will be in return! Ayee! He comes my way!"

Without so much as a glance at Jeanne, Black Eagle walked straight up to Sweet Breeze and tossed her a green silk ribbon. It fluttered, was caught and held aloft in triumph. This made everyone shout and yell and scream with laughter all over again.

The game lasted three more hours. Up and down the field. Up and down. Thin Man scored a goal for the Earth team. Buzzard scored a goal for the Sky team. When the cheers died away, Acorn rocked the piece of brightly colored cloth gallantly presented to her by Buzzard against her breast as though it were an infant.

Jeanne went through the motions of cheering and clapping. There was a hurt gathered together in one single frightening mass in her stomach. The hurt of rejection. Her eyes blurred, but she trilled as loudly as the others when Black Eagle sidestepped gracefully, spinning the ball to Little Bear with a deft flick of his wrist.

She gasped when Cornstalk struck No Bone in His Back with his body, tossing that young man head-over-heels into the earth. She cheered when No Bone in His Back rapidly righted himself to shoot the ball straight through the goalposts. She even managed to clap when he walked slowly to

Graceful One and gently tied his trophy, an azure-blue silk ribbon, around one long braid.

The Thunderers must have heard all the whoops and cries and been pleased, because, by the time both teams had scored five goals each, there was thunder in the sky, and rain fell, bringing an end to the game.

That night, Black Eagle did not return to the lodge. Jeanne cried herself to sleep. Next morning, there was blood on her legs. But there was no joy in her heart as she dragged herself to the women's lodge.

Chapter Eight

Jeanne stood before the ceremonial fire, quietly watching the festivities. She stared upward for a moment at the long fingers of sunset painting the deep gray sky with color, then let her eyes stray to the large group that had gathered around to observe a wrestling match.

Little Bear and Prickly Man sized up each other as they circled and watched for an opening. Prickly Man leapt on lithe, catlike feet, sending Little Bear flying over his head to land roughly on the hard ground. Rolling, Little Bear tripped his opponent, who fell facedown in the dirt. Little Bear dived on his adversary like a bounding animal. Prickly Man lunged upward. The two men grappled, rolling over and over again.

Her eyes swept over them, to the edge of the circle, locating Black Eagle where he stood between Thunderclap and Watchful Fox. She saw that he was staring straight ahead, not letting his eyes wander to left or right, but fixing them firmly on the wrestlers.

Jeanne was aware again, as she had been the first instant she saw Black Eagle, of the strength, virility and power that seemed to emanate from his body. Despite herself, she felt her heart leap into her throat at the sight of him.

"Look, but do not touch," a sibilant voice whispered in her ear.

Startled, Jeanne looked up to see the dusky face of Sweet Breeze.

"I did not realize that Prickly Man had been spoken for, Sweet Breeze! If he has, he does not know it, for he played his flute and sang outside the lodge of Singing Bird last night. Over and over again, he sang, 'I will keep on courting until morning,' until the crier came through the camp, telling all the young men that it was time to go home!"

Jeanne pushed past Sweet Breeze, whose mouth seemed to hang open. Her temper rigidly under control, she walked away, swaying a little, like a willow sapling in a light spring breeze.

The satisfaction of having bested Sweet Breeze in a battle of words was only momentary. She knew that Black Eagle was not going to take part in the dancing tonight. Had she not heard him say so to Cornstalk only this morning?

"I do not wish to be wed, and when I do decide it is time to take a wife, I shall choose who she will be. I do not play foolish games" were the very words he had used.

"That is all it is, a game," Cornstalk had protested. "There is no obligation on either the thrower or the catcher of the basket to marry!"

"Yes, but the cost of acceptance is high. For a woman to seek out a man and to ask for him in marriage, she must belong to him until his death. It is not a price I wish to pay to satisfy some childish amusement. I will take a lot of getting."

His words had slashed at her heart, and she had struggled desperately to keep her hands under control as she continued to rub sunflower oil into a small piece of hide. Her face had burned when Black Eagle and Cornstalk noticed her, only a few feet away.

Cornstalk had looked uncomfortable and become intent on the pattern and design of a wooden bowl nearby. Black Eagle had not seemed to notice. Folding his arms across his chest, he had leaned against one of the lodge poles. His face had had a hooded, secret look.

"It would seem that Sweet Breeze is to be disappointed." Jeanne had not been able to stay the words that burst from her lips.

Black Eagle had sighed deeply. "For a short while. But women stick like fleas on a dog. They come back for another bite!"

He had been laughing at her! Jeanne still felt hot and flushed at how easily she had fallen into his teasing trap. She drifted from group to group, watching a dice game, a peach-pit game, and several games between the young men anxious to show off their strength and agility.

Jeanne was surprised to hear Fierce Man being challenged by Dragging Canoe, husband of Red Leaf, who was many years his junior. It became a joking contest, many of the old man's former pupils joining in.

"Surely you have not forgotten how to toss a spear, when you taught each of us to do so!"

"I can recall how you refused to end a lesson until I had three times running hit the target you set me!"

"Yes, his arm still aches!"

Fierce Man was quite old, his face a wrinkled deep mahogany. A headband, decorated with feathers and small stones, fell from his roach over his neck to his waist. A short, sleeveless type of skin covering, beaded and tied with thongs, was draped over his shoulders. A pair of well-worn moccasins covered his feet. He looked from one to another of the young warriors, then nodded slowly.

"You think to avenge yourselves for the endless hours of practice I demanded?" His smile showed toothless gums as he accepted the lance from Dragging Canoe.

Too old to fight, close enough to the sunset to be wise, Fierce Man was not to be tempted into a hasty throw. He hefted the spear, squinted along its length, slowly approached the line drawn in the earth, and nodded to Musk-rat, who stood at the far end of the compound, to set spinning the small hoop that was the target.

Jeanne held her breath as the old man drew back his ropy arm and released the lance he held. The weapon flew in an arc to pass cleanly through the center of the revolving hoop and pierce the log behind. Amid the cheers and shouts, Jeanne heard Wise Speaker's voice beside her.

"Fierce Man may no longer have the endurance to hunt, but the old are granted wisdom to compensate for their creaking bones. He will have much meat this summer from the young warriors!"

"*Bonsoir,* Wise Speaker. How did Fierce Man hit the target, when his strength is withered?"

His finely wrinkled eyes took in Jeanne's keen interest. She lapsed into her old tongue now only when she was excited.

"Warriors seldom lose their command of the lance, so long as their vision does not blur."

"So a person—a young woman, say—who had no more strength than Fierce Man, if she practiced, could become accurate?"

"Practice is all that it takes."

Jeanne ran her fingers lightly along the soft folds of her elkskin tunic, which fell gracefully to her knees. The beaded ear decorations Singing Bird had given her jingled with every movement of her head. She would learn how to use all of the weapons. She would learn all that Fierce Man could teach her. She would practice and practice. She would call on the old tutor at the first opportunity!

A little while later, having checked the lodge where the infants were sleeping, Jeanne was walking through the gathering darkness with Rattle when she saw Black Eagle again. He was standing in a pool of moonlight by the lodge, his dark, striking features illuminated, talking to Brown Cloud. The maiden's moon-shaped face shone, and where the light touched her hair it looked like silver. Then Black Eagle took her arm and they walked away, heads close together.

The moon still shone after they had gone. But somehow a grayness had gotten into the light, dimming it. Jeanne could not understand that. All she knew as she turned away from the lodge and started back toward the festivities was that the edge of everything was unclear, that there was no purity to the moonlight, or even to the light of the stars.

For the first time in weeks, Jeanne's confidence left her, and she felt alone and destitute. She seethed with anger and a strange kind of pain. There were fishhooks inside her body. Fishhooks and brambles and knives.

Jeanne was staggered by how jealous she felt. Again and again the vision rose before her eyes of Black Eagle making tempestuous, passionate love to Sweet Breeze, to Brown Cloud. It was a vision that she almost could not bear. It was abominable, abhorrent! She felt utterly miserable, not only because of Black Eagle's amorous philanderings, but also because of her own startling reaction to them. She felt choked with anger and humiliation. Her mind raging with torment, she stood lost in her own turbulence.

Then anger exploded in her. He would be sorry. Jeanne's face took on a speculative look. A lot of getting, would he take? He had a high price on himself! But he was the man she wanted, even if his quick-moving dark eyes sometimes glinted with an intentness that scared her, as if he knew what she was thinking. It would be pleasant to see him suffer a little for her. She would sing, and dance, and throw her basket to Prickly Man! That would rile him!

People were talking and laughing as they found places on the mats laid on the ground. Conversation ceased when

Wise Speaker rose to his feet. Holding out a bag of sugar, he began to chant.

The wolf leads the man in begging from his friends.
I wish he would give me food—cornmeal with sugar
spread over it.

The drums began to beat, slow and even, as the People clapped and joined in the refrain. Each lodge ceremoniously received the gift of a sugar bag. The rhythm seemed to swell as more voices joined in. It seemed to Jeanne that the repetitive drumbeat entered her very blood, pacing her own heartbeat.

The women stood when the drumbeat became rapid, dancing in their places as the men moved around them. Cornstalk smiled at Jeanne as he circled past, his white teeth gleaming, his dark eyes flashing, laughing, coaxing, teasing. Jeanne knew he was only trying to make up for this afternoon, and she smiled back.

Jeanne watched Black Eagle as he came into her line of vision. She wondered if he realized how much his gaze and nearness affected her, for her body was trembling and tingling. She tossed her head in a defiant gesture, letting her hair fall free as a russet cloud down her back, revealing the slender curve of her neck. She was rewarded by Black Eagle's quick, barely perceptible intake of breath. In confusion, she lowered her eyes, not daring to taunt him further.

The drumbeat changed, became faster, the tones more rhythmic and appealing. The pattern of the dance also changed. The women began to move in a jig, their fringed skirts twirling. Of their own accord, Jeanne's little feet seemed to know the intricate steps of the dance. Who needed a dancing master here? The tempo increased. Soon, Jeanne was whirling, jumping, stomping, with the same complete abandonment as the other women.

The music slowed. Again the men circled, while the women swayed in a subtle form of body movement in time to the rhythm made while standing in one place. A flute joined in. As the men passed, they handed the unmarried women baskets. Those with baskets formed a circle. The others stepped back. Now the young men stepped into the center of the circle.

Jeanne stumbled and bumped into Brown Cloud, who was beside her. Black Eagle was there! How the music had changed! She did not know whether it was the flute or the blood soaring through her veins, but it was different! It tinkled. It fluttered like butterflies, softer than a breeze. It bowed and pirouetted like two partridges courting, feathers extended. It rose with the splendor of a sunrise, a waving, leaping flame. Holding her basket in both hands, Jeanne slowly raised it to touch one breast and then the other.

Willow fronds caught the breeze and moved, then froze again into a winter wonderland, icicles tinkling, hanging on a spruce. It was pure magic. The basket was lowered to touch the groin. The music soared, liquid silver, moonlight on a birch forest, an eagle soaring, watching, waiting....

The flute was drawing to a wailing stop. Jeanne moved to throw her basket. The music came to an abrupt stop. Brown Cloud crashed into her. Sweet Breeze jostled her on the other side. A deft foot tripped her. The basket flew out of her hands. Jeanne gasped, her face flushing hotly. Black Eagle had caught her basket!

She looked directly at him. Saw him smile. He was going to say something startling and insulting. Instead, he handed her the basket and spoke with good humor.

"It looks as though I have caught a wife!"

"You are all—all noise, and a great deal of smoke!" Jeanne retorted.

Black Eagle's hands went swiftly to his hips and then moved up and down his thighs, slowly, in the unconscious, angry gesture of a man who has been challenged and who is ready and eager to fight. He moved closer. Jeanne held her ground. She could see the faces on the men behind him, incredulous and delighted. One nudged another meaningfullyly with his elbow and grinned.

"What do you mean by that?" Black Eagle's dark eyebrows were a straight line across his forehead as he glared down at her.

"No gifts, you said!"

"Have I courted you with gifts?"

"No..." Jeanne's heart was thumping wildly. Her thoughts were confused, racing.

"Played the flute outside the lodge of Singing Bird?"

"No..." Jeanne shook her head. The crowd behind Black Eagle had increased, and the men were craning their necks to see.

"You were going to reserve your strength to better serve the spirits!" Jeanne said. Her voice was as forceful as it could be with those steady dark eyes fixed upon her.

"No stag ever found his antlers too heavy. His spindly legs can still outdistance the hunter. I will face my responsibilities as the spirit demands."

The people in the background moved forward slowly, listening with interest. Jeanne's chin went higher.

"You were not going to take part in the dance!" she reminded him.

For a long moment, Black Eagle stared at her.

"True. I have nothing to prove, no reason to celebrate. But Leaning Wood was concerned that I had somehow injured my foot while hunting. And Crayfish convinced me that if I were to dance, a stone would also be dancing, and the stone would be looked upon with more favor!"

There was a ripple of laughter, but Jeanne ignored it. "You have said you do not want a wife!"

Black Eagle shook his head. "No," he said flatly, "I did not say that. I said I would have a wife of my own choosing."

Jeanne's face flamed. Her thoughts were confused, racing. "You would not accept a wife in this manner. The cost is too high," she recollected, biting her lips.

Black Eagle stared down at the proud, angry little face. "But I do. You are the flesh of my dreams. And I accept, no matter what the cost."

"You accept?" She must be hearing things!

His eyes dark and intense, he dropped his voice so that it was very quiet. His words were a promise.

"I want you for a wife, Little Turtle. I have always wanted you."

For an eternity, it seemed, the words remained suspended between them in space. There was in his eyes a look, a flame that Jeanne had never seen before. As if all the power of his body had been gathered together in one single, frightening mass, and it was all directed at her. She had never seen fierce, frank hunger in a man's eyes before, never realized the primitive power of it.

The warmth of his low voice, his nearness, the vital, virile strength of him, shook her. She tried to step back, but his arms were already around her waist. Her resistance crumbled. Even as she nodded, unable to trust her voice, her arms lifted and wound themselves round his neck.

Shouts from the men, drawn out, ending in a yelp on a high note, made her hurriedly drop them. Then she heard the women trilling, especially Rattle's voice, loud with excitement and unmistakable delight.

"Oh, Little Turtle, I knew Leaning Wood was only teasing me when he said that Black Eagle would not dance with the maidens tonight! That one will eat nothing but clover for seven moons!"

As she turned, Jeanne saw the jubilation on Brown Cloud's face, saw her dark eyes dancing. "I was so busy watching your basket, Little Turtle, that I forgot to throw my own!"

"Little Turtle was fortunate. Mine was knocked from my hands and trampled in the rush!" wailed Sweet Breeze.

Jeanne felt overwhelmed by the merry jokes that were exchanged.

"Now you will begin to dance like a fish when your wife trails the bait!" Cornstalk announced, slapping his thigh.

"Or jump like the rabbit when he sees the wildcat coming!"

The laughing banter continued. "And Turtle will scream when she sees the little things that fly about in the nighttime!"

Black Eagle, ignoring the hilarious witticisms of his friends, replied, "The hunter grows strong in the sun. He rests in the shadow of the moon. Never fear, my friends, you will see me again next springtime!"

Thunderclap was grinning broadly. He slapped Black Eagle on the back. "The two sides of the heavens are coming together when you join with Little Turtle. There will be much noise and trembling when you clash. I can hear the Thunderers now, chuckling in anticipation."

Black Eagle smiled slightly, and when he spoke again, his voice was a slow, deep rumble. "My fire is in full blaze. Like a moth, my wife will flutter to my fire to seek my desire and cool the heat in my blood. To birth my sons."

"If that is all you want in a wife, Little Turtle is not the one for you! That one is all contrariness and contradiction. She has a restless spirit, the mind of a warrior. Not for her the waiting by the fireside. That one will walk by her man, or perish in the attempt!"

Jeanne missed Black Eagle's reply, for Acorn was there, at her side, bubbling over with exhilaration, wanting to talk, jumping up and down.

"Buzzard has caught my basket, Little Turtle. He has accepted!"

Many jokes were passed back and forth. Everyone seemed to want to speak at once. Jeanne looked for Singing Bird, her skin suddenly pale beneath the vermilion on her cheeks. In the past weeks, a closeness of a special quality had developed between Singing Bird and Jeanne, and yet the older woman had not come forward to greet either her or Black Eagle. Maybe it was not the custom.

For a moment, her brow furrowed with concern. Could it be that Singing Bird was not in favor of a union between Black Eagle and herself? Surely not! What difference could it make? They lived quite companionably now, the three of them in harmony. Singing Bird had given her the gift of earrings to wear tonight. She had helped paint her face. Jeanne's brow cleared.

She waited until the young people were through congratulating her and Black Eagle had been borne off by the young men, then approached Singing Bird. The old woman stood straight, head held high, amid a group of other matrons, her face impassive. Beneath the sagging flesh of her face, Jeanne could see strength and unyielding pride. Ignoring the coalition of women, Jeanne walked right up to Singing Bird and stared at her, her eyes troubled.

"Have I done something to displease you, Singing Bird, that you stand back and do not wish Black Eagle and Little Turtle well?"

Singing Bird lifted her hands as though she were going to say something, then changed her mind. She seemed nervous and uncomfortable. Her strange she-eagle eyes had an unaccustomed look of appeal.

Jeanne stood there, without moving, until the savage
cackle of Mountain Wolf Woman's laughter rode in upon
her.

"I told you to sell her, Singing Bird. Small and miserable
as she is, she would have brought a good price. Now, as wife
of Black Eagle, she will turn you out of his lodge, and you
will be homeless," she rasped.

Jeanne was stunned. She stared at Singing Bird, her mind
reeling with the impact of Mountain Wolf Woman's insin-
uation. This was the reason for Singing Bird's discomfort
and anxiety! How could she allay such fear? She bent her
head, applying rapt attention to the intricate beading on the
small, rounded toes of her moccasins. What would she have
done, if she had been wearing the moccasins of Singing
Bird?

Would she have been as merciful? Shown such generos-
ity of spirit to the one who killed her son? Her only son. The
son born after countless barren moons, when all hope of
bearing a living child had died? Would she, Jeanne de la
Rocque, have suckled an orphaned child, shared the last
drops of milk from her sagging breasts? Have shown char-
ity to her enemy? Instructed such a one in the curing of
hides? How to make them supple, yet strong? How to
smoke them so that they became waterproof? How to cut
and sew the skins to make garments? Her jaw clenched. No!
For her, revenge would have been sweet!

"Turtle," she heard Singing Bird say, and looked up. "I
am pleased the son of my heart and breast has decided to
wed. It is not right that the young live without a mate."

Jeanne finally broke the long silence, went to Singing
Bird, took her gnarled and wrinkled hand, held it tightly in
her own small palm and said softly, "Mountain Wolf
Woman has a viperous tongue, Singing Bird. There is no use
looking back, thinking what might have been. You have
done what you have done, and it was good. You protected

and defended Little Turtle when she was strange and did not know the ways of the People." Jeanne's voice stopped. She was acutely, painfully conscious of her critics.

She moistened her lips, started again, with slow, deliberate care. "There is a story I have heard, of a far-off time, a thousand moons ago, about an old woman whose husband and sons died. Filled with grief, this woman decided to travel back to the land of her birth. The wives of her dead sons resolved to accompany her."

Jeanne stood there, staring at Singing Bird, and her eyes were suddenly luminous. Her fingers tightened their grip.

"When they had gone some distance on the way, the old woman strove to persuade the wives of her dead sons to return to their own country. One yielded, but the other would not. Like that other girl, Little Turtle has been a stranger in a strange land. Like that other old woman, Singing Bird has taken the outsider to her heart."

Jeanne's clear, candid eyes rested on each of the women in turn. Then she smiled reassuringly at Singing Bird.

"The sound of the rapids no longer frightens Little Turtle, the woods are not so foreign. In the words that girl said to her dead husband's mother, I say to you, Singing Bird, *Whither thou goest, I will go. Where thou lodgest, I will lodge. Thy people shall be my people, and thy God my God.* You shall not want. And you shall dwell in the lodge of Black Eagle forever."

The joy on the old woman's face was no less than Jeanne's as they fell into one another's arms.

Next day, the women prepared their belongings to travel to the summer camp. Woven mats and furs from the beddings were rolled, bound tightly and placed with all their possessions until the lodge was empty. Within a short time, everything was loaded into canoes, which had great guardian eyes painted on bow and stern, and everyone was ready to leave.

Jeanne watched Black Eagle carefully place his weapons and sacred belongings beside him. The otterskin bag, which indicated his standing as a medicine man, was secured at his waist. A deep warmth curled inside her, like the flutter of unseen insects, as, wordlessly, his eyes, heavy with promise, drew an imaginary finger along her jaw, down her throat, along the slit at the neck of her tunic.

Five days passed swiftly, wearily, and uneventfully. A monotonous routine, one day blending into the next. Most of the time the People traveled in canoes. Sometimes on foot. The group moved slowly, allowing the very old and very young to keep pace. The men traveled both ahead and behind the main party, ever vigilant. Only occasionally did Jeanne catch a glimpse of Black Eagle.

Once she saw him speaking with Red Leaf and Bright Path. Both young women were heavy with child, yet they still diligently carried their share. Another time, he walked by Graceful One. The girl also carried a full load, skillfully, as though her body remembered having performed this task twice yearly since reaching womanhood. Jeanne watched as Graceful One lifted the arm from which the cast had been removed to Black Eagle, a small smile of greeting tipping her mouth. Then she dropped the limb, scowling, as though trying to remember why she had done so.

Even little She Is Playful assisted, carrying Fleecy Cloud for Sky Woman. Fleecy Cloud peeped over the rim of her cradleboard, crooning softly to herself, her little eyes round with wonder.

"I hope I have a girl-child," Bright Path said, her dark eyes wistful. "In my dreams, I see her, but when I reach to hold the infant in my arms, I become cold and wake up shivering."

Trembling, Jeanne felt at her neck for the leather pouch that lay against her flesh, reassured when her fingers found it, and followed the outlines of the little turtle shell and the piece of crystal.

"*Bon Dieu,* Great Spirit," she prayed. "Father of all. Do not listen to Bright Path. Listen to Little Turtle. Make it a man-child, in the image of Dry Man, a tomahawk for a nose, crow feathers for a brow."

Annoyed with herself for succumbing to the sinister, dark pictures in her mind if Bright Path's child was a girl, Jeanne concentrated on the women's conversation.

"Dragging Canoe is hoping for another man-child who can play with Little Shouter. I say two children as noisy as Little Shouter will drive me out of our lodge!" Red Leaf laughed merrily. "That one cried so constantly we had to call in Wise Speaker."

"Yes, I remember." Good Woman nodded. "He said the child was being called by the spirit women, and that they would take it away unless their bowl-and-dice game was played."

"Undoubtedly Little Shouter would have died if this had not been done," Red Leaf said.

The women's chatter faded, lost in the haze of Jeanne's daydreams. When the summer camp was set up, she and Black Eagle would be joined in a special marriage ceremony. She touched the colorfully etched armband he had given her, a smile curving her lips. It was his favorite.

Next moon, Black Eagle had promised her, he would take her to visit the Wolf River tribe, kin to the People. They would spend at least one moon, maybe even two, learning each other's ways, returning to help with the harvest and prepare for the return to the winter camp.

Three days later, the People reached the site of their summer camp. Everyone went to work immediately. While the women unpacked, the men cut poles for the frameworks of the new lodges. Jeanne helped Singing Bird push the poles into the ground, and cover them with strips of elm bark collected by Black Eagle.

The women quickly arranged the lodge in a similar manner to the familiar one at the winter camp, except that the private area set aside for Black Eagle had been enlarged to accommodate his bride. By late afternoon, all was completed, and Black Eagle's war bundle hung from a peg in its customary place.

Jeanne was standing outside, dreamily admiring the neat way she had attached the door flap, when Black Eagle approached her, silently, as usual.

She did not know he was there until he stood very near to her and said in a low voice, "Come, Turtle. The purification lodge is completed, and Good Woman says the sweat baths are hot. She wants you to get ready now. At the marriage ceremony, Wise Speaker wants to confirm your place as one of the People with formal adoption rites."

"Adoption?" Jeanne faltered. Her knees seemed suddenly weak, and she could feel the hot blood rush to her face. It was as though her thoughts had conjured him up, and for an instant she was not quite sure he was real.

"As a captured woman, you have no family to honor you with marriage gifts. Wise Speaker has decreed that you shall not lack such prestige. It is customary when someone is adopted for that person to receive gifts from everyone. As a daughter of the People, you will come to your husband as an equal, with respect."

"Are many prisoners adopted by the People?"

"Not unless they demonstrate they are worthy."

She met his gaze squarely. "How has Little Turtle, who sent On the Other Side to journey to the lodge of silent memory, whose deed caused Graceful One to walk through the lonely, eternally wasted roads of sorrow, proved worthy?"

"By your actions and words to Singing Bird, you have shown that you believe, as the People do, that outside show is a poor substitute for inner worth. You have learned the ways, the speech, of the People. If I closed my eyes, I could believe that I heard one of our women."

Jeanne's heart took wing. Adopted! To be truly one of the People! Her family was dead. France lost to her forever. Colorful turns of life, some new thing to be done, seen, admired, had been a part of her existence ever since she could remember. It did not seem odd how quickly she had adjusted and had begun to take for granted things that grew familiar. Servants and dancing lessons had been replaced by hard physical labor and this incredible feeling of homecoming, of belonging.

Black Eagle stared down at her, wordless, for a long minute, watching her vivid, expressive face, his eyes hot and shining.

"I will not see you until the celebrations begin."

A new and strange excitement stirred within Jeanne, and her pulse began to race. He watched her silently, and she could feel her cheeks burning. Her hands were shaking, and her throat was tight.

"You do not have second thoughts, Black Eagle? This is what you want?"

Jeanne watched the movement of his lips as he spoke. The little pulse that beat in his strong neck. Her breath caught at his words.

"It is what I want!"

Chapter Nine

"Never has there been such a celebration!" Good Woman straightened Jeanne's new tunic, making the elk-teeth decorations cascade and jingle. So many of them! And the hide was so soft and supple!

Skin pink and glowing, still flushed from the sweat lodge, her chestnut hair clinging in damp tendrils to her face, Jeanne clapped her hands and let out an infectious giggle. Her eyes twinkled with delight.

"It is so pretty, Good Woman. I am so excited, I know my face is as red as the eastern sky in the morning."

"Which is as it should be." Singing Bird added a dot of vermilion to each cheek. "It was the Spirit of the East, who moves across the sky in a day, who gave the People instructions for adoption."

Good Woman held out the stiff tail brush of a porcupine. "Come. Let me comb and braid your foxtail of hair."

"No!" Jeanne held out her hand. "I am sorry, Good Woman. I do not mean to offend, but I have noticed Black Eagle does not approve of my hair when I braid it. He does not say anything, but he looks down his long nose, like so!" She tilted her head back, in imitation.

The women laughed as Jeanne mimicked the haughty expression Black Eagle's face took on when he was displeased about something.

"Why not alter the armband you so favor, add a little piece, and wrap it around your head? That would stop the hair falling in your face and eyes, and it would still hang loose down your back!"

Good Woman's nimble fingers soon made the simple adjustment needed to convert Black Eagle's armband into a headband. As she gently teased Jeanne's hair, Jeanne admired the wampum necklet Stands Fast had given her. It shone by the fire as if it made its own milky light. It would look lovely resting on the soft mounds of her breasts, moving gently with her breathing. She would have to return it. Sighing, she laid it aside. She picked up a belt. The width of four fingers, the belt emphasized the slenderness of her waist, the slim curve of her hip.

Singing Bird sat on the edge of the bed, watching her every movement, her eyes darting back and forth like those of a fencing master. Jeanne smiled, a great feeling of contentment washing over her.

"Just think, Singing Bird. Is life not wonderful? I could have been burned, tortured, killed, but here I am, about to become wife to the son of your breast!" Jeanne knelt, twined her hands about the old woman's arm, hid her eyes in her skirt. "If you could find it in your heart to forgive?"

Singing Bird shook her head, puckered her lips, touched the long red hair. "You talk to me like the brook. What is done is done. Little Turtle delights this old one. I have her face, her scent, her touch, to remind me of my lost one. I see him reflected in her many-colored eyes. She is like a knot, another twist in the cord that binds the son of my breast and me."

With a wing quill, painted red to denote her new status, clutched in her hand, Jeanne felt as regal as the granddaughter of a duke should feel when the women escorted her to the medicine lodge. Her heart at ease, she stepped lightly, as softly as a dancer.

The arched lodge was packed, with the People seated along each side. Jeanne's eyes centered on Wise Speaker, who stood at the far end holding a hooked staff in one hand, a pair of heavy turtle-shell rattles in the other. He wore a horned-owl-claw necklace, and his moccasins were decorated with clipped moose-hair designs, fashioned after the motifs Black Eagle had shown her in the celestial cave.

Yellow Feather was also there, his scarred faced daubed in red paint, hands and ankles bright blue, two bear paws dangling from his staff. His red-dyed deer roach, drawn low, covered his scalp scar.

Cornstalk, Little Bear, Prickly Man and Stands Fast, each holding a gourd rattle in his left hand, the corner of a thin, membranous material of parchmentlike quality painted with strange geometric designs in his right, were gathered around a drum, humming. To Jeanne, the sound was reminiscent of the drone of wild bees.

The drum, fashioned from a hollowed log, was decorated with sacred drawings representing the earth and sky. One end was solid, the other covered with a heavy piece of deerskin held down with a wooden rim. Jeanne could see the hole in the side where water had been poured into the cylinder. The steady beat of a curved drumstick, wielded by Watchful Fox, produced on the dampened head a soft thrumming sound.

Jeanne recognized Black Eagle with a sudden mighty thump of her heart. He stood there, straight and tall, Thunderclap at his side, face painted, impressive in his best outfit. His tunic was embellished with lightcolored bone, shells, teeth, and yellow and red embroidery. Concentric circles of quillwork in the same colors were embroidered on his leggings. The stunning combination was repeated on his moccasins. His eagle feather lifted like a graceful wing from his roach. The banded snakeskin rattle trembled from his scalp lock.

She dropped her eyes in a maidenly fashion, but could not resist a second peek. Black Eagle was still watching her, jawline clenched, nostrils flaring like those of a stag winded after a swift race from the hunter's arrow. Ramrod-stiff, he gave no sign of recognition. Jeanne wished he would smile at her. She averted her eyes again when Singing Bird and Good Woman took their places, one on either side of her.

Yellow Feather held his hooked staff high, shaking it gently, making the bear claws dance. "In the name of the Spirit of the East, we are here to welcome Little Turtle, to make her one of the People. I, Yellow Feather, of the Great Ancestral Bear, leader of the war party that captured this woman, offer Little Turtle a place among the Bear Society."

"It is a great honor she is offered. What makes her worthy?" The chorus came from the four young braves holding the painted script.

"Outnumbered, she used her weapon like a warrior. By her courage, her fortitude, she ran faster than her shadow to survive the gauntlet of women. No person has lived to tell of a ride over the great falls but this one. She has had a vision. She has found a name. Her guardian spirit is strong. It looks with favor on this woman," Yellow Feather responded.

Jeanne's heart missed a beat. If she were adopted by the Ancestral Bear Society, she could not marry Black Eagle! She now understood why the women had joked when Black Eagle named her Little Turtle. By aligning her with the Turtle Society, he had repudiated kinship and, in effect, staked a claim, since marriage within one's own society was prohibited by tribal custom.

"Does any other wish to say something on behalf of Little Turtle?"

Black Eagle stepped forward. Jeanne looked at him. His body was as proudly erect as that of the guardian of a hallowed place. He did not even glance at her, kept his gaze rigidly in front of him.

"On the sun the spirits called the name of On the Other Side, I also swam in the river of light with the brother of my heart. But I was called by the voice of the turtle to emerge from the waters, compelled from within to recall the fasting dream of my youth, when the Great Black Eagle came to me and whispered to me of the pale daughter of the moon.

"When her blood mingled with mine, I heard again the words of Wise Speaker. 'The eye does not see. The ear does not hear. Only the spirit knows. . . .' She has won the protection of the Great Turtle, and should belong to that society."

Singing Bird's voice came softly into the silence that followed Black Eagle's declaration. "With the loss of her much-loved son, Singing Bird was bitter. But wisdom in love can grow in quiet places, as it has done for Singing Bird since Little Turtle came to our lodge." Singing Bird held a hand over her breast as if her own words had struck her there.

Back straight, Jeanne, swallowing the lump in her throat, stood very still and watched the face of Singing Bird.

"Singing Bird sees again the juices of her young womanhood flowing in the pale daughter of the moon." Quietly she made her point. "This old woman's hands and body do not work as they used to. Little Turtle has brought the gift of youth and laughter to ease Singing Bird's sunset years."

The four young braves called out in unison. "Who speaks for this woman? Who will offer her the kinship of the Turtle Society?"

Wise Speaker brought his staff forward, shaking the turtle-shell rattle. "The Wise Speaker speaks for Little Turtle! Neither the Great Ancestral Bear, nor the Snapping Turtle, will be responsible. The organization of the medicine lodge offers her the kinship of the People! Little Turtle will be a daughter of the medicine lodge!" The old man's voice was strong and deep.

Jeanne gasped, surprised. Why should the medicine lodge adopt her, when she had not even begun to know, or even understand, the use of the substances believed to have magical powers? Nor was she a teller of legends or one who remembers. She had no special talents to justify such an honor.

"Whether or not Little Turtle decides to be trained is a choice only she can make, but it does not matter in the least," Wise Speaker continued. "We do not know why this woman was chosen by one so powerful to be given the ability to recognize and sense things yet to be. We do know it was foretold many moons ago. We accept the choice of the spirits."

The drum was struck twice, signifying assent to his remarks, and the four choristers chanted, "Will the woman, Little Turtle, step forward?"

Jeanne's stomach churned and her knees felt weak as she walked the length of the lodge. She fixed her eyes on a point above the old medicine man's head, not daring to glance at Black Eagle or any of the others.

Wise Speaker conformed her fingers around his own so that they resembled the claws of a bird, and turned her around so that she faced the assemblage.

"Do you wish to become one of the People?"

"Yes." The sound of her own voice, soft but strong and clear, startled her a little.

"To live in peace and harmony? To ask the assistance and protection of your guardian spirit? To use the power given for the good of the People?"

Jeanne nodded her head respectfully in agreement, heard the drum beat, the rhythmic clapping and trilling, and was swept away by the four choristers. The dancers moved from the west toward the east, counterclockwise. As she passed each member of the medicine lodge, a long-tailed raccoon wand was waved over her head.

The adoption rites were now complete. As a daughter of the medicine lodge, Jeanne could go to choose her mate.

Out of the corner of her eye, Jeanne caught sight of Black Eagle. He watched her, his body held in relaxed control, a quality of his warrior training and practice. His lips were slightly parted, but his strong white teeth appeared to be lightly gripping the left corner of his lower one.

The dance swept him out of her line of vision, and then returned her to him. It seemed his need, his desire, focused on her, giving Jeanne the courage to hold out her hands. Without hesitation, he joined his hands with hers.

Jeanne led him toward the middle of the area. They circled the lodge three times before Wise Speaker signaled them to be seated on the woven mats that were spread along the walls. Jeanne made herself comfortable, legs modestly folded to one side. Black Eagle took a husband's place, in front of her, as was proper.

Jeanne stared at the wide expanse of shoulders that stretched his elkskin shirt taut as a drumhead. Her stomach fluttered as if it were full of tickling feathers, and her loins warmed with a strange heat that made her giddy. Acutely aware of Black Eagle's presence, she shook her head to avert her gaze, which had become almost hypnotized, and fastened her eyes on the old medicine man.

Wise Speaker shook his rattle and sprinkled some tobacco in the four directions. He chanted softly, thanking the spirits for the food and making a petition for a bountiful growing season.

That was the signal for the feast to begin. Mouth-watering aromas made everyone realize how hard they had worked that day unpacking and preparing for the celebrations.

As was the custom, the men were served first, the choristers acting as the food bearers. And what food it was! Fat blue grouse, stuffed with grain and pine nuts, baked slowly in the fire pit. Moose meat, brown and sizzling, dripping fat from its outer surfaces. Cattail and turnip bulbs, green onions and arrowhead root floating in a thick, mealy soup. The delicate eggs of wood pigeons. Steamed fish wrapped in skunk-cabbage leaves. Dried apples, roasted hazelnuts and preserved berries mashed with ground rice into little cakes.

Jeanne studied the jovial crowd. She could see Red Leaf, ungainly now, forced to kneel, the bulk of her pregnancy preventing her from sitting in the usual position. Sky Woman, nursing her baby, sat beside her. Fleecy Cloud nuzzled her mother's breast with the frantic racket of a being in danger of extinction if its belly is not immediately filled.

Sweet Breeze was there, watching Little Bear help serve the meal, her face upturned, sweetly carved. Rattle, her high-pitched laughter bubbling out of her throat, kept tapping Leaning Wood on the shoulder. The elders and matrons gathered at one end of the lodge.

After the meal, there was much merriment. Drumbeats filled the enclosed space. The pounding of feet, and the rhythmic clapping of hands, shook the medicine lodge. Black Eagle stood and turned to smile at her. Jeanne's heart raced when he leaned over, picked up his pelt cape, looked at her with his compelling eyes, and held out the fur mantle. Jeanne could not have resisted even if she had tried.

She stepped into the circle of his arms.

The folds of the robe engulfed her before he swept her off her feet and swung her around, and their laughter spilled forth to mingle with the sounds of the festivities. They danced slowly round the circle together, his arms about her. She felt the tickle of his breath, and when she slid her arms up his chest, as she might have felt the earth tremble faintly with the footfalls of a large advancing animal, she felt his heart.

Jeanne could feel the blood pounding to her cheeks, hear the jingle of the elk teeth on her tunic. People were calling to her, but she did not see them. There was only Black Eagle. His eyes, glittering like dark stones under rippling waters, seemed to hold her, draw her, weak and trembling, toward their depths. He pulled her closer to him, and their swaying steps became one.

As the evening wore on, the group began to diminish. Children dropped off to sleep and were carried to their beds. But the feast continued with singing, chanting, dancing, talking and eating far into the night, long after Black Eagle guided his bride to where a new moon shone like a bow at full draw.

Feeling as if she were in a dream, Jeanne followed his lead, her heart suddenly slamming into her throat when she realized they were at the door of their lodge.

"Come." Lifting the flap, he held it while she preceded him into the dimly lit interior. "We shall not be disturbed. Singing Bird is to stay with Good Woman and Yellow Feather for a few days."

Black Eagle carelessly tossed his war robe on the floor and bent to stir the embers in the fire pit. Then he stood and peeled off his tunic, which dropped to join the mantle in a puddle at his feet.

Jeanne swallowed to ease the dryness in her throat. There was only Black Eagle and herself, and the force that ran between them like a bolt of lightning. His night-dark eyes gleamed jewel-bright as he unlatched his leggings, slipped off his moccasins. A strange, half frightening, half thrilling shiver seemed to take hold of her, making her whole body shake as he stood there dressed only in his breechclout.

DOUBLE YOUR ACTION PLAY...

"ROLL A DOUBLE!"

Peel off label & place inside

**CLAIM 4 BOOKS
PLUS A FREE
GIFT**

ABSOLUTELY FREE!

SEE INSIDE...

NO RISK, NO OBLIGATION TO BUY...NOW OR EVER!

GUARANTEED

PLAY "ROLL A DOUBLE" AND GET FIVE FREE GIFTS!

HERE'S HOW TO PLAY:

1. Peel off label from front cover. Place it in space provided at right. With a coin, carefully scratch off the silver dice. Then check the claim chart to see what we have for you – FREE BOOKS and a gift – ALL YOURS! ALL FREE!

2. Send back this card and you'll receive brand-new Harlequin Historical™ novels. These books have a cover price of $3.99 each, but they are yours to keep absolutely free.

3. There's no catch. You're under no obligation to buy anything. We charge nothing – ZERO – for your first shipment. And you don't have to make any minimum number of purchases – not even one!

4. The fact is thousands of readers enjoy receiving books by mail from the Harlequin Reader Service® before they're available in stores. They like the convenience of home delivery and they love our discount prices!

5. We hope that after receiving your free books you'll want to remain a subscriber. But the choice is yours – to continue or cancel, anytime at all! So why not take us up on our invitation, with no risk of any kind. You'll be glad you did!

You'll look like a million dollars when you wear this lovely necklace! Its cobra-link chain is a generous 18" long, and the multi-faceted Austrian crystal sparkles like a diamond!

NOT ACTUAL SIZE

"ROLL A DOUBLE!"

PLACE LABEL HERE

SCRATCH HERE

?

SEE CLAIM CHART BELOW

247 CIH ANES
(U-H-H-03/94)

YES! I have placed my label from the front cover into the space provided above and scratched off the silver dice. Please rush me the free books and gift that I am entitled to. I understand that I am under no obligation to purchase any books, as explained on the back and on the opposite page.

NAME _____

ADDRESS _____ APT. _____

CITY _____ STATE _____ ZIP CODE _____

CLAIM CHART

	4 FREE BOOKS PLUS FREE CRYSTAL PENDANT NECKLACE
	3 FREE BOOKS
	2 FREE BOOKS

CLAIM NO. 37-829

THE HARLEQUIN READER SERVICE®: HERE'S HOW IT WORKS

Accepting free books puts you under no obligation to buy anything. You may keep the books and gift and return the shipping statement marked "cancel". If you do not cancel, about a month later we will send you 4 additional novels, and bill you just $3.19 each plus 25¢ delivery and applicable sales tax, if any.* That's the complete price, and – compared to cover prices of $3.99 each – quite a bargain! You may cancel at any time, but if you choose to continue, every month we'll send you 4 more books, which you may either purchase at the discount price...or return at our expense and cancel your subscription.

*Terms and prices subject to change without notice. Sales tax applicable in N.Y.

BUSINESS REPLY MAIL
FIRST CLASS MAIL   PERMIT NO. 717   BUFFALO, NY

POSTAGE WILL BE PAID BY ADDRESSEE

HARLEQUIN READER SERVICE
3010 WALDEN AVE
PO BOX 1867
BUFFALO NY 14240-9952

NO POSTAGE
NECESSARY
IF MAILED
IN THE
UNITED STATES

Her eyes shone as she gazed up at him, standing tall and proud before her, the powerful muscles of his body rippling in the amber light of the fire. Except for the turtle-shaped purple scar near his shoulder, his chest was smooth, inviting her touch and contact. With a gesture that was half pleading, half demanding, she held out her arms to him.

She had never experienced anything so exciting. The fingers of one hand wandered through his soft ruff of hair as the fingers of the other teased over his back. His hands eased beneath her elkskin tunic, sliding it over her head. His mouth traveled down her throat, pressing hot, gentle, quick kisses along the slender column and over her collarbone before his lips fastened over the tiny rosy bud of one breast.

Queer tingles raced from the stiff little peak in all directions, right down to her belly, which felt filled with tiny buzzing mosquitoes. Black Eagle held her utterly defenseless against his mouth, softly, completely devouring her. His tongue circled one nipple, his teeth gently raked, and she gasped as liquid fire streamed through her blood.

Jeanne squirmed with pleasure, grazing his shoulder lightly with her teeth. Deep in the soft, secret place between her thighs, she felt a slow, burning ache flicker, take flame, and begin to blaze like wildfire through her loins. With each tug of his mouth, each sweet stab of his tongue, the pleasure gathered. She felt her legs crumble under her and his arms strengthen and tighten until she was next to his heartbeat.

Slowly, gently, he eased away from her, drawing back until he could look down upon her once again. A smile slanted his mouth. He lifted a hand to trace the outline of her mouth with gentle fingers, then moved to tunnel through the heavy mass of coppery hair, releasing the band. Jeanne was so caught up in the strange sensations he was producing in her body that she was only dimly aware of him lifting her onto the platform bed, sliding off the remainder of her clothing.

His lips traveled downward once more, his mouth murmuring against her throat, before finding her breasts again. The touch of his hand skimming the rufous delta at the apex of her thighs made her gasp. His lips traced a burning path down the flesh of her breasts until at last they touched her where she had never dreamed a man's lips could rest.

The heat of his mouth against her inner thigh sent rippling sensations throughout Jeanne's body, echoing the supple dance of the firelight. A searing spiral of sensation whirled around her, driving her higher and higher with each caress until she twisted like fire within Black Eagle's grasp. Her whole small, fragile body shook.

No longer the master of her own responses, Jeanne felt her hips begin to undulate as her body swept toward some great height or depth, she knew not which. Some place she had never been or dreamed of. With a last surge of abandon, she let herself sweep along it with a moan of delight.

At her cry, Black Eagle made a low sound of satisfaction and triumph, eased her body beneath the burden of his weight. At the moment of their union, Jeanne felt a sharp stab of pain, quickly dwarfed by that other, all-encompassing torment, which filled her body with the sweetness of its agony.

All her energies were directed toward satisfying that ache, and with a sureness born of instinct, she let her hips begin to move in unison with his, slowly at first, then more and more frantically, until she was thrashing with an untamed urgency beneath his body. Sensations rushed through her flesh with a speed she would never have dreamed possible, as she felt the powerful, sharp contractions of his body joining with her own.

They did not speak, but lay in the darkness, their bodies damp from their lovemaking. Black Eagle's weight still

pressed down on her as they clung to each other, breathless.

Burrowing her head in his shoulder, Jeanne was glad that
Black Eagle could not see her face in the dark. Never, in her
wildest imaginings, had she realized that such closeness,
such personal touching, could occur between a man and a
woman. Never would she be able to describe the painful,
startling, tender, momentous thing that had happened between them.

"Turtle?" Black Eagle's voice was low.

"Yes?"

"I must be getting heavy," he said, pulling himself up to
partially support his weight on an elbow.

"No," Jeanne whispered. "You are not heavy at all. I do
not think I ever want you to get up."

Black Eagle bent down to nuzzle an ear and kiss her neck.
He disengaged himself slowly, as gentle as the winter sun
removing itself from the earth at day's end. He looked down
at the silken-smooth moon-gold skin, his hand running
lightly across her breasts, then down her belly. He stopped
abruptly when he caught sight of the bright red stain mark-
ing the darker red of his own flesh. Jeanne felt his muscles
tense. His face was surprised at first, then wary.

"Is it—?" He hesitated.

She knew he was about to ask if it was the time when no
man had a right to touch any woman. She could see by the
expression on his face that he already knew the answer.

Sitting up abruptly on the side of the platform bed, he
turned his face away from her and swung his legs down to
touch the matting on the floor. There was a curious look on
his face, remorse—resentment, tenderness, all mingled together.

"Why did you not—?" He broke off with a groan.
"What have I done to you?"

"You have made me a woman." Jeanne could not keep her hurt at his reactions from entering her voice.

"This is the first time you have taken part in the mating ritual! I never realized! I was so thoughtless, so demanding."

"I did not notice!"

"I was not as tender, as patient, as I should have been." His voice was contrite. His face bent into the hollow of her neck. "I will make it up to you."

"So soon? But how can you—?"

His laughter was filled with delight. "Do you doubt my manhood, Little Turtle?"

"I know little of such things," Jeanne reminded him gently, not catching the note of teasing in his voice.

"Of course not," he replied solemnly. "But you shall learn. Shall we start now?" His mouth brushed lightly over her cheek, moving toward her ear. Jeanne quivered in reaction.

"Now?" Jeanne's eyes opened wide with wonder. Involuntarily her breath quickened with the first beginnings of reawakened passion, causing her to tremble with anticipation. She wanted him. She wanted him inside her, lifting her up to breathless release.

"Now, Little Turtle." He took her hand, guiding it gently to the growing hardness that offered proof of his words. Jeanne felt her excitation increase at the thrill that ran like a shiver through his body when her hand came in contact with his warm flesh.

Folding her in his arms again, Black Eagle began to touch her with his lips and tongue. With a patient skill, holding the needs of his own body in check, he slowly savored the length of her body, his tongue lingering on her breasts, his mouth pausing to pull the taut nipples into its warm depth. Massaging, caressing, now teasing, now demanding, he led

Jeanne skillfully up the stream of light toward the sensual heights of the eagle's domain.

She gave herself up to the sensation, until all she knew was his arms holding her, his hungry mouth on her mouth, his body against hers, and a dizzying, demanding need. She met him at every crest, matching him thrust for thrust, arching to guide the pressure of his movements. Each time he filled her, she was conscious only of him. Her body—nerves, muscles, sinews—was filled with him, rising in an unbearable crescendo, until the explosion diffused through her body in a prism of color.

Jeanne awoke blinking. She lay still, eyes half-shut, listening to a rattling on the roof, trying to identify the source of the commotion. From the awful racket, flying squirrels must have jumped out of the big pine tree and flown right down on the wigwam cover and slid halfway around it! Like a lizard, she slithered down farther into the furs, curling against the solid warmth of her husband, her face pressed against his warm back. *Husband.* What a lovely word!

A further bombardment had Black Eagle rear up as violently as a soldier caught sleeping away his guard duty, to sit naked on the side of the bed, head tilted, face raised, listening.

"Hear them." He laughed, stood up, stretched his muscles. "Come," he said simply. He looked down at Jeanne, passed his thumbs gently over her eyelids, reached for his breechclout.

"What is it?" She looked uneasily at Black Eagle, pulling his shirt over his head, thrusting his feet into his moccasins. Her eyes stretched wide as another assault was made, accompanied by voices. A deep voice, a loud, low female voice, singing above the others, but so many others! There were several loud, strong males! And other females! And children!

"Calling the Eagle's head! Ayee!
Calling the Eagle's wings! Ayee!
Calling the Eagle's feet!
Feet turn toward us,
Bring the Turtle toward us.
You of the double trail,
Come for what we give you!
You whose trail crosses the sky,
Come for it! Come!"

A rattle on the roof, like pellets from a startled deer, had Jeanne hurriedly pulling on her clothes. "We hear you." Black Eagle's voice was loud in the lodge. He ran his thumb along Jeanne's jaw, lowered his voice. "If we do not go out, they will keep this up all day. Come." He grabbed her by the wrist, hauled her toward the door. In the transparent early-morning sunlight, people crowded in front of the lodge.

"What took you so long?" Little Bear called, a knowing smile on his face. "We have been waiting for you!"

"I think these two were trying to hide!" Cornstalk quipped, with a smile for Jeanne.

Jeanne's cheeks reddened as Stands Fast stepped forward, suppressed laughter in his voice. "I hope we did not interrupt anything!"

Black Eagle honored the joke with a wink at Prickly Man. The men shared a long laugh. Jeanne blushed to the tips of her ears.

And Rattle. Irrepressible Rattle. That one had both her hands at her mouth, trying to swallow the laughter that kept bubbling forth in snorts and giggles. "The women have come by the lodge several times to fetch water. There was no smoke from your roof. The sun has been up a long while. We thought you two were dead."

"Dead?"

Black Eagle caught Jeanne's eyes, yawned and stretched and grinned and laughed. Jeanne joined in. Their laughter joined the rest.

"Did you have a hard night, Black Eagle?" Thunderclap's face was solemn, but his eyes flashed like polished beads in the sunlight.

Black Eagle snorted and made a face that was like an opossum's when it smells a skunk. "I am so stiff and lame I can hardly walk!"

Jeanne's face creased into a smile. Black Eagle was a good man, without a doubt. No wonder all the men respected him. He did not mind their teasing, and they laughed cheerfully at his ready response, pressing forward to offer their gifts.

A beaded quill case, a sewing bag, a set of the long cherrywood skewers used for drying meat, a willow-rod backrest, handsomely decorated in wide bands of yellow and red, a shell paint container, willow paint brushes, cooking baskets and more were placed in the lodge.

Jeanne took a deep breath to avoid stammering from embarrassment and drew her teeth over her bottom lip. "I have no gifts to give in return. I own almost nothing, but you are welcome to join us, to share our first meal."

As many people crowded into the wigwam as it would hold. The rest squatted outside while Wise Speaker called to the spirits for the success, happiness and long life of the occupants. He asked that the new lodge might shelter them from storms and harm. He tamped his pipe with tobacco, lit it, took a deep draw, and passed it to Black Eagle, who was seated on his left. As the pipe was passed around, Black Eagle, head bowed respectfully, addressed the spirits. "Now I make you an offering of tobacco, my grandfather. Our lodge will grow and our children will be many. Find tobacco in the smoke as our thanks."

Following Singing Bird's directions, Jeanne carefully placed the sweet grass they had collected on the fire, offering it as incense to the spirits. Jeanne watched it burn, thinking silently, You can change the form of something, alter its structure, but you cannot deny its existence.

A fire, she reflected, is a portent, a kind of magic. The oldest magic. There are shapes in it. The ghosts of the past, the ghosts, too, of what has not yet been. Look into it and you see things. The years ahead, the good years, full of joy and peace. And it sheds its magic, sending it flickering over everything it touches, spreading liquid red and yellow over everything, even over the shadows hiding in the corners. Like splashes of blood. She shivered and pushed the thought from her mind.

Chapter Ten

Jeanne trotted down the slope of the hill easily, saving herself for the harder going farther on, turning in a wide circle toward the river, which she knew the women would already have left. Then, emerging from a deeply shadowed group of trees, she saw, fifty yards ahead, a single man. An elaborate roach of hawk feathers sat squarely on his head. A flicker of excitement ran along her spine. It was Fierce Man! Jeanne did not falter, but drew her tomahawk from her waist, dropped her hands to her sides and waited. The weight of Black Eagle's gift thrilled her. Lighter than a normal hunting weapon, but still a lethal missile, the little hatchet balanced lightly and perfectly between just two of her fingers.

"You are ready?"

"I am, my father."

Fierce Man secured several gourds to a tree with cord, grunted, walked backward for a number of paces and drew a line on the ground with a long stick. He gestured, with no more than a slight twist of the arm, for Jeanne to begin. She bowed her head in acknowledgment, shifted the weapon smoothly from one hand to the other, and moved unhesitatingly to the marker.

Standing sideways to the tree with the gourds, Jeanne drew in her breath, held it, pivoted and hurled her tomahawk. She was surprised when she saw it chop into the tree, a few inches from the largest gourd.

Fierce Man grunted. "You do not keep your eye on it, Turtle," he admonished her, his sunken eyes twinkling at her obvious discomfort. "Watch carefully." He spun his tomahawk, and it crushed through the largest gourd, scattering seeds and dry fragments of the hull.

Jeanne nodded and backed off a few steps farther. Fierce Man had thrown his tomahawk with an economy of motion. It turned no more than was proper. She took a stance, posing, and threw at the middle gourd. She missed not only the target, but the tree, too, and the tomahawk skidded out into the dirt beyond. Without a word, Fierce Man retrieved the tomahawk.

Jeanne's next throw splashed through the gourd on the right and buried itself solidly in the tree. She crowed with delight. Fierce Man nodded his approval. Like Yellow Feather, the old tutor used words sparingly, keeping his features placid, masking his feelings, but Jeanne could tell he was pleased. When approached, he had agreed to teach her the use of the weapon, in secret, so that the others would not learn of it and seek to laugh at her mistakes. He understood her desire to surprise the People.

For an hour she persevered, but mastery of the spin proved more difficult than she had anticipated. The muscles in her right arm cramped from hurling the missile, and her recently knit ribs ached throbbingly where sinews were stretched taut from the punishment she was inflicting. As Jeanne practiced with the tomahawk, Fierce Man stood near her, a patient, superior expression on his wrinkled features.

When Jeanne missed the target for the third time running, Fierce Man retrieved the fallen weapon, caressing it fondly, as though he recalled his own youthful training. His sunken eyes, infinitely wise and equally shrewd, seemed to strip away her inner defenses as he called a halt.

"It is time to go now. Come back tomorrow, Turtle, when you have rested. For now you have worked hard enough."

Jeanne sighed, her fingers closing tightly over the handle of the hatchet. "Do you think I will ever be able to use this instrument properly, my father? To be able to split a gourd with speed and unfailing precision?"

"Do not bow your head like a coward in defeat," Fierce Man chided her gently. "You have a good eye, but your aim is off, because you are impatient. Learn patiently and well those things I teach you, and your moccasins will follow the path you wish to tread. Practice, that is all it takes."

"Do you really mean that, Fierce Man? You are not making a joke?"

"Is there a shadow on the ground?" He smiled suddenly, an unexpected humor springing from his lips. "The midday sun does not tell a lie."

Praise indeed! Quietly pleased, Jeanne watched her instructor slowly wend his way toward the settlement. Carelessly draped over one shrunken shoulder and fluttering in the breeze, his intricately feathered cape managed to impart an aura of dignity to his withered frame. She looked at the sky. The sun was high, but gray clouds were beginning to form huge thunderheads. Her breath came in a choking gasp. Time to meet Black Eagle! Jeanne spun like a cat half falling from a tree and set off in the opposite direction.

She crossed a stream by a fallen branch and scrambled up the bank. Chattering birds took flight as she passed through the foliage. From the clump of trees on the rise, she had a splendid view of the terrain. Perched up here, she would see Black Eagle coming. No surprises today!

Sitting on a cushion of moss, she drew up her knees and clasped her hands around them. Below her, about a score of women were at work in a small clearing, preparing the ground with their short wooden hoes. Corn, beans and squash would be planted together when the leaves on the oak were as big as a mouse's ear. The People believed that the spirits of these plants were loving sisters who liked to stay beside one another.

Totally absorbed in their activities, she wondered if Mountain Wolf Woman was down there, directing and chiding the younger women. That woman used her tongue like a weapon, on all but her husband.

Only a little taller than Jeanne herself, with a long square face, his black hair partially shaved and tied in a knot at the top, Earth Trembler was not a formidable figure at all. But Jeanne had overheard him tell Yellow Feather that, since there was room for only one chief in his lodge, it might as well be him!

Jeanne hugged her knees more tightly, chuckling to herself as she thought how peeved Mountain Wolf Woman would be if she could see her now. She could almost hear the sniping remarks. *It is contrary to nature. Little Turtle should be with the women, doing women's work, not off wandering in the woods, playing games.*

Suddenly she was grabbed roughly from behind and thrown to the ground. A strong arm round the waist held her in a viselike grip. Her scream never left her lips, for a muscular hand clamped over her mouth and smothered any sound. The point of a sharply honed knife pressed gently against her throat as she stared with fright up into Black Eagle's dark eyes.

Had he taken leave of his senses? For two weeks they had made love every night before falling asleep, and now he was about to kill her!

"Do you surrender?" he growled, a threatening glint in his eyes.

For a moment, they studied each other, before Jeanne managed to say, an indignant edge creeping into her voice, "I admire you for taking such a strong stand, but I must ask you not to keep sneaking up on me!"

"Ah, it is good that you admire me, Little Turtle! A wife should always admire her husband!" Black Eagle grinned, rising, sheathing his knife and holding out one hand to help her up.

Jeanne doubled her fists and looked him straight in the eyes. Through clenched teeth she demanded, "What was that all about? Why did you attack me? Threaten me with a knife? Are you trying to frighten me to death?"

He tapped his chest. "That is just one of many such lessons you must master if you wish to become fully alert—fully alive—with all of your senses attuned to the art of survival."

"Say what you mean!" She gave him her most Gallic scowl.

"Keep your ears open! Every move, every gesture, every action, every reaction, has to become instinctive." Black Eagle put his finger to his temple. "If I had been one of the Red Earth People or one of the People of the Long Houses, you would not be alive right now."

Jeanne refused to back down. "No, Black Eagle! I would have known any other was near. It is only you, with your feet like the wings of the eagle and whose moccasin leaves no trail on the dew, who could creep up on me unawares!"

The edge of Black Eagle's teeth reflected his pleasure, and there was a wealth of satisfaction in his reply. "Be that as it may, to know the ways of the forest takes many lessons." He lifted his head slightly. "Follow me, if you wish to slither quietly through the grass like a snake to bring that battle-ax you carry down upon this unsuspecting victim's head!"

Black Eagle, unsuspecting? Never! While she could never hope to match Black Eagle's ability to glide noiselessly through the forest, Jeanne was determined to absorb as much of the art as she could. Eagerly she followed him into the forest.

Black Eagle did not speak, and Jeanne was quick to follow his example. She was careful, too, to turn her toes slightly inward as she placed her moccasins in the exact spots of his footfalls. That way, she knew she would not step on dead twigs or branches, much less make a rustling sound when they passed through mounds of dried leaves!

The forest woodland was alive with sounds, the chirping of crickets, the buzzing of insects, and the occasional faint rustle of small animals. There was a steamy, pleasant smell of soil and decayed leaves. Black Eagle pointed out numerous plants, some of them deliciously edible, like the small gray mushrooms they found in a pine grove.

Jeanne closed her eyes. Papa would have loved these. She could hear him now. Champignons *are a great delicacy.* She smiled with her eyes closed, and opened them to find Black Eagle silently watching her. Dropping to her knees, Jeanne gathered the mushrooms. Black Eagle gravely accepted the one she offered him, popping it into his mouth as she placed the rest carefully in her shoulder bag.

Jeanne stood and brushed herself off, keen to find plants to be used primarily as seasonings. Wild garlic was there in abundance, and Jeanne could not resist collecting a handful. Black Eagle showed her other plants that were utilized by the People for many purposes.

He pointed to a witch-hazel. "When the leaves are colored and ready to fall, the little black seeds of this tree will be harvested. They are important to the medicine man. If they float when placed on the surface of a bowl of water, the medicine man knows there is a chance that a sick person will recover, but if they sink, there is no hope."

Jeanne dug her fingernail into the soft bark of the tree. "After I have learned the ways of the forest, would it be possible to learn the mysteries of the medicine man?"

"Nothing is impossible. It is good that you learn many things. To judge from the depth and imprint of a bear's tracks how fresh they are. Scratch marks on tree trunks will tell you when raccoons are in the vicinity." Looking down into Jeanne's shining eyes, her lips slightly parted, half curving in a smile, he let out a long breath. "The patterns of disturbed leaves reveal the presence of birds' nests, just as bent blades of grass tell how recently deer have been in the area and in what direction they head."

Jeanne admired the symmetrical shape of his torso, the broad shoulders tapering to the waist. It was not nighttime. What would he do if she touched him, stroked her hand over the pads of muscle, under the gleaming skin and down his spine? The thought of caressing him kindled the flame of desire within her. It flared up painfully, seeming to scorch through her. She tried to concentrate on what he was saying.

"If you are a turtle, you do things the way a turtle does. Sometimes it is good to know the way of other creatures, too. If you know how to be as small and silent as a mouse, then the big cougar will not see you, and you will live to be a turtle again." Black Eagle lifted his hand and rested it against Jeanne's jaw, as if he were touching a small bird, something precious. "For such a frail shell, there is a fire that burns fiercely inside. Today Turtle is the hunter. See?"

He pointed to the footprints of a white-tailed deer. They trailed it, getting so close that the odor of their clothes and bodies, drifting on the windless day, alarmed the doe. It rose, shifting its ears, searching for danger with its great eyes. Jeanne tried to move closer. The deer wheeled away.

"Now look what you have gone and done!" Black Eagle's voice was thick with disgust. "You will have to do better than that, else you will starve to death."

Jeanne closed her eyes. "I am sorry," she managed in a strangled voice. It sounded breathless and thin. "I did not think you meant to kill the deer."

"I did not intend to do so." Black Eagle's voice was low and rough. He blew out a rasping breath. "I was only showing off, boasting to you of my skill, trying to get close enough to touch the animal. You did well."

Jeanne's eyes flew open. "I did?"

"Have I not said so?"

Black Eagle looked into her eyes with an intimacy that made Jeanne's toes curl. His lids half down over his eyes, a strange, intent look on his face, the corner of his mouth tilted—it was not quite a smile—that told her he, too, felt that burgeoning of throbbing excitement. She could feel the tenseness and longing in his body. He seemed to be having trouble with his breathing, but he continued to regard her with close attention, until Jeanne's cheeks began to color under his intent gaze.

One finger rubbed her neck in a soothing motion. A strangled sound came from Jeanne's throat, and Black Eagle crushed her to him with a groan. His hand caressed her neck, and his fingers softly twined in the tendrils of hair at the nape, then fluttered down her face, scarcely touching her flesh, evoking breathless whimpers from her.

Black Eagle's tongue followed the path his finger traced, his touch as light as a sigh. Jeanne quivered violently when she felt his hands move caressingly down her back, then slide up underneath her tunic. His hand curled around her breast, making it spring to life, and every nerve end in her being cried out in an agony of feeling so delicious that she whimpered without knowing that she had made a sound.

Black Eagle's tongue stroked the rounded flesh and probed the hardened peak before he drew it into his mouth. Jeanne gasped as a bolt of fire pierced her loins, rippled down her thighs, up her belly, leaving her quivering, her muscles trembling. She felt the strength in him, and her body responded to it positively, glorying in it. She moaned and dissolved into his body, raking her fingers through his hair, wanting him, needing him.

Jeanne curled her fingers in the thick ruff on his head. Black Eagle groaned, the sound emanating from deep in his chest. His hands were gliding along her skin, down her back, compelling her closer to the fiercely masculine outline of his body. He made no attempt to camouflage his desire as he pressed her to him. She could feel the passion rising in him, as his arms held her more and more urgently and his breathing quickened.

Lost to everything but her own searing need, Jeanne was shocked when Black Eagle suddenly froze. Grinding out an inarticulate curse, he pulled away from her. His muttered imprecation penetrated the haze of passion clouding her mind as he fumbled with the edge of his breechclout. His actions betrayed the effort he was exerting to corral his emotions, his sinewy knuckles were white with tension.

He lifted his eyes to hers. "This is not the time or place." He dropped his eyes away from hers, held out his hand. "Danger lurks in the forest."

Instinctively her teeth closed on his finger, silently demanding that he stay with her. Jeanne felt the response that ripped through Black Eagle at the unexpected caress of her teeth: a harsh intake of breath. She exulted when his hands shifted on her body, finding and stroking her breasts, the smooth, creamy curves of her body, sending burst after burst of pure delight through her.

Her response was instinctive, a supple movement of her hips. He lifted his head and let his breath hiss out between his teeth, arching against her in a sensual reflex. Making soft sounds of discovery and pleasure, Jeanne explored the texture of his body. His hand curled possessively around the rusty nest of curls as he began to explore with his lips the shadowed softness below.

He rocked hard against her, moving with a rhythm that was as elemental as the earth itself. Very slowly, propelled by something terrible and uncontrollable, her body began to dissolve as if it were made of mere wax. His passion was overpowering, and the strength of his body was frightening. Unable to leash her disarrayed, inflamed senses, she matched him caress for caress, giving herself to him in a surrender that was complete.

The following morning, as Jeanne hurried to join the women, she passed a litter of tumbling pups. She frowned. Why did she suddenly think of Black Eagle, bending to look at a small boy's pet, impulsively making a joke? Graceful One...Black Eagle...Owl... She picked at the thought like a knot, trying to unravel the threads in her mind.

Hunkering down, she waggled a finger in their midst. A spotted mite, braver than his fellows, reached up and caught the intruder with needle-sharp teeth. Jeanne picked up the wriggling bundle and rubbed it against her cheek. It tugged at her ear. "You are a bit small for a maneater, my friend." The pup butted its head into the curve of her elbow. She tucked it against her chest and stroked it. "But you are full of life. I think you should meet someone who has need of your vim and vitality."

Graceful One sat quietly on a rug of woven rushes in a patch of shade where the women were attaching newly prepared hides to the stretching frames to dry. Mountain Wolf Woman gave Jeanne a sour look that seemed to say, *Lazy good-for-nothing.* Jeanne ignored her, knelt and slipped the now-sleepy pup into Graceful One's lap, curving her hands over its warm fur, moving them to stroke the young dog's softness. There was no response. Graceful One gazed past her shoulder, as if at some distant cloud on the horizon. Leaving the pup in her lap, where it seemed content to sleep,

Jeanne joined the women, scraping and pulling the skins so that the hides would stretch evenly.

The pup dozed for a bit, then began to groggily explore his base. Nosing about, he planted his paws on Graceful One's chest and sniffed her chin, licking her cheek. He staggered, peered about, looking for further adventures, crept toward the dark braid, with its tormentingly bright silk ribbon. Growled. Head low, ears folded, he pounced.

Cord, tools, hides, even the stretching frames, went flying at the sound of the pup barking and, mingled with it, an urgent cry for help. Jeanne leapt toward the clamor. Graceful One was kneeling, crawling after the pup, who refused to let go of his trophy. Legs bent, the tip of his tail wagging, he was enjoying the game.

Jeanne grabbed the pup, which released the braid and promptly sank its tiny teeth into her hand. A sound suspiciously like a giggle spun her round. Graceful One held out her arms to take the small animal, cuddle and stroke it. Jeanne stared at the girl in disbelief, a long, slow time. The eyes that met hers were like sunlight on clear water, filled with serenity, with a great and abiding peace.

Her breath stopped, then hissed sibilantly out from between her teeth. Relief washed over her in waves. Of light. The bright spring sunshine seemed to have intensified, swirling in prisms of color. She had all she could do to keep from fainting. Suspended in time, aware of nothing and everything, she held out a shaking hand.

"Graceful One..." But before she could get the rest of it out, she was pushed aside by the excited women. They crowded around Graceful One, astounded, all talking at once, touching, marveling. Mountain Woman knelt, both arms around her daughter, shoulders heaving, head bowed in Graceful One's lap. Unnoticed, the pup fled back to his siblings as fast as his bandy legs would carry him, his treasure clenched in his tiny jaws.

Jeanne turned away, filled with a happiness so huge that
she knew she must find Black Eagle and share the good
news. She bent her head. Tears beaded on the rusty gold of
her lashes, turned her eyes into crystals, light-filled, brim-
ming. She shook her head to clear them. Blinked. Blinked
again.

There, on the ground at her feet, was a scrap of azure-blue
ribbon. Like an old woman, Jeanne bent over and retrieved the remnant. She gripped it tightly between her
thumb and forefinger, winding it round and round the in-
dex finger of her other hand as she stared at it, incredulous.

Was there any significance in the fact that the color of this
ribbon was an exact match of the azure-blue fleur-de-lis on
the de la Rocque crest? That it had been taken as a trophy
on the day On the Other Side joined the spirit world? Was
it only coincidence that this same ribbon had been, in part,
instrumental in returning Graceful One's spirit to her body?
It could not be accidental that the spotted dog had dropped
its prize just where she was to walk! No, there must be some
deep meaning intended for her guidance.

Were the manito, the omnipotent, unseen spirits of the
People, sending her instructions, asking her to do their bid-
ding? Jeanne felt their presence in the towering trees, and
she could imagine them listening to her, then whispering to
each other in the wind. But the question was, what was the
message that the spirits were sending?

Black Eagle said that no harm ever befell a warrior who
did what he believed was right, because the manito, who always knew right from wrong, would protect him from all
harm. She, Jeanne de la Rocque, now known as Little
Turtle, was a fighter, in spite of her frail exterior. Only the
inner strength of a warrior could have sustained her through
the trials she had undergone, could have enabled her to

shape, and revel in, a life totally different from anything she had known.

Jeanne pondered at length, and finally became acutely conscious of the fragment she held. She knew what was expected of her, what orders she was being given. She was being required by the manito to live up to the promise of her heritage. Putting the azure curl into her amulet pouch, along with the little turtle shell and piece of crystal, Jeanne formed a firm resolution. She would rely on the manito guidance to show her what was right.

Drawing in her breath sharply, she squared her shoulders proudly and rejoined the women. She saw that they were aware of her presence, for Singing Bird turned to stare at her measuringly. And Mountain Wolf Woman's eyes darted protectively to her daughter, then back. Graceful One's lovely face was calm, but alert. Jeanne swallowed hard, aware of tension in the air. She chose and spoke her words carefully and softly.

"I would hear from your own lips, Graceful One, that you understand what happened to On the Other Side. That your grief does not seek revenge."

Rigid silence accompanied her words, and there was a fleeting instant when time seemed to stand still. Jeanne met the other girl's clear eyes unwaveringly. Among the onlookers, not an eyelash flickered. No one breathed.

Finally, Graceful One whispered, her voice hoarse from disuse, "Speak of this no more. I have done with grieving. On the Other Side was a dutiful son, a good friend, a brave warrior. I understand now that the manito had need of such a man. They called to him. You were only the instrument to show him the way to the spirit world."

The others murmured agreement. Mountain Wolf Woman stepped forward, and looked at Jeanne long and thoughtfully. Then, suddenly, she bent forward to touch her cheek. "You did a great service here today. The life of my daughter is most precious to me, and your having saved that life erases many things."

There was a chorus of indrawn breaths. It was a moment before Jeanne could gather her scattered wits, so great was her relief. Encircled suddenly by the chattering women, Jeanne joined in the wonder and joy of the miracle that had occurred. In another moment, she knew, reaction would begin, and her teeth would be chattering as violently as a frightened ground squirrel. It was enough, for the present, to realize that she had read the signs correctly once more, and won a friend into the bargain. It was a day's work in any person's language.

The Corn Planting Moon grew aged and weary, and Jeanne's freckles blended until her skin was a golden bronze. Black Eagle continued teaching her the ways of the forest. He had also taken it upon himself to coach her in all manner of skills. She learned how to climb and jump, to tumble and fall, to twist and leap, to balance, until she was good enough to roll headfirst off one of the rocky ledges and land on her feet amid the dry brush and pine needles fifteen feet below.

And he tutored her in the ways of love. Lazy, lingering afternoons in the forest blended into a montage of perfect moments as their fingers and lips traced patterns on each other's bodies. And when the moon rose, pale and silver, over the dark blue hills, and they could hear the geese in the night on their way to their summer grounds, in the privacy of their partitioned space his arms would reach out eagerly to clasp her tightly against his body once again.

It seemed to Jeanne an almost perfect world. Her lessons with Fierce Man continued, but when the women took their digging sticks, picking, gathering, digging, Jeanne went, too, coming home with full baskets. She talked so much about Black Eagle that one day, when Good Woman was helping her weed the cornfields, the older woman laughed.

"You sound as though you and Black Eagle have never had harsh words with each other."

Jeanne felt herself turning red. "We have no reason to fight." Curiosity impelled her to ask, "Do you quarrel with Yellow Feather?"

"Often," Good Woman admitted cheerfully.

Jeanne could not imagine anyone disputing the word of the ferocious war leader. "Do you win?" She could hear the skeptical, incredulous tone of her own voice.

Good Woman lowered her voice to a conspiratorial whisper. "Always I allow him to think he has won. But very soon he does what I have wished him to do."

Jeanne shook her head. Her relationship with Black Eagle, which formed the core of her existence, was flawless. The thought of Black Eagle filled her with elation. She would never stoop to petty arguments, never criticize him, never try to bend him to her will. Unthinkable. She felt a cold shiver. It was as if she were walking along the edge of a cliff, blindfolded.

Coming back from tending the cornfield, Jeanne noticed Crayfish forcing Muskrat to trot, pushing him in the back with a stick if he faltered. A child of ten snows, Muskrat was small for his age, and relatively frail. He had trouble keeping up with the others when they ran, swam or engaged in games.

Grim-faced, Jeanne watched Sky Woman's husband prod the boy when he stumbled. Deeply disturbed, she watched as the pair disappeared down the path to the river.

"Is Muskrat being punished for something?" Jeanne asked Black Eagle, who was seated near the outdoor fire pit, whittling a piece of wood.

Black Eagle shook his head, unconcerned. "No. He is being trained to become a warrior." His calm response infuriated her.

"It is wrong to expect Muskrat to undergo trials of endurance like the other boys. He is too weak!" Jeanne could not stop the words, which seemed to burst out.

Black Eagle turned the wood over in his hand and carefully considered the eagle's head he had carved and the bear's head below it. "Muskrat must gain the strength of a man if he is to become a hunter, a warrior."

This was their first quarrel, but she did not care. "It is cruel to subject him to torment!"

"Life is cruel." Black Eagle fashioned a bear's paw neatly and carefully put the tiny shavings into the fire. "He who becomes a warrior must be strong and brave. He must know how to survive in the woodlands. He must protect himself and others from their enemies."

"Muskrat is too small! Why can he not wait a few years, until he has grown?" Jeanne heard the asperity in her own voice.

Black Eagle drew a burned twig from the fire pit and, with the charcoal, made geometric figures on the little carving. "Since the time of our ancestors, we have taught boys to test their endurance. There is no other way."

"How can you be so unfeeling?" She knew it was a mistake to insult him, but she could not help it.

For a fraction of an instant, his fingers paused. Then he picked up his carving again, studying it intently. "Warriors who cannot fight or hunt are soon killed by our enemies."

"I have been hoping that you would intervene. Maybe teach Muskrat yourself." Jeanne scowled down at his hands, her body stiff.

The knife moved slowly. He glanced at her out of the corner of his eye. "It is the task of Crayfish to test the boys. I will not interfere."

"Think of the boy!" She clenched her fists at her sides, and closed her mouth as fast and final as a snapping turtle's on a crayfish.

Black Eagle rose, brushed the shavings into the fire. His gaze was level, unblinking, and he did not smile. His voice was utterly without emotion. "Muskrat would be shamed if he were treated differently from the other boys. He would think he was being treated like a woman."

"Better that than to torture him!"

Black Eagle folded his arms across his chest. "It is not torture to make a man of a boy! A warrior knows what is best for those who will join them in the hunt and on the warpath. I do what a warrior must. Muskrat, too, will do what is necessary." He spoke with finality.

Chapter Eleven

Rain wept through the branches of the trees, and long streamers of moss hung down, unstirred by any wind. Black Eagle leaned against the dripping bark of a maple, unmoving, and watched the three women.

Red Leaf squatted upon the earth, bracing herself against Jeanne and Clear Sky. The midwife's mouth drew upward until her lips were pinched together like a hide pouch with the draw thong pulled taut.

"Blind the evil ones," she chanted to the spirits. "Confuse them. Make them run around in circles. Put the fear of the rabbit in their hearts. Let this child be born in peace, safety and joy."

Red Leaf's hair lay soaked and plastered against her forehead. Her eyes were shut, her face was twisted with pain, her lips were tightly compressed. She rocked on her haunches, shaking her head until her braids rattled against her fawnskin dress. Then, suddenly, she spoke, her voice soft.

"Manito who guide and protect the Bear Society, help me birth the baby of Dragging Canoe, hunter and warrior of the People."

The tiny head, with its fluff of black hair, appeared.

"The baby is coming," the midwife said. "We need birch fiber."

"I will get it," Jeanne volunteered.

She had taken only two paces when she heard the child give a lusty cry. A tangled rush of emotions flooded her senses, like blown leaves in an autumn gale. Involuntarily she glanced across at Black Eagle, who was standing guard. He was politely looking away from the women, his gaze fixed on the forest, silent and withdrawn, his face like carved marble. Her hand half rose in his direction before she pushed a straggling lock of hair out of her face with a forearm.

For three days, their relations had remained strained. Meals were eaten in eloquent silence. They seldom addressed each other, confining their talk to essentials. Jeanne felt alone, set on a path she did not understand, but from which she could not turn. She wanted to say many things to him, but they were beyond saying.

Even when all had been going straight and well, she could not have found words to tell him how she cherished his goodwill, how she treasured the way he held her when they fell asleep at night. And her feelings about their physical union! She could no more have spoken of that in words than she could have taken wing and flown from here to the faraway mountains on the rim of the sky.

Singing Bird had soon realized they were quarreling, but she wisely refrained from asking questions. At night, Jeanne claimed weariness and went to bed early, pretending to sleep. Black Eagle turned his back to her when he joined her on their sleeping ledge.

Still, he had come to their meeting place each day, stiff and cool, but prepared to honor his commitment to instruct her. This had lessened the sting of their argument. Black Eagle reminded her of Wise Speaker. That same mixture of common sense and straightforwardness, a complexity made simple because it dealt only with truth. And was

not marriage founded on tolerance and understanding? She
must teach him the art of compromise!

Today, the miserable weather had cut short Jeanne's lessons, and a short while ago, while returning to the camp,
they had come across Red Leaf, her face contorted from the
pains of labor. It was the custom for the women to go to a
special hut away from the main camp when their time came
to give birth. Red Leaf had been on her way there with Clear
Sky, the village midwife. But this child was in a hurry to be
born. It could not wait.

The newly delivered infant was cradled in Clear Sky's
arms when Jeanne returned with the birchbark. The midwife crooned over mother and baby. She paid no attention
to the rain that made her doeskin dress soggy.

"The manito," she announced above the sound of the
thunder, "have heard the prayers of Red Leaf. It is a man-
child." She bound him securely in the birchbark swaddling
and wrapped him in deerskin before taking the child to his
mother.

Red Leaf smiled as she took the child into her arms.
Raindrops glistened on her cheekbones and sparkled on her
long, sleek black hair. A look, completely private, crossed
her face, closing out the others. Jeanne stood still, head
bowed, feeling blessed relief.

What a wonderful thing was this gift of life. New life was
the true praise of God and the spirits. What had Papa believed? *Have we not all one Father? Hath not one God created us?* She felt whole and filled with warmth at this
thought. She gave thanks to *le bon Dieu,* to the Eternal
Person, for life—all life.

Black Eagle came forward. His long, sinewy fingers came
down on Jeanne's shoulder and tightened strongly. It was a
reassuring, comradely grip, an unspoken pledge. Jeanne
raised her hand and placed it on top of his. All her energy
seemed to have flowed back into her limbs, and her blood

was dancing through her veins. Without a word, he assisted her in burying the afterbirth. He said a prayer over the mound, asking the manito to watch over the life of the newborn child.

Jeanne felt a strange longing sweep through her body as she felt his nearness. She watched the steady rise and fall of his lean, muscular torso. She was utterly confused by her feelings toward this man. She bit her lip to hold back the tumble of words hovering on her tongue. She was terrified that the feeling was so strong.

She wanted to put her nose against his skin, press her lips against his mouth, taste his warmth. Would it be like his body, lush and salty, or would it be like the earth on a damp day, rich and fruity? The thought was rather alluring, in a strange way. A surge of anger ran through her at the waywardness of her thoughts.

She jumped when Black Eagle spoke. "We will wait here until Red Leaf has regained her strength."

Jeanne glanced up to meet Black Eagle's dark eyes and she started violently, wondering if he could read her thoughts. Their gazes clashed and held for a long, charged moment as she stared up at him.

Red Leaf's voice broke the spell. It seemed to come from a long way away, like an echo floating on the air from the other side of the valley. She lay back against the bole of a pine tree, resting.

"Be the first to look upon this little warrior." She gestured to Black Eagle and Jeanne to come closer.

"He is so small," Black Eagle muttered, staring down at the wizened face cradled within the folds of deerskin. He threw Jeanne a strange, sideways glance, taking in her narrow hips and slender frame. The fine hairs on her neck bristled, and she felt a chill ripple up her spine, as if she had been stroked with a feather. She smiled reassuringly. He took a deep breath, released a harsh sigh, and turned to Red Leaf. "Have you decided upon a name?"

Red Leaf held the tiny bundle up to him. "I thought perhaps you would sing prayers over the child and name him."

Before Black Eagle could object, Clear Sky had taken the infant and placed it in the circle of his arms. He held out one hand tentatively to the baby. Its little fist closed tightly around his finger. He looked up at the rain-laden sky, down at Jeanne. Although he chanted over the baby, it seemed he spoke directly to her.

"Little one, look at the trout, the sheen on their scales. Look at the shape of the clouds and the color of the sun as it sets. Remember the tracks and calls of the creatures of the day and night. Feel the wind on your cheek, breathe its scents."

Jeanne closed her eyes and absorbed his words, her supple young body quivering like an aspen in a high wind.

"Listen to the song of the redwing, the bark of the stag. Watch the snail, study its cast. Alone, each of these means little, but together they are the voice of the earth and sky, of which wind and rain are just a part."

Jeanne's eyes flew open.

"From them, and many other things, you will learn the secrets of the People." He paused, lifting an arm. "Until you find a vision of your own, you will be called Big Rain, for you have come to us upon the drops of such."

"Big Rain. It is a good name you have chosen," Red Leaf remarked proudly, and took the baby once again, huddled over him, protecting him from the drizzle.

Clear Sky nodded her approval. Silently agreeing, Jeanne passed the back of her hand over her lips, her misted eyes.

Jeanne knelt on the woven mats and sang to herself as she rubbed a fragrant oil of crushed almonds onto her arms, breasts, belly and thighs. The song she sang was a lullaby.

They had escorted Red Leaf home when the shadows were already long and thin across the ground. The storm that had swept over the forest had cleared with the same mysterious rapidity with which it had developed, making the journey to the camp a joyous occasion. Dragging Canoe was beside himself with delight, and Little Shouter had kept jumping up and down, wanting to see his new brother. Singing Bird, her weathered face creased into a smile, had offered to look after the little boy for a few days.

Realizing what tune she was humming, Jeanne blushed, as though she had been caught doing something wrong. She puzzled over this for a while. Red Leaf had a son. In two moons, Bright Path would also give birth. Already Acorn was complaining of a sickness each morning. It was time to mend this quarrel with Black Eagle!

There was only one way. Singing Bird had whispered, her leathery skin disintegrating into a field of wrinkles, *The best defense is a good offense.* And what better offense than to meet him on his own ground? Her stomach churned and her knees felt weak as she contemplated her plan of action.

Jeanne was determined to take advantage of her adopted mother's temporary absence and end the quarrel with Black Eagle. A faint trace of a smile appeared at the corners of her mouth. What had he advised? *Think like your opponent. Walk in the moccasins of your adversary. Be one with the enemy.* She played the part in her mind, chuckling a little as she dressed.

The odors of venison roasting, of vegetables bubbling over the fire in their own liquid, drifted through the lodge, mingling with the other scents. Jeanne loved the aroma of the lodge, the bite of smoke, the sharp spice of burning pine and basswood, hot resin, green and drying grass and bark, still-warm bread, and the different smells from the baskets that sat in a neat circle on the shelves. Dried salmon and deer meat, bulbs and fruit, pelts and woven rugs. The redolence of the tobacco and medicines and herbs that hung in bunches along the walls.

There was a rattle at the door covering, and Sky Woman came through the open doorway of the lodge, looking harried. She was holding Fleecy Cloud on one hip and a shallow wooden dish piled with deerskin and sewing implements on the other. Jeanne hurried toward her, put out her hands.

"What is it? Let me take the baby!"

"Oh, Turtle, thank you!"

Sky Woman handed Fleecy Cloud over to Jeanne, who hugged the child hard, crooning to her softly.

"I must finish making new moccasins for Red Leaf's baby, but I keep getting distracted. Crayfish is at a meeting of the senior warriors, and Fleecy Cloud woke up. I fed her, but she is not in any mood to go back to sleep yet."

"Black Eagle is also attending the meeting." Jeanne was puzzled. "What is the urgency to make moccasins for a newborn baby? Rain will not walk for many moons!"

"No, but to protect him from death, he must be given tiny moccasins with holes in the soles. Then, if death tries to lure the child away, Rain will be able to say, 'But I cannot come with you. See, my moccasins have holes in them!'"

Holding the baby, Jeanne watched Sky Woman work the bone awl through the softened hide. "Is the meeting about serious matters?"

Sky Woman shrugged. "It is a special meeting of the senior warriors regarding the training of the young boys."

Fleecy Cloud started to fuss a bit, and Jeanne bounced the child on her knee, then changed her position until she was looking at her. She studied the small face, talked softly, watching the little girl's eyes grow big and round. Fleecy Cloud blew bubbles, giggled, and pulled at Jeanne's headband with one chubby hand. That satisfied her for a while, but not for long.

When she got ready to cry again, Jeanne whistled at her. The sound surprised the tot, and she stopped crying to listen. Jeanne whistled again, this time making a bird's song. She had spent many hours, as she weeded or scraped, practicing brush talk. To entertain the baby, she squeaked like a field mouse, smacked like a rabbit and chattered like a squirrel.

To her surprise, Jeanne heard applause. The sound of thigh-slapping caused her to look up and see the faces of her husband and visitors smiling at her. Engrossed in entertaining Fleecy Cloud, Jeanne had not heard Black Eagle return, accompanied by Thunderclap, Cornstalk, Leaning Wood and Owl. Black Eagle stood there, filling the doorway, standing squarely on both legs, as if measuring the earth beneath him. As if he were not sure of his welcome.

His face, all angles and shadows, told her nothing. Shadows collected in the hollows of his cheeks, flickered through the fan of his lowered lashes. Jeanne could see no more than a glint of fire reflected in his midnight eyes, eyes that were like polished pebbles. Something deep inside those pebbles, though—a challenge, maybe—sent little frissons down her back. He lifted his hand in a stiff movement toward the hearth, as though to remind her of her position.

Embarrassed, she went to the pit where the food was cooking, checked to make sure there was enough for everyone, and turned and invited them all to stay for a meal. Sky Woman refused, taking the now-sleepy Fleecy Cloud and hurrying off.

Conscious of Black Eagle's eyes on her, Jeanne practiced her role as hostess. She murmured a greeting, her eyes modestly cast down, though alert and wary under her long lashes. Moving unhurriedly but not hesitantly, delicately but not timidly, she served the men large chunks of smoking venison and a gourd of vegetables.

As she watched Black Eagle bite into the succulent meat, Jeanne could no longer contain her curiosity. "What was the outcome of the meeting?"

Black Eagle's face darkened, but the change in his manner was so delicate that only someone who knew him well would have been aware of it. He leaned forward, added another turnip to his bowl. "There was much to discuss." His voice was bleak and fierce.

Jeanne was immediately conscious of the shift, and felt rebuffed. Her hands unconsciously clenched around the bowl. What had she done now? What convention had she breached? Surely a wife was expected to ask questions? To be interested in her husband's business? To be sure, Mama never had been. But Papa had talked to his eldest daughter about all matter of things. She could hear him now.... *I hold there is no sin but ignorance.*

"Yes, but what happened?" she persisted, knowing her curiosity was dangerous, yet unable to stifle it.

"Let me eat, woman." He paused. "Do not throw your questions at me like pebbles onto the lodge bark!" It was a reprimand. Given in the soft-spoken Indian manner, but a reprimand nonetheless.

Jeanne sat back on her haunches, stunned by his censure. She swallowed down a great lump in her throat. Ignorance was a virtue these men needed. She glanced over her shoulder, bright-eyed and guileless, the long mane of her hair swirling with the movement.

She shifted to another battlefield, lifted her hands to her face and turned, blushing and visibly upset. "How thoughtless of me. I have not given you a bowl, Owl." Her voice was high—unnaturally high.

Black Eagle's impassive eyes met hers. She read nothing there, no encouragement, no accusation, no denial. She clamped her hands to her legs and sought insight, tried a faint smile. His eyes shifted away from her. For the first time, he looked somewhat guilty. Now she could feel his moment of rebellion. He did not want her angry and troubled. He would fight against it. In a little while, he would make his case, and she knew his incisive, pragmatic common sense would prevail, so... She flashed Thunderclap a smile.

"The weather has warmed," she noted casually.

A distinct smile lit Thunderclap's craggy features. "The air hangs heavy and expectant."

Black Eagle's back straightened, his jaw jutted forward, but he said nothing. His silence sparked Jeanne's temper, but she fought it back under control. Well, she had silenced him, and she was glad. His voice was so deep, so melodious, so pleasant to the ear, that he might perhaps have persuaded her.... No. She jerked herself upright. She would show no weakness. She stiffened, took a deep breath.

"It is the rain. It brings a steamy, pleasant smell," she said.

Black Eagle sipped his mint tea, placed his gourd on the ground beside him and inclined his head a fraction of an inch in agreement. He was polite, he was reasonable—and he was unyielding.

Cornstalk nodded vigorously. His unease was obvious. There was a feeling of tension in the air. Leaning Wood stared at her. He seemed thoughtful and troubled. Jeanne picked at her food, irritated. The static in the room even set Owl to squirming.

They continued the meal in silence, but once, when Black Eagle reached over to toss a bone into the fire, he laid his hand on Jeanne's. There was no perceptible softening of his features, but somehow he had softened. She could feel his care for her, his anxiety, even though she had turned her face from him. *It is as if he were reaching out to enfold me in his arms.* She was confused. If she abandoned her dream of becoming a warrior, she would be forsaking her inner self.

She must stubbornly resist his subtle persuasion until he yielded to her terms. Could she do it?

He was a dangerous man. She must keep him at a distance, for her own sake. She would not show him that he had any power over her, any influence.... Instead of responding, she gave an eloquent shrug, lifted an eyebrow, sat back and folded her hands in her lap. The visitors exchanged knowing smiles.

Jeanne served a rice pudding sweetened with maple syrup and spiced with cranberries. It was his favorite. She felt him draw a deep breath. He released a harsh sigh, as if the air had been repressed and had finally burst out. He visibly relaxed. The tension dissolved from his figure. His furrowed brow smoothed, and the tightness of his jaws eased. She saw something in his eyes, a shining—like that of a smooth stone at the bottom of a stream—and felt such a flood of warmth and pleasure that she almost wanted to weep. Her ruse was working!

Heart pounding in her breast, Jeanne rose to tidy the lodge, rinsing the eating bowls, stacking them on the shelves. The men quietly discussed the prospects for the hunting season and speculated on the size of the grain crop. Bored, Owl started to fidget.

Black Eagle leaned over, cuffed Owl playfully, sent the boy tumbling into a pile of robes. "This one is to start training tomorrow."

Owl laughed and struggled like an overturned turtle.

"He will spend the entire afternoon running up and down hills, coached by Muskrat," Black Eagle continued. "That one has practiced incessantly. He understands that he who lags behind or falls by the side of the trail harms all his comrades. He will test this one's endurance to the utmost."

Jeanne stared at him, amazed. Maybe she had not heard right. She wrinkled her nose. Had she a fever in her blood? A chill from the rain? Muskrat was to coach Owl?

Black Eagle dragged Owl out of the pile and threw him upon his back like a cape.

"I will never slacken my pace, never pause for breath!" Owl declared bravely. He pulled at Black Eagle's ruff of hair, covered his eyes with small hands.

The warrior shrugged his shoulders, giving the boy a ride on his back as he hopped around the lodge.

The minute their visitors departed, Jeanne ran to Black Eagle, her eyes soft, her smile warm. She rested a hand on his arm. It was rock-solid with tension.

"No, Turtle." He moved away from her, crossing his arms. "Do not touch me. I do not want you to. We are through with that." The deadly monotone of his voice was low, and each word jarred, like a blow from a heavy fist.

She looked at him, both her hands on her middle as though he had hit her in the belly with his fist. Her eyes went very wide, stretched. What she saw was dark desire, like liquid smoke washing over her. The same throb of desire she felt in her own chest. Yet she recognized the crackle of tension that surged between them, the struggle to keep distance. The formidable, unbreachable wall of his defense.

"What—what are you talking about?" She heard her voice come out as a frightened squeak. She wanted to scream at him in her exasperation and frustration and alarm. Instead, all she could do was to croak at him. Like a silly, scared mouse.

"Did you not say that your mother died in childbirth, and the child with her?"

A chill shiver ran through her. Willing an inward and outward calm upon her body, she replied, "Yes, but she was ill beforehand!"

"You are so small. A half-grown fawn is heavier in the arms than you." He shuddered, uncrossed his arms, holding his fists clenched against his thighs. "Even though I wish for a son, I could not put you through such pain. Better to take a second wife." He spoke with only the slightest movement of his lips, slowly, deliberately, and clearly meaning every word of it.

Jeanne blanched, but her voice was as low and clear as his own. "My mother had six healthy babies with no difficulty!"

"I could not bear to lose you!"

Jeanne's whisper, her protest, sank away. She watched his eyes, dark, hooded in the flare of firelight, unsure if this was rejection. She could not quite see what he hid there, but she felt the disquiet, the ambivalence. As if it came from an impossibly great distance, she could hear Mama's voice, feeble with the effort of dying. *Children are the miracle, the jewels, of love shared.*

Ah! But she wanted his children! She wanted to feel his child move within her, to feel its mouth at her breast, tugging at her, the tiny fists kneading. She wanted to see the wonder and joy on Black Eagle's face, to feel his hand on her belly as he felt the child move within her for the first time. She wanted to see his face gentle with love and joy as he watched his child take his first steps, bring down his first deer. She shivered slightly. Children with night-dark eyes, his and hers.

She stepped back from him a little bit, raised herself on her toes, cupped his cheeks and pressed her lips to his, instinct, desire, driving her. He opened his mouth, breathing in, as she tasted the corner of his lips with her tongue. Sweet as the morning air, tinged with cranberry sauce. A deep pleasure flooded through her, and, what was more, a bold need. Jeanne could not think past wanting to dip her tongue in it and drink.

Soundless shudders ran through Black Eagle as she arched her body provocatively. She could feel them. The thundering of his heart against the solid wall of his chest, the tenseness and longing in his body, the hardness of his unsatisfied flesh, pressing supplicatingly into her belly. She rubbed herself against him, trembled at the controlled force of him, feeling her entire being burst into flames, willing him, wanting him to go on.

Slowly, carefully, before he could realize what she was doing or try to stop her, Jeanne leaned on him and with, a strength almost beyond her delicate frame, pressed his body down onto the sleeping ledge. She bent to cover his face with kisses, slowly working her way down his body, pausing to taste the flat masculine nipples, to savor the masculine smell of him. The bronze flesh, warm and vibrant, shuddered against the smooth skin of her lips, the insatiable swirl of her tongue.

She could feel her own restless excitement increase as, acting on instinct and a powerful love, she moved farther down his body, her fingers exploring the hard, ridged muscles of his rib cage, the indentation of his navel, the arch of his hips, the flat line of his stomach. His body tensed as she neared her destination, but in her own potent excitement she did not notice.

He said, in that low, raspy voice she found so attractive, "Do you have any idea what you are doing?"

Her hands slid over his hips, down his thighs to his knees. This was as far as she could reach. "No," she lied. "You do not like it?" It had not seemed to her it was an act that a man would dislike. Besides, it was so exciting when he did the same thing to her.

A muffled groan was her only answer.

"Do you want me to stop?"

She felt his fingers tremble as they threaded through her hair to hold her to him. "Not yet."

"You will tell me when?"

His arms reached out to clasp her tightly against his body. "Yes." And then he did not say anything else for a long, long time. And when he took her, it was with such force that she cried out in pain, but a pain so precious, so enchanting, that she savored it. For swept away with it were all the rancor, all the guilt, all the proud emotional dams. She clung to him, embracing him as fiercely as he was embracing her.

Jeanne lost all count of time, all sense of reality, as she floated through mists of half-consciousness, wanting never to return to earth. She did not know when she slept, but when she awoke, her head lay on his shoulder, and she could feel his warm breath lifting her hair at the temples. Their bodies lay only a fraction of an inch from each other, their skin glistening.

She raised herself on her elbow. His even breathing indicated he was still asleep. Jeanne looked down at the strong lines of his features, remembering the first time she had seen his face. She had feared it then, as she loved it now. This was the face she would one day see mirrored in her own son. The same high-bridged, strong nose, the same proud, high forehead, the same stubborn, arrogant jaw. She smiled at the thought of that little jaw, jutting out at her in moments of childish determination.

"I owe you an apology," she whispered softly. "I had no right to question your integrity. I was wrong about Muskrat, and you were right."

He opened one eye. "No, it is you who had the right feelings, Turtle. I was in the wrong. And I had no right to speak to you as I did."

Jeanne stared at him, her voice caught inside her.

"When I held Big Rain in my arms today, I suddenly realized how small and vulnerable he was. Muskrat is also small and vulnerable. But he will continue to become stronger, and grow to be a man, a warrior. Just as Big Rain will grow to be tall and strong as his father." He rolled over, drawing her with him. "As will our sons. I see them in the little pictures in my mind, training to become warriors."

Jeanne grinned. "And I suppose you will run effortlessly behind them, shouting, 'You are useless children who should be returned to the care of your mother!'"

He nuzzled his mouth against her neck. "No. She will be at my side, shouting, 'I am an old woman, ready for the long sleep. But I can do what these strong young braves cannot.'"

"I never expected both of us to insist we were wrong!"

"It is of no consequence." Black Eagle pulled her deeper into the curve of his body, playing with her hair, tousling it, smoothing it. "Did I mention we leave to visit the Wolf River People tomorrow?"

"No. I thought we were to wait until the new moon."

"It was an oversight." He lifted a fiery strand, running it along his cheeks, his throat. "I did mean to tell you, but you were acting the part of a snapping turtle, and did not seem willing to converse." He leaned one long arm over the ledge and picked up something. "I have been busy the past few days making you a marriage boon. I thought you could use this on the journey."

Jeanne took the article he extended and saw that the curved piece of turtle shell had been carved into a comb with a design of an eagle etched into the polished surface. She was overwhelmed. He had said, *No gifts.* But this gift, made with painstaking care, was magnificent by any standard. A gift of love. A warm glow suffused her.

She regarded his strongly planed face lovingly. "Black Eagle, I shall never quarrel with you again! We shall live in perfect harmony!"

"No, Turtle—" He raised himself slightly, as if on an afterthought. "I may not like it when you disagree. But I do like the way you say you are sorry. We must argue more frequently." In seconds he was sleeping.

Jeanne stared at his outstretched form, the guilt, anger and frustration she had harbored within her for so many days welling up into her throat to explode in a choking sob. This creature, this *cochon*, had tricked her! He had not teased and cajoled her out of her sulks. She had plotted and planned her gambit, only to be outwitted in the last trick. At this moment, she did not know whether she hated him or loved him more. And she was furious to discover that the feelings seemed to her to be lost in a vast tumble of emotions.

Chapter Twelve

"You are like the loon bird. She looks in the water to straighten her striped necklace and admire herself!"

Jeanne lay on her belly, watching her reflection in the river's surface. Under tawny brows that had a curious up-sweep, like the wings of a swallow in flight—graceful, elusive—two hazel eyes peered out from under long lashes. There was a resemblance to some beautiful forest creature in the high bones, the square chin, the rich coloring, the curve of the deeply indented upper lip outlining a wide, sensuous mouth. This folded back over small white teeth when she flashed a smile at Black Eagle.

"The water is so clear I can see the fish. Look!"

Black Eagle squatted and leaned over her shoulder to examine the long, sleek shapes. "Mmm...salmon trout. They make good eating." Within minutes he was looping thin strands of nettle stalk, winding the twine around a long, thin willow pole to form a seine. Dropping it into the shaded edge, where the fish were cruising to and fro, he announced that he would swim while she caught supper.

"Just remember to jiggle the trap up and down!" With one quick movement, he shed his garment and stood poised on the brink of the glistening sheet of water, stretched his arms high and lifted his face to the sun, listening to the breeze that rustled the tall reeds. His bared chest rose and fell steadily, and the muscles across his chest rippled with the gesture. His dark skin was smooth and slippery, stretched taut.

There was a rushing sound in Jeanne's ears as longing swept over her in a flood at the sight of the tall, lean body. She admired his sleekness and tone. Not an ounce of fat lived on that hard figure. Surely there were little birds fluttering on feathery wings inside her? Her breathing grew deeper. Slower. She felt rooted to the ground, could not seem to look away, his image frozen in her eyes. The water, green, cool and inviting, burst into an iridescent shower as Black Eagle cleaved the surface, breaking the spell.

A sudden swirl beneath the water returned Jeanne to the more mundane matter of supper. She scanned its surface in search of the undulating motion of a tail that meant a fish was entering the trap. No, the wretched thing was moving off, its jaws to the current. She looked longingly at Black Eagle swimming vigorously. *Sacre bleu!* Supper could wait! The fish could trap themselves! She removed her tunic and waded into the clear, knee-deep water. The smooth rock bottom was pleasant to her feet, and the rock-warmed water tickled the tender skin behind her knees.

Jeanne watched Black Eagle swim with powerful strokes from shore to shore, long, tightly corded muscular arms flashing, before she, too, plunged into the river's cool deeper waters. She shouted him a challenge, waving to the opposite shore.

As they raced, Jeanne was pleased to discover that, although he was a more powerful swimmer, he could not greatly outdistance her. They swam until exhausted and then, panting for breath, climbed out of the water onto a mossy bank to dry in the sun.

Black Eagle's limbs, glistening with droplets, were uniformly dark. Jeanne's arms and legs were a rich, tawny, sundarkened gold, but her body remained the creamy ivory of the habitually covered skin of her race. A film of moisture heightened the luster, the sheen, of youth, a glowing luminescence, an illusion of sun and moon locked in a loving, warm, living embrace.

"Shining creature!" Black Eagle looked at her. "I dare not touch you, lest you float away like a moonbeam!"

Flushing at the intensity of his gaze, Jeanne quipped, "Never will I float anywhere away from you, Black Eagle. I am very real, and will continue to be a burr in your breechclout."

She gave a little squeal when he made a deep noise in his throat and pounced on her. He put his mouth on hers, and she felt him put his arms around her and draw her closer. Soundless shudders of pleasure rocketed down her body. She leaned toward him, startled when his mouth opened and she felt his tongue lightly flick along her lips, tentatively tasting, testing. When she opened them, he applied more pressure, his tongue seeking entrance. She opened her mouth to receive it, to take the essence of him deep inside her. Their tongues explored, softly, gently.

Lost to the sensation, she closed her eyes, felt his hands caress her, and gave herself over to his wonderfully smooth touch, feeling every tingling sensation. Her breasts slid against his bare chest, and her breathing quickened to match his. He kissed her mouth, then each of her eyes, found her ear, breathed warm air in it, nibbled her lobe, and the tender, ticklish places of her throat. Then he returned to her mouth again, more fiercely.

Shivers, like lightning, raced through her body when he buried his face in her neck and sucked warmth to the surface. She quivered as he touched the rounded smoothness of her breast, the dip of her waist. When he moved down to the smooth curve of her stomach, the taut muscles of her thigh, she moaned in anticipation. One hand brushed the triangle of soft russet curls, while the other curled around the turgid swelling of her breast. Her whole body fluttered.

He tasted the rosy crest with the tip of his tongue, swirling in decreasing circles, slowing drawing the nipple into his mouth, suckling gently. She pushed herself against him, wanting, and shuddered when he answered with a deep pull. Every nerve, muscle and sinew taut, she could feel the pressure, the tension gathering, building, mounting, surging. His name was released in a gasp as she enfolded him with joyous abandon, taking his full, proud manhood into her eager warmth.

For an eternal instant, his deeper, throatier cries rose in harmony with her breathless sobs, repeating her name as pleasure shuddered through them. Together they entered that sweet oblivion where every need has been mutually satisfied, where words are only superfluous, where body is joined to body, mind to mind, spirit to spirit.

The sun was setting behind the blue-ridged hills, its last rays turning the edges of the gathering clouds to liquid gold, when Jeanne and Black Eagle stirred. Two spotted salmon trout had trapped themselves, and Jeanne kindled the fire while Black Eagle gutted the fish, threaded them on skewers and proceeded to roast them over the flames.

By the time the preparations for the meal were completed, an occasional firefly glowed greenish-yellow in the soft darkness. Somewhere upstream, a frog croaked to its mate. There was only a thin shell of new moon, but the sky was brilliant with stars. Legs folded beneath her, Jeanne sought the familiar stars, her eyes and mind drawn away from the present.

Mama had told the children the stars were peepholes in the floor of heaven, through which dead souls could watch those they had loved and left behind on Earth. Papa had laughed at the notion and tried to tell Mama that they were firmaments, other planets, just like Earth.

Staring at the stars above until the edges of her vision darkened, Jeanne closed her eyes, expelling a long breath, a faint gasp, like a wordless sob. She gave her head a little shake. Groaned. It was a visceral sound, full of guilt and contrition, shame. She had all but forgotten France in the bliss of the past months! Her expression changed to one of intense remorse, her face so mobile it took the imprint of each passing thought.

Oh, Papa, forgive me. If you are up there watching, you will know I can never carry out my promise. You will know how much I love this man, this life. *If I have no love, I am nothing.* I could not ever return to *Grand-père* and the old ways.

Black Eagle's voice, curt, remote, intruded into her thoughts.

"I have decided that we will use the half-moon of time along this trail to Wolf River to show you how difficult it is to be a *real* warrior, how much it is better for you to behave like a woman than a man."

She raised her eyes in inquiry, her cheeks suffused with color. That tone of voice did not sit well with a proud female, but she wisely, though resentfully, refrained from making a harsh reply. Instead, she smiled with innocent gravity, straightened her shoulders in an effort to appear relaxed, and nibbled at the trout he passed to her.

He was watching her steadily, his face a hard mask, his jaw flexed, as if she had done something that he did not like. Did he guess that she had been thinking of the past? Did he worry that she might still yearn for it? What a goose she was! Such fantasies belonged only to a woman, not a warrior!

Black Eagle took a breath. "You will learn to track me while I evade you, and then I will try to track you while you avoid being caught." He brought his lips gingerly down on the fish and grimaced. It was still too hot to eat.

Jeanne watched his strongly planed face, returned his intense look without a blink, and moistened her lips with the tip of her tongue. A thought occurred to her. "Is there danger from the animals here?"

Black Eagle's eyes met hers, dark and deep. He shrugged. "No more than anywhere else. There is no need to display your brushy tail as a warning, like the striped skunk. If you are frightened, say so."

Face flaming with hurt pride, she fumed for a moment, then remembered the teasing habits of the People. Perhaps he was only having fun with her? Bright spots of color high in her cheeks, she eyed him warily and, switching tactics, taunted him in response.

"Does it not concern you that a snapping turtle may outwit an eagle's fledgling? Escape the trap?" She let her low, husky laughter beat against the night air like the wings of captive doves, allowed her long, tawny lashes to beat a tattoo over her half-closed eyes. "Or, worse, could it be that such a small creature will remove the eagle's claws and tame it?"

A tight white line formed around Black Eagle's mouth. His deeply etched scowl was thunderous, and his liquid eyes glittered. "You will learn to be still, be silent. To use your eyes and ears, and not make questions out of the emptiness of your head."

"Beware of the sting of hornets!" Jeanne snapped, exasperated, her eyes flashing with a sudden burst of fire. Though she was careful to keep her voice low, she could not prevent the anger invading her voice. Still, she was startled when Black Eagle jumped to his feet and pivoted to stride off into the darkness.

Baffled, she peered uneasily into the darkness, filled with a mixture of anger and remorse at the tiny impulse of mischief that had made her taunt him. A brisk breeze carried the scent of water past her hot face. Her mind echoed his words. *Be still.* Was she such a distraction, with her lively ways and ready laughter?

She scowled at the thought of a major flaw in her character and her thinking. Was she an empty-headed flibbertigibbet? The very thought dismayed her. *Be silent.* Did she really chatter so much? *Behave like a woman.* Was she a forward hussy, as that dreadful Madame Guibert, the governess, had suggested to Papa that his eldest daughter would become if she did not mend her ways? Perhaps Black Eagle's words had been merely zealous endearments, not jokes or insults? Was that why he had overreacted and been hateful? Would she ever understand this man?

Dawn was just a pale ghost when they set off the next morning. A faint purple mist webbed the distant, shadowed mountain peaks. Black Eagle had returned with a canoe. Though Jeanne was bursting with curiosity, she did not ask where he had obtained such a vehicle in the wilderness.

The river was alive. Perched in a riverbank aspen were a pair of horned owls. Sandpipers and yellowlegs flitted and hopped about close to shore. Around almost every bend they came on flights of larger birds resting on their flyway routes. Black ducks, goldeneyes and mergansers rose flapping from the surface and flew swiftly over or around them, resuming their journeys. Far down the glassy stillness of the water, a great blue heron spread its huge wings and lazily disappeared.

Jeanne watched Black Eagle dip the paddle in a smooth motion, the water scarcely rippling. Silence crackled between them. She had drifted off to sleep before he returned, her last waking thought concerned with the sudden realization that he had deliberately picked an argument. Her dreams had been fractured and elusive, disturbing her rest with distorted visions of nameless, faceless shadows, leaving her unrefreshed.

It was much lighter now, broad bands of purple, crimson, orange and yellow lying along the eastern horizon. Black Eagle paddled steadily, his gaze straight ahead, but seemingly unseeing. His entire body was uncompromising, his attitude unbending.

A movement near the bank caught her eye, causing her to turn abruptly. A pair of loons was holding an early-morning race across the water with several downy blackish-brown chicks. In a general babble of noise, they seemed to be congratulating the young, and each other, as well.

Jeanne risked a glance at Black Eagle. "Wise Speaker says the loon is a messenger from the Eternal Person." Opening her eyes very wide, she ventured a peace offering. "He says whenever a loon cries at night, it is to deliver a secret message to his master in the sky."

Black Eagle shifted in his seat impatiently, his eyes scanning the area around them without interest and shrugged, but his glance rested on her a second longer than necessary, and he seemed to relax.

As they approached a rocky promontory, they surprised three handsome, husky white-tailed deer that eyed them briefly, then clattered up the rocks and were gone. Jeanne shifted position, tilting her face to the sky.

A still, small voice inside her was mockingly calling her a fool, but Jeanne could not suppress her excitement when a flock of passenger pigeons flew overhead. There were so many of them, they ate up the sun, darkening the sky. Nowhere could she look without the flash of wings.

She rose, weapon gripped in one hand. The bow, carved of the finest ash and rubbed to a soft sheen, felt alive to the touch. Slipping an arrow into the notch, she spread her legs for balance and released the shaft. Another.

There was a whistle as the arrow cut the air, followed by the solid and satisfying sound of connection. Plop. A fat bird landed in the canoe. The other splashed into the water, to be retrieved on Black Eagle's paddle. Jeanne straightened up, proudly. She wrinkled her small nose toward the dead birds, looked sideways at Black Eagle, tossed him an impudent smile, and giggled. It was a very young giggle.

"Do not say it, Black Eagle! I know! With so many targets, how could I not succeed!"

"Nevertheless, your aim is true, and you have provided us with enough meat for a hearty supper." His stiffness melted away like a deer in flight as she bounced in excitement. "Sit down, Turtle, you are rocking the canoe!"

Jeanne could not suppress the grin that she knew was spread all over her face. "Do not tell me to sit quiet like a stone and let thought come to me, or I will snap a hole in it!" she threatened.

He laughed, showing all his strong white teeth. "You heard the words in my head! Took them right out of my mouth!"

The tension broken, they settled back into their old camaraderie. It became a game to see how close they could get to flocks of aristocratic buff-and-black long-necked geese before they honked their displeasure and flew off, forming chevrons in the sky.

When they abandoned the canoe, leaving it carefully hidden for another time, they tracked each other and small game. Jeanne brought down squirrels and birds, as well as an occasional weasel or raccoon, and, on one special day, a red fox. The warm summer days had an unending quality, one so like the next that time seemed held in suspension.

One morning, when the sky was streaked with yellow and hot rose-pink as the sun nudged open the eastern door, Jeanne filled a water skin at the edge of a small lake, washed her face and combed and braided her hair. On her braid, she tied her embroidered headband. Black Eagle was honing his weapons in readiness for their journey through the muskeg.

Suddenly she froze. She heard the crackling sound of someone, or something, approaching, occasionally stepping on a dead branch that cracked underfoot. Dropping the water skin, she drew her tomahawk, grasped it, and braced herself. Through the underbrush, a black bear approached. The beast was old and tattered, but stout and solid. Long, sharp, wicked claws hung from its huge paws. Tiny, malevolent red eyes peered from beneath a bushy brow.

The animal stopped, considered. Jeanne knew she could not kill the bear with a single blow of the tomahawk, and her bow, made for a boy rather than a man, while large enough to bring down small game, would be ineffective against so massive a beast. The bear pawed the ground, sending a cascade of pine needles behind it, sniffed, raised its head, growled, and pawed the air, swinging its head blindly as it prepared to attack.

Jeanne stood frozen, numb with fear. *Think!* She measured the distance to the branch of the pine tree above her head. Then, just as the bear started forward, she leapt, terror giving her strength. She caught hold of the moisture-laden branch with both hands and managed to pull up her feet and legs, which she also wrapped around the branch. It dipped and swayed. She clung to the branch with all her might.

The bear, demonstrating remarkable agility and speed, barely missed her and charged through the open space. The animal halted and looked around in myopic confusion. Its enemy had suddenly vanished, but it could still smell human beings.

Jeanne's hands were slipping, sliding, losing their grip. An arrow flew through the air with a slight singing noise and penetrated between the bear's eyes, and the animal, bleeding heavily, collapsed.

Black Eagle stepped into the clearing. He held his heavy bow in one hand, and with the other dropped a stout arrow back into its quiver. He reached up, caught hold of Jeanne, imprisoned her in the circle of his arms. He leaned against her, his forehead resting against her neck. Faintly, so faintly that she was not sure it was not her imagination, she felt him shaking. He was shaking with laughter. He pushed her away, expelling a long breath.

"Turtle, you are the equal of most warriors in your knowledge of the forest, but do you not yet know that bears are good climbers? If this one had not been so old and decrepit, he would have shared the tree limb."

Jeanne did not know whether to be thrilled at his praise or irate at his tender teasing. Before she had made up her mind, they had reached the swamp. Scrub gave way to withy and reed as they entered the muskeg. A sharp breeze swayed the rushes, bringing with it a rustle, a stirring, the staccato boom of a bittern and the cry of geese rising, honking, into the lowering sky. Water lapped around them. It gradually deepened as they plunged farther into the marshes.

They splashed through the shallows. No wonder the People did not visit the other tribes very often! Twigs clawed at her tunic, caught at her hair. Every plant had thorns, and mud plastered her legs, her haunches. Frogs croaked in the swamp, a cacophony of sound, an out-of-rhythm chant. A flicker of movement alerted her to a snake slithering through the mud toward her. It was small, no more than two feet in length, and about as thick as her thumb. She slapped the water. *Go away. Chase the frogs.*

Insects rose up. The sound of their buzz, a wing-drumming, a long, tearing whine, filled the heavy, hot, wet, stench-laden air. Indifferent to the bear grease she had rubbed on it as protection, a hundred hot needles plunged into every visible, uncovered inch of her skin. Their whirr merged with her curses as she floundered, stumbled, clutched futilely at some rushes and sank up to her belly in the marsh.

"Come along, Turtle. You are putting your feet in the muskeg like a raccoon that dabbles its paw in the water until it gets a bite!"

Jeanne gulped and began scrambling over the rotting bog-oak, green-slimed and fetid, that lay waterlogged in the swamp, trying to keep pace with Black Eagle. "Now you are trying to provoke me again!"

In places, withy and sedge rose high overhead into a canopy of green. In others, they vanished to reveal an open stretch of water, or a heron, its wings brushing the surface, flapping lazily to a nearby perch.

"There are several islands high in the marsh. We will make camp there for the night."

Jeanne sighed with relief at the prospect of rest. "Good. My feet are swollen, and I am dotted with itchy red splotches from insect bites. They are tiny, but fierce. They sting like hornets!"

A fallen tree blocked their path. Black Eagle climbed onto its trunk and held out his hand toward Jeanne. She took it. And when she jumped and swung up beside him, their two bodies touched, skin meeting skin from waist to shoulder.

"Oh!" Jeanne gasped, looking at his body, strong, muscled shoulders, narrow, flat waist, well-muscled thighs and bulging breechclout. "Such surprises are becoming a habit with you! You might at least wait until we are clean. From toe to temple, there is no part of me that does not reek of swamp."

A grin escaped Black Eagle at her openly assessing gaze. He took both her hands and touched them to the inside of his thighs. His skin felt warm, alive to her touch. Her fingers tingled. She trailed them along the smooth muscles until, in her delicate exploration, they curled over the thick stalk of his manhood, round the edge of his breechclout, up to the cord, which was around his waist, and down to the several knots where it ended at his buttocks. His back stiffened, and he arched back and away from her.

Frantic, she sunk her teeth into his muscled shoulder, and heard him chuckle. Slowly he lowered his face to hers until the tips of their noses touched, pecked her parted lips briefly, several times, in kisses so delicious and teasing they set her heart pounding. Then he surprised her with a hard, relentless kiss to the mouth, as if to make an irrevocable imprint, before he straightened again.

The abrupt sensation of passion was dizzying. Jeanne felt her knees go wobbly. "You could test the passions of the dead! I suggest you try mine no further." She felt the heat of his breath as his face came close to hers, but the kiss he brushed her lips with had only the weight of a feather. His fingers slanted across her cheeks, edged to the corner of her mouth. His eyes filled with promise. "When we have prepared our camp and bathed, then I will see if you are so bold!"

They made camp on a tiny, tree-clad cone fringed with white cedar. Jeanne took the brace of ducks they had killed and baked them in thick bog marl. The moon rose clear of a low cloud that hugged a distant mountain and flooded the clearing with silver light as Black Eagle removed the two hard-baked clay balls from the fire and, after they had cooled, cracked them open with his hatchet. The odor of duck cooked in its own juices was delicious. Delicious enough for Jeanne to forget—for a short while, at least—the mosquitoes that attacked her tender skin with ferocious abandon.

"We need a canoe to travel through all this water," she said.

"There will be one concealed at the cone with the poplars. We will use that."

Jeanne did not think she had ever spent such an uncomfortable night. She slept fitfully, kept awake by the gusting in the reeds, the crying, hooting clamor of waterfowl echoing in the dark sweep of marsh and sky. The fire was small, doing nothing to ward off the dampness, and in the early hours of the morning it flickered sporadically and died. Black Eagle lay beside her, exuding a sense of security, of comfort, but he, too, dozed only briefly. They were up and eager to leave at first light.

The journey that day seemed endless. They retrieved the canoe, which had a small leak. When sufficient water seeped through to slosh over her moccasins, Jeanne began to bail with her cupped hands. They made their way slowly, painstakingly. At times, Black Eagle, with one edge of the canoe balanced on a shoulder, waded through the quagmire of ankle-deep mud and lush waterlogged reeds until eventually the mud gave way to water and they were able to resume their seats in the canoe.

The sun was tipping westward when Black Eagle halted. He studied the morass that lay ahead, then headed the canoe into a narrow channel. Gradually the waterway became wider, with foliage increasingly confined to the banks. However, although the flow was still sluggish, Jeanne noticed that the water became increasingly clear. One of the myriad of small freshwater streams that fed the marsh must be nearby. The familiar chill of premonition that she had experienced so frequently since her capture returned now in a gripping flash.

Uneasy, she put her arms around herself. "This muskeg is not as bad as the one we left behind us." Had that casual comment really come from her lips? Her voice sounded perfectly natural, not stiff or forced.

Black Eagle turned and grinned at her. "Perhaps the worst of the journey is over."

"Look—blueberries." Impetuously Jeanne swung her legs into the calf-high water, intending to wade to the bank to gather some of the berries growing along the sandy edge.

To her astonishment and dismay, the ground under her feet gave way, and she began to sink lower. The sand sucked at, oozed around, her legs, drawing them farther into the quagmire.

Terror boiled in her stomach. Arms and legs thrashing, like a fish struggling away from the bait although the hook is already embedded in its flesh, she sought to release her imprisoned limbs. The more she struggled to release herself, the deeper she sank. She bucked and heaved when strong arms cut into the soft flesh under her armpits.

"Hold still." Black Eagle lay stretched flat on the prow of the canoe, clasping his hands in a suffocating grip behind her back. In spite of his considerable strength, Jeanne sank deeper.

"I cannot breathe." In a frenzy, she pulled at the constricting pressure, hands like sharp claws, scratching, fighting, as viciously as a wild creature.

Black Eagle did not release his firm grip. "It is all right, Turtle," he said softly. "It is the fear of the trembling earth that puts a tight band around your chest."

The edge of her vision condensed, darkened, wavered. Oblivion beckoned. She gulped a breath.

"Do not try to pull yourself out. You will only sink deeper. Be still. Be silent. Think of the leaf on the pool."

Black Eagle's deep, hypnotic voice penetrated the pernicious haze of Jeanne's terror. In the midst of shuddering, hysterical confusion, her mind focused on one thing only. She fixed with preternatural intensity on him—his words, his voice, his energy.

"Gently now, gently. Look at me." His eyes held hers, infinitely deep, infinitely dark. All else was mist.

I see my death in your eyes.
Keep the fear inside you. I have enough of my own.
Do not leave me.
Be still. Be silent. Be strong. Show no fear.

She clung to him and obediently stopped struggling, lost herself in his eyes, in his silent command, concentrating instead on the pains deep in her chest every time she sucked in a breath.

Black Eagle held her in a viselike grip until the veins stood out at his temples, and his face and torso were drenched with sweat. She could feel it dripping in runnels onto her upturned face, its salt on her lips. Still he held her with his steady gaze. She was being drawn no deeper. Little by little Jeanne felt herself being released. Inch by inch, more and more of her body appeared.

"Do... not... move... yet...." Black Eagle's voice was only a thread, a gasp.

Jeanne nodded, too frightened to speak. Pain stabbed in her chest like a jagged knife. She willed her energy to flow into his. He seemed to be calling on his last reserves of strength as she felt herself come free, her legs floating to the surface. Now, in spite of her numbness, she kicked with her remaining might, launching herself toward the pull of his arms to land on top of him. For a few moments they sagged at the bottom of the canoe, locked in each others' arms in a deathlike embrace.

Gradually the strength began to come back into her limbs. Her vision began to clear. She sat up, chest heaving, stared hard at the ribbon of trees that marked the edge of the swamp. Birds whirled in clouds, flying in a ghostly silence. Each separate bush seemed to waver. Swamp and sand spit merged, a curdled green, as though the land itself were staging an earthquake to match her exploding brain.

Then the horizon settled into its unkempt tranquillity again, unmoved by time or change, supremely indifferent to the dilemma of one Jeanne de la Rocque, whose own small world had turned over and then righted itself in a space of minutes. Jeanne shuddered, even as she felt its magic.

She forced her trembling legs into action, used the paddle to maneuver the canoe back into the current and staggered to kneel beside Black Eagle, who still lay in a crumpled heap. Head tipped back, eyes closed, taking in great gulps of air, he struggled to sit up, in time to be almost knocked down again by the force with which Jeanne hurled herself on top of him.

"You will be the death of me yet, woman!"

But he folded his long arms around her and crushed her to him with a sound curiously like a sob.

Chapter Thirteen

It was the water that woke her. Water, sloshing over her legs, the back of her neck, in her ear. Wearily Jeanne opened her eyes. The whole bottom of the canoe was full of water, making it slew sideways and lurch ponderously in the tug of the current.

Licking her parched lips, she pushed herself up on one elbow and looked over the side. Shivering, she realized that the sun's last light was dissolving over the ridge of mountains. The spine of the ridge was cleanly etched against the red anger of the dying sun. Soon, the muted half-light of a summer night would enclose the world in soft purple shadow.

During their exhausted sleep, the canoe had gently drifted out of the muskeg into a small stream, slowly taking in water all the while. She struggled to a sitting position and nudged Black Eagle, who came awake in an instant, ready for action.

"What happens now?" Jeanne breathed in a choked voice.

Black Eagle's tone, though very quiet, was rough with some emotion that feathered her spine. "Can you swim with your bag and weapons?"

"I think so."

He picked up the paddle. "I will try to nose the canoe out of the channel, toward the bank. Once free of the main current, even if the canoe capsizes, we can swim ashore. Be prepared."

The blade was dipping into the water before he had finished speaking. She felt him stroke hard and, with his paddle, turn the canoe until it pointed at the bank.

Fortunately, the channel's course was close to the bank. A dogleg break in the flow sent the canoe careening toward a small clearing. Water poured over the bow, and the canoe settled down its whole length, to wallow in the riverbed. They waded easily to shore.

A cloud of egrets, settling to rest for the night, spouted from some tall saplings at the edge of the clearing. Surprised by the movement, a deer on higher ground translated abruptly to a vanishing white alarm signal as the creature plunged into the underbrush. Several turtles slid quietly from the embankment into the water.

Turning to Black Eagle, Jeanne felt her eyes widen as she took in his appearance, from the top of his thick hair, down the impressive width of his shoulders, to his trim waist and flat stomach, to the muscular tension of his well-shaped thighs, all the way down to his mud-stained moccasins.

Silhouetted against the furnace-glow light from the west, he looked funny. For one thing, his scalp lock was stiff with brown mud and silver-gray moss, runnels of which had dripped in streaks down his shapely head to dry in mock decoration on his strongly marked nose and chin. For another, he stank. Worse than a spotted skunk after it had erected its white-tipped tail to warn off a would-be opponent. Jeanne could see greenish-black tide lines of fetid dried slime glistening in the creases of his neck and along the edges of the ridged scar tissue that marked the place where she had shot him.

But she liked what she saw. She had a feeling that she would go on liking it forever.

"Black Eagle—?" Jeanne's voice, sounding as if it came from deep within her, cracked somewhere in the middle of saying his name. She put out a small, trembling hand, and tentatively touched those greenish-black lines. They felt sticky.

He did not say anything, only leaned forward, pinpoints of fire in his midnight eyes. He hung there a moment, staring, searching her face, drinking in her features. *I need you.* She stood frozen to the spot as his gaze swept over her from head to foot and back again, her breath coming faster and faster as his gaze roamed every inch of her.

There could be no mistaking his feelings at that moment. He wanted her. Drowning in his hungry eyes, Jeanne felt as if her insides had begun to melt into an indistinguishable mass, and that at any moment they would start to flow out through her feet.

A spasm of some indefinable emotion slid like moving water across his face. The tension in him became more pronounced as he stood rock-steady, his whole attention focused on her until she found it increasingly hard to breathe. It was as though he had to hold himself back with all his considerable will to keep from devouring her whole.

Then he caught her hand, turned it palm up, and held it to his mouth, tracing warm wet, tingling little circles on it with his tongue tip.

"You taste and smell like the muskeg, Little Turtle."

Jeanne's lips formed a smile—a weak and tender effort, but authentic. She could feel life in herself again, slow-creeping, soft and warm, along all her veins, her nerves. She threw herself upon his long, lean, rock-solid frame, her arms wrapping themselves around his neck, almost strangling him.

"Oh, Black Eagle. I did not think I would live to see another sunset. You were so strong, so brave." Her hands
came up to his chest. She kissed his eyes, his mouth, his
throat, all permeated with the miasma of bog slime. Tears
spilled over her dark-gold lashes and arrowed her mud-
streaked cheeks.

He groaned aloud, with a queer sort of intensity, bent
down and found her mouth, wildly but ever so briefly, pulling her lower body closer to his in an instinctive movement
of relief and gladness. As her lips slackened, parted, became fiercely demanding, he straightened, thrust her from
him and held her inches away in a hurting grip that told her
how hard it was for him to break contact with her. His dark
eyes held her huge, tear-washed ones, locking them in a gaze
of such intense unspoken communication that Jeanne went
weak at the knees.

"Gently, Little Turtle, gently. Brave tales do not always
have a happy ending. Stinking and miserable as you are, you
have the power to arouse me, if you do not suffocate me
first! The fire in my veins tells me I am still alive. Let us find
shelter and get ourselves cleaned up." His voice was hoarse,
but a smile played about the corners of his mouth.

He wrapped one arm tightly, companionably, around her
shoulders, gave a quick squeeze and turned away. Released
from the spell, Jeanne came to herself with a start. A glance
at the strip of sunlight that pierced the clearing reminded her
that the day was far advanced. Her attention reverted to
Black Eagle as he retrieved their accoutrements, his body
expressing inexorable purpose with every movement. Prepare a camp!

The smell of the bird roasting over the small campfire
tormented Jeanne unmercifully. A mouth-watering, stom-
ach-cramping smell. But the need to get rid of the stench and
filth of the swamp overrode her hunger.

After only a short trek they had come across an escarpment, jutting over an ancient, wave-cut cliff, that revealed an ancient forest bed of logs, branches and upright stumps, contorted into shapes, then fused together by some primeval force. From tiny cracks between these rock columns, a soft mist of rising steam created little rivulets of moisture on the limestone cap. These, in turn, dropped to the sandstone floor to form shallow steaming pools of hot water, an irresistible invitation to the travelers.

Jeanne had wanted to bathe immediately, but Black Eagle had insisted they prepare the camp first. While she had collected brush and began a fire, he had taken time to pull a lethargic bird from its resting place and prepare it for their supper. She tipped out the contents of their bedraggled carry-bags. Some things she laid out to dry. Other items, ruined by moisture, were discarded. Unraveling her soggy braid, Jeanne followed Black Eagle's movement with her eyes as he adjusted the makeshift spit on which the browning bird rested.

Overpowered by the lure of the steamy water, Jeanne began shedding her clothes. The water was startlingly warm as it covered her feet, tingling, tickling, caressing. So sensuously pleasant did she find it, she lowered herself slowly, allowing herself the torture of slow submersion.

The mineral-laden water was buoyant, pushing her body to the surface. She submerged herself again, this time sliding under the surface until her hair was completely wet, emerging with a gasp when Black Eagle joined her with a splash, a piece of soaproot in his hand.

Jeanne slid onto her back and allowed the water to support her. Her eyes followed his body down his strongly muscled torso, past his navel, to the physical evidence of his excitement. She shifted position, raising her hand to brush a strand of hair from her forehead. She made a choking sound of stifled mirth, recovered, but her voice trembled with laughter.

"The women say that hot springs like this drain a man, make his manhood soften," she managed to say.

He leaned back, shook his head confidently. "Believe me, that will not happen tonight." His eyes were fixed on the spot where her legs joined her body, on the russet curls nesting against the moon-pale flesh, an opalescent invitation sweetly rimmed by the shallow water. They held the hungry look of the hunter. The bold stare of a young eagle. His eyes met hers with a flash of heat. He took a deep breath. "Maybe I will need a little extra measure of control, but just in case . . ."

Purposefully, he gathered her to him, dragged her into the cradle of his legs, pressed her against the strong, erect shaft of his manhood. One strong hand crept round her belly, molding its heat to the shape of her, enfolding itself against the feminine core of her, sending a wave of feathery sensations to her toes that spiraled upward to start a quaking deep inside. The other hand moved in slow, sensuous circles up her arm.

Jeanne felt excitement flow through her. She threw her head back, allowing him to lift her hair, kiss her throat, her chin. Her breathing accelerated. She felt as if her body were flying out of her control. She arched her back, her hips lifting to his fingers. A deep pleasure flooded through her, and she twisted to meet his lips. He tasted her own with small, nipping, teasing kisses, as if he were savoring the sweetness of ripe fruit.

At the same time, the smooth touch of his hand moved gradually across her shoulder, over the pale mounds of her breasts, the rosy, rigid points, to the curve of her slender hips, to trade places with his other hand. Leisurely, he repeated the procedure, with tantalizing slowness.

Urging her body closer with the gentle pressure of his palm, he exposed the center of her being, the bud of her desire. Squirming, bucking, Jeanne tried to avoid the persistent, gentle ministrations of the fingers that slid between her legs to find every tiny crevice, every tender fold, but he held her firmly, her legs securely fastened by the long, thick muscles of his own legs, his feet pinning her slender thighs open to his meticulous attentions. His fingers on her, probing, teasing, made her rear up in pleasure.

She sucked in her breath when she felt his hand cup her buttocks, lift her, rub her against his burgeoning masculinity. She let it out again in a gush as she buried her nose in his neck, nipping the smooth warmth of his skin. His groan was one of sheer delight.

Her sudden move to withdraw surprised him enough that she was able to break free from his embrace sufficiently to lower her arm and slip her hand between their bodies. Her fingers slid over his tight, smooth skin, then curved around that hard, throbbing part of him. She could feel his pulse beat strongly in his bold man root as it rose against her hand, surging into her palm. She grasped him in her hand, pressed her fingers inward, and it was his turn to suck in his breath. His breath caught, and then came quicker. He moaned into her mouth as her hand fondled him, thrusting his hips forward.

Then, somehow, with single-minded vigilance, he managed to turn her around, dislodging her marauding hand. Trembling visibly, his warm palm still moved efficiently, effectively, down her spine, massaging the small of her back gently with the soaproot before including her firm, rounded buttocks in his ardent attentions.

He pulled her up to close his lips around her turgid nipple, tickling it with his tongue, sucking, drawing, summoning her very spirit to the site of his mouth, and also to that other, secret, moist place, where he had changed the rhythm of his fingers. Jeanne closed her eyes helplessly against the voluptuous tremors that rippled through her body.

All wild urgency, she touched his cheek, his lips, his nose, the pulse throbbing in his neck. His mouth covered hers, seeking, demanding, his tongue darting, plunging, tasting, feeling. Her hands trembling badly, Jeanne reached up to smooth the heated water across the breadth of his shoulders, her resolve almost destroyed at the first touch of his smooth flesh, the ripple of muscle.

His heart was throbbing wildly, reverberating, ricocheting, echoing under the hand she moved up over the broad column of his throat. The dark eyes regarding her intently were half-lidded, expectant. Lowering her mouth to his chest, she touched the ridge of scar tissue with her tongue, drifting slowly down in light, lingering, moist kisses toward her quarry, his potent loins.

Delighting in the sensation of running her hands and lips over the rigid, swollen member, she did not acknowledge the deep, responsive shuddering that began in Black Eagle's strong frame, though it set her own body trembling, set it on fire. A low, hoarse, unintelligible whisper escaped his lips, and he pulled her on top of him. Holding her hips, he lowered her onto himself, thrusting upward as he did so, to be caught and held in that wonderful, warm-soft, enchanted place.

Exquisite rapture spread from between her legs through her whole body as she accepted him and surrounded him with her warmth. She clung to him, hugging him as fiercely as he was hugging her, molding her body to the heat of his.

Frantic, she sank her teeth into his muscled shoulder and heard his rumbling laugh. Their voices mingled in incoherent, yet totally meaningful, gasps and murmurs of love, while their bodies arched, demanded, molded and melted. Spiraling out of control, her back arching, she began to lose all sense of self, all lucid thought, and still he pushed her, drew back, pushed her again, pushed her over the edge, like a burst of white light.

She gasped out his name as the surge of his passion overtook him. Trembling and convulsing, he poured himself into her, took her into himself, inseparable, a part of him.

Later, when they lay quietly side by side by the fire, drained, in an island of time that held only them, beyond the reach of anything else—even reality—Jeanne watched Black Eagle. His eyes were closed, and his breathing was regular. He rested with his hand relaxed upon her belly, relaxed, yet possessive.

Her eyes searched the night sky. Brightened by a huge golden moon that hovered just above the horizon, it was crowned by a million diamond stars, hazy with distance. The south wind brought the sound of geese talking far away—like the future. That, too, was veiled, imperfect, but she knew as surely as she knew that the sun would rise on the morrow that there was nothing else in the world more important to her than this man. He was her love, her passion, her only desire.

The sun was weary next day, casting long shadows, when a distant drum began pounding. Black Eagle paused, his head tilted. He took Jeanne's hand and led her to a glade by the edge of the stream they had been following.

"The Wolf River People have sent a welcome party. We are to wait here." He squatted, cross-legged, on a carpet of silver-gray pine needles.

Jeanne sat facing him. "How do you know?"

"The drums speak."

She listened to the rhythm, but could not discern any pattern. She soon lost interest and looked around. Behind them, on all sides, the black-brown trunks of the conifers stood guard, like giant warriors. Here and there, rose-colored shafts of sunlight pierced the thick canopy of leaves, casting blushing pools of light on the sea of ferns that washed against the gnarled roots of the trees.

The drums throbbed furiously. Suddenly, a tall, older warrior wearing an elaborate feathered bonnet appeared on the trail. His face was painted a garish red, his cheeks highlighted with long, straight streaks of black and white, his eyes resembling the core of huge concentric circles. A collar of bear claws surrounded his neck, and several large necklaces of wampum hung on his breast. Jeanne could see the bones of his ribs, and his neck was very thin, the skin wrinkled like the throat of a lizard.

Black Eagle rose lithely to his feet. "Slanting Eyes," he acknowledged.

Slanting Eyes nodded a greeting. "I have come to greet our honored guests. Welcome to the Wolf River summer camp, Black Eagle."

While he spoke, the warrior's eyes slid to Jeanne, then politely away again. In the months since her capture, she had become one of the People to such an extent that she had forgotten the curiosity her vivid hair and pale skin had initially aroused.

"We have been awaiting your coming. We knew it was this day." Slanting Eyes pointed south. "Arrowheads were seen in the sky, where the dark rain clouds and the thunder are stored beyond the rim of the world."

They must have been close to the encampment, because shortly a vanguard of children and curious adults surrounded them. It seem to Jeanne that everyone in the village must have turned out to greet the newcomers.

Senior warriors appeared, as did their juniors, who were distinguished by a lack of paint. They smiled and called to Black Eagle happily, then stared at Jeanne.

The women stood silently, scrutinizing her with great care. Their look was curious, but not unfriendly, as they stared at the peach-gold of her skin and the delicate modeling of her bones. The color of her eyes, in particular, intrigued them. She could hear their whispers behind her back.

Children, most of them boys, joined in the procession, accompanied by dogs that barked furiously but amicably wagged their tails.

A tall warrior broke out of the forest and came to a halt. Jeanne turned to Black Eagle in surprise. She watched the men exchange glances. Nonplussed, she stood still. Was this in truth Watchful Fox? The same Watchful Fox who had bidden farewell to Black Eagle and herself a half-moon since?

Jeanne took another look, and saw the sapling straight woman at his side, mouth wide and ready to smile, a beaded wampum band around her two long, night-black braids. Brown Cloud? What were they doing here? How had they arrived ahead of those who had left before them?

Brown Cloud, brown face beaming, ran towards Jeanne. Her delightful smile lit up her dewy-soft face with a blooming, radiant beauty Jeanne envied. She glanced at Black Eagle. He had a guarded look, as if he were concealing something. It was gone in a blink. His eyes avoided hers as he nodded abruptly to Brown Cloud, then strode, at the stately pace expected of a senior warrior, across to clasp arms with Watchful Fox.

"I am so happy to see you arrive safely," Brown Cloud exclaimed joyfully. "Where have you been? We have been here for ten suns!"

Jeanne responded absentmindedly, her mind skipping round and round, trying to solve the puzzle, not concentrating at all on Brown Cloud's effervescent conversation.

The answer hit her as she dipped her head to enter the visitors' lodge. An answer that exploded inside her and sent both force and weakness to her fingertips. *Black Eagle had taken her the long way round.*

Jeanne's fingers curled into her palms. She felt an emptiness in the pit of her stomach as she continued to listen to Brown Cloud and to smile politely at the wife of Slanting Eyes. She nodded and agreed vaguely to Summer Night's suggestion that she and Black Eagle join them for the evening meal. She even smiled into Brown Cloud's anxious eyes.

When they had gone, she paced back and forth. Blood washed up to stain her face. It seemed to throb across her cheeks in waves. Bitterness rose in her throat like a green tide, and she nearly choked on it. *He had deliberately exposed her to exhaustion, to danger.* She felt herself sway, her leg muscles threatening to give out.

Loud, angry voices pounded through her head. *No, Jeanne. He was merely making every effort to develop both the stamina and the technique you need to become a warrior. Yes, Jeanne. But remember that dreadful swamp, the insects that stung like a thousand whiplashes, the leg ache, the bone-deep exhaustion, the sharp, sickening sensation of certain death in the quicksand.*

The coals of the fire had retreated behind white ashes when Black Eagle joined her in the lodge. Without a word, he stirred the embers and added a log. The anger, which had been building up in her like thunderclouds massing before the storm, broke.

"You went to a great deal of trouble to bring me here. May I ask why?" She eyed him balefully, aware of the sulky tone of her own voice, like a spoiled, thwarted child about to throw a tantrum. The sound irritated her.

The paralysis of surprise was very brief. His black eyes glittered, a midnight void. His voice grated with vexation. "You are wasting your substance and your time in trying to pick a fight with me, Turtle."

Ashes, sparks, and smoke erupted skyward as flames started attacking the dry wood. They seemed to add fuel to Jeanne's blind fury.

"You inflict pain and punishment upon me at a whim, and do not even try to excuse yourself?"

Black Eagle shrugged. "You have arrived intact. Do not complain, else I become impatient with your snapping ways."

Jeanne ground her teeth to prevent the irrational words that welled up within her, but they could not be stopped. "Did you take me through the swamp to be bitten raw, itchy, red as a spotted deer, so that you would have an excuse to lie with Brown Cloud? Is she to be your second wife?"

His look was suddenly cold. "Your words are beneath contempt." The subject was obviously closed, for he picked up his war bag, sat, and began to paint his face.

Jeanne stood stunned, felt her face grow hot with mortification. Tears pricked her eyes. Angrily she blinked them back. The *cochon!* She hated him. She only hoped that one day she could even the score with him.

Too late she remembered Papa's oft-repeated words of warning: *Do not ever wish for things in anger, because you just might get what you asked for!*

Black Eagle was saying something to her, something about taking care, about Bird Hawk, a bad man, a mischief-maker, but she did not even hear him. She could only hear the voice in her head cursing the tongue that always wagged before thought caught up with it.

Silence fell around them. Darkness settled in the lodge like a heavy cloak. Seething, Jeanne knelt on the sitting mat. Began combing the snarls out of the tangled web of her hair, watching it intently as it sprang away with its own ebullient life when she let it go, as if that were an interesting and absorbing occupation.

The moon was edging a glowing silvery fingernail over the top of a far hill when a polite cough sounded outside the lodge. Black Eagle called out an invitation, and an aged man stepped inside. His scalp lock was entwined with iridescent turkey feathers that fluttered with each motion of his head. Following etiquette, he came around the right side of the fire pit and took a seat near Jeanne. His many bracelets of shell and polished stone and seeds jangled impressively.

"There will be feasting tonight at the Lodge of the Porcupine, and storytelling. Juggler asks that the visitors of Slanting Eyes come and join him in pipe-smoking and stories."

"Black Eagle and Little Turtle will come," Black Eagle said. "We are grateful for Juggler's invitation."

The old man seemed pleased, and passed a few more minutes with Black Eagle in polite conversation, then left. The tension remained unbroken when, in angry silence, they strode to the lodge of Slanting Eyes.

The meal was delicious—a fish soup as thick as porridge, followed by roasted turkey, which had been first smoked in order to preserve it. Stuffed with rice meal and small onions, it was served with squaw cabbage and a concoction of boiled cranberries sweetened with maple syrup.

In the shadows, Jeanne could see the proud angles of Black Eagle's profile, and the way his strongly muscled chest rose and fell with his breathing. She could feel his eyes on her in the flickering firelight, felt their serious intensity—a faint, cool challenge. *He is afraid I will embarrass him. As I did by chattering like a chipmunk the night Big Rain was born.* She simply stared at him, a long, hostile look.

After the meal, the party trooped to the lodge of Juggler. Jeanne found herself sitting opposite Bird Hawk, a huge, bearlike man with a thick chest and broad shoulders, the five feathers of his high rank protruding from his scalp lock.

There was, perhaps, a hint of the dog fox in his face, a quickness, a shrewdness, an instinct for survival that spoke of storms weathered and chances taken. Something about his faint smile, the gleam of his yellowed teeth, the tone of his voice, made Jeanne feel uncomfortable.

She dared a quick glance in Black Eagle's direction. He was leaning over to talk to Brown Cloud, looking into her glowing face. Pain raged through her body, barbed and bitter. With effort, she returned to the conversation.

"Tell us, Black Eagle, how do you come to be sitting in the Lodge of the Porcupine Clan with a pale daughter of the moon?" Juggler asked, handing Black Eagle a long red pipe.

Black Eagle ran a finger over the smooth mouth end, took a puff, exhaled and waited interminable moments. "It is a long story that only the spirit knows," he began. Those present nodded. It was what they wanted to hear. A lengthy story. For a moment, he closed his eyes, and then he began, slowly, hesitantly, to tell of his boyhood revelation.

Fascinated, Jeanne listened as he recounted his vision, his secret dream. He was a good storyteller, with a flair for drawing out suspense.

"Stands Fast and Little Bear struggled with the Algonquin. On the Other Side, Thunderclap and I went toward the canoe, thinking we would take the woman captive. Then we heard the roar of her firestick...."

"What happened then?" Slanting Eyes asked, shaking ashes from the straight shankbone pipe into a neat little pile.

"Little Turtle will have to tell you the rest. That is her story."

All eyes turned toward her. There was something hypnotic about their fixed regard. It took an effort to look away from her silent audience. She looked down at the rush mats. Across to Black Eagle. She saw nothing. No truth. No illusion. Only a mouth set in implacable lines, a stiff jaw, opaque eyes. Jeanne tried to speak, fumbling for words, but her tongue felt too heavy, too thick. In the little pictures in her mind, she could see her father, cradled in her arms, the ominous silence around her, the eagle riding the wind, watching…waiting…abruptly she recovered the use of her tongue.

"My people lived a long way from here, far, far beyond the rising sun, even beyond the source of the Great Lakes that empty into the Great Waters. We lived near a river, too, as you do, but our river flows into the Great Waters from the other side…."

She held the group enthralled as she recounted her adventures. There were nods, murmurs of approval and words of encouragement, often shouts of excitement.

"They were pressing close, so I swung the weapon, and one warrior fell—"

"Ha!" a voice said derisively. It was Bird Hawk. He stared at her openly, frankly, almost rudely. "Are you trying to tell me a little thing like you killed a warrior of the People? I do not believe it."

There was a strained silence. Then Black Eagle spoke. "You do not believe it?" He sounded angry. "Little Turtle does not lie." He pulled his deerskin shirt to one side and exposed the shoulder disfigured with the ridged purple scar. "Black Eagle does not lie. I almost followed my brother to the river of light. Little Turtle is the equal to any task set for a warrior."

No one moved. It was as though Black Eagle had given the man a weapon to use against him. Bird Hawk raised his hand, curved like talons, against the flickering firelight. His eyes flickered over Jeanne's face.

"In the Porcupine Clan, the women tend the fires of the lodge," Bird Hawk said. "They do not fight at the side of the warriors. They do not bring shame to their husbands by acting the man."

As ice cannot stop the river in the spring, Jeanne could not stop her words. "I am the mate of Black Eagle. I bring him no shame."

"Women are not warriors. A spear is not a sewing needle."

"But the People need both." She raised her chin defiantly. *Be still. Be silent.* Black Eagle's words rang in her ears. She ignored them, just as she ignored his sharp indrawn breath. She heard herself counter. "It makes sense that the more skilled a man or woman is, and the more watchful, the less danger and the more food there is to all. Women are equal to men!"

Bird Hawk glanced uneasily at the others. Silence followed. Then a mutter rose and ran round the lodge. Emboldened, he turned back to her, a wicked smirk on his face.

"Then I, Bird Hawk, challenge the warrior woman, Little Turtle, to hand-to-hand combat."

Chapter Fourteen

The wind was keen and sharp. Far through the woods behind her the wind whistled and hummed among swaying tops of giant fir and cedar. Young sugar pines, as light and feathery as squirrel tails, were bowing almost to the ground, while the old patriarchs, whose massive boles had been tried by a hundred storms, waved solemnly above them, their long, arching branches streaming, every needle thrilling and ringing, shedding keen lances of light, like a diamond.

There was a heady freshness in that rollicking wind, an odor resinous and pungent, mingled with that elusive smell of green growth along the shore. On the broad front exposed to the river, the women were winnowing grain harvested from the grassy marshes below. Taking advantage of the gusty air, the women tossed up the grain from wide, shallow baskets, letting the wind carry away the chaff before catching the heavier seeds.

Jeanne swallowed. Soon the woman would join the men and watch her foolish body be battered to pulp by Bird Hawk. Her heart slammed against her breastbone, while the rest of her body froze. Why had she been so imprudent? Why?

Why had she brought so much trouble to her husband when she would only have given him happiness? There had been no dark or disloyal thoughts against Black Eagle in her mind when she accepted Bird Hawk's challenge. Only sheer, ungovernable fury.

She had drawn back, horrified at Bird Hawk's words, at the eyes filled with hunger and hate that leered down at her cruelly. As though he wanted to feel her struggling against him or wanted to revenge himself against Black Eagle for some long-standing grudge. Why had she not listened to Black Eagle, heeded his words of warning?

A tremor of fear had run through her, yet her pride had not allowed her to show it. *La malédiction de la famille de la Rocque.* She had looked around at the shocked faces gaping at her and felt herself shaking, her stomach roiling.

With a small gasp, once she had recovered from her initial shock, she had felt her lips curl in a feral snarl, had leapt to her feet and crossed her arms angrily. She had heard the voice, heavy, resonant, insolent, too mocking a voice, too loud and too barbed a voice, to be hers. But those two short, merciless words had in truth been her own. They echoed now in her head.

"I accept!"

And Black Eagle! She could see his face as it had been last night. Sallow, angry. Not pleasant, or friendly or forgiving at all, his mouth a tight, grim line. When she had offered a tentative apology, he had said, flatly, "The challenge has been met. It is done."

But he had sat late, polishing the blade of his knife with his rubbing stone. Only when he touched the tip with his finger and drew back in pain had he laid it with her effects.

His own knife! One of his most prized possessions, made of a smooth black substance, hard as stone, but not stone. And when he dropped his breechclout and climbed into bed, he had held her and whispered muffled, intimate things to her, and then joined his body to hers, until there was room for nothing else in her mind.

Now, she remembered, she had not even told him that she loved him, loved him to distraction. *Mon Dieu!* He was her saviour, her protector, her teacher, her friend, as well as her lover and husband. She turned toward him. He was standing so solemnly at the edge of the circle outlined in white.

Too late. Slanting Eyes was already reminding the combatants of the rules.

"You will meet in the center of the circle. If you are thrown or pushed outside the circle by your opponent, you are disqualified."

Jeanne faced Bird Hawk, suddenly terrified, paralyzed by her opponent's terrible, jeering grin. It was natural, she knew, to be afraid. But she resented it. She might lack physical strength, but she did not lack courage. Her body was lithe and well muscled, her reflexes were sharp, her mind was alert, but up to this moment she had never faced anything as lethal as this seasoned warrior. She could feel hostility, his rancor.

Her eyes glared with fright, the strength slipping from her body as she fearfully studied the huge mountain of muscle that was Bird Hawk. His arms were as thick as the branches of an oak, and nearly as long. Massive shoulders, dark and weather-creased, a broad, solid chest, heavy thighs with muscles that rippled and danced with each movement. His whole body spoke of strength and power. A colossus of a man, compared to her own slight frame. She circled him warily as his hands went up.

The giant, Goliath, whom no man dared to meet, had been defeated, shamed, by a boy with a sling. That boy had feared not. But she was not a boy! No, but remember Black Eagle's training. Be strong. Show no fear.

She cast one frantic look at her husband. His face betrayed no emotion. Only his eyes, bleak, fathomless, turned on her, spoke a silent message.

Know your enemy. Cunning will overcome strength and muscle.

With a whoop, Slanting Eyes let his hand fall, the signal to begin. The deadly quiet surrounding her slackened her fear. It vanished totally when a large hand seized her by the braids. Instinctively she brought up her knee, catching Bird Hawk in the groin. His eyes rolled in anguish, and he released his grip, then grunted, groping for her wrathfully as she whirled away from him.

Free now, she twisted her body and drove the heel of her palm as hard as she could into his face. His head snapped back, blood running from his nose. He drew back his arm to hit her. Swung. But Jeanne was not there. She twisted, diving sideways, avoiding the blow.

Bird Hawk's eyes were bulging with fury. His thin lips were drawn back into a snarl that turned his face from human to demonic. A harbinger of death. He charged her, head down. His right hand came up, with the thumb extended. Jeanne dodged beneath its thrust. Before he could brace for the next gouge, she smashed her foot into his belly with enough force to send him reeling. He dropped his arm as promptly as though a rattlesnake had nested in his breechclout.

Look for a weakness. She danced away. She had to keep out of his grasp. If he should get his hands on her, he would separate her from her spirit as neatly as one squeezed a hogpeanut between the fingers.

Bird Hawk took a step forward, the great sinews of his arm tensing as he curled his fist. He sprinted forward like a bounding animal. With a bloodcurdling yell, he leapt toward Jeanne. A split second later, she dropped to the ground. Bird Hawk tumbled right over her body and continued to roll to the very edge of the circle. Rapidly he righted himself and grabbed for her ankle. Blinked like a molting owl. She was not there.

It was soon evident that Jeanne possessed the quickness, while Bird Hawk had the greater strength. He began to grunt, but Jeanne never made a sound as she circled warily, struck and ducked, sidestepped another great blow. Once again her foot flew so quickly that Bird Hawk could not dodge, and there was a grunt as her foot sank solidly into his belly.

A buffet to the head sent Jeanne off balance. Red fire exploded behind her eyes. A hot multiple stabbing pain, searing, biting her jaw. Her vision erupted into a galaxy of shooting stars and dancing sparks, which twirled, rotated, spun into a vortex of concentric circles, whirling there from the dark epicenter of her head. The world rolled, receding into an onrushing darkness.

Jeanne desperately fought to keep from falling into that bottomless void of blackness. Her sight was blurred, blinded by sweat, her ears were deafened by roaring blood, her lungs labored. She could taste her blood, bittersweet, in her mouth, but she paid no heed. *Be strong.*

Bird Hawk tried to follow his momentary advantage with a kick, but Jeanne recovered, shifted her body, caught his foot in both hands and lifted, sending Bird Hawk toppling onto his back with a crash. In one smooth roll, he regained his feet.

Think. Know your enemy. Without conscious thought, Jeanne moved, turned like an otter, stooped down and scooped up a handful of dirt and pebbles. She knew it was her one and only chance. Hurling the handful of dirt at Bird Hawk's face, she kicked him once more, driving her foot straight up between his legs.

This time her foot delivered the coup de grace, and connected in the heavy place between his thighs. He leapt back in clumsy panic with a grotesque jerk of the legs, like a jester dancing, to shield his manhood. He tripped himself and fell crashing, sprawled on the ground outside the circle, limbs thrown wide, stunned, making no effort to rise.

Shaking and gasping, Jeanne stood there. There was movement. Voices raised in shock, released from their tension in thunderous shouts of mirth. The roaring in her ears was only an echo of the roar of laughter and ribald joking that would sweep across the rivers, lakes and woodland forests, as the tale was told of how Little Turtle had solved the dilemma of getting past Bird Hawk's defenses.

That a senior warrior would challenge a woman, little more than a child and smaller than a half-fledged youth, was outrageous. That the challenge had been accepted was surprising. That he had been humbled, brought to his knees, humiliated, was disgraceful. Watching the mortified warrior stagger self-consciously through the surrounding group, Jeanne knew she had made an enemy, a dangerous enemy.

Bit by bit the circle began to break up as she moved toward Black Eagle, forcing herself to walk calmly, proudly, her head held high, in keeping with the People's customs, although she wanted more than anything to run to his waiting arms.

She came to him. Stood there, very close to him, but not touching, not even trying to, though she had a foolish wish to touch him. She could not speak. His look, his stillness, unnerved her. They stood, mute, gazing at each other. She licked bone-dry lips, smiled nervously up at him, made a small movement with her hand, and tore her voice from its captivity.

"That was an unexpected victory!" Her voice surprised her, it sounded so loud and firm. Both Slanting Eyes and Juggler looked expectantly at Black Eagle. He did not move, just stood there, rigid as stone, looking at her, at the tiny trickle of blood at the corner of her mouth, at the purpled flesh along one side of her jaw.

A very long silence passed. Everyone crowded round, waiting for him to speak. It was like a dream. The silence, the anticipation, the endless waiting. He exhaled sharply.

"I do not forgive you easily, Turtle, for what you have put me through!"

In his face she caught a suppressed passion, controlled as always, but betrayed by the deep, luminous gleam behind his eyes, the tension of his mouth. Jeanne's faint smile admitted her own emotional turmoil. The little knob in his throat moved up and down. She stared at him, not knowing if she should speak, or what to say if she did. He was breathing hard, as if he had been the one fighting.

He was trembling inside himself. With fear. For her. He wanted to put his arms around her, hold her, tight and close, know that she was whole.

Jeanne looked at him with understanding, her voice soft. "It was nothing. You have trained me well." Her eyes still on him, she tipped her head sideways, and wrinkled her nose. "Did I do well?"

Black Eagle was looking at her in a new way, a way that was hard to define. Shaking his head slowly from side to side, as if he could not believe what he saw. His eyes clouded with the satisfied shadows that fill a father's eyes when his son grows straight and tall as a lodgepole pine, and begins to show muscles in his legs, like the deer, or in his arms, like the sleek ripples under a cougar's skin.

Turning to Slanting Eyes, he said, with what sounded strangely like pride, "Does not Little Turtle awe you, Slanting Eyes? She stands there, aching all over, muscles jerking from fatigue, and says it is nothing! It is nothing that she has proved Bird Hawk is all hot wind! That he has nothing in his breechclout! And that he sits down to urinate!"

It was enough. Jeanne's head came back. Her laughter floated upward, silvery and sure. The joy of release. The sky gave it back, the mountains. Then Black Eagle started laughing, and Slanting Eyes. And Juggler. He did not want to laugh, but he could not help it. His old, lined, seamed, gnarled face fought his laughter, but the laughter won. All the compound was loud with their laughter.

The soft, steady thrum of a muffled drum was picked up by another rhythmic beat, then another, and another, until the air, brisk and biting, was filled with a steady throbbing cadence. The sunlight had long since disappeared, and now the shadows were darkening like a bruise. In the center of the compound, a huge fire flickered and danced in the sable twilight, casting a soft yellow glow over the merrymakers, creating an intimate, exciting atmosphere.

Food in vast quantities was spread out on endless mats in front of the Lodge of the Porcupine. Games and dancing had been under way for some time, with people drifting from one form of entertainment to another.

Some of the older people gathered in small groups, idly watching the dancers as they laughed and talked, while the younger ones clapped in rhythm and, with their feet, kept time to the pulsating beat. There were delighted smiles on the dusky faces, white teeth flashing and dark eyes sparkling with satisfaction as Jeanne wandered through the camp.

Pausing to speak with Summer Night and Brown Cloud, she was filled with a warm feeling of happiness as she watched the dancers, her feet moving in rhythm and her slim hips swaying in answer to the pulse-quickening sound.

A circle of warriors with painted limbs and torsos, clad only in doeskin breechclouts, had begun to rotate in a slow, almost spiritual, rhythm, pausing, at wide-spaced intervals, to utter a low, rumbling shout that seemed to issue from their toes.

The turtle does not run away when one comes upon her anywhere.

Suddenly, a feeling of warm affection for Brown Cloud—for all the People—flooded through her. They were singing her praises! Heads nodding in unison. Honoring her victory! She belonged here as surely as if she had been born of them. They were her people!

Black Eagle was among the dancers. His body gleamed rich and dark in the firelight. His scalp lock was adorned with a single feather of the black eagle, and his face and torso were smeared with paint. His eyes flickered over her face. She could almost feel his gaze.

With good-natured enthusiasm, Brown Cloud pushed her toward the circle of dancers. "Last time you danced, Black Eagle asked me to trip you so that he could grab your basket." She gurgled gleefully at Jeanne's jerk of surprise. "This time you dance, and you still need some help. Go to him of your own accord!"

Jeanne opened her mouth to protest, but shut it again. Looked down, as if to examine her soft leather moccasins, ornamented with colored seeds and porcupine quills. A tendril of suspicion curled in her mind. Brown Cloud laughed merrily, the tufts of red woodpecker feathers stuck in the mink strings that tied her hair fluttering like tiny birds about to take flight.

Her mind still busy, Jeanne ran the tip of her tongue along the arch of her upper lip. The joke was on her. It always had been! Something dissolved inside her. Her eyes slid upward. She took a backward step, met Black Eagle's eyes steadily, lifted her chin and straightened her back, her eyes crystalline, light-filled. She heard the hiss of indrawn breath. His? Hers? Jeanne smiled. A wide, white smile. Her heart sang.

Black Eagle had not been cavorting with the lovely young maidens. Rather, he had connived with Brown Cloud so that he would catch her basket in the Beggar's Dance. How could she be angry at his deception? He had truly wanted her for his wife! Further pressure at the small of her back sent her two steps forward. They stood less than a foot apart, still not touching.

She smiled again, broadly. There was a look on his face that caused a shiver of pleasure to course through her. Holding his eyes for a moment, she winked audaciously.

Mutely, as though incapable of speech, Black Eagle held out his hand, clasped hers and drew her into the dance. He faced her, his gaze bright, unwavering, and began to stamp his feet.

Never taking her eyes from his, Jeanne did the same. She felt the hypnotic pull of his eyes and, trapped by the enchantment of the night and the lure of the drums, was deaf to all but the music, and the stamp of moccasined feet on the earth.

The pattern of the dance was in full swing now, though the performers still moved slowly, chanting in the same nasal monotone. The step itself was a peculiar one. Between the drumbeats, each foot stamped out a kind of alternate counter-rhythm. Bit by bit, the shouted monotone rose in volume as the dancers cupped their left hands to the lips.

"When you shoot, your arrows will glance off my shell,
And you will get hit by your own shots.
I am the chosen one!
The chosen one am I!"

Against the clear night sky, the chant seemed older than man. Dancers and onlookers had long since joined in the chorus,

"A warrior hero
Am I!

A warrior hero
Am I!''

Even the children's treble voices were mixed in the chant.
Rising on the shout of *Am I!* they made a shrill *obbligato* to
the compulsion of the drums, the thud of feet that seemed
to shake the leaves on the trees, the fires that surged and
wavered in tune with the passionate, wild music.

Black Eagle pranced, leapt in the air and pirouetted.
Swept away by the rhythmic beat of the drums, Jeanne followed his lead, her willowy figure swaying seductively in
time to the cadence. The tempo was like fire in her veins,
and, as the momentum increased, she swirled and danced in
compulsive, uninhibited, sensuous movement. Her chestnut hair, a warm bright glow in the firelight, rippled with a
life of its own as she threw back her head, raised slim, sun-
browned arms high, pivoted and stamped.

From the moment she caught his eye, Jeanne saw no one
but Black Eagle. The flames leaping from the fire pit, the
rumbling background beat of the drums, were ignored.
There was only Black Eagle and herself, and the current
which ran between them as strong as a river. Sometimes they
danced far apart, then moved closer, clapping their hands
together, their faces and bodies not quite touching.

The soft fawnskin tunic Jeanne wore molded itself to her
pliant form from breast to hip, then spilled out in long embroidered fringes. She bobbed and stooped, twirled and
bounced. As she danced, the colorful strips spun out and
swayed with her almost frenzied movements, giving tantalizing glimpses of pale, slender legs.

As the drums beat more rapidly, Black Eagle and Jeanne,
bodies gyrating, flew back and forth across the open area,
their legs moving in unison, their bodies swaying. Around
and around she danced, faster and faster—a creature possessed—until faces were a blur and blended into one an-

other like falling leaves in autumn. Faster and faster, until
she could hear her heart roaring in her ears like the beating
wings of an eagle. She lost awareness of time, and of the
laughing, thigh-clapping crowd.

All the dancers were shining with sweat now, the central
fire pit making writhing, sinuous live mahogany of their
limbs. Beat by beat, the tempo increased. One by one the
warriors reeled from the ring, exhausted by the pace the
leaders had set. In the end, the ever-narrowing circle seemed
to graze the fire. Finally only Jeanne and Black Eagle remained.

For an instant they faced each other across the hot coals,
capering like a pair of partridges courting hysterically. Then,
as the entire assembly lifted its voice in a delirious shout,
they leapt as one from the circle of flames. The drummers
halted. The noise of the crowd, an intolerable hum, faded
and was gone as, exhausted, Jeanne sought the visitors'
lodge.

Breathless, she slumped against the wigwam wall and
closed her eyes. Her chest felt oddly hollow, a vast, empty
cavern. She breathed deeply, trying to fill the space with air.
The strength in her legs seemed to have vanished like summer rain, and her vision was washed with red mist. Her
loosened hair flowed all about her.

There was sweat on her face, tiny droplets, gathering,
beading, to fall into her eyes, to sting the livid bruise on her
jaw. She felt disheveled, weary, light-headed, yet exultant,
exuberant.

"That was a day and a half!" Was that thread of sound
her voice?

Strong fingers gripped her upper arms. "The way you
incite the manito, you need an extra portion in each day!"
The deep rumbling of Black Eagle's voice was a windfall
delight.

Jeanne's eyes flew open. The world ceased its endless spinning to come to a standstill. Their faces were only a few inches apart. She gave him a slow, warm, triumphant smile, her heart full.

The black eyes suddenly blazed. He gave her a little shake, and hesitated, as if searching for words. "Do not bait me with the sunshine of your smile. To goad Bird Hawk was not a lark for untried youths, or women, even if they are filled to bursting with heavy instruction and tedious practice."

Jeanne watched the firelight playing on his face, and something in his expression gave her pause. She bit her lip, giving him a sidelong look. "I am sorry I upset you. Forgive me."

With a small, muffled groan, he slid his hands up her shoulders, drew her to him and pressed her close. She felt his heart pounding in counterpoint to her own, and the involuntary quivering of his muscles as his manhood thrust hard against her. A shudder of anticipation rippled over her body. She could feel the desire for him building inside her. Her blood, hot and sweet, sang in her belly, hummed in her ears.

"What matters now is that you are not tempted again to pit yourself against a warrior." His whisper was hoarse, full of anxious doubt. "Do not even consider it!"

Jeanne shook her head, a smile forming on her lips that had no reason to be there. She swayed against him, wanting to be closer to his masculine strength, certain she could never be close enough to satisfy the longing he roused in her.

Shadows pooled in the hollow of his throat like dark water, and she could not think past wanting to dip her tongue in it and drink. She really heard nothing but the sound of his voice, imagining the touch of his lips against hers, the taste of his flesh. Then, realizing how far her thoughts had wandered, she tried to pay attention to what he was saying.

"I have this recurring vision that you will challenge all comers just to thwart me, demand wrestling matches—or, worse, that you will take pride in the hard and bulging muscles all this will obtain you." There was mock resignation in his tone, as though he were in contempt of his fears, and could dismiss his uneasiness with ridicule.

Jeanne giggled. Understood his apprehension. Kissed his neck, light as the wings of a butterfly. Became sober, wistful, bereft when he released her. Until she heard his words.

"Turtle, I do not know why you did this, but it is over now. Not to embarrass you, or distract you, I said nothing before. I say it now. It is not the custom for women to fight as a warrior. It is not to happen again."

"Who is to say what will or will not happen? You are foolish in your fears." Her face felt stiff. Hurt and anger gave her voice a sharp edge. "Today I proved my substance as a warrior. Let us not have differences here at the Wolf River."

Black Eagle's mouth thinned, lengthened, and Jeanne was hesitant to say more. The silence was so deep, it was as though she could taste it. They stared at each other as if they could do nothing else. The somber shadows of his eyes seemed part of the night's blackness.

Jeanne found herself unable to look away, yet she did not know what else to say. Black Eagle neither stood back nor stepped aside.

"It does not make me happy, to cause you pain," she said finally. "But you must understand my wish to be a warrior." Jeanne's heart took on the weight of a stone as she noticed the slight flaring of his nostrils, the intensity of his brooding stare. She let him see through her eyes what her spirit contained.

Black Eagle swiveled his head away from her, and the tendons in his neck swelled. "When you look at me that way, I glimpse a future so filled with torment, today is pale by comparison." He sounded frustrated, angry. "Surely what I ask is not too much?"

"Why do you simply *ask?*" Jeanne's temper flared for a moment, and her voice rose, tightened. "Why not order this? Force me to your will?"

Black Eagle narrowed his eyes, but his voice was low and calm when he finally spoke. "Force is not always the fastest or the best way, Turtle. Observe the gentleness of the wind, and yet its ceaseless blowing changes the way a tree grows. Sometimes, Turtle, a feather's touch may bring better results than the beating of a fist."

Jeanne shook her head, unconvinced. She reached for the amulet hanging around her neck. "The eagle flies high. It sees many things, but only from a far distance. It sees this one as rash, impetuous, ready to preen its feathers, when it knows the turtle is slow, ponderous. This confuses the eagle. That one never gives its back to an enemy. But the turtle has many sides, an inner sight no one knows. The spirit of the turtle is to endure, to lead others to safety."

Black Eagle considered this carefully. He ran a finger over her bruised cheek, and she winced. "Be careful the manito do not become weary of your provocation and retaliate by thinking that if you act like a man, they will treat you as a man." He put his hands on her shoulders, stared at her for a long moment. When he spoke, his voice was very soft, and his smile was menacing in its gentleness. "I want a son, and only a woman can give me a child. I do not wish my seed to be wasted. A warrior wife offers nothing I desire."

Jeanne digested this idea in silence. Touched her stomach—flat, lifeless, empty. If she did not give Black Eagle a son, he would soon tire of her or find another to replace her. She felt the trap close in around her.

"To be made barren would be a terrible revenge," she said.

Black Eagle continued to look at her with that strange expression. Her sight blurred, her head seemed to be spinning around. Why did it seem that she was back on the rocks by the waterfall, sliding, sliding, over the edge? Though the lodge was warm from the banked fire in the central hearth, for some reason she felt cold.

"Turtle, are you all right? *Turtle!*" There was a note of unease in his voice, and he sounded farther away. His shadow loomed over her, wavered; it was all around her, blinding and choking.

Without warning, flowing out from deep within her, came an unbidden explosion. Suddenly there were stars dancing in a field of midnight. Stars fluttering high above a place she loved more than she could ever say. Slowly, one detached itself from the rest.

Jeanne could see it clearly as it took the form of a young man, a warrior. Black Eagle, yet not Black Eagle. In a strange cap and deep blue costume, with shining fastenings, gleaming wings on his shoulder decorations. Another time, another place?

"You are exhausted. You need to rest." The voice echoed in the stillness.

She looked up at the face of the warrior, but his features were hidden in the shadows beyond the realm of the fire pit. Jeanne composed herself and tried to open her mind to receive whatever thoughts came to guide her. In perfect stillness, the silence spread like warm water, dissolving the last traces of disharmony within.

Although he did not speak, Jeanne could hear the young man's words. *Individual lives are like the individual leaves of a tree. No tree has leaves so foolish as to fight among themselves. Hold steadfast to this truth, though the tree will seem to die. Even when roaring ships of magic stone fly with people in them across the skies, that ember will hold still its tiny glow. Know this, a great fire can be ignited from a single, glowing ember!*

Her head hurt. Every part of her hurt. Jeanne opened her eyes, squinted and, with painful effort, rolled over. She raised up on one elbow. Through the open flap, she could see the moon rising in the east. It looked so close she could almost touch it. The night was star-blazed, the wind cool and pine-scented as it whispered through the trees. A large pot steamed over the fire pit, and enticing odors blended with the drifting fragrance of basswood smoke. In the background could be heard the faint throbbing of a drum. The sound was quiet yet intense, even though the drummer did not increase his volume.

"You are awake! You have slept the sun around." Black Eagle's smile was tender, his hand on her shoulder warm. Kissing her cheek gently, he pressed her shoulders back to the headrest. "Rest, Turtle, and stop worrying about the future. It will look after itself."

With a sinking heart, Jeanne shivered involuntarily, and lifted her chin. The manito had spoken, but did she have the courage to obey them? With nervous, desperate urgency, she made her decision.

"It is wise to be alert, to see danger before it is upon you," Jeanne said carefully. "It will be as Black Eagle says. The manito will not be confused by a man in woman's dress. Little Turtle will return to the duties of a woman."

Chapter Fifteen

As Jeanne toiled in the cornfield, enjoying the freedom of sky and wind, she was engulfed in a flood of recollections. The whole sweep of sky, the limpid, dancing wash of sun, were filled with them. Sweet things. The curious little intimate details that a woman remembers.

A man's warm breath stirring her hair. The feel of hands, callused yet soft, brushing as gentle as a mother's touch against breast, shoulder, thigh. The feel of skin—silken, solid heat. Her finger tracing the ridge of bone and muscle that ran from shoulder to groin, learning each of them like a map, a living thing. The cool, sweet taste of his mouth, the wholesome musky scent of his flesh filling her nostrils, the ruff of black hair, a thousand little gestures, inflections that belonged only to Black Eagle. The passion that burned endlessly within him, the insatiable, eternal, demanding fury of his love.

The joy, the enchantment, of being his woman. Like smoke in the wind, her ambition to be a warrior disappeared when he touched her. Only to return when she was alone. Like now. Although she knew great happiness lay in her future, yet she felt uneasy and strangely fearful. The manito had not yet granted her desire for a child. What could be wrong?

She had rapidly recovered from the fatigue and weariness that had assailed her. Peace reestablished with Black Eagle, she had genuinely tried to conform. When the women took their digging sticks, picking, gathering, digging, she went with them. Picked irises and ferns and went back to the lodge with a full basket. With the other women, she dug young bulbs, gathered clover and other greens.

A full moon had passed. The days grew shorter. Already there was a chill in the air. Slowly the bright green foliage of the larch dulled. Poppies and lupines faded. Seedpods formed where blossoms had been. The papery winged seeds of the pinecones were being scattered by the wind. Still they had lingered at the Wolf River camp. Watchful Fox was courting one of the local maidens, Brown Cloud wooing one of the warriors.

Even during the last deer hunt before their return home, Jeanne had dutifully remained with the women, cutting up meat and scraping skins, when she longed to be with the hunters. So hard had she worked to prove herself, that when the women took up their packs, hers was so heavy she could not lift it off the ground. Summer Night had to help her get under it. Tumpline cutting into her forehead, she had followed the women, thankful that the way back to the camp was mostly downhill.

Even so, she soon dropped far behind the others, until she was out of sight and even out of earshot. She rested against the granite face of a flat-topped boulder, easing the pack until it gripped the rock in its embrace, like a papoose on its cradleboard. Behind a cloud, the sun lay hidden, making the clearing alive with shadows. Shadows that danced and twisted like spirit lovers in a mad embrace.

Although she had managed to brush away some of her uneasiness during the hunt, her dark forebodings were steadily growing stronger. She did not fear the whispering, rustling language of the trees, or the sudden shrill cries of the birds. It was the knowledge of something, someone, watching....

Jeanne shivered slightly at the memory. When had she realized she was not alone? Had it been when a silt-stained salmon broke the surface of a nearby pool, idly slapping the water as it flopped onto its belly? Or when a line of ducklings bobbed astern of their mother, leaving a shallow wake behind them? The awareness, the knowing, had crept upon her silently. For a long, long time, she had remained completely motionless, listening, sniffing the air, watching for the smallest movement of a leaf.

Until it became too quiet. No sound broke the silence. No rustle. No birdsong. Chilled to the marrow, she had turned to face Bird Hawk. She could see him now, in her mind's eye, standing where the clearing met the forest edge, a bow in his left hand, quiver and arrows slung over his right shoulder for instant access, tomahawk and knife at his waist.

She felt her cheeks flame as she saw that his eyes were looking, not into her own, but much lower. She looked quickly down and gasped. Her tunic had caught in the pack, exposing her legs right to the juncture of her body.

A tingle of fear, originating somewhere near the base of her spine, ran down her thighs to make her grow weak at the knees. Her heart beat irregularly and her mind struggled like a badger in a snare when she noticed the sudden bulge in his breechclout.

His small, closely set eyes had glinted with bottomless blackness. His voice had been mocking, vicious, as he whispered, "It will not be my pointed arrow that bites you, woman of Black Eagle, but the rounded spear of my manhood."

Her scornful reply echoed in her mind. "A swaggering braggart will receive only contempt from Little Turtle. This one has shown the People how strong are your threats. If necessary, she will do so again. The woman of Black Eagle sees no worth in the limp and flaccid lance of Bird Hawk! She has no taste for pliant men who have nothing behind their breechclout but the fat cheeks of a ground squirrel.''

They had stood glaring at one another. There had been no sound as she stared him down. His eyes had lost their heat, flickered. Confidence had surged in her, intoxicating and sharp. She had straightened, clasping Black Eagle's knife, warm and comforting in her hand, when Bird Hawk turned and melted into the trees. He had fled like a hare to his hole! Ignominiously, she, too, had fled, to the security of the women.

These thoughts evaporated, like the dew on the morning grasses, at the muted sound of a cry, a shriek, beyond the path. Jeanne stiffened, and listened carefully. Her ears filled with the sounds of the hills, the faint breeze rustling the corn, the meadowlarks trilling with the shrill tongues of happy girls, the incessant leg-rub and groan-buzz of insects.

A gray squirrel rippled up the trunk of an old silver birch and disappeared in a hole. A black-capped chickadee flitted from branch to branch. The call of a dog fox echoed around her, and she smiled at it, savoring the normality of the sound.

There is no danger, she assured herself. Nothing untoward. Nothing to rouse this steady commotion in her mind. Above the squash blossoms fluttered several butterflies, whose orange-and-brown wings reminded her of the patterns she was learning to weave into baskets.

The breeze that blew in from the west lifted her heavy red hair and fanned it out around her face, draping her eyes like a silken mantle. Impatiently she pushed it back. In the distance she could see the lazy gray curls that rose from the smokeholes of some lodges. She heard the faraway voices of small children playing, the sharp whack of their sticks clacking together like teeth, the thunk of wood against hide balls, and the yap of dogs. Reassured, she continued hoeing.

A cloud crossed the face of the sun. The buzzing of the insects on the sweet-scented air seemed intolerably loud, and the birds suddenly quiet. A shudder of foreboding chased its icy way across Jeanne's skin. Abstract images formed, then, as quickly, faded.

One impression danced across the edge of her consciousness, making her tremble with fear at the implications. Black Eagle. A girl. Her face hidden on his chest, clinging to him frantically, sobbing convulsively. As he lowered her, gently, to the ground, Jeanne saw the girl's face. It was a mask of tragedy, contorted with grief, the eyes red and bloodshot, the full, moist lips working, wild black hair blowing back from a wide forehead.

Jeanne stood, breathing heavily, her eyes closed, her muscles turned to water. She could feel the sweat running down her body in tiny, tickling streams, between her breasts, between her shoulder blades. She stood very still, barely breathing, until the shadow of the cloud receded.

The wind caught her loose hair and spread it in all directions, making the skin on her back crawl as if someone had tickled it with the tip of an eagle's feather. *There is no danger. Of course, it was the wind, not stealthy footsteps around—*

"I will not be afraid," she said firmly, aloud. "I will not be afraid."

As she continued to weed the vegetable patch, Jeanne did her best to bury the strange, troubling feelings that assailed her. But they would not be quashed. She checked instinctively when a shadow darkened a patch of sunlight at her feet. She looked up. An eagle soared above. Suddenly it folded its wings and dived straight for her, talons outstretched. She brought her arms up to shield her face as the eagle extended its wings and drenched her in shadow, blocking out the sun for a moment, before it wheeled away, as if it wanted her to follow.

Jeanne watched the bird's flight, over the field, beyond the trees, toward the encampment. She glanced uncertainly toward the field, then back again to the eagle's path. The sense of something wrong plagued her, and she lifted her head, alert. It was as if she heard someone calling. Drawn by an instinct she could neither comprehend nor evade, she dropped the hoe and hurried towards the path. She went up the steep, hardly visible track almost at a run, as swift and light-footed as a hare.

As she scrambled up the slope, her mind shed its confusion with every step. The wind slapped at her hair and brought a shiver to her cheeks. Smoke tasted sharp in her throat. Drums filled her head. She stumbled, straightened, started to move on. . . .

Faintly she heard a moan. She waited, and it came again, from the deep brush at the side of the path. A throaty moan, a ghastly gurgling noise that made Jeanne cringe. Hesitating, she drew her knife from her waistband and moved cautiously toward the sound.

She stopped in horror at what lay before her. Her cry was sharp and quickly bitten back. She felt as if a fist had been slammed into the center of her chest.

Bright Path was lying crumpled like a discarded deerskin in a massive puddle of blood, body twisted with pain and the agony of death. Her once-sweet face was almost unrecognizable, a flower bruised by vicious blows. She had been battered, beaten, her belly ripped open wide, split like a rabbit, by the sharp blade of a knife.

Jeanne dropped to her haunches and stared blindly at the tumbled heap of flesh. Tears stung her eyes. The air she gulped down burned her throat like red-hot ashes. For a moment the bright red spurts still gushing like flames from that great open wound drowned shape and shadow, even their own stream.

Hair, face and limbs all fused and became one. Then Jeanne found focus, and saw that Bright Path's spirit was almost free of her body, off for the sun's place in the west. Her face lifted, tilted, as though to some uncanny music none but she could hear. For a moment the heavy eyelids stirred.

"Was it a girl-child?"

With a hand that trembled, Jeanne picked up the tiny pale form, so soft and limp. Tears silently slid down her face. The little girl lay perfectly still, with a huge, twisted cord attached to the middle of her belly.

"Yes." Was that anguished croak her voice? Her throat felt as if it had been reamed out with red-hot fish hooks.

Lips quivering, Bright Path gave a half smile, sighed. Then her face was empty, an abandoned vessel, bare and barren. Her eyes frosted over with the glaze of death, her spirit fled.

For a moment, Jeanne was numb to sorrow. It was overwhelmed by an all-consuming black hatred, so great that it swept everything else before it. Who had done such a terrible thing?

With eyes that flamed, she looked at the blood-covered infant, with its clenched fists, its face with closed eyes. A drop of moisture fell like rain on its crumpled face. Her heart slammed itself against her ribs like an angry caged animal. Oh, Great Turtle, could you not, just this once, help the hopes and dreams of Bright Path to live?

More drops fell. Faster. Angrily Jeanne brushed the eyes, pressed the puny chest, then put her face to its face and breathed into its mouth. Again. And again. Dense air, thick and stifling, filled her lungs. Eyes slitted in concentration, her mouth pursed to a bow, she exhaled slowly, blew gently.

Suddenly the baby trembled and gasped, the sound very faint. It lived! Panic, a hot, violent taste, rose in Jeanne's chest. Her teeth were chattering with tension, grief and fear. The small face slowly wrinkled, and the baby began to cry, squalling in protest against the chill and harshness of its new environment. Jeanne held the baby close to her, feeling its small movements and listening to the sounds it made.

What to do? Where to get help? She knew so little about babies. Acutely aware of an odd resentment, a sudden fury at her own inexperience, she looked frantically toward the encampment. Faint, confused cries floated up from the direction of the settlement. A cold fear crept across her skin. *Bébé Jésus* help me! Where was her knife? Holding her breath, Jeanne brought the blade down, severing the now-limp cord.

Tucking the soft, warm, still-wet little body inside her tunic, Jeanne ran toward the camp. She could feel the baby there, tickling softly as she moved, its mewling sounds muffled by her shirt. It felt smooth and soft to her skin. Apprehension followed her like a dark thunderhead, spurring her onward.

Sounds of screaming, smells of burning, carried on the wind. *Many things burn. Canvas, rope, wood, cloth, straw. And flesh. Yes, flesh burned too... pungent and sickly...* The blood gushed and pounded in her ears as she ran, and her body raged with tumult. Her tears made a prism of all she saw, so that her surroundings became a multitude of colors that kept splintering and adopting new forms. The pounding inside her head blotted out the thud of her feet.

Jeanne could hear a voice in her head. It sounded like Black Eagle's. Find sanctuary! Go to the river! *Be secret! Be silent!*

Her resolve faltered momentarily, but then, without breaking her stride, she began to work her way back towards the river. She was breathless and her heart was pounding painfully by the time she reached the watercourse. In time to see three shadowy figures, their faces striped with vermilion, violent yellow and blue, wildly racing along the riverbank to their painted canoes.

Jeanne dropped down, cradling one arm protectively in front of her. *Do not cry, baby. Please do not make a sound.* Moving only one hand or foot at a time, she crawled slowly backward until she reached the protection of a fallen log. She lay there, straining to catch the slightest sound of movement. All she could hear was her own heartbeat. A deep, squeezing ache that seemed to push outward from the center of her chest. The baby had stopped making noises. Was it dead? Jeanne rolled over on one side, shoulders hunched and tight, biting her lip.

The river ran black and as smooth as glass between its banks. There was no wind here. She lay there, too frightened to move, watching through the thick waterfall of her hair. Where was Black Eagle? Singing Bird? A frog croaked nearby, hopped past, a handsome wood frog with a black eye stripe like a robber's mask. It brushed the grass, scattering fluffy clouds of white dandelion seeds across the soft air. The baby stirred, but was silent. Frightened by the movement, Jeanne's nails dug into her palms, drawing blood.

Everything seemed to be moving slowly, too slowly. The sun was dipping low in the west, but color still gilded the few places where its light still ventured, the ragged crown of the forest, the smooth, mottled bark of an elm, the angled corner of the path, framed in a crimson shaft. A blackish porcupine with white-tipped quills lay dozing in a motionless ball, making the most of a weak ray of sun. Inches from her nose, a beetle climbed a blade of grass.

Suddenly a figure loomed out of the trail, silhouette cloaked in shadow. Moccasins whispered against the earth. Jeanne huddled lower. She tried to keep herself very small, as small as the stump left by the gnawing beaver. Through the screen of her hair, she could see the warrior move. He was tall and stately, but difficult to see among the leafy shadows.

Eagle feathers tied below the chipped flint blade of his lance fluttered, twirled on thin, bloody sinew. In his right hand he swung a ball-headed hardwood club. In his waist belt was a tomahawk, across his broad shoulders a familiar quiver of otter skin, with a bow and arrows. It was Black Eagle! Her voice caught inside herself, came out as a croak.

"Black Eagle!"

The still, shadowy figure galvanized into action, spun round, poised, lance drawn back, raised, waiting. The dark eyes staring down at her were hard, unblinking, and for an instant Jeanne closed her own. She shuddered convulsively, but managed to keep her voice soft.

"It is only me, Little Turtle!"

"Turtle! What are you doing here?"

Black Eagle stepped into the dappled green and gold of the sunlit glade, naked except for breechclout and moccasins. His body gleamed with a sheen of sweat, and the sinews, each trained and obedient to its purpose, stood out on chest and limb. His eyes, red-rimmed, flashing with a deep emotion from cheekbones that stood out in sharp relief, were like the slashing of a knife. He breathed deeply.

"Are you all right?"

"Yes. I am, now."

There was something in his eyes that made her obscurely uneasy. An intensity. A severity. But this was not anger. Even in the shadows, she could see the suspicious glistening that matched the tears welling up in her own eyes. He, too, was shaking, his face tight-skinned. His countenance was not his own, but angles of dark skin stretched over the bones of his face. A muscle jumped high on one cheekbone. He looked shattered.

Jeanne faced him, her eyes blind, scalded. She swallowed, croaked, "Bright Path... What has happened?"

The barest flicker of a smile touched the masklike face. His black eyes lost their disquieting gaze. He took her hands in his, drew her closer, rubbing his chin against her hair.

"Assault."

The single word, spoken flatly and without inflection, fell like a stone into a silent pool. It seemed to echo, reverberating through Jeanne's mind. She buried her face in his shoulder, squeezing her eyes tightly shut against the sudden sting of tears. After her fear and cold loneliness, it was a miracle to feel his warm vitality, to be comforted by his solid strength. He could not be too close for her to feel safe enough.

A gurgling cough, a muted mewl of sound, then an angry bellow of surprising volume, answered the indignity of being squashed. Black Eagle leapt back as though scalded. He lifted a sinewy hand, pushed back the fawnskin tunic and stared at the wizened, tiny countenance, at the head covered by a bristling mop of jet-black hair. At that wisp of a brow that soared across the red, wrinkled face like crow's feathers. Saw that tiny mouth come open, heard the angry howl.

He drew his dark brows together, and his voice was gruff. "This is a complication we could well do without!"

Jeanne's eyes widened in apprehension as they met Black Eagle's. He pulled the edges of her shirt together, his lips slanting in a rueful smile.

"The little one could be the least of our problems," Black Eagle said. "Come, let us find out what awaits us."

Black smoke billowed. A hut was burning, its roof a single sheet of flame as molten wedges of bark collapsed into its blazing shell. The smell of roasting human flesh assailed their nostrils. Bodies, blackened and charred, lay across the compound in hideous confusion, merged with the blazing embers of wood.

Jeanne stood like a woman carved of stone, her lower lip between her teeth. Black Eagle dropped a hand to her shoulder. She shook it off, never glancing his way. Took a step forward, toward the carnage. Then she was running, not away from the horror, but toward it.

"Singing Bird!"

She could hear the voice screaming—her voice—edged and shrill. She could feel waves of heat from the flames, and was beginning to choke on the acrid smoke drifting over her.

"Singing Bird!"

Shielding her face against the heat, she plunged toward the group of singed, smoke-stained women now gathered with their babies and children in the compound. The fires lit their faces and burned bloodred in their eyes. Singing Bird was not there!

She saw the sprawled figure of an old man. A spear pinned him to the ground in front of his still-smoldering shelter. A gray-headed woman lay facedown, a hand outflung by her cheek, huddled in the odd angle of death. A sob caught in Jeanne's throat.

Icy with apprehension, hands shaking, she turned the body over with infinite care, afraid to look at what she might see. A sharply honed stone blade was plunged deep in the old one's chest. Her hand went to her mouth in shock, but it was not Singing Bird! Jeanne shuddered uncontrollably, throwing the body from her, drawing clenched fists to her mouth.

"Turtle," someone whispered softly.

Jeanne spun, disbelieving, and stared into the face of her adopted mother. Black Eagle was there, also, his strong young arm supporting the trembling old woman. When Singing Bird's dazed eyes met Jeanne's anxious ones, her face crumpled into a thousand crinkles. That smile spoke volumes, and in it Jeanne saw genuine love, and a warmth and relief that would not be denied.

"My prayers are answered! You are safe!" Jeanne shouted.

The sudden cessation of the nightmare banished reality. The figures before her blurred, became indistinct outlines. Jeanne knew she was sinking, sinking, into some dark, fathomless pit without an end. She tried to stop herself, gasping for breath, but it was too late.

When Jeanne came to her senses, she was propped against the side of a lodge, and the center of the compound seemed filled with people. In the center of the clearing stood Yellow Feather, arms folded, blinking back the thoughts crowding his mind. His face wore a look Jeanne had not seen since the death of On the Other Side, dangerous—malevolent. The puckered scar at his mouth showed livid against lips compressed with a blend of rage and concern.

"What happened?" Yellow Feather raised his long arm, pointed down the slope in the direction of the lower line of trees. Three columns of smoke rose where the lodges still burned.

Fierce Man stepped forward. He spoke so low that Jeanne could barely hear the words.

"The evil ones crept into the village after the warriors had gone hunting," Fierce Man began. "Thin Man and Stands Fast remained on guard duty." His voice was heavy with sadness, slow, careful. "Thin Man was ambushed at his post, and now walks with the spirits. Stands Fast was grievously wounded. There were many renegades, only a few defenders. No Bone in His Back and Muskrat were the only strong young ones capable of using weapons. They acquitted themselves well."

The very silence of the warriors expressed to Jeanne the awful social implications involved in this breaking of a taboo by No Bone in His Back, a warrior discredited and dishonored. The air fairly crackled with tension, with horror.

No Bone in His Back faced the group of vengeful warriors. He seemed to drag the words out of himself. "I know I have been forbidden to carry weapons," he responded bitterly, "but, even if I should be punished with banishment or death, I could not obey that order!"

The words were simple, but charged with meaning, and a murmur of anticipation went through the People, like wind in the river weeds, hungry, alive. Muskrat took up the story, telling the fascinated audience of the heroic deeds he had witnessed.

It seemed No Bone in His Back had followed the retreating renegades, hurling tomahawk and knife, shooting arrows and bringing down a number of the enemy. He had decided to give up the chase only when he discovered the body of Bright Path and realized the danger that still faced the unprotected camp. His belt laden with fresh scalps, he had accompanied Muskrat back to the settlement, where Fierce Man was directing the defenses. Without the old warrior's expertise, casualties would have been much worse.

Yellow Feather, arms folded, absorbed the story of the disgraced young man's bravery in silence. He looked at No Bone in His Back, his expression noncommittal. All eyes were fixed on the dripping scalps that dangled, as casually as an amulet or a water skin, from his waistband. Jeanne saw the young man's haggard expression, and, conscious of the anxiety in his eyes, she felt desperately sorry for him. Surely he would not be punished for using weapons in the defense of the women and children?

Slowly the war leader's arms dropped to his sides. Then he raised them again, inch by inch, and extended them. "Welcome to the land of the People, Roused Bear," he said, a trace of huskiness in his voice. He gave an approving nod, his smile open and candid. "No Bone in His Back is no more. Now the Roused Bear is invited to join the hunt. May your arm strike hard and true, may your heart be strong, and your name be honored in the fire-songs of the People. Welcome home." He walked over to Roused Bear and folded the newly identified young man into his arms.

Muskrat, too, was honored, receiving the name of Little Cat. As a junior warrior, Little Cat would now be able to join the men's secret societies, their dances, their war parties. He stood there, stiff and proud, as the warriors roared his new name.

Only one man remained completely calm. Fierce Man behaved as though such a victory were an everyday occurrence. When the warriors learned of the wonders he had performed in saving the settlement, Yellow Feather tried to find appropriate words to express his feelings.

"You are unique among the warriors of the People," he declared.

Fierce Man smiled and shook his head. "For an old man," he said dryly, "I have not done badly."

Dry Man, ashes smeared on his forehead, the bridge of his nose and the backs of his hands—signs of mourning he would leave on until they wore off—rocked to and fro. "The enemy took everything when they took Bright Path. I was so full of love, and now I am empty. I have nothing left. How can she be gone?" His eyes were lost, lonely, the reflection of his wretched grief.

Graceful One laid a gentle hand on the grief-stricken young man's arm and tilted her head, revealing the long, curved line of her throat. "Bright Path's spirit lingers on, like smoke in a long valley, like the mist that rises from the grasses in the early morning, when the sun is born again in the east. As long as you remember her, she will be with you."

"It is more likely that Bright Path's spirit lingers, waiting to accompany the child, to guide it to the land of the spirits," Dry Man said, grim-faced and sullen.

Carefully, slowly, so as not to wake or frighten her, Jeanne rose, went to Dry Man, and held out the baby. He glanced down at the little face, at the shapeless nose, the swollen eyes, the fine black hair, his eyes bleak.

"I do not want to see the girl-child that helped to kill my woman."

A spasm of anger slid like moving water across Jeanne's face. How unfair! The baby had not killed Bright Path. The murderous renegade band had committed the deed! Jeanne looked down at the small, thin creature.

Its knees were drawn to its chest, its tiny ankles were crossed, its flower-face was dark and wrinkled, and its eyes were squeezed shut. The dancing shadows of the fire gave its steep-planed face an unearthly look. Perhaps the child was tiny, but it had a right to life. Its mother dead, rejected by its grieving father, would no one give it sustenance?

Jeanne felt her eyes burn with tears and a swelling grow inside her throat, so tight that she could not swallow. The manito had not yet given her a child, but instead had given her to the child.

This child was hers as surely as it was Bright Path's. Not the child of her body, but the pulse that beat at the top of the fragile skull, the pulse that made the black hair gently flutter—the pulse of her spirit. Excitement, and a strange kind of fear, thudded her heart.

She looked around for Black Eagle and bit her lip. He stood there, tall and stiff, fists clenched, jaw shut hard, eyes hooded, a message in his eyes, a message that puzzled her. It held urgency, wariness, anger, a deep and powerful passion, a warning, and something else she could not decipher.

So tiny and pale the wind would carry her with the seeds. Is this the warrior son you would give me?

On one side of Black Eagle was Wise Speaker, his painted face giving nothing away. And Yellow Feather, the puckered scar that pulled at one corner of his mouth twisted in a tight awareness of trouble. No one moved, no one spoke. Each was busy with private thoughts.

Chapter Sixteen

"This child, torn from the living body of Bright Path, would be dead if I had not tended to it." Jeanne spoke slowly, clearly. "Surely that was not wrong? For reasons only they know, the manito have denied a child to Black Eagle and myself. Maybe this child is the reason!"

For a moment, Jeanne's gaze moved to the formidable figure of Black Eagle. Fireglow slid over the planes of his forehead, shadowed the strong, proud nose, lit the stubborn line of jaw, where a muscle twitched, traced the mouth set in a grim line.

"My breasts are dry. But if someone will nurse the child until it can live on hard food, then it will be our child to have, to hold, to keep. Without milk to feed her, with no one to help, this child will die!"

There was a murmur in the crowd, a rumble, like distant thunder across the uneasy faces. Wise Speaker raised both hands, in an imperious order for silence. The wrinkles on his face deepened as he stared at Jeanne. A hint of admiration flickered, then was gone. Holding his arms wide, the old medicine man spoke quietly.

"It is understood, Little Turtle. Well do I see what has brought you to this moment. We will do what we can. We will do what we must."

She heard one of the women mutter, "No woman can feed two children at the same time, or not for long, so the spirit of this child knows it has made the long trip from the spirit world for nothing. It must go right back again."

"No," Jeanne whispered brokenly, panting, breathless.

Wise Speaker shook his head with a patient sigh. His even voice continued gravely, "This could not be advisable or proper. The manito will know of this and think the People are playing with them, disrespectfully, accepting a child born to a woman already dead, birthed by one still unclean from the women's lodge."

The words iced the blood in Jeanne's veins, puckered the flesh on the nape of her neck. She stared at Black Eagle blindly. Why did he not say something instead of standing there so stubbornly silent? Face set, dark, inscrutable—like a log! Why did he not come to stand by her side? *Know who you are! Think!* Hands trembling, she tightened her grip on the baby. "It is not the child's fault. It should be given the chance of life, to know the colors of dawn, the first song of a fledgling bird, the feel of grass beneath its feet, a warm breeze, the soft sound of running streams."

She could hear her voice, brittle and edged with resentment. She brushed her hand gently over the dark, downy hair of the baby. Its face was still puckered and spotted with blood. But its dark eyes were wide open, and they stared up at her with a wisdom and clarity that seemed to pierce her to the core.

Jeanne closed her eyes as the pain bit deeper; she opened them to meet Black Eagle's dark gaze. *Let this cup pass from me.* For the first time, the planes of Black Eagle's face shifted. His eyes widened, and Jeanne, watching, saw the honest bewilderment there, the love, the hate. She saw her own face reflected in the black eyes, her eyes stretched to impossible limits, huge dead lakes rimmed with tears, emphasizing their upward slant.

The confused emotion raging within him drove straight into her heart with the unerring accuracy of an arrow and lodged there, tearing at her, urging her to take the initiative. *Not my will, but thine be done.* He opened his mouth, but she forestalled him, addressing the assembled crowd, her words clear, calm.

"What you feel in your spirit determines what you see. Fear rides upon the spirit as a canoe rides upon turbulent water. Your understanding has become jumbled, confused. You perceive through the waves of illusion. Recognize it for what it is—fear."

There was a sudden, breathless hush, then a gasp, sending Jeanne's words like the wind rippling across the fields of corn. She held the baby close, holding in the sobs that threatened to break free. "This child's spirit has been given to my trust."

Once more her eyes met Black Eagle's. She knew that the private longings of her spirit lay naked in her eyes. Knowing that it was wrong to press the matter, but that she could not stop herself, her eyes willed him to exhale his doubts. *Weeping may endure for a night, but joy cometh in the morning.*

Neither of them breathed or spoke or moved. They existed only in this moment of wordless communication, of intimate silence. And then the spell woven of unuttered meanings deepened into action. Jeanne stepped into the halo of light cast by the fire, determination in her stance. Her words echoed eerily.

"Nothing ever really dies. From every death, does not some form of life arise? Leaves fall from trees and are reborn in spring. The manito have given a life and canceled a life." Her voice took on color and strength. "Return, like the salmon, to the place of your origin, to the place of everlasting mist, to the dawn of the birth of your own inner spirits. As the sun rises, the shadows become sharper and more clearly defined.''

Jeanne was clinging so tightly to the baby that her breast had flattened beneath it. It whimpered slightly, unclenching a fist, and then the tiny throat gaped open and the whimper gave way to a bellow. The baby's voice was sharp.

Jeanne continued. ''As the energies of love grow stronger, the shadows of fear become more visible than before. To some of you, it may even appear that they have grown in number and strength, but this is not so. What was hidden has simply become revealed—that it might be healed and brought to peace.''

There was a long silence, a silence that ran into itself and held. She closed her eyes as Black Eagle moved to stand beside her. A hand brushed hers. Encouraged, she tried to find the right words, groping, uncertain.

''As the birds welcome the morning sun with their song, invite this child into your awareness. In the whisper of the pines, in the gentle call of the mourning dove, in a child's sleepy yawn, the spirit lives. Accept this child, Always Day, as you accept the circle of stars in the night sky, the circle of seasons, of fruit ripening on the vine, the circle of the honest and open eye.''

There was movement at her side. For a moment she thought Black Eagle was leaving. She let her head drop lower, biting her lip to keep from calling him back. She lifted a hand to hush the thump of her heart. Then his fingers knit with hers, applying no pressure, but willing her to face him. Her eyes flew open. There was something in his countenance that brought her heart into her mouth, a hunger, a desire, that could mean everything, or nothing at all. She looked up at him, her eyes fixing his in helpless thrall.

Black Eagle spoke slowly, his voice thick, every word seemingly wrung from his throat, though they came with deliberation: ''To every good place, a trail leads!''

Jeanne knew he meant that if you need something, a way to get it becomes clear. The words had a certain rhythm. Like Papa's proverbs. Maxims to be recalled countless times. A song would come from these simple words of Black Eagle, whatever else happened, a song for legend, to be passed through the land, mouth to ear. Would there be a trail between Always Day and the chance to live?

"A man without a child is as a tree without a leaf." Slowly, as if it were poison being drawn from a deep wound, Black Eagle let some of the bitterness leave him, something of his grief. "Many couples never have children, no matter how they try, and—"

"But sometimes they do, long after hope has died!" Singing Bird interrupted Black Eagle quietly. "And sometimes the manito are good. They give an old, barren woman a son of her body, then the chance to hold another, to sing to him, to feed him with the milk from her own breasts."

Jeanne ran the tip of a dry tongue over drier lips. "Singing Bird, you understand the need, the joy, the privilege, of watching a child grow with each passing day!"

"The spirits have not always been kind," Singing Bird answered with a sigh, her she-eagle eyes cloudy with pain. "Yet I have not been entirely cheated of a son, since I have Black Eagle." She turned to Wise Speaker. "Would you deprive Little Turtle and Black Eagle, then, of the chance to see a child grow? For this child would be theirs, Wise Speaker, because of the great love that they will bear it."

Mountain Wolf Woman stepped forward. "There was a time when I bitterly resented Little Turtle, but now I see that Singing Bird is fortunate that Black Eagle has found a generous woman." She bravely touched the child's hand. "In her old age she will be surrounded by young ones." She smiled kindly at Jeanne, her voice oddly tender. "You and Black Eagle have not been together for a full turn of the seasons. Give the manito a chance! As you would give this little one the chance!"

It was a statement, not a question. The baby's face twisted into a smile, and the little fingers clutched at one gnarled finger as though, like a wise, aged person, it understood.

Red Leaf stepped forward and laid a hand on Jeanne's shoulder. For a long, tense moment, their eyes met. Wordlessly she took the baby in her hands, cradled it gently, sang a little and, lifting her shirt, put it to her milk-filled breast. Like a starving beast, the infant latched onto the nipple and began to nurse.

Wise Speaker's sunken eyes flashed with anger for an instant. Then, as he accepted the fact that the slip of a girl in front of him had effectively won over the women, they began to gleam with grudging respect. Finally his thin mouth curved into a reluctant smile.

"You have learned your lessons well, my daughter," he admitted with a sigh, preserving his dignity in defeat.

Jeanne bowed her head in a gesture of respect. "Yes, Grandfather," she agreed quietly. "And one of the most important things the People have taught me is to live in harmony with all creatures. The child, Always Day, completes the circle of life into death, of death into life."

The old man smiled slyly, his eyes twinkling at Jeanne's subtle point. "Yes," he allowed with an emphatic shake of his head. "It is true, in a circle there is no beginning and no end." He watched Stands Fast, lifted on a stretcher of wood and skins, carried to the lodge of his parents. He looked at the women clustered around Red Leaf, and gave another sigh of resignation.

Fixing Black Eagle with a look of affection mingled with complacent self-satisfaction, he said with thin humor, "I know people, Black Eagle. It has always been my strength." But then he looked at Jeanne, without rancor, and muttered, "Though even I can miscalculate upon occasion."

He held out a trembling, aged hand to Jeanne, then tittered, looking at Black Eagle like a small boy with a delicious secret. "You will need to appease the manito every day for the rest of your life if you wish to live in peace, my son."

Black Eagle nodded. His eyes, dark and accusing, locked with Jeanne's. Unable to hold his gaze any longer, Jeanne lowered her head.

"I bow to the will of the manito, Wise Speaker," Black Eagle uttered in a tone devoid of all animation.

Jeanne understood what he was suffering, and knew the reasons behind his feelings, although she gave no indication of her knowledge.

By the time he held the door flap aside for her some hours later, and then hung his war bag on its hook, his air had become gloomy. She pretended to be unaware of his mood as she fastened the leather flap over the door to ensure privacy and then lit a wood fire for warmth in the stone pit in the center of the lodge.

Singing Bird had taken her basket of healing herbs and was helping to tend Stands Fast. Jeanne knew that the activity would help the old woman overcome the trauma of the day. The memory, fresh and vivid, taunted Jeanne. She, too, needed some activity to take her mind off the day's events. She needed Black Eagle. She longed for him, ached to have him touch her, to drive away all thoughts but those of him.

Instead, she calmly tended the fire! While he was prowling with the faint exasperation that she was learning meant he was upset, or uncertain. She had to bend low to hide her own uncertainty.

"I think in a little while the People will choose not to remember that Always Day is not of our flesh."

Black Eagle kicked a stray log back into the heart of the mounting fire, as though it offended him. "I hope you are right," he said, his tone ragged, despite his efforts to control it. "There will be none who did not see me step into the trap you set, who is not secretly laughing at me."

Jeanne knew precisely what troubled him, but she feigned surprise. "No, Black Eagle." She spoke with soft certainty. "You do not bow to my will, but your own. It is true that I proposed the burden. But it is also true that you took it up of your own free will. You are a strong man, Black Eagle, a man of conscience. You know, of course, that I counted on that."

He grunted in a gesture of morose acknowledgment. Realizing he was not about to come to her, Jeanne shifted to another battlefield.

"I had left the women's lodge and was on my way home when I saw some weeds in the field that needed clearing!" As she spoke, she tilted her head to one side, so that her hair caught the glow from the fire. Its light mirrored her eyes and played on one cheek, giving her a soft, lambent beauty.

He did not move, though Jeanne's eyes grew hot under his probing gaze. She began to feel somewhat dismayed at his stiffness.

"The squash is in flower, and the corn is budding," Jeanne said, hesitantly.

"They do at this time of the growing season."

The seed of anxiety grew. He was courteous, he was rational, and he was unbending. She gazed at him, her certainties sliding.

"Black Eagle," she whispered, draping herself around him bonelessly, fitting her slim, incredibly supple form into all his hollows, "Love me now."

"No." Just like that. Flatly.

"Why not?" He had to be joking!

Black Eagle peeled her off him and jumped back, holding her away with one arm. He faced her resolutely, a trifle defiantly. "Turtle, I do not feel like it. I am tired, weary. It has been a long day. It has to be mutual, or it is no good."

He saw the direction of her gaze, and drew his dark brows together.

His voice was gruff, almost accusing. ''Besides, I want you to think about a couple of things, Turtle. Really think. You defy me! Today you risked life and limb by going to the fields. You defy convention! You want to use weapons, to hunt. And I have been weak enough to throw caution to the winds, for a little while even to encourage you!''

She saw him hesitate as he searched for the words to express his frustration, and in one swift moment realized the enormity of what she had done.

But it was too late. If her position had been precarious before, how much more so was it now!

''As a result, you and I have no ordinary marriage. In this lodge there is an old woman, a wife and, now, a female child, for which I alone must be responsible. You are likely to defy me, if you do conceive, by presenting me with a lodge filled with female warriors. I am like to become suffocated by women!''

All the love and desire she had ever felt for him, every laugh they had shared, each kiss and caress, even the cross words that had passed between them, welled up within her.

''I am your mate. You are mine. We are partners in all that we do.'' She moved to the side of the bed and stood beside him, grinned at him like an imp, her eyes alight with mischief, with a tiny bit of trepidation and, curiously enough, with joy. Winding both arms around his neck, she hugged him fiercely.

''I will help you hunt, to care for Singing Bird and Always Day, and, if you lack the physical strength to make love to me, then it is my duty and my pleasure to make love to you!''

Giving him no chance to protest, she unfastened the loops that held his breechclout, knelt and pressed a kiss on the arch of his foot.

"Turtle?"

Without answering him, she continued to slide moist kisses along his strong, smooth leg, slowly rising to her knees, her hands curling around his ankles. Her kisses wound ever upward, serpentine, around his leg, with the heat of little leaping sparks, and she came underneath his body through the opening of his legs. His hands clenched in her hair as she moved under him, holding his thighs in the palms of her hands, gently pressing her lips against the soft, full hang of the sac between his legs.

Her own breath coming in short, heaving gasps, she continued frontward and, never ceasing the light pressure of her lips, kissed the stiffening excitement of his manhood. Her light, hot caresses seemed to hold Black Eagle in suspension. He did not move or change position at all, though his body trembled for release. He did not interrupt her wandering over his body, but when her warm tongue lazily curled over first one flat nipple and then the other, while her hand slid gently over the sensitive tip of his manhood, he groaned and pulled her up tight against him.

The deaths cast a dark shadow over the village, and the next four days were ones of mourning. The settlement reverberated with the soft, steady thrum of a muffled drum, the shrill wails of those lamenting the dead. But in assessing their losses, the People were philosophical. It could have been worse. Other than Bright Path and Thin Man, all of the dead were old people already close to the sunset. And Stands Fast would recover.

Luckily, Thin Man had been a young brave who had not yet married. His parents cried loudly and made some mutilations in their mourning, but at least he did not leave a wife and children with no provider. For seven suns after the burials, Dry Man spoke to no one. Not one morsel of food or sip of water passed his lips while he grieved, alone, in the lodge he had shared with Bright Path. Jeanne lived in constant trepidation, lest he came to claim his daughter.

A drifting blanket of ground mist was swirling in the deep purplish grayness that precedes the dawn when the lodge door rattled. It was Dry Man! What could he want? Surely not to claim Always Day! Not now! Jeanne reacted as the People did in moments of great stress. Her face betrayed no emotion, and her voice was calm as she bade him welcome.

"I have come to say farewell. I know I will never see Bright Path again, but her spirit is near me, like breath inside me. I had a vision last night. I saw the colored bow that arches across the sky after a rain to remind us to honor the ways of the manito. I was reminded how, like the rainbow, the colors of Little Turtle's eyes touch and intermingle."

Dry Man was silent for a moment, then continued. "Know you both, the spirit of Bright Path is content that the child of her belly will grow in peace under Little Turtle's eyes of living color, and the watchful eyes of Black Eagle. The child belongs with you. I have said it."

Black Eagle struck his chest. "My spirit is heavy at your loss, my friend. I shall be sorry to see you go." His dark eyes were filled with sorrow. "But you must do as your spirit wills. Only the spirit knows what is right. Go in peace, my warrior brother, and may the manito walk beside you to give you strength."

Jeanne's heart ached, and tears were a hard lump in her throat. She laid a hand, light as a leaf on water, against Dry Man's face.

"The ways of the manito are strange. But know this— Always Day will also understand the source of her being. In the scent of the breeze that fills her nostrils when she breathes, in the mists that rise up from the earth, she will know the spirit of Bright Path is nearby."

When Dry Man had departed, Jeanne's tears could no longer be held back. They slid down her cheeks, great salty drops. She lowered her head so that Black Eagle could not see them. Silently he wrapped his arms around her, held her close, hard against him. Let her cry, for all that was and is no more. They were good tears, cleansing tears, which broke the long-held-in tension and grief. Gently he put a finger under her chin and lifted her face. Lowered his head very slowly, kissed her mouth, softly, tenderly, with what was less passion than an aching sense of loss, less desire than pain shared.

It was not until much later, as she spread black raspberries and blueberries on mats in the sun to dry, Jeanne wondered why she had the strange feeling her life had suddenly taken a strange new course. A course she could not control.

As she checked the smoking and drying frames, she stirred the berries with a wooden paddle so that they would dry evenly. As soon as the fish and meat was dried, taken off and stored, the frames would be refilled. She could see, squatting motionless on the high ground around the settlement, several warriors doing guard duty. Since the assault, these sharp-eyed sentinels had been increased.

A hunting party was to leave next morning. The baskets she and Singing Bird wove would soon overflow. Some would be stored in pits until spring. The remainder would be taken to their winter camp. Would Black Eagle take another wife then? Lie in another woman's arms? Beget a son? The thought made her stiffen.

Uneasily Jeanne glanced at him. Sitting at the door of their lodge, he was tying fresh feathers to the otterskin wrapping of his war club. How could she bear to share him? She must show no signs of the pain she felt.

"There is enough wood ash to treat a batch of acorns," Jeanne said. "I will go tomorrow to gather some."

There was a noticeable hesitation, as if some inner struggle were taking place within him, but at last he shook his head. His expression set tight, his eyes grim, he made the bald announcement. "You will not go alone into the forest. I shall not permit it."

Startled by the unexpected statement, Jeanne was momentarily at a loss for words. "But—"

"I have spoken."

Black Eagle's statement was pronounced with a finality that allowed no further room for discussion, and, feeling suddenly trapped by his determination, Jeanne stumbled for a response.

"These words are heavy."

Black Eagle laid down his war club and stood, proud and silent. What could she see enshrouded in those dark eyes? Resentment? Rejection? When he spoke, he did not even raise his voice. But there was the crackle of lightning in it, the boom of sudden thunder.

"When I go hunting, I do not want the added worry of whether you are safe. I want to know! You nurture needless fears. It is not a son I need, Turtle. It is you. I could not live without you. You will be my one and only wife. This I promise."

How had he known of her fears? Her unspoken thoughts? He loved her! Truly loved her! The sudden blaze of joy that surged through her must surely be reflected in her face! She lifted a hand to him.

Misunderstanding the gesture, he jerked his head, sending the eagle feather in his scalp lock lifting, hovering, like a graceful wing.

"If—" he began, but she put her hand over his mouth.

"It will be as you say, my husband. And while you hunt, have no fear. The spirit of Little Turtle will be with you when we are absent from one another. Her eyes will be your eyes. Her ears will be your ears. Until you send for her, she will await you here.''

His face was blurred by too much nearness as she went up on tiptoe, tilting her head sideways. His kiss drew every hurt she had ever known, every disappointment, chagrin, anguish, defeat, shame, loss, along with whatever residual scattered, shattered grains of rationality, of will, she had left by then, out through her suddenly assaulted mouth.

The fire blurred before her eyes. Everything went still, except for the deafening thud of her heart. And then she was sitting still, not breathing, her eyes fixed on the flames, yet seeing it not. Seeing a broken arrow, smelling the odor of blood, while a voice filled her brain, praying for courage.

And the voice and the smell faded, and she was looking at the circle of women, accepting a wooden bowl, and Singing Bird was looking at her with shrewd black eyes, eyes that saw everything and noted everything.

Acorn and Sweet Breeze, Graceful One and Rattle were setting out the pitch-stuffed acorn dice. Mountain Wolf Woman and Clear Sky were arguing about something. Could they not hear, see, smell, the danger?

Black Eagle! Jeanne wanted to scream to everyone to be silent, to cease their noise, so that she might think. Quiet! she said to the hollow space inside herself. Quiet, Black Eagle! *I heard you.* . . .

She felt herself divide into two. There was her body, sitting with the women, watching, waiting for the game to begin, idling away the evening while the men were absent at the hunt. And there was her inner self, calculating, planning, vigilant . . . holding Black Eagle wrapped in her arms, trying to tell him that she was doing what she could . . . trying to give him hope and patience and courage.

The dice rolled in her favor. And the pain stabbed her. She could feel the burning of the cord against her wrist, yet nothing had touched her. Quiet! she said to herself again. Quiet, Black Eagle . . . *I am coming.*

Suddenly there was warmth around her. She closed her eyes for a moment, and let out her breath, the tension leaving her . . . and letting him in . . . relaxing, feeling his strength around her, his self-control, his clear, uncluttered mind.

Jeanne opened her eyes and looked about her, seeing everything now as if through his eyes, making calculations as if with his mind, noting that Graceful One was talking with Acorn and that they were both turning to look at Sweet Breeze.

She retreated from her vision, heard the soft drumming of rain, the distant rumble of thunder. Lightning flashed, and the sky danced with the brightness of death.

Dreams troubled Jeanne's sleep, disturbing her rest with distorted visions of nameless, faceless shadows. Once, she rose, lifted the door flap and peered into night, seeking she knew not what.

The wind gusted, wailed, rattled the door flap, the sound half impotent rage, half despair. The rain seemed endless. The night was pitch-black between the moments bleached by the lightning that moved about the sky in an aimless, wandering pattern. And then a column of azure-and-silver light shot down out of the sky and exploded a clump of lindens in the dell. White bark and large tooth-shaped leaves tilted every way, erupting in a ball of fire.

Jeanne's mind cleared, and she knew what she must do. She knew what Black Eagle wanted. She could do it. A pouch of cornmeal and pemmican were dropped into her pack. After all, this could be no worse than many other dangers she had met. She picked up her weapons.

By the time the sky was beginning to lighten, the rain had gone. Jeanne paused, looking around her, searching the forest for signs of danger. The forest was waking up, with animated chatter about the previous night's storm. Birds called, and squirrels gossiped in the trees.

She passed through a field of goldenrod, careful to sway in and out to avoid trampling down the flowers and leaving marks that could be seen instantly. Like a deer, she paused in the trees to look back on the open ground she had crossed. All was peaceful, nothing moved. The sky overhead was clear and just beginning to be tinged with blue.

Jeanne went on, moving swiftly, carefully. She crossed a stream, stepping out where she would leave no mark of her passing. Every crackle, every wisp of wind, sent chills up her spine. Tirelessly she continued, instinctively avoiding the soft places where her moccasins would leave a trail, listening, ever alert, vigilant.

She had told no one where she was going, and she was thankful for this, for although there was no sign of life in the dripping forest, lying on the rain-flattened grass beneath a dogwood bush she found a black feather with a white tip. It was a feather such as Bird Hawk had worn on his hair to show his rank. The crested hawk did not live in these parts. It was found only in the higher mountains. So the feather must have been dropped by a human agent.

Doubling back around a rise, she made a complete circle, crossed a fallen tree, leapt off and then returned to it. Ran along the tree in the opposite direction and then returned to it.

From somewhere there came a bird's trill, high and clear. It was almost true, but lacked the hard purity that comes from the throat of a bird. A prick of fear assailed her. She could smell danger.

Caution held Jeanne still. She did not move, but her eyes probed the shadows around her, and the certain sense that she was in danger grew.

Chapter Seventeen

The man came from nowhere. One moment Jeanne was staring vaguely between the trunks of oaks thirty feet away, the next moment the big coppery figure had drifted into her line of vision. She saw the long, flat muscles of powerful arms, the heavy set of his neck and shoulders, the ridges in his back as he turned to look behind him.

She melted into the shadow, still as death itself. To her heightened senses, the rustle of cloth against skin, of moccasin against grass, and the pounding of her heart against her ribs, were magnified to deafening proportions. He must be able to hear her! Desperation balled tight inside her. She held her breath, and only by conscious effort kept her hand from going to her mouth.

The man moved on silently. He was behind trees for a moment, and then he came into view again and stopped. He must know she was there!

But no. Incredibly, he did not turn his head, did not budge an inch. Jeanne's breath was burning in her chest. She let it out slowly, and the releasing made a sound that she could hear, a sigh that seemed to flow past her lips forever.

Terror made cold knots inside her. She saw the yellow and black and red smears of his war paint. Something in the opposite direction from Jeanne held his attention, for he kept looking that way, and once he crouched as if to get a better view along the ground.

She took a deep breath and instantly she found herself holding it again. She pressed her body tight against a tree bole, breathing short and hard, and watched, listening with every nerve. The man had turned and was looking toward her. His gaze swept across the deadfall with terrible deliberateness. He was looking straight into her face, she was sure.

Jeanne knew an insane desire to scream, and stifled it. *Think!* This was no time for panic, no time to submit to the rigors of terror. Better, far better, to keep one's nerves intact and concentrate the mind on finding Black Eagle. She was nearly panicked into making a scramble to run, but she held still as some reserve of coolness restrained her. It took all her willpower. *Motion is always the betrayer.*

Lying rigid, as still as a nesting bird, face pressed against the bole, she lived a long, terrifying moment. Willed herself to become one with the spirit of the tree. There was no sound more desolate than the roar of the silence now ringing in her ears. Her heart shook her body with its ceaseless pounding. Surely the noise it made in her ears must be audible across the forest!

He turned away. Even then, she was not sure he had not seen her. But his profile as he stared ahead showed the same fierce concentration he had turned her way. He went on. Craning and peering, she saw just a dim glimpse of him once more between the trees, and then he was gone.

Jeanne let her breath out slowly. She remained perfectly still for a long time, her mouth dry. Each moment of inaction heightened her unease. Her heart thudded when she heard a chipmunk chattering. Was it a chipmunk? *Be still. Be silent.* She caught a glimpse of squirrels scurrying around in the underbrush near a pair of towering oaks, searching for nuts to hide away for the winter.

In the distance, barely discernible in the underbrush, she saw a fox that halted and froze. Jeanne's heart missed a beat. It was only when it moved on, a rabbit dangling from its mouth, that she felt the tension begin to ease out of her limbs. She filled her lungs with air, went on.

Approaching a castellated ridge, Jeanne hesitated. Which way? She surveyed the terrain. She saw a rock pillar whose capping rock layer still connected with the main cliff. A narrow, rocky gorge. Shrill yells behind warned her that she had been seen.

Looking back, she saw two men scrambling down the bluff. She headed along the ridge slope, keeping to the thickest line of pines and sheering around the clumps of spruce. As she ran, her mind whirled with the need to find Black Eagle and the hunting party.

She knew the course ahead soon ended in an abrupt declivity too precipitous to descend. An arrow flew past her head. It lent wings to her feet. Like a deer, she sped along, leaping cracks and logs and rocks, her ears filled by the rush of wind, until her quick eye caught sight of thick-growing spruce foliage close to the precipice.

She sprang down into the green mass. Her weight precipitated her through the upper branches. But lower down, her spread arms broke her fall, then retarded it until she caught.

A screaming in her ear, the sudden beating of wings in her face, nearly sent her plunging to the earth below. A bird, in its summer-checkered plumage, had been so perfectly camouflaged that she had brushed against it. It shot straight up through the trees, calling in panic, seeking its mate and the open skies in its terror at her intrusion.

Jeanne hugged the tree, trembling, and watched it go. When quiet fell again, she turned to regard the abandoned nest and its two small eggs, olive-brown, dark-spotted.

She looked down. Very gently, she bounced her weight against the thick branch that supported her. Her sharp eyes caught another tree that appeared to be growing right out of a huge boulder, elevated as if on a platform a good eight feet above the ground. If she could reach it, swing herself to that tree, she might well climb down in safety.

A long, swaying limb let her down and down, and she grasped another, and a stiffer one that held her weight. Hand over hand, she worked her way toward the trunk of this spruce and, gaining it, she found other branches close together, down which she hastened, hold by hold and step by step, until all above her was black, dense foliage, and beneath her the brown, shady stone.

On one side, the tree seemed to have only a tentative hold on the rock. On the other, Jeanne could see two massive roots winding like tentacles down the stone to anchor themselves in the soil. She sat for a moment, motionless, letting her breathing steady, before sliding down the exploring roots, right down the granite face, to the soft earth below.

Sure of being unseen from above, she glided noiselessly down under the trees, slowly regaining freedom from that constriction of her breast.

Passing on to a gray-lichened cliff, overhanging and gloomy, she paused there to rest and to listen. It was as though the ancient trees did not want an intruder in this secret place. Shadows grew and walked long. The tiring day spoke of danger, but the compressed feeling held on. Birds murmured sleepily. She heard the whooshing of a hawk. A herd of deer stepped lightly down an unseen trail hard by, and somewhere an opossum scratched bark.

Jeanne rose and glided down under the spruces toward the level, grassy opening she could see between the trees. As she proceeded, with the slow step and wary eye of a warrior, her mind was busy. *Know your enemy. Think.* The enemy had seen her. Knowing she was alone, they would expect her to flee. They would track her.

Black Eagle had taught her to follow the trail of a feather across stone. He would, somehow, leave a mark for her to follow. If she could do the same, only delude the enemy, she might also be able to outwit them. Save Black Eagle from death's dark wings. She did not have the physical strength of a man, but she had quickness. She did not dare let fear or the sick dread that lurked in the back of her mind take hold.

She *knew* what she had to do. Find Black Eagle!

Jeanne was aware of an odd sense of security, a feeling that she was protected. One corner of her mind picked at this sensation, even as the rest of her concentration focused on the task at hand. First she made an obvious trail toward the north, then she backtracked quickly, leaving no sign. As silent as the ghost of a departed spirit, she moved from tree to tree, from concealment to concealment.

She traced the feeling to its source, just as she came to an abandoned wildcat's lair. It came from the amulet at her throat, not from its size or strength, but from its content, the fact that she carried something of Black Eagle with her. Each article, the crystal, the turtle carapace, the strip of ribbon, held memories of Black Eagle, his touch, his hold, his vision.

She held the pouch tightly, a talisman against fear. Prayed to the God of her father. *Let this cup pass from me.*

Something rustled in the bushes. She jerked to attention, listened. A wildcat? A bear? Or, worse, a man with muscles and weapons? She froze in place, instinctively remem-

bering her lessons in camouflage, silence, immobility. *Be
still. Be secret.* Far away, a cougar cried, and another, farther still, answered. Or *was* it an animal? An owl hooted,
another replied, and then there was heavy silence.

Jeanne began to shake with a chill, violent, convulsive,
her teeth chattered like angry red squirrels, and she was no
longer certain if it was she or the wind who moaned.

She let out her breath raggedly, feeling the harsh pain of
terror and relief as her constricted heart relaxed. Only a
porcupine! She leaned against a tree bole, trying desperately to calm herself, to still the trembling in her hands, the
paralyzing weakness of her knees. The panic eased.

The canyon wall above Jeanne on the right grew more
rugged and loftier, and the one on the left began to show
wooded slopes and brakes, and at last a wide expanse with
a winding willow border on the west and a long, low, pine-
dotted bench on the east. It took several moments of study
for Jeanne to recognize the rugged bluff above this bench.
It was where Black Eagle had said he had seen his vision!

Even now, there was an eagle, soaring high in the still
summer air. With tail spread and head arched, it swept effortlessly on, scanning the earth below for any sign of
movement. It circled again, then steadied. Suddenly it collapsed its wings and began falling, sheering earthward in a
plummet of black and brown. She lost sight of it. Then it
rose from a patch of timber and flapped ponderously
northward towards the blue-ridged hills, the dun shape of a
hare clenched in its outstretched talons.

Jeanne smiled as it grew smaller. An eagle seen with its kill
was a good omen. Confidence restored, she proceeded with
the utmost stealth, absolutely certain that she would miss no
sound, no movement, no sign, nothing unnatural to the wild
peace of the canyon.

The eagle's eye was hers. Signs of a scuffle. A depression in the soil. A footprint! A broken thornbush. A drop of blood on a leaf, and farther on a similar drop on the stem of a small bush. As surely as if they were signposts, Black Eagle was leaving a trail. It had to be him! It had to be!

Jeanne scanned the earth. Green twigs on the ground and small pieces of dry bark indicated the way, hardly more than a thread among the brushwood making for the cliff wall. Surely only a fox or a wolf could have used it?

Soundlessly she glided around the jagged rocks, turned a shoulder of crags. Froze. Melted into the shadows. It was Black Eagle! Tied to a stake like a bear! Another pulsebeat and she would have betrayed herself. She looked down. The ledge had come to an abrupt end, and beyond that was a sheer drop of crumbling perpendicular shale rock face that no living thing larger than an insect could have managed, and even an insect only with appalling difficulty!

Jeanne's sight blurred. Her head seemed to be spinning around. She shut her eyes and made herself breathe steadily till her heart quietened. Then she inched backward along the rock ledge until she reached the shelter of the overhang. She pulled herself up slowly and peered down. Two men were squatting, exulting about something, grunting and laughing softly. They were full warriors, scarred and powerful.

Black Eagle drooped against the stake, watching them from beneath heavy lids. The warriors rose, circled, mocking, yelping like frightened coyotes, jabbing him with the points of their lances until his torso was streaked with blood. He spat on the ground in front of them. Tiring of the sport, the warriors returned to their squatting positions. They seemed to be waiting.

Knowledge rose like water in a spring. Their companions! The two men she had seen earlier! Once they returned, Black Eagle would have no chance! Could she defeat two men? Jeanne would have started from her hiding place, but Black Eagle lifted the fingers of one hand. It was the slightest of gestures, but it checked her.

He knew she was there!

Jeanne waited and listened. The shadows lengthened. A trickle of perspiration slid between her breasts. Her legs cramped. Several times the warriors returned to torment Black Eagle. Jeanne felt a sick sense of dread seethe through her body. What did they have in mind for him?

A turkey gobbled. The renegades lifted their heads. Turned to the sound. Gave birdcall signals. Suddenly Black Eagle sprang lightly upward, gracefully, like a cougar, the muscles about his shoulders bunching into knots. As he descended, knees raised almost to his chest, he wrenched his hands together with every ounce of his strength, his arms twisting.

Incredibly, the cord parted from his wrists, leaving bloody bracelets. The braided fiber twanged back into position like a released bowstring, and Black Eagle, crouching, was free.

Before the renegade could draw a weapon, Black Eagle's foot had smashed into his painted face, shattering nose, teeth and cheekbone. The man grunted, spun like a dancer and fell in a crumpled heap on the ground. The second warrior, hatchet raised, ran at Black Eagle. He hesitated for a single moment, and was lost. He was swept aside like a doll in the hands of a petulant child, disappearing headlong over the cliff.

A movement behind her had Jeanne spinning to face a new threat. The rest of the party! Bird Hawk! She stared at the painted face, as sleek, hard and handsome as a well-gorged buzzard. The black eyes glittered with lust, with malice. The humiliation, the ignominy of his defeat at her hands, had sent him over sanity's edge. His spirit had fled to join the crazy ones!

His companion launched his long lance at Black Eagle. As the weapon seemed about to hit his chest, Black Eagle pivoted. The lance slid past him, tearing the flesh of his arm. Blood gushed, a thick film of red.

Black Eagle leapt high, swinging his tomahawk while he was in midair, the momentum of his rotating body adding force to the blow that took the renegade in the upper part of his chest. Black Eagle staggered, dropped to one knee. Jeanne could hear the harsh, rhythmic, tortured contractions of his lungs as he gasped painfully for breath.

Bird Hawk grinned, his lips pulled back in a sneer. His small eyes, beady, hungry, calculating, brimmed with venom. "Does the spotted deer outwit the cougar?" he taunted, sliding his own weapon from his shoulder.

Crouching low, Jeanne slowly drew the tomahawk from her waistband. She balanced it lightly in both hands, carefully gauging the distance. It was about the same as the distance to Fierce Man's practice block. *Remember your stance. Balance your feet. Position yourself properly before you throw.*

Recollecting everything Fierce Man had taught her, Jeanne stared at an invisible target just above the bridge of the man's sharp, predatory nose. She did not move her eyes from his forehead as she exhaled and straightened, sweeping the tomahawk and throwing it in one quick blur of movement.

For an instant she thought she had not snapped her wrist down at the right second, and that the weapon would strike head-on. Then she and Black Eagle would be doomed. But the turn was right. Her aim was true. The tomahawk hit its target and chunked solidly into bone.

Bird Hawk did not know what hit him. He crumpled up, with his legs bent under him, still clutching his tomahawk. A deep gurgling sound rose in his throat. A whispered, grunting sound, a soft thud as his head struck the ground, and his unused weapon dropped from lifeless fingers.

There was a moment of silence. Jeanne was shaking too much to move.

"Can you do it again?" Black Eagle asked dryly.

"I do not want to try!" Jeanne ran to him, like a quail for cover, throwing herself into his open arms.

"Once convinces me," he murmured into her hair, his good arm tightening about her. "You have earned the right to wear the eagle's feather. I think you are equal to any warrior."

Silence fell, a silence like nightfall, heavy and thick. The ground below, the sky above, seemed to hold their breath as she clung to him.

"Where is Thunderclap, Turtle?" He spoke distantly. The blood from a long gouge on his right forearm was running over his wrist and between his fingers, congealing stickily.

Jeanne gazed at a point between his feet. "I do not know. You needed me. I came."

The grip on her arm tightened painfully, dropped away.

She tilted her head sideways and froze when she saw Black Eagle's grim face, anger, raging red anger, evident behind his war paint.

He is only angry because you have placed yourself in a position of nearly being murdered!

Black Eagle was silent for several moments. "Come," he said, the blood lust gone, but anger still glittering in his eyes. "There is moss and healing pine here. Wipe the blood from this arm, and bind it tightly."

Obeying Black Eagle's instructions, Jeanne gathered some moss and swabbed clean the dirty, bloody forearm he offered her with the fibrous material. She could feel his eyes on her, but she kept her face low, packing fresh moss against the laceration.

She ran her hands over his arm, testing the strength and resilience of his muscles. Her fingers itched to savor the texture of his shoulders, his cheeks, his midnight hair. She tore a strip of inner bark from a nearby pine tree, and bound the wet strip tightly until he winced, the corded muscles rippling in his throat.

When she felt Black Eagle's hand at her throat, she gave him a startled look. Black Eagle did not notice. He was carefully lifting her hair, his hand gently sliding up beneath her chin.

"Prepare a sleeping pallet. We will rest for a while." Releasing her, Black Eagle leaned against the tree, as if needing the support.

The rush of cool air against her throat was disorienting. Silently Jeanne scraped aside the top layer of pine needles that covered the ground until she felt the warm, dry humus underneath.

With a grunt of acknowledgment, Black Eagle, exhausted, lowered himself to the indentation and rolled over until his back was to her.

"You would do best to remain here. Guard my back. Should there be other enemies lurking, I would know that my spirit is here to protect me."

His voice slurred, faded, drifted into an incoherent, febrile mumble. Jeanne exhaled a long, soundless breath of release and took up her guard post, waiting, watching.

Black Eagle's soft, slow laugh circled the lodge. Jeanne could not help but notice the change in him. Like a boy, he was joking, laughing, his face no longer still and pain-filled, but moving and alive.

Jeanne had enjoyed the night of listening to the men's quiet voices as they ate and played ring and pin, swapping tales about their ambushes and escapes, their skill at hunting and gambling. She spent the time carefully punching the designs she had drawn in charcoal onto a strip of hide. Black Eagle's new mink medicine bag needed pouches and pockets to hold his charms and medicines.

He had enchanted her! Before she had known Black Eagle, she had not truly realized what she was capable of doing. She was no longer Jeanne de la Rocque, daughter. She was Little Turtle, warrior and wife.

Weakened by blood loss, Black Eagle had been delirious with fever by the time Thunderclap and Little Bear found her. They had explained how the hunters had become alarmed when they found two sets of alien tracks they knew were the renegades.

One set of tracks had strategically been covered, yet Black Eagle's astute gaze had caught it. They had followed one set, Black Eagle the other... Back at the camp, Black Eagle's wounds had healed quickly.

A small smile just barely turned up the corners of Jeanne's lips. She dropped her eyes to Always Day. The child lay back in her arms, small mouth pursed, still working in sleep, a drop of milk on her lips. Jeanne looked at the small, compact body. The shell-shaped curve of lip, the fat little fingers curled trustfully around her own, brought a surge of emotion, warm and soft, within her.

She placed the child in the finely carved cradleboard Black Eagle had made. An amulet, decorated by Sky Woman and blessed by Wise Speaker, hung on the hickory hoop. A necklace of bear claws was also attached to the hoop. The large claws rattled when the necklace was moved, attracting Always Day.

This gift from Black Eagle had more than sentimental meaning, since the bear was the chief totem of Black Eagle's clan group. It meant total acceptance of Always Day as his child.

He often held the child in his strong arms, talking to Always Day as he would to another adult, telling her the lore of the woods, pointing out the moss on the trees, and holding up to the sunlight various leaves, pointing out the different shapes and colors, stopping to let the baby touch and pull at the yellow and red leaves. Laughed with her when they rustled and fell.

And Singing Bird! The eyes Jeanne had once thought resembled those of a she-eagle were soft as maple syrup when she played with the baby, gave her a piece of bone to chew on. It was good to have the old one in the lodge. She laughed and sang and told stories.

Maybe it was time for Little Turtle to learn all the many legends, the secrets, of the People. Words, not weapons, were the way of a woman. Used skilfully, they could be carried on to future generations, thousands of moons hence, when her spirit was no more than a breath on the wind.

Words were powerful, strong, influential. Could this daughter of the medicine lodge be the eye of the eagle, the shadow of the moon, the voice of the wind? She remembered her father's words. *Many are called, but few are chosen.*

Was she Black Eagle's secret dream, the choice of the manito? Had all her life been directed toward this one purpose? To live in peace and harmony? To use the power given her for the good of the People? A warrior whose weapons were words? Was she ready?

When you know the way your moccasins must tread.

Black Eagle's low voice seemed to come from far away, although he sat only a few feet away. There was mock resignation in his tone.

"Since she earned her warrior's feather, Little Turtle neglects her wifely duties. Do you see how her mind wanders to further conquests while a guest wrecks her husband's lodge?"

Thunderclap made a disrespectful noise and rubbed his temple. The corn he was roasting had popped, sending hot, fragrant golden bubbles shooting in all directions.

Jeanne's face was solemn, but she could feel her mouth widen, ready to smile. "A wife has many weapons. It is time Thunderclap discovered this."

"I have no taste for women who seek to use weapons." Thunderclap winced when an accurately aimed bubble of corn flicked his ear.

Black Eagle sighed, gave Jeanne one private glance, swift and secret, looked away and rolled his eyes airily. "A husband encourages his wife to use her weapons, especially inventiveness and imagination."

Early the next morning, they stretched their net across the stream. It was the last venture before the People prepared to return to their winter camp. Black Eagle and Crayfish took one end to the far shore. Black Eagle waved. The women and older children began to wade into the stream. One child, knee-high to a grasshopper, started to follow.

"No, Grasshopper," Good Woman said. "You must stay, you are not old enough."

"But She Is Playful is helping," the child pleaded, her lips trembling.

"She Is Playful is older than you, Grasshopper. You can help later, after we bring the fish in. It is too dangerous for you. Stay here."

Noticing the disconsolate expression on the small child's face, Jeanne crouched down to whisper. "It is important that the babies be tended. See Fleecy Cloud, Big Rain, Always Day and the others in the shade by the tree? Someone must guard them from harm. Are you equal to the task?"

Grasshopper nodded gravely, and moved to stand beside the cradle boards, happy with her new task.

"You have a way with young ones, Little Turtle. May your fireside be blessed with many."

Jeanne blushed, embarrassed at Mountain Wolf Woman's smooth words. Praise indeed, from that feisty old bird!

They moved into the water slowly, creating as little disturbance as possible as they fanned out to form a large semicircle, then waited until the sand stirred up by their movement settled down again. Jeanne stood with her feet braced against the strong current surging around her legs, her eye on Black Eagle, waiting for his signal. He was the anchor man, standing on the bank to control the guide cord, which released the net.

Fascinated by the intensity of concentration reflected on his face, she allowed her eyes to move slowly over the taut, sharply angled planes. The dark brows were drawn together in an intense frown, the midnight eyes were bright with subdued excitement, the powerful muscles in his arms and chest were corded with strain. So caught up had she become in her admiration of Black Eagle that she did not realize they were waiting for her to indicate her readiness to commence the fish drive.

In mid-channel, she was equally distant from both shores and nearest to the channel drawing the water that poured over the limestone lip. She had a glimpse of the limestone channel behind her, glass-smooth as a millrace, and the silent crystal current that was a synonym for extinction. She watched a large, dark shape glide past a few feet away. A pike! She nodded to Black Eagle.

He raised his arm. As he brought it down, the women began to shout and beat on the water. What appeared to be a disorderly chaos of noise and splashing was soon revealed as a purposeful drive. The women were driving the fish toward the net, drawing their circle in tighter. The men moved in from the far shore, bringing the net around while the churning confusion created by the women stopped the fish from returning downstream.

Suddenly Jeanne heard a loud cry.

"Turtle! Turtle!" Grasshopper shrieked.

Jeanne turned to look, and barely caught sight of a dark head bobbing up once before it disappeared under the water. It resurfaced, went under, skipping downstream as gaily as a stone on a millpond, a patch of color, bobbing on the water.

In the confusion of the hauling in of the catch, She Is Playful had been overlooked. Only the small child, watching her older playmate from the shore, had noticed She Is Playful's desperate plight. The tug of the current had already pulled She Is Playful dangerously close to the falls, where the bottom shoaled abruptly.

Rattle gave an agonized fluting cry, her outstretched hands spread wide in horror as she scanned the water. She screamed the child's name over and over again, until her voice broke in a shrill falsetto.

Without thinking of the consequences, Jeanne took a deep breath and dived. Those far-off days in France when she had dived for copper coins thrown by Pierre from the bank into the millpond now came back to her. Her arms flailed through the water with speed and certainty. She lost the floating patch of color, then saw it again. Stronger strokes brought her nearer, and she saw the girl's head.

When her head burst into the light, the water was boiling at her armpits. She was able to hook her foot against a knob of limestone a few feet downstream. Near enough to hammerlock the child's shoulder as her windmilling body rushed by.

The force of their collision shook Jeanne free of her temporary anchor, and the two seemed helpless now against the current sucking them toward the brink. Through the centuries, the water had worn an ever-deeper channel in its wild plunge to lower ground. Now no swimmer under heaven could hope to make headway against it, even without a burden such as Jeanne was supporting now.

One last obstacle remained, and she swam for it with all her fading strength. It was a rough outcrop that half spanned the waterfall almost at the chasm's rim. With one final burst of strength, she flailed her feet together, cradling She Is Playful's head in the curve of one arm as she struck out with the other. The crash came before she had time to tense against it, so rapid was the tug of the cataract. The rock scraped Jeanne's chest as she clung grimly to the rocky spur that anchored them to the bank.

Suddenly Black Eagle was there, taking the child from her numb grasp. Hand over hand, he worked his way from the deep drag of the channel. In a few seconds, his feet touched the shelving bank. In a moment more, he had dumped his burden on the grass and returned to give Jeanne assistance. She felt the pressure of hands in her armpits. She was gasping as they made the shore. Together they crashed to the ground.

The misty haziness left her eyes, and she could see Black Eagle looking down at her. His eyes caressed her, and she realized her head was resting on his lap. Yellow cattail pollen clung to his hair, his eyelashes, his hard and corded body. She lifted her hands, sought her own face, warm and silky beneath her palms. Looked at them in wonder. Golden pollen. Symbol of fertility. Of healthy babies. A sign from the manito.

Black Eagle's eyes met hers, gleaming, elated. *Did I not tell you? During the Long Snows Moon, bears sleep and women conceive?* He rose, set her on her feet.

"Come, Little Turtle. If you are to show me all your secret weapons and insist we practice training diligently until I am exhausted, we must first listen to the People sing your praises, and then catch some fish!"

Serene, confident, hand in hand, they turned to face the future.

* * * * *

Take 4 bestselling love stories FREE

Plus get a FREE surprise gift!

HARLEQUIN SUPERROMANCE®

TIRED OF WINTER?
ESCAPE THE WINTER BLUES THIS SPRING WITH HARLEQUIN SUPERROMANCE AND

_MARRIOTT'S_____

Camelback Inn
RESORT, GOLF CLUB & SPA

Mobil Five Star, AAA Five Diamond Award Winner
5402 East Lincoln Drive, Scottsdale, Arizona 85253, (602) 948-1700

March is **Spring Break** month, and Superromance wants to give you a price break! Look for 30¢-off coupons in the back pages of all Harlequin Superromance novels, good on the purchase of your next Superromance title.

April Showers brings a shower of new authors! Harlequin Superromance is highlighting four simply sensational new authors. Four provocative, passionate, romantic stories guaranteed to put spring into your heart!

May is the month for flowers, and with flowers comes ROMANCE! Join us in May as four of our most popular authors—Tracy Hughes, Janice Kaiser, Lynn Erickson and Bobby Hutchinson—bring you four of their most romantic Superromance titles.

And to really escape the winter blues, enter our Superromantic Weekend Sweepstakes. You could win an exciting weekend at the **Marriott's Camelback Inn, Resort, Golf Club and Spa in Scottsdale, Arizona.** Look for further details in Harlequin Superromance novels, beginning in March.

HARLEQUIN SUPERROMANCE...
NOT THE SAME OLD STORY!

HSREL2

When the only time you have for yourself is...

Spring into spring—by giving yourself a March Break! Take a few *stolen moments* and treat yourself to a Great Escape. Relax with one of our brand-new stories (or with all six!).

Each STOLEN MOMENTS title in our Great Escapes collection is a complete and never-before-published *short* novel. These contemporary romances are 96 pages long—the perfect length for the busy woman of the nineties!

Look for Great Escapes in our Stolen Moments display this March!

SIZZLE by Jennifer Crusie
ANNIVERSARY WALTZ
by Anne Marie Duquette
MAGGIE AND HER COLONEL
by Merline Lovelace
PRAIRIE SUMMER by Alina Roberts
THE SUGAR CUP by Annie Sims
LOVE ME NOT by Barbara Stewart

Wherever Harlequin and Silhouette books are sold.

SMGE

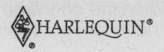

Harlequin proudly presents four stories about *convenient* but not *conventional* reasons for marriage:

- ♦ To save your godchildren from a "wicked stepmother"

- ♦ To help out your eccentric aunt—and her sexy business partner

- ♦ To bring an old man happiness by making him a grandfather

- ♦ To escape from a ghostly existence and become a real woman

Marriage By Design—four brand-new stories by four of Harlequin's most popular authors:

CATHY GILLEN THACKER
JASMINE CRESSWELL
GLENDA SANDERS
MARGARET CHITTENDEN

Don't miss this exciting collection of stories about marriages of convenience. Available in April, wherever Harlequin books are sold.

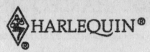

HARLEQUIN®

Don't miss these Harlequin favorites by some of our most distinguished authors!

And now, you can receive a discount by ordering two or more titles!

HT#25409	THE NIGHT IN SHINING ARMOR by JoAnn Ross	$2.99	☐
HT#25471	LOVESTORM by JoAnn Ross	$2.99	☐
HP#11463	THE WEDDING by Emma Darcy	$2.89	☐
HP#11592	THE LAST GRAND PASSION by Emma Darcy	$2.99	☐
HR#03188	DOUBLY DELICIOUS by Emma Goldrick	$2.89	☐
HR#03248	SAFE IN MY HEART by Leigh Michaels	$2.89	☐
HS#70464	CHILDREN OF THE HEART by Sally Garrett	$3.25	☐
HS#70524	STRING OF MIRACLES by Sally Garrett	$3.39	☐
HS#70500	THE SILENCE OF MIDNIGHT by Karen Young	$3.39	☐
HI#22178	SCHOOL FOR SPIES by Vickie York	$2.79	☐
HI#22212	DANGEROUS VINTAGE by Laura Pender	$2.89	☐
HI#22219	TORCH JOB by Patricia Rosemoor	$2.89	☐
HAR#16459	MACKENZIE'S BABY by Anne McAllister	$3.39	☐
HAR#16466	A COWBOY FOR CHRISTMAS by Anne McAllister	$3.39	☐
HAR#16462	THE PIRATE AND HIS LADY by Margaret St. George	$3.39	☐
HAR#16477	THE LAST REAL MAN by Rebecca Flanders	$3.39	☐
HH#28704	A CORNER OF HEAVEN by Theresa Michaels	$3.99	☐
HH#28707	LIGHT ON THE MOUNTAIN by Maura Seger	$3.99	☐

Harlequin Promotional Titles

#83247	YESTERDAY COMES TOMORROW by Rebecca Flanders	$4.99	☐
#83257	MY VALENTINE 1993	$4.99	
	(short-story collection featuring Anne Stuart, Judith Arnold, Anne McAllister, Linda Randall Wisdom)		

(limited quantities available on certain titles)

	AMOUNT	$
DEDUCT:	10% DISCOUNT FOR 2+ BOOKS	$
ADD:	POSTAGE & HANDLING	$
	($1.00 for one book, 50¢ for each additional)	
	APPLICABLE TAXES*	$ _____
	TOTAL PAYABLE	$ _____
	(check or money order—please do not send cash)	

To order, complete this form and send it, along with a check or money order for the total above, payable to Harlequin Books, to: **In the U.S.:** 3010 Walden Avenue, P.O. Box 9047, Buffalo, NY 14269-9047; **In Canada:** P.O. Box 613, Fort Erie, Ontario, L2A 5X3.

Name: _____

Address: _____ City: _____

State/Prov.: _____ Zip/Postal Code: _____

*New York residents remit applicable sales taxes.
Canadian residents remit applicable GST and provincial taxes.

HBACK-JM